THIRD EDITION

The Family

An Australian Focus

LOIS J. ASPIN

LONGMAN

Addison Wesley Longman Australia Pty Ltd
95 Coventry Street
Melbourne 3205 Australia

Offices in Sydney, Brisbane and Perth, and associated companies throughout the world.

First published 1982
Reprinted 1983 (twice), 1984, 1985
Second edition 1987
Third edition 1994
Reprinted 1995, 1996

Edited by David Lowe
Designed by Judith Grace
Set in 11/13 Goudy (DTP)
Produced by Addison Wesley Longman Australia Pty Ltd
Printed in Malaysia through Longman Malaysia, TCP

National Library of Australia
Cataloguing-in-Publication data

Aspin, L.J. (Lois J.).
The family: an Australian focus

3th ed.
Bibliography.
Includes index.
ISBN 0 582 80242 3

1. Family–Australia. 2. Australia–Social conditions–1990–. 3. Australia–Economic conditions–1990–. I. Title.

306.850994

Acknowledgements
The author wishes to thank the various organisations and individuals who contributed visual and other material to accompany the text. They are acknowledged on the pages their contributions appear.

The
publisher's
policy is to use
paper manufactured
from sustainable forests

FOREWORD

Since European settlement, the family as a social institution of Australian society has undergone many changes and has had to adapt to many social, legal, political and economic changes. Although some of these changes may have been similar to those which have occurred in other countries, it cannot be assumed that their effects have been the same in Australia as they have been elsewhere. The lack of research data on the family in Australia prior to the Second World War, and particularly during the nineteenth century, makes it difficult to identify all the unique and specific factors that have influenced the development of the family in Australia.

During the last two decades there has been much concern expressed about the stability of the family unit; it is often claimed that the family, a fundamental unit of our society, is breaking down and ceasing to perform the functions necessary for the wellbeing of its members, and indeed for its own survival. Some argue that the influence of the family is declining, traditional values are disappearing and there has been a loss of parental authority.

During this century, and particularly since the 1960s, there have been many broad social changes which have influenced the nature of family life. As a result of these changes there has been a general reduction in family size, more children are born and raised outside marriage, the divorce rate has risen, an increasing proportion of children live in single-parent families and blended families, increasing numbers of mothers remain in or re-enter the workforce, and there are more social services available to assist the family and its members. More recently, there has been a trend for young adults to remain with the family for a longer period of time; to delay or postpone marriage, or to enter into living-together relationships in preference to legal marital relationships.

While the changes outlined above have been significant, and by no means exhaustive, evidence still suggests that marriage and family remain popular social institutions. However, changes in values over the last few decades has meant that a greater variety of behaviours and lifestyles are tolerated. The family may now exist in a wider variety of forms than it did one hundred years ago, but then society has also changed dramatically in this same period. Despite the changes that the institution of the family has endured, it must still be regarded as one of the most important social systems, as most individuals spend a large proportion of their life in some type of family situation. During the last few decades the diversity of family forms has increased significantly and it cannot be assumed that the majority of children will grow up in a nuclear family with only the father–husband in the workforce. It would appear that many children will experience more than one family situation during their dependent years, and many adults will choose not to marry or to have children.

This book will explore not only the changing nature of family life in Australia, but also the interrelationship of the family with other social systems and institutions. It is important to note that as individuals and families adjust to changes occurring within society, society must also adjust to the changes and demands of the family and its members. The book outlines and discusses not only the many changes that have occurred within the family unit but also the issues and problems that confront the family in Australian society today.

An examination of the structure and composition of the family prior to 1900 and the political, social, economic and legal factors which have affected the family in Australia during this century may reveal relationships between broad social changes and family formation and dissolution. However, causal connections between changes in society and changes in the family are less easy to establish: the variables are complex and interrelated and no one factor can be said to be responsible for a particular change within the family. As a result of industrialisation and the massive developments in technology, society has become increasingly complex and individuals and families are faced with many decisions and choices concerning interpersonal relationships, utilisation of resources and the achievement of individual and family goals.

When studying the family as a social system of society, it is difficult to ignore our beliefs about what a family is, what a family should be, and what a family should do for its members. The majority of the population have been socialised in some form of family group, and through living in a family individuals form certain ideas about family life and what is thought appropriate or inappropriate or desirable or undesirable. Values that we hold to be important with regard to family life are difficult, if not impossible, to ignore. However, it is necessary to be aware of these values and how they may bias any investigations and study of the family.

THEORETICAL PERSPECTIVES ON THE FAMILY

A sociological study of the family may be approached from a number of theoretical perspectives or frameworks. Three major theoretical frameworks or perspectives include *functionalism*, *the conflict perspective* and *the femininist perspective*. None of these perspectives or frameworks have really found answers to the universality or continued popularity of the family in society. Many sociologists use parts of many theoretical perspectives to study and analyse the family and to explain its persistence as a social institution. While a brief outline of these perspectives has been provided, it is important to remember that within each perspective variations do exist.

The functionalist perspective views the family as one of several basic structures or units that make up a society. Other structures include the law, economy, polity, education and government. The family is seen to be a functionally necessary unit, occupying a central position in society: producing new members for society and teaching the behaviour, attitudes and values considered appropriate and necessary for the continuation of society. The family consists of a set of different status positions occupied by family members who each perform a number of different roles—the most important role being that of socialisation. The family unit is constantly changing in the sense that it is adapting to change, often performing new or different functions. However, it is also thought that too much change to the institution of the family may lead to instability in society. Many functionalists believe that traditional family values are necessary in order to maintain the integrity of society, and that family instability may lead to major social and psychological problems.

The conflict perspective views the family, along with other institutions, such as education, as an exploitative and repressive mechanism of the capitalist system, used to perpetuate the unequal allocation of economic resources within society. The family socialises children to accept prevailing social values, and strengthens the power of the upper classes by reinforcing the relationships found in the wider society, e.g. the dominance of men over women and adults over children. Women work as unpaid housekeepers, providing men with the comforts that allow them to go out and work to produce goods and services, thus making profits for the upper or capitalist class. This view sees the family as outmoded as it restricts individual behaviour and freedom. The more families there are, then the greater the number of goods and services there are to be produced, and the greater the profits for the capitalist or the owner of production. The average family in a consumer-oriented society cannot hope to accumulate the economic resources required to become a member of the upper or capitalist class, and so the existing social inequalities are perpetuated.

The feminist perspective views women as individuals within a family and examines their role both within and outside the family. Many feminist writers argue that there has been a glorification of motherhood and a view that all families are harmonious units, free of conflict. The modern nuclear family has made women dependent on their husbands, and they have not had the access that men have had to the social and economic resources of society. While the family may be supportive and caring to its members, it can also be oppressive. Feminist writers have focused on the problems of families, and in particular, on the inequalities experienced by women in society. Issues of child care, lack of social supports, workforce participation of women and the division of labour within the household are major concerns of feminists.

The following discussion of the family does not focus strictly on any particular perspective, although it draws on some aspects of each of the above perspectives. Discussion of structural and role changes within the family will necessarily involve certain assumptions of the functionalist perspective. On the other hand, any attempt to demonstrate that the family as a social unit or social system is not breaking down may mean a focus on the conflict theory: society has mechanisms to ensure that the family does not break down, because it is one of the systems required for maintaining existing economic relationships and social stratification within society.

Some theorists who approach the study of the family from a feminist perspective maintain that the relationships of power and dependence that are the basis of class relationships in our society are mirrored in the family. As long as these relationships exist within the institution of the family they will exist within the larger social structure, and vice versa. As has been suggested above, a conflict theorist would maintain that those people in society who hold the majority of power would not like to see the family breaking down as it would mean relationships in society would also break down. This would be a threat to their existence and lifestyle.

It is not the intention here to explore all the perspectives that are used by social scientists to study the family but rather to bring to the attention of the reader the diversity of perspectives that are sometimes used in the study of the family. Rather than focus on a particular perspective it is perhaps more useful to adopt a critical approach when studying the family. Rather than take at face value the changes that have happened to the family, it is also useful to think about why these changes have taken place, and to consider the implications for both individuals and society. Often, those changes which appear to be positive for some people have negative consequences for others, and of course the reverse also applies. Assumptions about ideal family structures, roles and functions, appropriate family relationships and the division of labour within families requires critical analysis in order to obtain a true picture of the family in Australian society today.

The use of the term 'the family' should not mislead the reader: it is not intended to convey an image of a specific type of family or an ideal family formation. Rather, 'the family' is used in the broadest sense; it refers to the social institution of the family, embracing all family types and formations. It provides a framework for a study of family relationships, changes experienced by families, and the interaction that occurs between families and other social institutions. Within this context, attempts are made to identify changes experienced by families and to find explanations for these changes.

Contents

1

THE FAMILY AS A SOCIAL SYSTEM

Societies are made up of *social systems*. Social systems are concrete forms of social organisation: they are the units in which individuals live, work and interact. The family is an important social system: some form of family life has existed in virtually all known human societies since man first inhabited the earth. There are many reasons why humans organise themselves into family groups and, although the dynamics and structure of family groups may vary from culture to culture, each human society appears to have some type of *family formation*.

Some types of family formations found in primitive or in other contemporary cultures may seem very different from what we regard as a family group. As discussed later in this chapter, there are many types of groups that can be regarded as a family: family structures and formations are not the same for all families, nor for all cultures. Similarly, what was once regarded by many people in our society as a typical family may no longer be regarded as the typical or only type of family formation. Indeed, changes in society during this century have meant that other types of family groups have become more common and no single family form can be regarded as inevitable, or as more natural than any other form. Despite the changes to the family unit it still remains an important social system or social institution in Australian society and most other societies. The family remains the primary place where social behaviour is transmitted from one generation to the next.

Why do individuals organise themselves into family groups? One theory is that in pre-industrial times, when agriculture was the main means of production, the family could produce more as a group than as individuals. The group also offered individual members protection from external factors, as well as providing emotional support and security. Families were the legitimate means for the bearing and rearing of children, and marriage was the socially approved union for sexual relationships between adults.

These reasons however may not have been applicable in all cultures and societies. Why do the majority of people in society still wish to form—and remain in—family groups? Do the same reasons still exist, or have they changed? Are new family groups formed as a result of individual desires, or are individuals socially conditioned to believe that the formation of families is acceptable and appropriate?

Definition of terms

To study the family and be able to analyse the changes occurring in family life, it is necessary to become familiar with the meanings of the various terms and concepts used, many of which are given in a generalised form. Sociology, psychology and anthropology are *disciplines* or *schools of study*, and each has a different approach or emphasis in the study of the individual, the family and society.

Schools of study

Sociology

Sociology is the study of human social relationships, social groups, social institutions, social systems and social interaction. Sociology views the family as a social system interacting with many other systems in society.

Psychology

Psychology is the study of various aspects of the behaviour of individuals, with some study of interaction between individuals and groups.

Social psychology

Social psychology is concerned with both individual and group behaviour. While the study of the family in this book has a basic sociological perspective, it also focuses on psychological aspects of individual and family behaviour.

Anthropology

Anthropology is often difficult to distinguish from sociology. Anthropology studies the social and cultural factors in human behaviour, often with a historical perspective: an anthropologist may be more concerned with studying primitive societies and the social evolution of humankind, whereas a sociologist may concentrate on studying individuals and groups in existing societies.

Some specific concepts

Outlined below are explanations of some of the concepts that are used extensively throughout this book. It may be necessary to refer to other chapters for a more thorough explanation of some of these concepts.

Norms

Standards or rules of behaviour, expected ways of behaving in certain situations and within groups in society. Norms may be *formal* or *informal*. Formal norms are those which are written down; rules which apply to the whole of society and are referred to as *laws*. Norms which are informal are unwritten rules and are regarded more as *expectations* rather than as rules. Societies, communities, families, schools and peer groups all have specific norms to which individual members are expected to conform. Some of these norms will be formal and some will be informal. Many theorists maintain that acceptance and sharing of norms is essential for the maintenance of a stable social system, whether the system be a social group, a family or a society.

Norms will vary in different groups and in different social situations, and tension and disagreement may result if there is a deviation from the norms of the group. For example, one of the norms of a family may be that the children behave in a respectful way towards their parents. If the children do not display the expected behaviour, conflict and punishment may occur. As society and parts of society change, so too will norms. What was expected behaviour of children in the family fifty years ago may not be the same today, as norms have changed. Similarly, norms surrounding the tolerance of homosexuality have changed significantly during the past fifty years. Over time, the formal norms or laws of society will also change.

Mores

Unwritten rules of behaviour. They are very similar to norms but not as exacting. If an individual does not conform to the mores of a group, culture or society he or she can expect some disapproval, but this will not be as strong as in the case of a failure to comply with norms. Today, for example, having an 'ex-nuptial' child may be a violation of the mores of our society; fifty years ago it would have been considered a violation of the norms of society and the child would have endured the *stigma* of being regarded as 'illegitimate'. Both mother and child would have been subject to far greater social disapproval.

Sanctions

Rewards or punishments that an individual may receive when he or she rejects the group norms. A *positive sanction* is reward or approval for appropriate behaviour. A *negative sanction* involves disapproval or punishment for inappropriate behaviour. There can be varying degrees of both positive and negative sanctions, for example a negative sanction may range from the raising of an eyebrow or a disapproving look to actual physical punishment, for example the smacking of a child.

Culture

The way of life of a community or society. It is the way people think, interact and produce goods. It includes knowledge, values, beliefs, norms, customs, attitudes and language. Culture represents a shared way of life, more or less shared ideas about what is known, how things ought to be, and how things ought to be done. Culture is transmitted through the process of socialisation. From birth, individuals *internalise* consciously and unconsciously the culture into which they were born and live.

Socialisation

An interactive process whereby individuals learn and become aware of the patterns of behaviour expected by society. It is a dynamic process through which individuals become familiar with the norms and values of their culture and society. Socialisation is a developmental process as it continues throughout an individual's life-span, as he or she encounters new social situations and must learn new norms and accepted standards of behaviour.

Environment

Includes all the external conditions and factors which may influence an individual or group. Thus, everything which is not contained within the actual family unit may be regarded as the external environment.

Social stratification

Refers to the arrangement of individuals or groups in a hierarchy *on the basis of money, status or power*. Hierarchies exist among families: families with the highest incomes, and usually the most power and prestige, are at the top while those with the lowest incomes, and usually the least amount of power and prestige, are at the bottom. Thus, social stratification is the distribution of inequalities within society.

Life chances

The chances an individual has in sharing in the economic, political, social and cultural resources of the society in which he or she lives.

Social institution

Defined in a number of ways. A *social institution may be a group, an organisation or a social practice which has significance for the majority of individuals within a society*. For example, celebrations such as Christmas may be regarded as an institution, as may the education system, the economy, the legal system, the political system and the family system. The latter are often referred to as the *institutions* of society, the *subsystems* of society or as *social systems*. Throughout this book these three terms are often interchanged, as all terms refer to forms of social organisation, units in which individuals live, work and interact.

Role and status

The terms *role* and *status* are defined and used in many ways.

Status

Sociologists use the term *status* in two distinct ways. First, status may be used to refer to the esteem or prestige an individual receives as a result of his or her position in society. Secondly, status is used to refer to the various positions an individual occupies within society.

Individuals may occupy many status positions and for each status position there is an accompanying *role*. Role can be defined as the duties, obligations and rights associated with the status position. While these terms have been defined independently in this instance, when the term *role* is used it is meant to encompass both the status position and the accompanying role.

In relation to the family, each individual will occupy several status positions, both within and outside the immediate family. Many individuals who do not live in a family situation will still occupy status positions in relation to their family—son, daughter, brother, sister, uncle, aunt etc. As shown in Table 1.1, a mother may have the status not only of mother, but also of wife, sister, daughter, niece, aunt, worker etc. With each of these status positions there will be an accompanying role. In Table 1.1 the status positions and roles of a *nuclear family* are shown, and these are quite straightforward. However, in a *blended family*, or stepfamily, the status positions tend to increase, as do the roles and the potential for conflict among roles.

Status, and thus role, may be *ascribed* or *achieved*. Status is *ascribed* when an individual acquires it by birth or inheritance and masters the role afterwards. Thus, the Queen of England occupies an ascribed status position: it was not earned through her own efforts, but was obtained by virtue of her birth and position in the royal family. Status is *achieved* when the position requires the individual to have special skills, abilities

Table 1.1 Status positions of each member of the Clarke family

Mrs Alice Clarke	Mr Gary Clarke	Angela Clarke	Tim Clarke
Wife	Husband	Daughter	Son
Mother	Father	Sister	Brother
Daughter	Son	Cousin	Cousin
Sister	Brother	Niece	Nephew
Niece	Uncle	School student	University Student
Aunt	Purchasing Manager of chemical firm	Member of netball team	Part-time worker
Accountant in office	Member of fishing club	Casual worker in shop	
Treasurer of Parents & Citizens Association			
Member of tennis club			

and experience obtained through his or her own efforts, for example the manager of a company has to demonstrate that he or she can competently perform the duties or fulfil the role that the position entails. If this does not happen, the position and thus the role will be taken away. Individuals who are retrenched from employment often sustain a large amount of stress when a significant status position and role is taken away.

ROLE

Roles can only exist in relation to other status positions and roles. Roles are *complementary*: a woman cannot have the role of mother without a son or daughter. Similarly, an employee cannot have this role without the existence of the role of an employer. Much role behaviour is learned within the family through the process of socialisation. Children internalise the way in which their parents undertake roles and often use this to model their future behaviour. This can have desirable or undesirable consequences. Children socialised in a family where the role of mother and father are performed in a way that is very satisfying for the children may undertake these parental roles in a similar way later in life, if they choose to have children. This learning of role behaviour can also be illustrated by studies which show that adults who were abused as children are more likely to abuse their own children when they are parents.

Each role has certain *expectations*, i.e. what other people expect of the role and what the individual expects from other people when he/she is undertaking the role. Role expectations may vary from family to family: the duties and obligations expected of a mother in one family may not be the same for all other families. Over time, the expectations of a role may change, which means the duties, rights and obligations may change. However, this is usually a slow process, as a change in norms is necessary and norms which have been in existence for a long period of time are usually resistant to change. To some extent changes have occurred to the wife-and-mother roles during the past few decades, although many would argue that these roles have not changed, but rather women have simply taken on another role, that of employed worker.

Roles are *differentiated* or *allocated* within society and within the family. Traditionally, roles have been allocated or differentiated on the basis of sex and age. Women in the family were expected to perform certain roles and tasks, and men were expected to perform other roles; older people were usually given tasks requiring less physical activity, while younger children were regarded as too unskilled for certain duties.

Roles allocated on the basis of sex are often referred to as *sex-linked roles*. In many societies, including Australia, this stereotyping of roles is gradually changing. For example, the role of wife and mother has traditionally included the performance of all household and domestic tasks. This has changed a little as men have become more involved in household tasks. However, the re-allocation or redistribution of duties and tasks is not as significant as the work role now undertaken by a majority of mothers. That is, women with children are now fulfilling a role that was for a period of history reserved almost exclusively for the husband/father of the household. In some families there are clearly defined roles and each member is assigned specific duties and tasks. In other families there is a greater overlap of roles and the attached duties, tasks and obligations. The changing roles of men and women are discussed in greater detail in later chapters.

ROLE CONFLICT AND ROLE STRAIN

Each person undertakes many roles at different times, in different places with different people. As the individual acquires more status positions and thus more roles, conflict can occur within and between the roles in the following situations:

1 *If the obligations and duties of one role conflict with the obligations and duties of another role*. In the example of the Clarke family in Table 1.1, Mrs Clarke may find that her role as mother conflicts with her role as worker (i.e accountant). Mrs Clarke's employer may expect her to work back at certain times, but Mrs Clarke may feel she should be at home with her family. Similarly, Angela Clarke may experience this type of role conflict if the obligations of her casual job interfere with her obligations as a student. Conflict between two roles may occur only at certain times or it may be everpresent if both roles are demanding. Many women, particularly those with young children experience this type of role conflict and it may lead to tension, stress and feelings of guilt.
2 *If the duties of one role conflict with each other*. A mother may find that some of the duties of a particular role conflict with each other, either temporarily or permanently. A mother may experience conflict when she has to assist a child with homework while a small baby is crying and requiring her attention.
3 *When the expectations of others are different from the performance of the individual in the role*. The role performance of a wife may not be what the husband expects: the wife may not expect to undertake all household tasks, while the husband may have been socialised to

expect his wife to perform all these tasks. If conflict is to be avoided, the partners will have to make some adjustments.

TYPES OF FAMILIES

While this book focuses on the family as a social institution it does not intend that the family be seen as a social unit uniform in structure and functions. The term *the family* is used in the broad sense to refer to the social institution of family. It encompasses all types of family formations and relationships. There is great diversity of family forms and relationships in Australia.

Before examining the various definitions of a family it is necessary to look briefly at the types of families that have existed and do exist in Australia. Approximately 90 per cent of Australians live in family

Figure 1.1 Although the nuclear family is the dominant family formation in Australia, there are many other types of families. (Photo: M. Partridge)

households, although over the past two decades there has been an increase in the proportion of people who live alone. This increase has been largely due to the growth of the aged population.

Nuclear and two-parent families

This family formation consists of husband and wife (*de jure* or *de facto*) and their own or adopted children occupying a separate residence from other kin. Approximately 80 per cent of dependent children live in families where both adults are their natural parents. In this type of family, members traditionally undertook roles that were fairly clearly defined by the norms of our society. In recent decades traditional roles have been challenged, and in many families, roles, and the attached duties and tasks, are increasingly negotiated by the adult partners. In the nuclear family prior to the Second World War, it was rare to find the wife/mother in the workforce; now it is rare not to find the wife/mother in the workforce, at least in a part-time capacity.

Couple families

As an increasing number of people choose not to have children or to postpone having children, the number of couple families who have not produced children has increased over the last decade. The increase in the number of couple families without children is shown in Table 1.2.

Table 1.2 Family type, proportion of all families, Australia, 1986 and 1992

	1986	**1992**
Couple families	*86.4*	*84.7*
With children	38.2	35.5
Without children	48.2	49.2
Single-parent families	*6.6*	*7.5*
Female parent	5.8	6.8
Male parent	0.8	0.7
*Other families**	*7.0*	*7.8*
Total	*100.0*	*100.0*

* *Includes families comprising a parent and children aged 15 years and over.*
Source: Australian Bureau of Statistics data

Also, a significant number of aged married couples live together, although their children may have left home to live alone or to establish another family. The number of aged couples is expected to increase as Australia's population ages and life expectancy increases.

SINGLE-PARENT FAMILIES

In Table 1.2 the proportion of single-parent families in 1992 is shown as 7.5 per cent. However, this figure does not include single-parent families where children are over 15 years of age. These families are included in the classification of 'Other families'. If these families are counted in the single-parent family classification the figure is likely to be closer to 10 per cent. While some single-parent families are formed as a result of a woman choosing to have a child and raise it by herself, the majority of single-parent families arise as a result of separation or divorce of parents.

Figure 1.2 A single-parent family. A group of people can be regarded as a family without conforming to the nuclear-family pattern. (Photo: M. Partridge)

Blended families and stepfamilies

Of all families with dependent children, blended families comprised approximately 7 per cent at the 1986 Census. At the time of writing figures for the proportion of blended families at the 1991 Census were not available. However, it is expected that this figure has remained fairly constant because there has been a decrease in the proportion of divorces involving children and a consequent decrease in the proportion of remarriages involving children. A significant number of children may move from a two-parent family to a single-parent family and then back to a two-parent family. Blended families have varying characteristics: they may consist of children of both partners, children of only one partner and/or children of the new union.

Extended residential families

The traditional or ideal extended family consists of several generations living in the same household. Traditional extended families were characterised by a large number of children, close ties with neighbourhood and relatives, interdependence of family members, traditional sex-linked roles, acceptance of the authority and control of the family, and strong family unity. As will be discussed in the next chapter, it is doubtful, however, whether this type of family was ever as common in pre-industrial times as is sometimes believed. It has certainly not been common since European settlement of Australia.

It is difficult to estimate the proportion of families in Australia which could be regarded as extended. Extended family situations may include adult brothers or sisters living with kin, or a widowed mother or father living with an adult son or daughter and their children, or a young married couple sharing accommodation with one spouse's parents. However, such family compositions could not be regarded as traditional or ideal extended families. Extended families of three generations may increase in number if the trend continues for adult children to remain at home for longer, and the ageing of Australia's population means many families encounter a situation where aged relatives are living with them as well as adult children.

Extended families and kinship groups

While the number of residential extended families may be small, there is a significant amount of regular interaction that occurs among related kin who do not live together. While members of the family may not live in the one household, kinship bonds and reciprocal rights and obligations exist among related kin. Indeed, many people regard their family as including not just their spouse and children but other members such as parents, grandparents, sisters, brothers, in-laws, etc. They may not live with these relatives but they do have regular contact and interaction with them, and many social occasions involve family gatherings. Ethnic families have traditionally placed great importance on the kinship group, and while smaller family units may not co-reside, they often live in close proximity and social activities tend to include all relatives.

With the increased number of mothers with young children in the workforce, grandparents and other related kin are being called upon more to help in the care of children. Similarly, while aged relatives may live apart from their children they are often reliant upon them for their help and assistance. The Institute of Family Studies Australian Family Formation Project has found that according to family members born after the Second World War strong family links do exist between generations within Australian families. Older and younger generations do take responsibility for one another, supporting each other financially, practically and emotionally.[1]

Aboriginal society was traditionally, and to some extent is still, based on an extended family or kinship system. In Aboriginal society the extended family often includes friends as well as blood relatives, operating within a network of mutual responsibilities and obligations. The communal social structure of traditional Aboriginal society was destroyed to a large extent by European colonisation.

COMMUNAL FAMILIES

An example of a communal family is the kibbutz in Israel. Communal settlements consist of clusters of nuclear families which are dependent upon each other and who share both domestic and work tasks, and child care. Many of the tasks undertaken by the family as we know it are taken over by outside agencies or by other members of the settlement. Children do not necessarily live with their parents. They may live in separate dormitories and be cared for during the day by other people. Time is usually allocated each day for parents and children to spend time together. Women are free to work and to enjoy leisure on the same terms as men.

In certain areas of Australia, such as the northern coastal regions of

1 H. Glezer, 'Cycles of care: Support and care between generations', *Family Matters*, Australian Institute of Family Studies, no. 30, Dec. 1991, p.46.

New South Wales, there have been some attempts, particularly during the late 1960s and early 1970s, to establish communal settlements where families engage in cooperative productive work. These arrangements were not as formal as the kibbutz in Israel and success with this type of family formation has been fairly limited.

DEFINING THE FAMILY

While the majority of Australians live in a family situation, it is difficult to find a definition that can be applied to all families living in Australia. Some definitions of the family state what the family ought to be rather than what it actually is: that is, what is defined as the family may be someone's conception of an ideal family. Families are not fixed groups of people; their structure and composition are constantly changing, and it is difficult to find a definition that accommodates all groups of people who are, or wish to be considered as, a family unit. A *plurality* of family forms exists within Australia and it may not be possible to find one definition that fits all types of families. When examining various definitions of the family ask yourself the following questions and think about the reasons for your answers:

- Does a couple need to have children to be classified as a family unit? What of an aged couple whose children have left home but visit regularly?
- Can an unmarried mother and her child be classified as a family?
- When there is only one parent in the group, is this group a family?
- Can homosexual couples with children (either belonging to one partner or adopted) be classified as a family?
- Does the family consist only of the group living within a household? What about absent family members or kin who visit regularly?
- Do adults who live together have to be legally married to be regarded as a family?
- Can a couple or group of people who live together but do not interact with each other be regarded as a family?
- Does an individual who lives alone but interacts with kin belong to a family?
- When a young adult leaves his or her family group to form a relationship with another person, is the original family group still regarded as his or her family?
- Does the definition take into account multiple family memberships?

First, a definition of the family needs to be broad in order to cater for a variety of family formations including two-parent families, single-parent families, couple families without children, blended or stepfamilies, aged families, extended families, de facto relationships and related adults living together. Secondly, a definition of the family needs to consider not only the structure and composition of the family but also the roles that are undertaken in the social unit. Thirdly, a definition also needs to take into account the extended family relationships that may exist outside the immediate family unit but which are an integral part of family activities.

What *is* a family? Can you provide a definition to cover all types of families? To demonstrate the problem of defining the family several definitions are included below. Examine each definition carefully to see if it allows for a diversity of family formations. It may be also useful to note the year in which each of these definitions was published and observe if there have been any obvious changes in how the family is defined.

1 *A group of related individuals living under one roof as a household.*[2]

2 a *The family consists of persons united by the bonds of marriage (husband and wife), or blood and adoption (parents and children).*

  b *The members of the family typically live together as one household. The size of the household may vary from the extended family to the marital group of the husband and wife.*[3]

3 *The family institution is a small kinship-structured group with the key function of nurturent socialisation of the newborn.*[4]

4 Sometimes social surveys use a specific definition of a family so family characteristics can be compared and conclusions drawn. A 1976 national family survey, for the purposes of its research, defined a family as *a child or children and the adult or adults responsible for their care.*[5]

5 *The family is that group of kin who live together in a household and who are usually caring for, or have in the past cared for, the material and emotional needs of children.*[6]

6 The Australian Census defines a household as a person living alone or two or more people who live and eat together in private residential accommodation. A family is defined as *two or more people*

---

2 Family Research Unit, *Australian Family Research Bulletin*, no. 1, (Sydney, 1973), pp.13–14. E.F. Young, *Dictionary of Social Welfare*, University of Southern California, 1948, p.77.

3 Both from E. Burgess & H. Locke, *The Family*, New York, 1950, pp.7–8.

4 I.L. Reiss, 'The universality of the family: A conceptual analysis', *Journal of Marriage and the Family*, vol. 27, no. 3, 1965, p.449.

5 Family Research Unit, *Australian Family Research Bulletin*, no. 3 (Sydney, 1976), p.8

6 B. Cass, 'Family', in S. Encel & M. Berry (eds), *Selected Readings in Australian Society*, Longman Cheshire, Melbourne, 1987, p.182.

related by blood, marriage or de facto relationship who live in the same household. [7]

Three major types of families have been identified by the Australian Census: couple families, single-parent families and families of related adults.

The Australian Census, while providing reliable national data, is limited in the sense that it defines family structure on the basis of co-residence. However, prior to the 1986 Census, family members who were absent on the night of the Census were not included as part of the family, and this tended to overestimate the number of single-parent families. Since 1986 censuses have included people who usually live in that household but were absent on the night of the census.

It becomes obvious that it is virtually impossible to find a definition that can be applied to all types of family formations. Some of the

Figure 1.3 A family can be defined as a social group with or without children.

7 Australian Bureau of Statistics, *Australian Families and Households*, Census 86, Canberra 1989, p. 1.

definitions outlined above concentrate on the structure and composition of the family and do not make mention of roles or functions that are undertaken by the family, or the relationships that exist within the family unit and with other related kin. The family is more than just a structure: it consists of interacting players, and a definition needs to take this into account. Can a group of people be regarded as a family if:

- there are at least two members, comprising either two adults or one adult and one child; or if one adult lives apart from the family group but regards the group as his or her family?
- the members are related to each other through marriage, blood ties, adoption or interaction?
- the members hold certain positions and undertake certain roles?

This is not an ideal definition of the family, as it is rather cumbersome, but it may allow for a greater variety of family formations. Can you think of a definition that can be applied to all families?

Functions and Tasks of Families

The aim of this section is to discuss the functions and tasks that families may perform in everyday living. Some of these functions are idealised, that is, they may be what we think families should undertake, not what they actually do undertake. It may also be the case that the family never did perform all these functions completely by itself, and that it does not undertake all of them today because some have been taken over (in full or in part) by other institutions in society. The degree to which the family actually performed such functions in the pre-industrial era will be discussed in later chapters.

The size, structure, composition and resources of each individual family will also determine the extent to which it undertakes the functions outlined below. During the various stages of the family life-cycle, families will have different needs to satisfy and different goals to reach, and thus different functions and tasks to perform. Families will need to make decisions as to how to undertake these functions. For some families, access to social and economic resources may be so limited that it is impossible to provide for basic needs, let alone undertake all the functions outlined below. Unfortunately, children who grow up in families where economic and social resources are inadequate may not acquire the education and skills required to participate effectively in society. Families existing on very low incomes may rely heavily on other institutions in society for assistance with physical, economic and social functions.

Family self-sufficiency is a myth, and even those families who have the economic resources to provide for their needs will find that reliance on outside institutions is necessary to undertake some functions. Many sociologists and social workers maintain that in today's complex society, all families need support and assistance at some stage in rearing children, caring for family members and coping with stressful situations.

A *function* may be defined as an activity carried out by members of the family or by the family unit as a whole. Whereas a function is defined in broad terms, a *task* may be defined in narrower terms, as something more specific which contributes to the fulfilment of the function. Families tend to make decisions about which tasks to undertake, rather than which functions to undertake. For example, a social function of the family is to provide opportunities for individual and family recreation. Tasks that form part of this function may include taking the children to a park, going on a picnic, socialising with friends etc.

While some functions listed below have been taken over in full or in part by other social institutions, there are certain functions that must be undertaken if the family is to survive as a social system.

Physical functions

- To provide shelter, food, clothing and some health care.
- To protect their members from the physical environment through adequate housing.

Economic functions

- To consume and produce goods and services (although they tend to consume more than they produce).
- To allocate economic resources within the social unit.

Social functions

- To provide new members for the population through reproduction and adoption.
- To socialise children, by providing situations where individuals can interact with each other and learn the behaviour and values expected in society.
- To provide frustrating situations so that children may learn to tolerate such circumstances in society.

- To act as a mediator: they link the individual with the larger social structure.
- To provide social support for their members and give them a feeling of social identity.
- To provide individuals with a status position within the family and within society.
- To maintain order within the group by encouraging communication, interaction and decision making.
- To provide opportunities for individual and family recreation and leisure.
- To allocate roles and tasks.

Emotional and psychological tasks

- To provide emotional support and affection for each family member.
- To allow sexual expression between adult members.
- To give personal security and loyalty to each member by providing a place where the individual feels protected and relaxed.
- To encourage the development and realisation of the individual's intellectual and social potential and self-esteem.

Cultural functions

- To teach the norms and values that are part of the society in which they live.
- To pass on the language, customs and traditions of their culture.
- To teach children to use the equipment and tools that are part of their culture.

Moral, spiritual and religious functions

- To teach children attitudes, values and standards of behaviour. In some families this may extend to teaching of religious beliefs.

Adaptive functions

- To assist members to adjust to a changing and increasingly complex environment.

FAMILY DEVELOPMENT: THE LIFE CYCLE

From marriage (whether de facto or legal) to the eventual death of both partners, families pass through a number of developmental stages and substages. This development is often conceptualised as a *family life cycle*, and basically consists of three phases—the *beginning* stage, the *expanding* stage and the *contracting* stage, each stage containing a number of substages. While the life cycle framework may be useful for studying resource management and decision making in families, it is only a guide and many variations to the pattern will occur in individual families.

In the period following the Second World War in Australia, there was a fairly typical life cycle which could be applied to the majority of families. During this period the first child was usually born soon after marriage and childbearing was usually completed before the age of 30 or 35 years. The life-cycle as shown in Figure 1.4 was typical for the majority of families. However, current trends in family formation include later marriage and childbearing, an increase in divorce rates

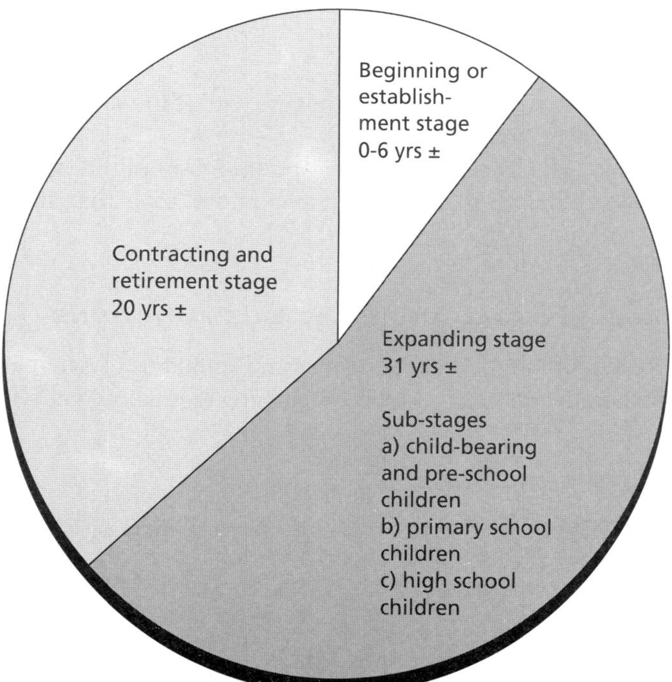

Figure 1.4 The family life cycle.

and an increase in both the number of childless families and blended families. Consequently, the family life cycle framework is valuable only if a flexible approach is adopted. The diversity of family types is such that families will spend significantly differing amounts of time in each stage of the life cycle; some families may not experience all stages of the family life cycle, while other families may repeat stages.

The life cycle approach can be used to develop individual life cycles for families. For example, in a blended family, overlapping stages may be experienced, while other couples who have children later in marriage may find they have retired from the workforce yet they still have adult children living at home. It is difficult to generalise about the types of problems and conflicts that families will face at each stage of the life cycle because the resources available to families will vary considerably. As circumstances of families will differ, so too will the decisions that are made. In families where both partners are in the workforce, or in a single-parent family where the custodial parent is in the workforce, resource allocation and the types of decisions that are made are likely to be different from a couple family where only one partner is in the paid labour force.

At each stage and substage of the life cycle, families will have adjustments to make and new functions and tasks to undertake. Apart from the biological time changes of childbearing, growing up, maturing, ageing and dying, families will experience other developments, including structural and role changes. Such changes may include the mother re-entering the workforce, one partner becoming unemployed, or an adult child or grandparent returning to live with the family. It is for these reasons that people who write about families often prefer to talk not about a family life cycle but rather a *life course*. The term 'life *cycle*' implies stages; 'life *course*' does not. However, for the purposes of this discussion 'life cycle' is a convenient framework.

Developmental stages in the life cycle of families

While the life-cycle stages of families have been discussed in terms of beginning, expanding and contracting stages, it has been done for convenience of discussion, and it is important to remember that significant deviations to this framework will occur.

The beginning stage

This is the period from marriage to the birth of the first child and traditionally this length of time was only one or two years, but now the trend in Australia is for couples to have children during the second five years of marriage. This change has occurred as a result of improved methods of contraception, economic pressures and the desire of many women to establish themselves in a career prior to having children. While this may be a period of relative affluence if both partners are in the workforce, it may also be a time when there are heavy commitments to housing mortgages.

Some families may not experience this stage, for example a woman choosing to have an ex-nuptial child as a single parent, while other people may experience this stage more than once, as in the case of remarriage. In blended families, stages may overlap, for example the beginning stage and the expanding stage may overlap if the new couple decide to have children.

Couples living in de facto relationships will be involved in making many of the same decisions that married couples will make; decisions may include whether to get married and whether to have children. During this stage, partners will need to adjust to the relationship and this may require negotiation of roles in order to minimise conflict and tension. During this stage decisions may be made concerning the allocation and management of financial resources; the allocation of responsibilities and setting and ranking of goals.

THE EXPANDING FAMILY

One of the major adjustments required in the family life cycle occurs with the birth of the first child. Caring for children consumes physical and emotional resources of parents, and often restricts involvement in other activities. To meet the demands of children a mother may leave the workforce, although this may be only a temporary situation. Families will have to adjust to the increased economic costs of children as well as to the loss of income. For this reason, many mothers will return to the workforce, although work-related costs and child care will also utilise economic resources. Whether a family is dual-income or one-income, the birth or adoption of children will mean that a re-allocation of economic resources is necessary.

The expanding family may pass through a number of often overlapping substages—when the children are of pre-school age, when they are in primary school, when they are in secondary and post-secondary education, and when they are in the workforce. Family resource utilisation and decision making will vary with each substage, for example the costs of feeding and clothing a pre-school child may be less than for a teenager, but the younger child will require more access to the parents' physical resources. Further, a family with pre-school children will be involved in different activities to those of a family with teenage children.

During this child-rearing stage there are added economic responsibilities and a restriction of leisure time, either alone or with the partner. Food, clothing, transport, educational, medical and dental expenses all increase as the children grow older. It may be necessary to change housing to accommodate a larger group of people, although availability of economic resources may mean this is not an option. It is important to note that while the costs of children increase as they get older, the costs of child care are such that very young children may require a greater expenditure than do older children. During this period the drain on economic resources can cause stress within families and often two incomes are needed to provide for needs and wants.

While the number of children per family has decreased, so too has the period of physical dependency of young children on parents. However the period of emotional and economic dependency may be higher. With the demand for higher educational qualifications and high youth unemployment rates, many young adults will be economically dependent on their parents for a longer period of time than they were a few decades ago.

The expanding stage places the greatest demands on both the human and non-human resources of families, and is therefore the period in which the most critical decision making occurs. Decisions made during this time relate to the allocation of resources, allocation of roles and responsibilities, and to housing, parenting, education and the achievement of individual and group goals.

Families without children will not be involved in the management problems that occur during the expanding stage. Childless families are likely to be more mobile and have greater flexibility of economic resources, and it is more likely that both partners will be involved in work outside the home.

The contracting and retirement stage

As life expectancy increases, it is to be expected that the number of years spent in this stage will also increase. While this may be so, it must also be recognised that many couples are having children later in their life span and children are remaining at home for a longer period of time. The age at which parents have their children and the age at which children leave home will have a large bearing on the decisions that are made. For some families, children may be leaving home when parents are in their forties, while other parents may be in their sixties.

Although children may leave home gradually, for parents who have spent a considerable part of their life raising children, a major social and psychological adjustment is often required when this happens. While it was once expected that parents would spend a considerable time alone after children had left home, this assumption can no longer be made. Parents who may have looked forward to a time when they were alone again may encounter a 'never-empty nest' situation. The contracting stage may be a period of financial recovery for families as their children become economically independent. On the other hand, inflation may mean that superannuation is insufficient for a comfortable life in retirement.

Retirement from the workforce presents another major adjustment for either or both partners, and as they grow older problems related to health, mobility and housing may arise. Decisions made during this stage relate to role changes, death of partner, resource allocation, physical and mental changes, health and mobility and dependency and isolation. (These issues have been discussed in greater detail in Chapter 8.)

Review questions

1 Outline some if the reasons that may account for the continued popularity of the family unit.
2 While the family continues to be a popular social institution, more individuals are choosing to live alone. Why may this be so?
3 Distinguish between *norms* and *mores*.
4 What does the term *culture* mean?
5 What is meant by *social institution* and *social system*?
6 Outline the difference between *role* and *status*.
7 How may roles be allocated within families?
8 What is *role conflict*? When may it occur?
9 Explain the difference between the extended residential family and the extended kinship group.
10 Distinguish between the terms household and family.
11 Why is it so difficult to develop a definition which will fit all families?
12 Outline the main functions that families may undertake in our society.
13 List those functions that you think are undertaken to greater extent by other social institutions.
14 Some families may rely more on other institutions to assist in providing for needs. Why may this be so?

15 The family life-cycle is often used as a framework for studying family development. Outline the advantages and disadvantages of using this framework.

Case Study 1.1

A Blended Family

Ann and Robert married when she was 18 and he was 22. They had two children, Sally and Tim, within the first two years of marriage. When Sally and Tim were in primary school, Ann and Robert separated and eventually divorced. The children live with Ann although they have regular contact with their father. After the divorce, Ann returned to the workforce and eventually formed a relationship with Ken, whom she lived with for two years prior to marriage. At the time of remarriage, Ann's children were in secondary school.

Ken had one child from a previous marriage, Julie, aged six years, who lives with her mother but has regular contact with her father. Two years after Ann and Ken married, they had a child, Peter.

Questions

1 What is the relationship between:
   a Sally and Julie;
   b Tim and Julie;
   c Sally and Ken;
   d Tim and Ken;
   e Ann and Julie;
   f Sally and Peter;
   g Julie and Peter?
2 In terms of a life-cycle framework, describe the developmental stages that this family has experienced and may experience.
3 Outline the management decisions that this family may have made or may have to make during the various life-cycle stages. How may these decisions vary from a nuclear family?

2

HISTORICAL DEVELOPMENT OF THE FAMILY

INDUSTRIALISATION AND THE FAMILY

Industrialisation affected Australia much later than Britain and it was not really until the last decades of the nineteenth century that secondary industries began to expand in Australia. During the eighty or so years between the arrival of the First Fleet and the real beginnings of industry in Australia, the economy was based on agriculture and the majority of the population lived in rural areas. As there is a shortage of records and research on the Australian family during this period, it is necessary to examine family life in other countries. Family life in Australia during the nineteenth and twentieth centuries will be discussed in the next section, but a brief look at family life in pre-industrial Britain will give some insight into the nature of family life before 1800.

The Family in Britain

In pre-industrial Britain many families lived on their own farms, and those who did not have the resources to purchase a farm were employed by other farmers for wages. The size of the farm and landholding was determined by the wealth of the family. Each farm was an industry, producing goods for its members, and any surplus was sold or exchanged for other needed goods.

Although the farm provided the family with many of the resources needed for survival, household activities such as cooking, gardening, spinning and weaving were considered to be equally important in the production of goods. In the lower and middle classes, women were involved not only in these household activities but also in the care of animals, the dairy and the orchard. Women from the wealthier classes may have had the benefit of household help and may therefore have spent more of their time supervising staff rather than performing economically productive work.

In pre-industrial times, the social position or status of the working woman was not considered to be lower than that of a man. Unlike today, household tasks and other work undertaken by family members were regarded as part of the overall productive activities of the household and were undertaken by both sexes. This applied not just to farm families but to all cottage industries in both rural and urban areas. Many families earned their living through such home industries as spinning, weaving, leather manufacturing, boot- and shoe-making, cabinet-making and baking, and all members of the family were involved in household as well as income-earning tasks.

With the spread of industrialisation and the growth of factories, the family found that even with the cheap labour of its members it could no longer compete with output from the factory. Thus, in order to support the family group and provide for basic needs, men were forced to find employment outside the home. Women remained at home to look after the children. It eventually became uneconomical to spin and weave at home, as textile factories could do it more cheaply, and women lost more and more of their productive tasks to the factory. As industry grew, so did the separation between home and work and wives became financially dependent upon their husbands.

Although household tasks were necessary for the survival and wellbeing of the family unit, as is the case today, such tasks came to be regarded as a lower-status activity. Housework, although still productive, became an activity that did not directly provide the family with any economic resources. Wifehood and motherhood emerged as full-time careers for women. Furthermore, many of the men were unemployed, because there were not enough jobs in the factories, and women found it virtually impossible to obtain employment. If men were unemployed, it was felt, why should women be employed! Also, when child labour was abolished by law, women had no choice but to stay at home and look after the children.

CHILDREN

In pre-industrial England, children of the lower and middle classes were involved in work activities at an early age. As soon as children were old enough, they were given tasks to perform on a regular basis. Boys ran errands and fetched tools, and as soon as they were old enough they would be made responsible for the care of animals and ploughing the field if they lived on a farm. Girls were taught the skills related to the role of motherhood. While many of the tasks undertaken by family members were sex-linked, tasks were allocated on the basis of age rather than sex. Children made a valuable contribution to the productive work of the families and thus to their economic resources.

It must be remembered that the role of children, as of all family members, was closely linked to a family's resources: children of upper-class families were obviously not required to perform productive work within the home. After birth, many children from wealthy families were sent to a 'wet nurse' in a nearby village until they were weaned. At about two years of age they usually returned home, where they may have spent a few years before being sent to a boarding-school or they may have remained at home to receive schooling from a tutor or governess.

It was not really until the middle of the nineteenth century that society realised the need for affection and positive physical interaction with children. In pre-industrial times, many children did not have basic needs satisfied, and a significant number died as a result. Prior to the eighteenth century it was believed that children should be brought up with little freedom, much discipline, and strict obedience towards elders. Regular beatings were considered a necessary part of their upbringing.

Prior to industrialisation, the majority of English children were educated by their parents. Schooling was not really considered necessary, as all skills required for work and survival could be taught in the home. With the spread of industrialisation, children became a cheap source of labour for factory owners and many families were dependent upon the money this brought into the household. Children were exploited as factory workers: they were made to work extremely long hours with inadequate food and rest, and consequently a large number of them were neglected and died. Laws were passed in the early nineteenth century to limit the number of hours children could work, but these laws were not really enforced.

With the introduction of laws preventing child labour, making school attendance compulsory and enforcing a minimum school-leaving age, children ceased to be an economic resource for the family. Many families in England during the 1870s were so dependent upon the small amount of money their children contributed to the family income from factory work that they campaigned to have the school leaving age lowered.

Thus, with industrialisation the role of both children and parents within the family changed. As children were no longer involved only in household and productive work, they had more contact with other people, particularly children of their own age, and became subject to more outside influences. Many anthropologists believe that it was this separation of children from the home, and the grouping of children in schools, that eventually led to the formation of the *peer group* and the *generation gap*.

The larger families of the pre-industrial era often meant that children grew up with a number of brothers and sisters, and were therefore exposed to a greater number of role models during the socialisation process. The family provided support for the aged, sick and disabled—if there was no family, the individual depended on assistance from charity organisations or the Church. Rural families, however, were

Figure 2.1a An upper-class family of the nineteenth century. (Photo: Tyrell Collection/Australian Consolidated Press).

at the mercy of the weather and the environment and floods, droughts and disease forced many families into poverty. Welfare services as we know them were virtually non-existent, and families with few economic resources were dependent on the charity of others for their survival.

Industrialisation altered the nature of extended family systems in most countries. With the growth of factories, many families moved from rural to urban areas in search of work, and this mobility tended to break up large extended family units.

The Family in Australia in the Nineteenth and Twentieth Centuries

While the family in Australia has experienced similar developments and changes as in other developed societies, the family in Australia is unique in several respects. In the early years of settlement in Australia, the majority of the population consisted of males: only 15 per cent of the 150 000 convicts transported from Britain to Australia during this time were females. Schemes to encourage families to migrate from England to Australia were not widely supported until about 1850 and males outnumbered females throughout the nineteenth century.

Mateship

In the first few decades of Australian settlement, the majority of the population remained close to the Port Jackson (Sydney) region. When migration to rural areas began, there were so few women that approximately 75 per cent of the rural population consisted of males who had to rely solely on the companionship of other males. It was not until the latter half of the nineteenth century that the sex imbalance lessened as the rate of free settlement increased.

Many sociologists have suggested that it was this high concentration of males in the early years of settlement that encouraged deep bonds of friendship among males. This bonding has come to be known as Australian mateship. Although many decades have passed since that era, norms and values concerning both male and female behaviour are often passed down through successive generations, including the norm of mateship. Many sociologists maintain that mateship is alive and well

Figure 2.1b A mother and child of the early nineteenth century (thought to be the wife and son of explorer Gregory Blaxland) (Photo: Tyrell Collection/ Australian Consolidated Press)

in Australia, and is evident in many aspects of life e.g., male-dominated clubs, hotels, and social and sporting events.

Extended families

As industrialisation affected Australia later than it did Britain, rural families in Australia remained self-sufficient for a longer period of time. Even so, the traditional extended family was not really a common feature in rural Australia as it may have been in other societies. First, so few families migrated to Australia in the early years there was not sufficient time to develop extended family networks. Early settlers were either single people or young married couples. Secondly, very few families had the economic resources to support large families on large properties. Rural families were very isolated during the nineteenth

Figure 2.2 A nineteenth-century working-class family group, in the Rocks area of Sydney (Photo: Tyrell Collection/Australian Consolidated Press)

century, as transport systems—including roads and railways—were poorly developed and interaction with kin and other families was very limited.

Under these conditions it was very difficult to maintain family cohesion even if there were other kin living in Australia. Extended family systems may have existed in the sense of emotional bonds, but it is unlikely that there were many families with three generations living under the one roof. It is more likely that two generations may have lived on the same property, sharing in the work and profits, but living in separate houses. It has often been suggested that it was this initial isolation of rural families and the strong tendency towards nuclear family formation which led to the modern tendency for Australian families to maintain an isolationist existence even in suburban areas.

There is some evidence to suggest that extended families may be more common now than they were in the past. Increased life expectancy, the ageing of the population, longer periods of economic dependency of youth, early retirement and the increased workforce participation of mothers may place heavy demands upon the family and contribute to family cohesion through greater reliance on all family members. Further, since the Second World War, immigration has contributed significantly to Australia's population and extended family networks are a feature of many ethnic groups. Migrants may not form extended families in the sense that they share one household, with many generations living together; however many ethnic groups place great importance on family and kin networks. This is evident in the emphasis that migrants place upon family reunions; that is, relatives migrating to Australia to join families who are already settled here, as well as the tendency to live in the same neighbourhood as relatives.

Social structure

During the nineteenth century, Australia did not have the rigid social structure that existed in Britain. The bulk of the population was working class, and there were fewer families who had the socioeconomic resources to belong to the middle and upper classes. Those who did so could not enjoy the same lifestyle as well-off women in England—for example, the shortage of females in Australia often meant that household help was difficult to acquire.

Living standards and conditions

Conditions in rural Australia during the nineteenth century were very harsh. The climate was unpredictable, housing was inadequate, sickness was prevalent, and people were often isolated from their relatives, friends and neighbours. Although some Australian women may have been involved in productive activities on the farm, men did not participate in domestic tasks. For the majority of women, their place was in the household—cooking, cleaning and caring for children—and their role came to be regarded as of lower status compared to the external role of men.

Life was also difficult in the towns and female employment was menial, usually in poorly paid domestic service. Living costs were high in the towns, and in times of high unemployment or economic depression many men deserted their families to search for work or gold. A middle class in Australia did not really appear until the middle of the nineteenth century.

Fertility patterns

Throughout the nineteenth and during the first half of the twentieth centuries, rural dwellers produced more children than city dwellers, Catholics more than non-Catholics, and immigrant Europeans more than Australian-born. While fertility rates have declined generally, it is difficult to determine whether these trends will continue.

An important change in fertility patterns is the increase in the number of *ex-nuptial births*, that is births occurring outside marriage. In the period 1956–60, 4.5 per cent of births were ex-nuptial; in 1971 the proportion was 9.3; in 1992 it was 23 per cent. While the proportion of ex-nuptial births has increased significantly, there has also been a

Figure 2.3 A middle-class family group of the mid-nineteenth century.

steady increase in the number of these births where the father is acknowledged.

Contrary to popular belief, the most dramatic decline in fertility rates (number of births) occurred during the second half of the nineteenth century, not during this century (see Table 3.1). The family of five or six children had nearly disappeared by the turn of the century, and family size declined gradually from approximately 3.5 children in the early 1900s to approximately 2 children per family by 1990. It is important to note that the figures shown in Table 2.1 refer to *total fertility rates* and not the number of children per family. Total fertility rate is an estimate of the number of children which would be born to a woman if she were to live out the entire span of her childbearing years.

Although fertility decline has been occurring since the 1860s there have been some stages in Australia's development where fertility has increased slightly. The period of economic prosperity following the Second World War coincided with rising fertility rates, much of which was due to the postponment of childbearing during the war. Fertility increased until the mid-1960s and then declined fairly steadily since, although there was a slight upturn in the late 1960s and early 1970s,

Table 2.1 Total fertility rates in Australia 1921–89

Period	Number of children
1921–25	3.03
1926–30	2.73
1931–35	2.19
1936–40	2.21
1941–45	2.54
1946–50	3.02
1951–55	3.18
1956–60	3.41
1961–65	3.29
1966–70	2.87
1971–75	2.48
1976–80	1.97
1981–85	1.92
1987	1.85
1989	1.85
1991	1.85

* *Refers to the average number of children that would be born to a woman throughout her child-bearing life*
Source: Australian Bureau of Statistics data

and again in the early 1980s. This upturn in fertility rates has been called the 'echo effect' of the 'baby boom'. That is, these short-term increases in fertility are due to the increase in the size of the childbearing population as a result of the 'baby boom' generation born between 1947 and 1961, as well as to the large number of young women who migrated to Australia during the 1960s.

In recent years there has been a trend to increased fertility rates at older ages: in 1991 the median age of mothers at first nuptial birth was 27.8 years. Women in the 25–29 years age group have the highest fertility rate and the group with the second highest fertility rate is the 30–34 years age group. This latter group has replaced the 20–24 years age group who until recently had the second highest fertility rate. The proportion of births to mothers under 25 years of age has declined from 47 per cent in 1971 to 26 per cent in 1991.

Reasons for declining fertility

The downward trend in fertility rates has occurred in most other developed countries and Australia's fertility rate is higher than many other developed countries. Increased life expectancy has compensated to some extent for the declining total fertility rate. The economic and social reasons for declining fertility are complex and interrelated, and no single factor can be held responsible. The following changes have contributed to declining fertility rates.

- *Industrialisation* required the family to be more mobile—to be able to move to areas where there were work opportunities—and in order to be mobile, families needed to be smaller. Reduction in family size did not happen immediately following industrialisation; it took several decades to occur.
- With the *introduction of compulsory education* and the *abolition of child labour*, children were no longer regarded as an economic asset to the family. Children are economically dependent on parents for a much longer period of time. Slowdown in economic growth also limits job and career opportunities and the costs of raising children will increase as young people remain in the education system for a longer period of time.
- While the *standard of living and quality of life have improved* this century, many families maintain that in order to provide more opportunities for their children, families need to be smaller. Fertility rates have traditionally been lower during periods of economic recessions and economic depressions. During the depressions of the late nineteenth century and the 1930s, birth rates fell dramatically as families could not afford to have children.

- *Contraception* is often cited as a factor contributing to declining fertility rates. However, significant reductions in fertility rates occurred before reliable methods of contraception were available. Reliable methods of contraception do allow greater control over fertility as choices can be made regarding whether to have children, when to have children and how many to have. Further, the *availability of abortions* has meant that both married and unmarried females have a choice concerning unplanned pregnancies.
- The *increased desire by women for self-fulfilment*, independence, economic freedom and stimulation through a career outside the home has indirectly affected fertility rates. It is not easy for women to participate in the workforce if they have more than two or three children.
- The *opportunity costs* (loss of opportunities to earn and spend an income) *of childbearing* have increased greatly. The economic implications of a mother's withdrawal from the workforce have become increasingly significant, particularly since the advent of equal pay, increased career opportunities and rising housing costs.
- *Social attitudes regarding the role of females* have changed. It is more acceptable for a mother of young children to combine motherhood and paid employment. *Availability and affordability of child care* also make paid employment a viable proposition for many women with young children. However, the costs of child care for more than one child may mean that employment is not economically viable.
- As birth rates have fallen *new norms* have been established and accepted by society, including the acceptable number of children a family should have—which is currently two or three, but preferably two.

The decline in fertility rates is not due specifically to the numbers of people marrying in Australia, but there is an increasing tendency for couples to delay having children or to choose not to have children. Forty years ago, a couple was most likely to have its first child during the first year of marriage. Today it is not uncommon for a couple to live together prior to marriage and to have the first child in the second five years of marriage. A woman now spends fewer years in child-bearing and child-rearing, because fewer children are produced and child-bearing is concentrated into a shorter period of the life-cycle.

Migrant Australians and fertility patterns

Immigration contributes to population growth directly by providing new settlers, and indirectly by providing new settlers who will have children and further increase the population. For most of the large migrant groups in Australia, total fertility rates have not varied much from the rate for Australian-born women. The common belief that many overseas-born groups have large families is not true, except for Lebanese who have significantly higher fertility levels. For Australian-born and overseas-born women, the peak age for childbearing is in the 25–29 years age group. However, for Lebanese, Turkish and Yugoslav women, the peak age is the 20–24 year age group.

Immigration has contributed significantly to Australia's population. In 1991, 22 per cent of Australia's population were born overseas. While Australia's early settlers may have been of predominantly Anglo-Celtic background, this is not so of recent arrivals. The ethnic and cultural diversity has been an important influence in determining the nature of families in Australia.

MARRIAGE PATTERNS

Prior to industrialisation, most marriages were arranged in relation to family rather than individual needs. Love was not the prime motivating force for marriage as it is generally assumed to be today. Marriages were planned for economic reasons and for the production of offspring. During the pre-industrial era, marriages were more likely to end with the death of a spouse than with divorce.

In the early years of European settlement in Australia, marriage was encouraged, as it was believed it would promote stability. The English Marriage Act of 1753 which was also applied to the Australian colonies had little significance for the Scots and Irish convicts. Thus, as the population increased, control over marriage was lost and by the first decade of the nineteenth century de facto relationships were widespread. It was not really until the second half of the nineteenth century that civil marriages and marriages by churches other than the Church of England were possible.[1]

Early marriage patterns in Australia were influenced by the adult sex imbalance and economic conditions. The substantial excess of males over females continued until the mid-nineteenth century, when free settlement increased considerably. Consequently, during the period when there was an excess of males over females there was a significantly higher proportion of females than males married, or living in a de facto relationship. Even when the sex ratio evened out in the 1870s and

---

1 G.A. Carmichael, *With This Ring: First Marriage Patterns, Trends and Prospects in Australia*, Australian Family Formation Project Monograph No. 11, Department of Demography, Australian National University and Australian Institute of Family Studies, p. 3.

1880s, significant numbers of men never married. One of the major reasons for this was that males still outnumbered females in rural areas. Further, it is possible that the cult of mateship which had developed earlier in the century continued for some decades, and many men chose not to marry.[2]

The Australian Marriage Act of 1963 placed marriage laws throughout Australia on a uniform basis. Marriages may be celebrated by a minister of religion, an authorised celebrant, or other person authorised by the Attorney-General. Since 1963 there have been several amendments to the Marriage Act and in 1991 the minimum marriage age for females was raised from 16 years to 18 years, and the minimum marriage age in exceptional circumstances was raised from 14 years to 16 years. Thus, the legal marriage age for both males and females is now the same, that is 18 years of age.

INFLUENCES ON MARRIAGE PATTERNS

It has been proposed that economic considerations are the most important influences on marriage patterns. In periods of economic recessions and depressions, people postpone or delay marriage. This occurred during the depression of the 1890s and as shown in Table 2.2

Table 2.2 Average age of first marriage in Australia

Year/Period	Males (years)	Females (years)
1926–30	26.35	23.37
1931–35	26.47	23.40
1936–40	26.66	23.72
1947	25.30	22.50
1954	25.00	22.00
1961–65	24.20	21.30
1966–70	23.50	21.20
1971–75	23.30	21.00
1976–80	23.90	21.60
1981–85	24.90	22.70
1988	26.10	24.00
1989	26.30	24.20
1990	26.40	24.30
1991	26.70	24.50

Source: Australian Bureau of Statistics data

2 G.A. Carmichael, *With This Ring*, p. 5.

this trend was also evident during the Great Depression of the 1930s. Traditionally in Australia, when the economy has been prosperous and employment levels high, people have married at a younger age. This occurred in the period following the Second World War, which was an economically prosperous time for Australia and many other countries.

From the postwar period until 1975 Australians married at progressively younger ages. However, since 1975 this trend has reversed, and generally, the age at marriage for both females and males is increasing. Teenage marriage is now at its lowest level in Australian history. Less than 9 per cent of females turning 20 years of age in 1986 had been married, compared to 31 per cent in 1971.[3]

While economic considerations, including employment opportunities and housing costs, may be major factors contributing to the increase in age at first marriage, there are other factors which have also influenced the tendency to delay marriage. The reasons for delaying marriage are complex and interrelated, and reasons other than economic ones include:

- Social attitudes towards males and females who have never married have changed and there is a greater acceptance of people who have chosen not to marry.
- Marriage is no longer seen as the only legitimate means by which to leave the family unit and live independently.
- The current generation has, through socialisation, internalised values of personal autonomy and independence. These values may not be consistent with early marriage. Both males and females may wish to establish a career and enjoy a period of independence before making a commitment to a long-term relationship.
- There is an increasing tendency for couples to live together before making the commitment of marriage.
- Both males and females who have chosen not to have children may see little need to legitimise a relationship through marriage.
- Traditional attitudes to marriage were based on religion, and the influence of religion over the lives of young Australians has diminished significantly. This is evident in the increased proportion of couples who choose to marry in a non-religious ceremony.
- Social attitudes to ex-nuptial pregnancies have changed, and pregnancy is no longer generally considered as a sufficient reason for marriage.
- The availability of contraception as well as legal abortions have provided other options apart from marriage.

---

3 P. McDonald, 'Families in the pursuit of personal autonomy', *Family Matters*, no. 22, December 1988, p. 41.

- The increasing trend to higher education for both males and females means that many individuals are still undertaking full-time education at an age when their parents would have been married.
- Females may be rejecting the roles of wife and mother, and the associated tasks that marriage has traditionally encompassed. Many females no longer view marriage as a passport to economic security; they have acquired the educational qualifications and jobs to provide for their own economic wellbeing.
- The increase in the divorce rate since the mid 1970s may have caused many young people to question the virtues of marriage and thus reject early marriage.

For the past fifteen years, the total first marriage rate has been below 80 per cent. This figure may indicate that 20–25 per cent of this generation of Australians will never marry.[4] While individuals are marrying later in Australia, the institution of marriage still remains popular, although the 1991 Census recorded the lowest marriage rate since the Second World War.

Migrant Australians and family formation

Immigration policies have traditionally encouraged migration of young families and information from the 1986 Census and 1991 Census shows that overseas-born Australians are more likely than Australian-born to be married, and this is particularly the case for Greeks and Italians. Early marriage is more likely to occur among Southern Europeans, particularly among Greek, Lebanese, Maltese and Yugoslav females. However, during the last decade there has been an increase in the age at which marriage occurs for females in families of Southern European background. This increase in age at marriage may be due to the trend to complete secondary education and higher education as well as to a change in social attitudes regarding early marriage.

Remarriage

In one of three marriages today, one or both of the partners has been married before. This compares to only one in seven marriages in 1971. While a large number of people remarry following divorce, remarriage rates in 1990 were considerably lower than they were in 1971, indicating a declining popularity of remarriage. It is important to note that men are more likely to remarry than women.

---

4 McDonald, 'Families in the pursuit of personal autonomy'

WOMEN IN AUSTRALIAN SOCIETY

The major change in family life during this century can be summed up in one word: women. As discussed earlier in this chapter, in the pre-industrial era women were involved in the productive work of the family, but with the growth of factories, the home and workplace were separated and women remained in the home. The status of women changed from being equal to that of men, to being lower to that of men. Because the labour of women in the home is unpaid, household labour is seen as unconnected with the economy and lacks the prestige that is given to labour in the paid workforce. For this reason, the status of women in contemporary society has often been seen as inferior to that of men.

In the nineteenth century in Australia, as in other industrialised countries, there was only one possible role for women—wifehood/motherhood. The alternatives to marriage were spinsterhood, prostitution, or work for very low wages. None of these alternatives were socially acceptable. Women from lower socioeconomic groups may have obtained work in factories but this meant working very long hours for very low wages in appalling conditions. Women from the middle socioeconomic strata may have been able to obtain work as governesses or by giving music and drawing lessons to children from wealthy families.

During this century there has been some return to the egalitarian roles of males and females in pre-industrial times, and thus an improvement in the social status of females. Factors which have contributed to this include: *legal*, *political*, *educational* and *economic reforms*, as well as *changing social attitudes* and *technological developments*. These factors, which are each discussed in turn below, have also directly and indirectly contributed to the increased *workforce participation of women*.

LEGAL REFORM

Since European settlement of Australia many laws and practices which have discriminated against women have been challenged. Consequently, many significant changes have taken place which have improved the status of women.

During the 1880s and 1890s, Australia introduced legislation which allowed married women to purchase and dispose of their own goods and property. The Sex Disqualification Removal Act of 1923 legally stopped discrimination against women. Unofficially however, discrimination has continued throughout this century. As late as 1969, some department stores would only issue credit cards to a married woman in her husband's name. During the 1970s, many financial institutions lending money for housing to married couples would not take the wife's income into account when a loan application was made. If the income of the wife was taken into account, it was only a very small proportion, usually about one-quarter.

The Family Law Act of 1975–76 improved the legal, economic and social position of women to a great extent, as have Anti-Discrimination Acts which have since been passed in the various states and territories. The Family Law Act addressed many issues pertaining to women, including joint rights to property, joint bank accounts, custody of children and financial maintenance of children.

Political reform

Australia legislated for female suffrage (right to vote) earlier than any other English-speaking country, although it took over fifty years of campaigning by women to achieve this right. However, the suffragette movement was not as strong or as influential in Australia as it was in the United States America or the United Kingdom. Females were given the right to vote at Federal Government elections in 1902 and at the state level, female suffrage was granted in South Australia in 1894, Western Australia in 1899, New South Wales in 1902 and Tasmania and Victoria in 1903.

It was not until 1943 however, that the first female entered Australian Parliament, and in 1990 the first female was elected State Premier: Carmen Lawrence in Western Australia. This was followed by the election of Joan Kirner as Premier of Victoria. While the number of females in the political system has increased during the past sixty years, the proportion of women in local, state and federal politics has remained fairly small, although the proportion is higher in local government than at other levels. Political involvement requires a support system, and this support system is usually in the form of a wife who assumes responsibility for the care and organisation of the household and its members. Married women who may wish to become involved in the political system usually do not have a comparable support system to enable them to do so.

In 1976 the Office of Women's Affairs was set up in the Department of the Prime Minister and Cabinet. In 1978, the National Women's Advisory Council was established to advise government on matters of concern to all women.

EDUCATIONAL REFORM

Until the latter half of the nineteenth century, education for females concentrated on preparing them for wifehood and motherhood with instruction in feminine accomplishments. The University of Sydney, established in 1850, and the University of Melbourne, established in 1853, both resisted pressure for over twenty years to accept female enrolments, and even in the 1880s attempts were made to legally exclude females from the medical faculty at Melbourne University.

While primary school education became compulsory for boys and girls in 1872, until the Second World War boys continued to remain at school for much longer than girls. However, for the past two decades, school retention rates for females have been increasing at a faster rate than have retention rates for males. Currently, more females than males complete secondary education.

Despite the rapid growth of tertiary education since the Second World War, some faculties in tertiary institutions have remained dominated by males. There has tended to be a higher proportion of females undertaking courses in the humanities and social sciences, and a lower proportion of females undertaking courses in the areas of science, engineering and law. However, since the early 1980s the proportion of females in traditional male faculties has increased significantly, as has the number of females undertaking both undergraduate and postgraduate courses and degrees. (See Table 2.3) In 1990, figures released by the Department of Education, Employment and Training revealed that women accounted for over half the graduates at both undergraduate and postgraduate levels. However, women still dominate the arts and education fields, accounting for over 68 per cent of arts graduates and nearly 75 per cent of education graduates. In 1990, less than 40 per cent of science graduates and only 9 per cent of engineering graduates were female.

Table 2.3 Higher education: Course completions by level of course and by sex, 1981 and 1989

	1981		1989	
	Males	*Females*	*Males*	*Females*
Bachelor degree programs	20 929	17 172	25 554	28 539
Postgraduate degree	4 388	4 965	6 648	9 380
Higher degree	2 438	852	3 427	1 858

Source: Australian Bureau of Statistics, Year Book Australia, 1992

Since the 1970s, the federal government and most state governments have implemented *gender-equity* programs aimed at encouraging girls to complete secondary education and undertake tertiary education. Initially, these programs were aimed at removing sexism from teaching materials and courses taught in schools. In the last few years, these programs have been expanded to encourage girls to undertake a wider range of curriculum choices, including those traditionally dominated by boys.

While many parents are concerned that their daughters complete secondary education and some form of tertiary training, they may be less ambitious regarding the type and extent of tertiary education undertaken by their daughters than they are for their sons. Some groups in society often see education as being more important for males than females, as it is expected that males will spend their working years in paid employment. It is not always expected that females will do so. Despite the increasing number of females choosing not to marry and/or have children it is still generally assumed that daughters will marry and have children. It is therefore considered desirable that girls have a career they can work in prior to having children, as well as after having children. However, it is often assumed females will work only to supplement the family income and that the family will take precedence over a career, particularly when the children are young.

As will be discussed in Chapter 6, the reality is that more than half the mothers with dependent children are in the workforce in either a part-time or full-time capacity. However, the lack of social and domestic supports for women undertaking two roles—at home and at work—has meant that educational qualifications of many females are not fully utilised.

ECONOMIC REFORM

For most of Australia's history, the national arbitration system has reflected the attitudes of the rest of society—that the place of women was primarily in the home, not in the workforce. These attitudes were apparent during the struggle by women for equal pay and working conditions. While the principle of equal pay for equal work was operating for females in some occupations as early as 1901, females were limited to certain occupations and it was not until the 1970s that all females received equal pay for equal work in all occupations in Australia.

In 1907 Justice Higgins introduced the concept of the 'living wage', an amount of money determined as adequate to support a male breadwinner with dependent wife and three children. In 1912, the Arbitration Court stated that equal pay would only be granted in male industries, in order to protect male workers from cheap female labour and prevent females from being employed in preference to males.

In 1918, the first 'living wage' for females was introduced at 30 shillings per week; this was half the male 'living wage'. Apparently, it was thought that women could live more cheaply than men, and it was assumed that the male, rather than the female, supported the family. By 1926, wages for females had risen to approximately 65 per cent of the male wage, but during the Great Depression of the 1930s all wages were severely affected and many were reduced. Female wages suffered the greatest setback, and it took many years to recover the gains made in earlier years.

In 1930 it was ruled that fruit-picking was no longer regarded as a man's work and was therefore not subject to equal pay for women. Female wages in this occupation were subsequently reduced by 7 per cent—only one example of occupations being reclassified so that females could be employed more cheaply. Indicative of attitudes towards females during the 1930s depression, a newspaper correspondent wrote that it was a strange society where 100 000 men were out of work while 200 000 women were working in factories. This male correspondent had no complaints about women working in personal and domestic service, because they were 'fulfilling duties which amply lay within their scope and function'.[5] Obviously, it was assumed that women working in factories had fathers or husbands who were financially supporting them.

In 1942 the Women's Employment Bureau was established on the understanding that it would be disbanded when the war finished and the men returned to take their 'rightful' place in the workforce. While this Bureau managed to have some female wages increased to 90 per cent of male wages, many female wages remained at less than 60 per cent of the minimum male wage. In 1950 females were awarded 75 per cent of the basic male wage but it was not until 1972 that the Australian Conciliation and Arbitration Commission accepted unconditionally equal pay for equal work.

Social attitudes

During the late 1940s and 1950s a large amount of work appeared in academic circles which proposed that children would not become

5 P. Spearitt, 'Women in Sydney Factories c. 1920–50', in A. Curthoys et al., *Women at Work*, Canberra, 1975, p. 89.

'normal' adults unless they had the care and attention of their mothers, both day and night. It is interesting to note that much of this information appeared during a time when women were being encouraged to return home, following their participation in the workforce during the Second World War. Many women had little choice, as creches and child-care centres which had been provided during the war were closed down.

The 1960s and 1970s saw the rise of the Women's Liberation Movement in most developed nations, including Australia. During this period many women's organisations were formed which focused on specific issues such as law reform, child care, equal pay, family planning, and refuges for women and children. During the last few decades significant progress has occurred in improving the status of women, and there have been changes in social attitudes regarding the role of women both in the home and in the workplace.

While in theory women have the same opportunities in education, in work, and as far as the law is concerned, in everyday life it is not always the case. Nevertheless, the Women's Liberation Movement has challenged traditional assumptions about the roles of males and females and has secured many legislative changes and removal of discriminatory practices. This has contributed to a change in social attitudes regarding the role of women in society.

Technological developments

While technological developments are often cited as having contributed to the changing status of women, controversy surrounds the degree to which technology has actually freed women from household work in order to allow them more time to participate in the paid labour force. Technological developments in contraception have to some extent allowed women a greater control over their fertility and consequently allowed more choices in all aspects of their life.

Workforce participation of women

The improvement in the social status of women has been a result of complex and interrelated factors, although the increased participation in the workforce of women has been a major contributing factor. At the beginning of this century almost half of the paid female workforce was involved in domestic service. A large proportion of the other 50 per cent were working as dressmakers or in factories, particularly in the textile and clothing industries. Gradually, single females began to be drawn into other forms of paid employment, including teaching, nursing and clerical occupations—all of which have remained predominantly female careers.

In Britain, the First World War helped society realise that females were capable of far more activities than those they had been involved in previously. With a large proportion of the male population at war and the expansion of factories providing military equipment, it was necessary to employ more female labour, and thus females became involved in new areas of industry, transport and communications. The First World War had little effect on Australia's industrial expansion and Australian women were not needed in the workforce to the same extent as they were in Britain.

The Second World War was really the first time Australian women were given the opportunity to work in occupations that had been traditionally regarded as reserved for men. This situation extended into the postwar era, when there were labour shortages and the economy was prosperous. However, it was still expected that once the men returned home from the war, married women would return to their 'proper place' in the home. Automatic preference in employment was given to male members of the armed forces returning home. Traditionally, women have been accepted more easily into the workforce when there were labour shortages and when the economy was prosperous, but the Second World War broke down many employment barriers for women and gave married women with children the incentive to re-enter and remain in the workforce.

As Table 2.4 illustrates, the participation of females in the workforce increased only slightly between 1856 and 1901, but during this century there has been a steady increase in the proportion of females in the workforce, with a corresponding decrease in the proportion of males in the workforce. For females, the increase in the past few decades has been largely due to the increase in married females remaining in or re-entering the workforce. In 1992, of the total workforce, females comprised approximately 41 per cent and males 59 per cent. In 1954 the corresponding figures were 22 per cent and 78 per cent. Further details and figures relating to the full-time and part-time participation of married females in the workforce are provided in Chapter 6.

Occupational structure

It has only really been in the last two decades that females have been actively encouraged to enter occupations traditionally reserved for

Table 2.4 Proportion of females in the Australian workforce, 1956–1992

Year	**Per cent of total workforce**
1856	18.1
1901	20.4
1911	20.1
1921	20.3
1933	21.8
1947	22.4
1954	22.8
1961	25.1
1966	29.1
1971	31.7
1976	35.9
1981	37.0
1986	39.0
1988	40.0
1992	42.0

Source: Australian Bureau of Statistics data

males. While some progress has been made, even in the professions men dominate the higher positions. Women are concentrated in the occupations of clerks, salespersons and personal service workers, whereas male employment is more evenly spread among industries and occupations. In 1992 approximately 76 per cent of employed females were in four major industries: community services; finance, property and business services; recreation and personal services; and wholesale and retail trade. In 1982 approximately 72 per cent of employed females were in these four major industries. While the number of females in professional and para-professional occupations has increased, females are still confined to a narrow range of jobs within these broad occupational classifications, including teaching, nursing, social work, clerical work and child care.

INCOME

While females have the right to earn the same income as males, in practice this is not always the case. Female earnings are on average lower than male earnings, as females predominate in middle and low-income occupations. On average, females earn 30 per cent less than males. The average wage earned by males is higher than that of females because a higher proportion of males are employed in higher-paying occupations. This may change as the proportion of females obtaining tertiary education qualifications increases; although evidence suggests that even when women do possess equivalent qualifications men may be promoted in preference to them. Further, females often lose both seniority and experience if they leave the workforce temporarily to have children.

DEVELOPMENT OF SOCIAL WELFARE SERVICES

Social welfare refers to the benefits, services and programs provided to individuals and families in order that they can satisfy basic needs and maintain an acceptable standard of living in our society. Social welfare provisions include monetary benefits, housing assistance, child-care facilities, community facilities, health care and education.

There has existed in Australia a belief that individuals and families should assume responsibility for their own welfare, because government support would undermine self-reliance and initiative. There has always existed a tendency to 'blame the victim' for their poverty or misfortune, although this was possibly more apparent in the nineteenth century.

During the nineteenth century assistance was provided through charity and voluntary organisations.

Voluntary organisations have played an important part in the provision of social welfare services throughout the nineteenth and twentieth centuries. The oldest voluntary organisation in Australia is the Benevolent Society of New South Wales, founded in 1818 to relieve the poor, the distressed, the aged and the infirm. In the nineteenth century, voluntary agencies were active in all States, providing homes for orphans and abandoned children, food and clothing relief for widows and the aged, hospitals for the impoverished sick, and institutions for the aged and disabled.

In the middle of the nineteenth century, New South Wales, Victoria and South Australia felt obliged to do something about the many wives and children who were left destitute when their husbands and fathers deserted to search for land and gold. However, the aid given to such families was very limited and there was no obligation for the government to provide it. It was not until the beginning of this century that state governments really introduced welfare benefits for the aged, invalid and unemployed. The amount paid was extremely low and insufficient to provide for basic needs. Prior to the Second World War, the Commonwealth government played only a small part in the provision of social welfare services, but after 1945 it expanded welfare provisions and assumed responsibility for the aged, handicapped, migrants and Aborigines.

WELFARE PROVISIONS

Outlined below are some of the major social welfare services available in Australia. Many of these services, and other benefits and provisions, will be discussed in greater detail in later chapters.

CHILDREN'S SERVICES

Social services are not directed at the family as a whole, but rather at individuals who are in need of assistance. The State has certain controls over the family—including legal marriage age, compulsory school attendance, child labour laws and laws requiring financial support for children—but it is believed that each child is part of a family unit which should protect and care for its members. The State will only remove a child from the family unit when it is absolutely necessary for the child's total wellbeing.

Until the late nineteenth century, the aim of child welfare services was to protect children from abandonment, destitution and vice. While children's institutions and orphanages were established, they were not very satisfactory. It was not until late in the nineteenth century that there was a definite move to provide care for children in foster homes and family group homes rather than in large institutions. Many of the children who were fostered out and boarded in cottage homes were seen as a source of unskilled labour, either as farm labourers or as domestic servants.

By the 1890s there was the beginning of a more enlightened view of children, and in 1896 the New South Wales government initiated a program of subsidising mothers, in order that children could remain with their mothers as an alternative to fostering or boarding out. Similar schemes were adopted in other states. In 1895, South Australia established a Children's Court for children up to 18 years of age and other states adopted similar reforms shortly afterwards. Children were no longer regarded as criminals and no longer appeared in adult law courts. The emphasis had partly changed from punishment to rehabilitation. Early in the twentieth century legislation was enacted concerning compulsory school attendance and minimum leaving ages.

This legislation to some extent protected children from exploitation in the workforce.

FAMILY ALLOWANCE AND CHILD ENDOWMENT

When child endowment was first introduced in 1942, as a method of supplementing the basic wage of the breadwinner with a large family, many argued that it would undermine parental responsibility and remove the incentive to be thrifty and work hard. This was a common argument against many social welfare provisions. Initially, payment for child endowment was to be made to mothers following the birth of the second and subsequent children. In 1950 the benefit was extended to include the first child. In 1976 taxation deductions for children were abolished and child endowment was increased significantly. At this time the benefit was renamed family allowance.

In 1987 the federal Labor Government introduced income-testing of this allowance. Family allowance is payable, subject to an income test, to a person with children under 16 years of age or dependent full-time students aged 16 to 24 years who are not in receipt of a pension, benefit or educational allowance.

FAMILY ALLOWANCE SUPPLEMENT

This supplement was introduced in 1983 as the family income supplement in order to provide additional income support for low-income families. In 1987 it was replaced with the family allowance supplement and the amount of financial support was increased. In 1988, 9 per cent of dependent children were receiving the family allowance supplement.

AGE PENSION

This pension was introduced in New South Wales and Victoria in 1900, Queensland in 1907 and South Australia in 1908. Until 1908 differing amounts of pensions were paid in the various states and different conditions of entitlement applied. In 1908, Commonwealth legislation replaced state pensions, and the pension was means-tested and subject to residence qualifications. Entitlement to this pension has changed considerably throughout this century. From 1985 payment of age pensions has been both income-tested and assets tested, and is generally subject to residence qualifications. (For more details see Chapter 8)

Unemployment benefits

Unemployment relief was provided by most state governments prior to the Great Depression of the 1930s, although it was insufficient to provide for basic needs. There was a major expansion of the social security system in 1945 with the introduction of Commonwealth unemployment and sickness benefits. At the same time, the Commonwealth Employment Service was established to administer employment assistance and benefits. Unemployment benefits are paid to unemployed persons over 18 years of age. Job search allowance was introduced in 1988 and is payable to unemployed persons aged 16 and 17 years to encourage active search for employment. This allowance is subject to both a parental income test and a personal income test. A young homeless allowance is available to recipients of job search allowance, who are homeless and without parental or custodial support.

Sickness and special benefits

These benefits were introduced in 1945 and are subject to an income test and an assets test. Special benefits are granted to people who do not qualify for the aged pension or unemployment or sickness benefits and who are not eligible for any other pension. Often persons who qualify for a special benefit are those who have not met residence requirements, e.g. newly arrived migrants.

Invalid and accident pension

This was introduced in New South Wales in 1907 and while there were limitations on who was entitled to the pension, the legislation was ahead of other countries. Commonwealth legislation was introduced in 1908 to provide this pension in all states.

Sole parent's pension, widowed person's allowance

Widows' pensions were first introduced by the New South Wales government in 1926, and by the Commonwealth government in 1942. The amount of money paid was barely enough to support a subsistence level of living, and there was no similar benefit available to lone fathers until 1977. It was assumed by governments that men could support themselves and family, and that the natural place for children was with their mother.

In 1973, a new Social Services Act was introduced, providing for the supporting mother's benefit. This was payable to unmarried mothers, deserted de facto wives, de facto wives of prisoners, married women not living with their husbands, and wives who had been separated for other reasons. To be eligible for this pension women had to have the care, custody and control of at least one dependent child. The benefit had the same conditions, and paid the same amount, as the widow's pension. In 1977 the benefit was extended to male lone parents and became known as the supporting parent's benefit.

The sole parent's pension was introduced in March 1989 and it incorporated some widow's pensions and the supporting parent's benefit. In general, a sole parent's pension may be paid to a person who has the care and custody of a dependent child. A widowed person's allowance provides short-term assistance for recently bereaved widowed persons. It allows a period of adjustment to make funeral arrangements, settle financial matters or seek employment.

Carer's pension

This pension was introduced in 1983 to provide financial support to a person who stays at home to care for a spouse or near relative, including a child or grandparent who is severely handicapped or in need of constant care and attention.

Double orphan's pension

This pension is payable free of means test to guardians of, or institutions caring for, children under 16 years of age or dependent full-time students aged 16 to 24 years whose parents are both dead, or one parent is dead and the other missing, imprisoned, or in an institution.

Handicapped child's allowance

Parents or guardians of a child under 16 years of age or a dependent full-time student who is severely disabled mentally and/or physically, is living in the home, and needs constant care and attention, are entitled to a handicapped child's allowance. The allowance is not subject to an income test, but a residence qualification does apply.

Department of Veterans' Affairs

This was established in 1920 as the Department of Repatriation. The principal functions of this department are the payments of disability and dependent's pensions (war pensions), medical treatment for veterans with injuries and illness caused or aggravated through their war service and medical treatment for widows and dependents of deceased veterans whose deaths were service-related.

Reciprocal social welfare arrangements

Australian pensions, with the exception of widows' pensions for non-de jure (not married) widows, supporting parents' benefits and carers' pensions can be transferred overseas once they have been granted. The amount of pension paid to the recipient is dependent upon the length of residency in Australia. Australia has comprehensive reciprocal social security agreements with the United Kingdom, New Zealand, Italy and Canada. Negotiations are occurring with other countries to establish agreements.

Voluntary organisations

Many voluntary organisations were established in the latter half of the nineteenth century, including the Salvation Army. Like other charitable organisations they relied heavily on government subsidies for their operations. During the 1880s and 1890s voluntary organisations became less selective and less morally judgmental in whom they assisted, although help was often accompanied by religious counselling. Voluntary organisations established soup kitchens and night refuges for the poor, and assisted in obtaining employment for the unemployed. During the depression of the 1890s voluntary organisations were no longer able to provide the degree of assistance required, as the unemployment rate was very high and charitable donations decreased.

During the twentieth century many new voluntary organisations were established, including The Smith Family, Red Cross, Legacy, St. Vincent de Paul Society and the Brotherhood of St. Laurence. These organisations have provided substantial assistance to many individuals and families in need, as well as lobbying governments to provide more services and assistance. Many agencies cooperate with the government in supplementing social welfare services. They are involved in the care of the aged and the sick, meals-on-wheels, senior citizens' centres, home-help services, sheltered workshops, aged persons' homes, services for the mentally and physically handicapped, children's homes, pre-schools, counselling services etc.

While the state governments and federal government may have taken over the role of some voluntary agencies, it is obvious that society cannot do without voluntary help and support. This has been very evident in the economic recession of the late 1980s and early 1990s, when the resources of voluntary organisations were severely stretched. Traditionally, local government has only played a small part in social welfare but in the past few decades there has developed a community-oriented approach to social welfare, with an increased involvement of local community groups.

Review Questions

1 In the pre-industrial era, why did working women have a similar social status to that of men?
2 Explain how the growth of factories caused the separation of the home and the workplace.
3 When did wifehood and motherhood emerge as a full-time career for females?
4 Describe the role of children in the pre-industrial era.
5 When and why did children cease to be an economic asset for families?
6 How did industrialisation in Britain affect extended family systems?
7 In Australia during the nineteenth century, men greatly outnumbered women. What effects may this have had on the role and status of women?
8 Why were traditional extended families not a common feature in Australia during the nineteenth century?
9 During which period in Australia's history did fertility rates decline most rapidly?
10 Outline the major reasons for the decline in fertility rates.
11 Outline the reasons that may contribute to people postponing marriage or choosing not to marry.
12 Outline the major factors contributing to the increased workforce participation of women.
13 When did women in Australia obtain the right to vote?
14 What proportion of the total workforce is now female?
15 What effects has the feminist movement had on the status of women?
16 In what year was the principle of equal pay for women finally accepted in Australia?
17 Throughout this century, which occupations have females dominated?
18 When did social welfare services really start to develop in Australia?
19 How have the attitudes towards children's services changed this century?
20 Explain the important role that voluntary agencies play in the provision of social welfare.

3

Socialisation and Individual Development

The process of socialisation

If individuals are to interact satisfactorily with other members of society, and be accepted by the society in which they live, they must be *socialised*. That is, individuals must undergo a developmental process whereby they learn and become aware of the patterns of behaviour expected in society. Through interaction with other people, individuals become familiar with the norms and values of their society, and learn the language and other symbols peculiar to their culture. For a society to continue, socialisation must be effective for the majority of members. If the majority of members choose to reject prevailing norms and values, society as we know it may cease to exist and a different society may emerge. If a serious disagreement about norms and values exists in a small social group such as a family, or in the larger society, it is very likely that tension and conflict will result.

Although the most intensive socialisation occurs in childhood and adolescence, the process continues throughout life. Each time an individual encounters new experiences and social situations, he or she has to become familiar with another set of norms and learn the behaviour expected in that situation. For example, the behaviour expected of an individual at home will be different from the behaviour expected in a work situation, and this will be different again from the behaviour expected of a member of a basketball team. Each group or situation has different norms and thus different expectations of appropriate behaviour. To be accepted as part of a group it is necessary to accept the values of the group, conform to the norms and behave accordingly. In learning and conforming to the norms of a group, whether the group be a family, a class or a sporting team, the individual is undergoing a process of socialisation.

Unconscious socialisation

Even before children can speak or understand language, they learn about the social world by observing the behaviour of others. Through the facial expressions and voice tones of parents, a toddler learns quickly which behaviour is regarded as good and which is bad. When children are old enough, they imitate the behaviour and actions of family members, and of other people with whom they come in contact. Children grow and develop in a learning situation, and they must learn to tolerate frustration if they are to acquire acceptable patterns of behaviour. The process of socialisation occurs both consciously and unconsciously; children internalise many norms, values and behaviours without realising it.

Identification

An essential part of the socialisation process is *identification*. Children model their behaviour on that of people with whom they form close attachments. Children need to have continuous and consistent relationships with family members in order to identify with and imitate them. Unfortunately, children can also learn unacceptable patterns of behaviour in the home. Children raised in an atmosphere of conflict and violence may identify with such and regard it as normal. When they transfer this learning to other social situations, they are likely to experience disapproval. Nearly everyone a child has contact with plays a part in his or her socialisation—it is through interaction with other people that children develop acceptable manners, attitudes and skills, at the same time as learning the culture of their society.

Inadequate socialisation

For a child to achieve independence via the socialisation process, certain basic physical, social, and psychological needs must be satisfied. A child is completely dependent upon the family or other caregivers to satisfy these needs and when they are not met, a child may not undergo normal development and may fail to learn the behaviour expected by society.

In 1938 in America, a social worker visited a farm and found a girl named Anna who had been kept in an attic since she was about 5 months old. Anna was an illegitimate child who lived with her mother and grandfather, but the grandfather did not want her in the house. Her living conditions were filthy and she was badly undernourished; she received very little affection, had no contact with other people, and could not walk or talk. Anna, aged 6, was taken to a home and during the next two years she was taught to walk, feed herself and understand simple instructions. She was them moved to another children's home for special treatment, where she lived until she died at the age of 10 years. Before she died, she had learnt hygiene practices and could talk in phrases.

While Anna's case is an extreme example of inadequate socialisation, there are also children in our society who do not have basic needs satisfied and/or have not been taught behaviour appropriate to the society in which they live. Sometimes, poor health of the parents, repeated illness, inadequate housing and insufficent income can mean that children do not have the opportunities to grow and develop in a stimulating environment. This can affect the socialisation process and ultimately the opportunities children may have in life.

Norms

Norms are standards or rules of behaviour; expected ways of behaving in social situations and within groups in society. When people interact with each other many norms are taken for granted and individuals are often not aware that they are acting in accordance with unwritten rules or norms. As norms are internalised gradually by new members of a society, they are usually not seriously challenged. However, norms can change over time, and what was regarded as a norm a few decades ago may not be regarded as a norm today. Norms vary from society to society, and therefore what is regarded as acceptable behavior in one society or culture may not be regarded as acceptable behaviour in another society or culture.

SANCTIONS

When an individual does not conform to the expectations of a particular social group, *negative sanctions* may be imposed. Thus, when a member of a basketball team intentionally hits another player during a game, he or she may be punished by being removed from the team, temporarily or permanently, as such behaviour does not conform to the norms of the group. Similarly, when an employee refuses to work, he or she is not conforming to the expected patterns of behaviour and may be subject to negative sanctions by the employer. This may involve temporary suspension and loss of pay or it may involve a more severe sanction such as being dismissed.

Although an individual has to learn some new patterns of behaviour in each new situation, it is often possible to transfer behaviour from one situation to another. Through socialisation during childhood an individual becomes familiar with what is, and what is not, acceptable behaviour in society generally. A child will soon realise that when he or she hits a brother or sister, punishment may result. The child may not be removed from the family group for this behaviour, but is likely to sustain some type of sanction such as being sent to his or her room. Similarly, if a child does not observe a particular norm (rule) at school, a negative sanction or punishment may result. The more severe the breach of norms, generally, the more severe the punishment.

AGENCIES OF SOCIALISATION

The child and adolescent are subject to many socialising influences other than the family, including the school, the peer group and the mass media. However, the family or primary caregivers are the child's first contact with the social world. It is the family which is still seen as having the primary responsibility for socialising children so they fit into and can participate in society. Within the family situation, the role models for a child are usually the parents, and a child will usually internalise parental role performances and regard them as normal and appropriate. The people with whom children and adolescents form close attachments are often referred to as *significant others*. Significant others may include parents, caregivers, teachers and other authority figures. Such individuals are significant because it is through them that we learn norms, values, attitudes and skills. Even in adulthood there are significant others, and adults learn skills and behaviours from other adults.

The three stages of socialisation

Socialisation may occur in three stages:
Primary socialisation occurs in early childhood and mostly within the family, although children may also be strongly influenced by other caregivers in child-care situations. Because of the strong emotional ties that a child has with his or her family, the family has a powerful and long-lasting influence on the socialisation of an individual. The large number of migrants in Australia means that children will be socialised into a variety of cultures. While some aspects of socialisation will be the same for all children, there will be some significant cultural differences.

Secondary socialisation takes place in middle and late childhood and occurs mainly at school, although other groups to which a child or teenager belongs are also influential, e.g. sporting groups and clubs. Secondary socialisation cannot be completely separated from primary socialisation as it tends to reinforce what has been, or is, learnt in the family. Education serves an important function as an agency of socialisation, as young people spend a substantial part of their formative years in school. The school is an important influence on the lives of young people as it tends to reinforce values and beliefs taught in the family. As children grow and encounter new situations and different people they may experience a conflict of values. It may also be that they reject some of the values and roles they internalised in their early years.

Tertiary socialisation occurs mainly in adulthood, and in circumstances in which individuals encounter new social situations, for example the workplace, clubs, voluntary associations etc. Socialisation continues as adults learn new skills and roles associated with work, marriage, parenthood etc. As society becomes more complex, so too do work roles, and as work roles change individuals are expected to adopt new roles. This often involves socialisation as new skills and behaviours have to be learnt. Also, the mass media have become important socialising influences, transmitting fads, fashions and norms, and providing role models. It should be noted that tertiary socialisation is not always distinguished from secondary socialisation.

Children in migrant families

The way in which children are socialised will vary over time among societies and among cultural groups within the same society. In 1989 it was estimated that approximately 7 per cent of Australia's children were born overseas, and over one-third of all Australian children had at least one parent born overseas. It is difficult to generalise about the child-rearing and socialisation practices of ethnic groups. However, many ethnic families try to retain customs and values of their country of origin and may mix socially only with the members of their own ethnic community. Children of overseas-born parents may grow up in a society which allows, and promotes, freedom and independence for its youth, but often in a family and ethnic group which wishes to retain the customs and culture of their country of origin, these different norms, values and expectations may create conflict for children, particularly during adolescence.

Children in Aboriginal families

Generalisations about socialisation of Aboriginal children and youth is difficult due to the diversity of family formations and social groups in which they live. Also, living patterns range from traditional tribal life to urban living. As a result, family customs and the way children are raised varies greatly among Aboriginal families. Traditional Aboriginal culture places a high value on extended family and kin networks, and this aspect of culture appears to have been retained in many Aboriginal communities, including urban communities. Thus, it is likely that Aboriginal children may be exposed to a variety of role models from which to learn behaviour.

In traditional Aboriginal society, children learned about their culture through everyday activities of hunting and gathering food. When food is readily available and there is no need for Aborigines to hunt and gather it, education of children about their environment and culture diminishes.

Aboriginal children may experience conflicts between the values of their traditional culture and the culture of the larger society. Such conflicts can create confusion for children who may be raised in a family with some traditional Aboriginal values yet are exposed to different values at school and in the wider community.

For many Aboriginal children, poor health, malnutrition, inadequate housing and poverty mean that many basic needs are not met. When basic needs are not satisfied, physical, social and emotional development may be inadequate, and full potential may not be realised.

The role of school and community in socialisation

For the child under five years of age, the family is the main influence in the socialisation process. However, once children have contact with other adults and children outside the family group, they will start to learn how to behave and interact in other social situations. The behaviour learned at home will be transferred to other situations and, similarly, children will learn that different standards and norms are appropriate in different groups and situations.

Children who attend playgroups or child-care centres or pre-schools are provided with the opportunity to learn to become part of another group. Depending on the age of the child, this may be a difficult transition, as he or she is separated from the primary caregiver (usually the mother). At the same time, a child has to learn to share and cooperate with other children and accept authority from other adults. This experience provides the child with a variety of adult role models outside the family unit and a wider variety of people to imitate and observe. Children will eventually become part of a peer group and learn to interact in a socially acceptable way with other children.

Child-care centres and pre-schools will help children acquire many of the skills they need at school and will usually reinforce those values, norms and standards considered appropriate in society. These organisations usually complement the role of the family in the socialisation process. Early childhood experiences can help ease the transition from home to infant's school. It is difficult for the family to provide all the different types of play, situations, activities and people that children experience at such centres. Unfortunately, not all families have access to pre-schools, kindergartens and child-care centres.

The influence of infant's and primary school in the socialisation process is fairly significant as a child spends a considerable number of waking hours in this environment. Apart from the educative function of the school, many aspects of the school assist in the socialisation process. Different role models are provided; children have access to the school library; to sporting activities; to school excursions and to clubs and activities within the school. Such experiences often cannot be provided by the family.

The community in its broadest sense supplements the role of the family in the socialisation process. The local and wider community of which the child will eventually be a member provides many resources which may influence the development of the individual. Perhaps the earliest contact a child has with the community are visits to the park, the local shops or the shopping centre. A child can observe other people, and whilst he or she may have little direct interaction with them, he or she is starting to internalise the nature of the outside world and the larger environment. Such outings provide stimulation for a child and allow observation of behaviour of people outside the family group.

As a child grows older it is likely that he or she will have more direct interaction with many aspects of the community. Apart from the school, which is also part of the community, the child may join sporting clubs or youth groups and may attend entertainment provided in the community. As families have grown smaller, it is likely that more reliance has been placed on the use of community resources. Similarly, the influence on children of the mass media and the peer group may mean that the family has no choice but to utilise community resources and become involved in at least some aspects of the community.

SEX-LINKED SOCIALISATION

Babies are born male or female, but they learn from birth their respective male and female roles; babies are not born knowing how to behave in a 'male' or 'female' manner. From birth, the majority of children are socialised into sex-linked roles, i.e. they are taught consciously or unconsciously certain roles, tasks, activities and skills that society regards as appropriate for their sex. Boys are usually expected to behave in a 'masculine' way and to be involved in activities that are traditionally regarded as male. Girls are usually expected to behave in a 'feminine' manner and to be involved in activities that are traditionally regarded as female.

GENDER

The term gender is used to distinguish the biological attributes of sex from the social and cultural attributes of sex. Gender denotes those aspects of male and female behaviour that are not biologically determined, but rather socially and culturally determined. Gender differences are found in modes of dress and speech, in behaviour, in roles, in emotions and in skills, many of which are regarded as belonging predominantly to either the male or female sex. Male and female stereotypes have been questioned in recent years, because traditional female stereotypes have assisted in perpetuating the inequality experienced by females, particularly in the workforce.

NATURE VERSUS NURTURE

During the 1970s, when the femininist movement gained momentum, many people argued that all gender differences were due to social conditioning. Lately, it has become acceptable to suggest that there may be inborn differences among the sexes, and that these inborn differences may in part be responsible for the tendency of males and females to adopt different roles in society. However, many people would argue that this is not so; genetic differences are insignificant and the major differences among females and males occur as a result of *sex-linked socialisation*. This is the basis of the *nature versus nurture* argument. It may be that there are some genetic differences in abilities and that these can be minimised through socialisation and education if girls and boys were treated with greater similarity and provided with the same opportunities.

Figure 3.1 Sex-linked stereotypes are being challenged. (Photo ©*The Mercury*, Hobart.)

SEX-LINKED ROLES

Over the past two decades many people have become increasingly concerned about the socialisation of children into traditional male and female roles. As discussed in Chapter 2, many initiatives have been taken, particularly in education, to ensure that females are not treated differently and that they are afforded the same opportunities as males. While many parents make a determined effort not to socialise their children into definite sex-linked roles, it is often difficult to avoid. The reasons for this are outlined below.

1 The biological differences between males and females mean that females must undertake at least one role that is unique to females, i.e. child-bearing, although more and more females are choosing not to undertake this role. As women must bear the children, they tend to become more involved with child-rearing and the tasks of child care.
2 Children learn sex roles in the same way they learn other things—through imitation. Girls will identify with their mother, and will often imitate the tasks and duties that their mother undertakes as part of her role; similarly, boys will identify with their father and will imitate his activities. In families where parents have not adopted completely traditional roles, e.g. where both parents are working outside the home and share household tasks and child care, identification with traditional roles may not be as great. However, as discussed in Chapter Seven, research indicates this is not necessarily the case.
3 While parents may make a conscious effort not to socialise children into traditional sex roles, children will become aware of these roles through interaction with other people in society. The influence of other children and other significant adults can be very strong in this respect. Children who attend child-care centres or pre-schools will likely be cared for by females, and will be socialised into regarding this nurturing role as belonging predominantly to females. Role-play is an important part of the play of young children, and they may accept their playmates attitudes towards roles in order to be accepted by the group. Advertising and the mass media also tend to reinforce the traditional role of the mother/wife involved in child care and household activities, with the husband/father involved in earning a living outside the home. While advertisers have made some effort to avoid stereotyping of roles, an analysis of television advertisements will show that it is still mainly females who are associated with food and household products, while males are associated with goods and services external to the home.

Sometimes parents are so concerned that children should not be socialised into traditional roles that they go to the opposite extreme, for example girls may not be given any dolls to play with at all. It is interesting to note however, that boys are rarely denied the opportunity to play with traditionally 'masculine' toys such as Lego. It is probably best for the development of children if they are given a variety of toys with which to play, although evidence suggests that when this is the case, the choices made by children are still traditionally sex-linked.

The list below illustrates various ways in which males and females are socialised into sex-linked roles. Although some of these practices are changing, examine each one carefully to see if you have observed it in the world around you. Try to think of other ways in which males and females are differentiated on the basis of sex.

- When a baby is born, friends and relatives usually wish to know if the infant is a boy or a girl.
- Sometimes colours are used to differentiate sex—blue for a boy and pink for a girl.
- Parents, friends and relatives often use different phrases with boys and girls, for example: 'Little boys don't cry', or 'You must act in a more ladylike manner' etc.
- Children are often given toys that are linked to their future role in society: girls are given dolls, dolls' houses and tea-sets, while boys are given trucks, train-sets and building sets. Toys for girls are related to the adult role of wife and mother, while toys for boys are related to the adult role of breadwinner and employed worker.
- Boys and girls are often dressed in a different manner.
- Boys are often encouraged to be aggressive, while girls may be encouraged to act in a 'feminine' or more demure manner.
- Advertisements often show females involved in traditional household activities (e.g. washing the clothes), while men are shown in more overtly active household tasks (e.g. mowing the lawn or painting the house).
- At school, boys and girls may be segregated in different ways, e.g. lining up separately, playing different sports. However, educators and teachers are more aware of differentiation on the basis of sex, and this is less likely to happen.

There are many people who believe that gender differences are unavoidable and not to be regarded in a negative manner, provided females have access to the same opportunities as do males. Further, many sociologists are concerned that much attention has been paid to females entering courses of studies and occupations traditionally reserved for males yet little attention has been paid to males undertaking courses of studies and entering occupations traditionally reserved for females. For example, if children are to be socialised perceiving males and females as having equal responsibility for nurturing and child care, a higher proportion of male staff is needed in child-care centres, pre-schools and kindergartens. While programs have been developed to encourage more girls to undertake studies in the areas of mathematics and science, little attention has been paid to encourage more boys into studies in the humanities areas.

Read Case study 3.1, 'A Fabulous Child's Story' at the end of this chapter and you will see how difficult it is to avoid sex-linked socialisation.

THE NEEDS OF INDIVIDUALS

All human beings have certain needs which must be satisfied in order to ensure physical, social and psychological wellbeing. Infants and children are almost entirely dependent upon the family to satisfy these needs, but adults also have certain needs which cannot be satisfied without interaction with other people. The needs of adults and children are basically very similar, although they may be satisfied in different ways. Unfortunately, not all families have the necessary resources to satisfy the needs of all family members. At certain stages of the life cycle some families may require greater assistance from other institutions in society in order to provide for basic needs.

To some extent, all families rely on external agencies and institutions to help satisfy needs, e.g. education, health care, community facilities etc.

PHYSICAL NEEDS

An individual needs:

- Adequate nourishment for normal growth, development and good health. Children and adolescents have specific nutritional needs during periods of rapid growth.
- Adequate sleep and rest for good health.
- Regular health care, beginning before birth. Children must have the opportunity to avoid physical illness through protective measures such as immunisation.
- To be safe and protected from external hazards and the weather. Children require protection from substances and materials that may

cause them injury, e.g. poisons, cleaning materials. Children require safe and sensible clothing that will not contribute to accidents,
- Comfort in his or her environment.
- The use of certain amounts of closed and open space. (The physical environment—housing and its location—also affects the social and psychological wellbeing of individuals and families.) Children need space to explore the world and develop skills through play.
- Special treatment and help for disabilities and handicaps.

Psychological and Intellectual Needs

An individual needs:

- To feel secure within the family unit. It is necessary to create a stable and consistent environment where children can feel as though they belong.
- A certain amount of independence to develop his or her skills, abilities, interests and activities. Children require encouragement when they experience failure and praise when a task is accomplished (e.g. feeding and dressing themselves). The fostering of independence makes adjustment to the outside world easier.
- Love and affection from family members. This should be consistent so a child does not find it difficult to form attachments later in life with other people.
- Stimulation from the physical environment and from interaction with other people. Toys that are suitable to the age of the child provide a valuable source of stimulation.
- The opportunity to express himself or herself and to be creative.
- A good self-image or self-concept. A child's self-image is formed through others' apparent impressions of him or her: a child who is continually punished and criticised will form a poor self-image. A child needs care, encouragement, love and guidance to develop a positive self-image and thus gain confidence in performing tasks independently of others. Children with a positive self-image will find it easier to interact with other people.
- Access to educational facilities.

Social Needs

An individual needs:

- An environment where socialisation, interaction, companionship and friendship can be fostered and encouraged. Children need the

physical and emotional communication of holding, cuddling, lifting and touching, as well as verbal interaction. Interaction with other children is an important part of socialisation.
- Privacy, seclusion and quietness when required.
- Opportunities for leisure, recreation and relaxation both with, and independently of, the family.
- To be able to identify with the family and with others outside the family unit. This promotes a sense of belonging to a particular group or community.

Needs are also often classified as primary needs and secondary needs. Primary needs include food, clothing and shelter; secondary needs include safety, comfort, security, independence, love, affection, sexual satisfaction, opportunities for creativity and education, privacy, status etc.

GROWTH AND DEVELOPMENT OF CHILDREN AND ADOLESCENTS

From the creation of a new family unit to the dissolution of that unit, the group passes through various stages. This is known as the family life cycle. Just as a family passes through a life cycle, an individual passes through a life cycle or life span. During the life span an individual moves from a state of complete dependency to independence, and will most likely eventually live independently of the original family unit into which he or she was born.

Erikson[1] has identified the following stages in the life span of an individual:

- infancy
- early childhood
- play age
- school age
- adolescence
- young adulthood
- adulthood
- mature age

For an individual to achieve independence, growth and development must occur. Growth refers to changes in the size and structure of

1 E. Erikson, *Childhood and Society*, 2nd edn, W.W. Norton, New York, 1963, p. 116.

Figure 3.2 Children must reach a certain stage of physical development before they can master the task of walking. (Photo: John Fairfax & Sons Ltd)

the human body, while development refers to the sequence in which individuals master certain tasks such as talking and walking. Both growth and development depend upon the satisfaction of basic needs and upon interaction with other human beings.

At each stage of the life span, there are various developmental tasks that have to be mastered if an individual is to be well adjusted, happy and accepted by society. In this chapter the developmental tasks associated with infancy, early childhood and adolescence will be briefly discussed. Different authorities often use different terms and categories to describe developmental tasks, but these definitions are all very similar. R.J. Havinghurst defined a developmental task as:

> a task which arises at or about a certain period in the life of the individual, successful achievement of which leads to his happiness and to success with later tasks, while failure leads to unhappiness in the individual, disapproval by society and difficulty with later tasks.[2]

The achievement of one task (e.g. walking) is often necessary to perform other tasks (e.g. running and playing), and when an individual does not master the task he or she is hindered in performing others. This can produce frustration, unhappiness and problems of adjustment. Some tasks cannot be learnt until a child is physically mature enough to cope with the task, while mastery of other tasks requires social and psychological maturity. For example, children reach a state of readiness to walk when the skeletal and muscular structure is strong enough to support the body in an upright position. Similarly, children need to have developed some degree of social maturity in order to interact and play with others of the same age. While children should be encouraged to master tasks, if parents or other family members try to make a child master a task before he or she is ready, frustration will result for all concerned. On the other hand, when a child does not master a developmental task at the appropriate stage, the task may never be mastered satisfactorily. This is likely to happen when children are abused or neglected.

Not all children and adolescents develop at the same rate. Individual differences, level of maturity, interests and environment will all affect the age at which an individual masters certain tasks. Development is not smooth, and many tasks will overlap. In childhood, the developmental tasks are more related to physical development; while tasks in adolescence are more related to social development.

Development during infancy and childhood

Generally speaking, infancy refers to the first few weeks in a child's life; babyhood covers the period from infancy to approximately 2 years; and

2 Quoted in M.W. & H.E. Draper, *Caring for Children*, Illinois, 1969, p. 116.

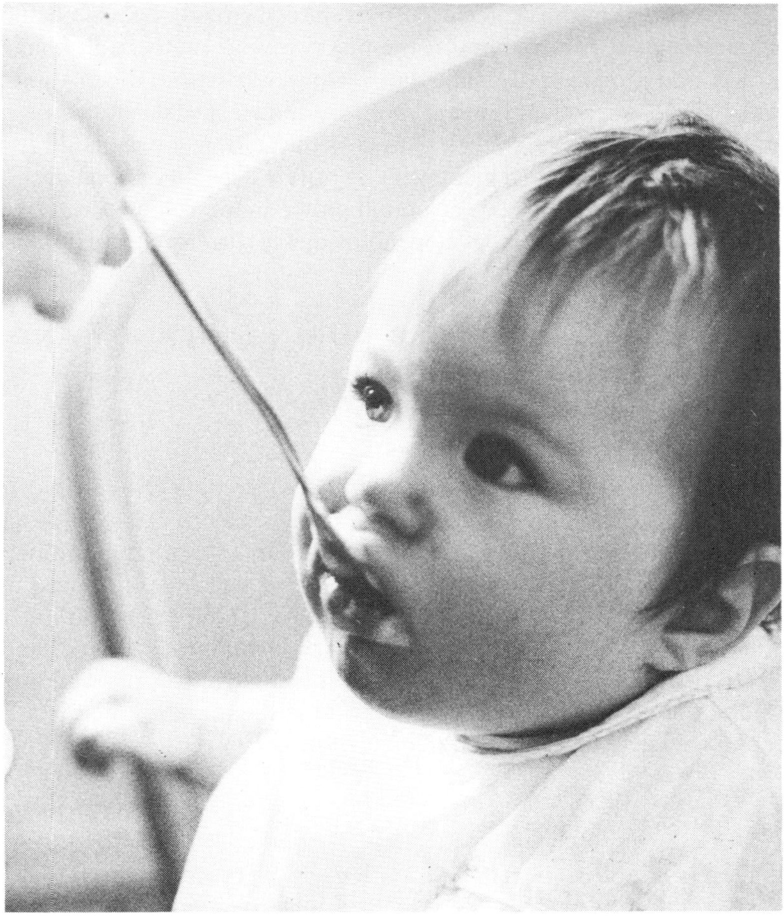

Figure 3.3 Children cannot feed themselves until they have acquired the physical ability to hold and use eating utensils.

childhood the period from 2 years to adolescence. The early period of childhood is one of intense socialisation, where children learn tasks through trial and error, imitation, and identification with another person. Physical, social and psychological stimulation, and adequate nourishment, are necessary if a child is to master developmental tasks and realise his or her potential.

Many studies have produced evidence to show that seriously deprived infants and children experience difficulties in relating to other people later in life. Children who are deprived of basic needs may not master the tasks required for normal development. When children have to accomplish these tasks at a later stage, there may be problems relating to mastery of the task.

Babies differ in the degree of activity, rate of growth, behaviour and physical appearance. Generally, the first two years is a period of rapid growth and babies usually triple their birth weight within the first year. As a baby grows, body size and proportions change, facial features alter, and the child begins to develop a personality. A new-born child has very uncoordinated movements and is entirely dependent upon others to satisfy his or her needs. As a child grows and develops during the early years, physical skills develop more quickly than intellectual skills.

Developmental tasks during infancy and early childhood

Learning to walk

When a baby is about 4 months old, he or she likes to see what is happening around him/her. At about 7 months a baby can sit without support for a short time, and by the age of 10 months can pull himself or herself into a standing position. Although a baby does not need to crawl before he or she can walk, crawling usually begins between 7 and 9 months. Between the ages of 9 and 15 months, muscles, bones and nerve tissues develop sufficiently to allow a child to start walking. Walking is a gradual process and a child will experience many falls before complete mastery of the task is achieved.

Learning to take solid food

Weaning—the change from bottle or breast milk to semi-solid and solid foods—is a gradual process. Children are able to eat more solid foods as their teeth grow and harden. Babies often reach a stage where they can hold their own bottle, and eventually they show a desire to feed themselves by reaching for the spoon. At about 15 months of age children can hold a cup and spoon but will usually make a mess in the feeding process. It is not until after 4 years of age that children acquire the physical ability to use a knife and fork. By the age of 10, children have improved eye–hand coordination and can use a knife and fork as proficiently as adults.

Learning to talk

In the early months of life a baby makes his or her needs known by crying. By the end of the first year a child's throat and mouth muscles and teeth have developed physically to the point where some speech

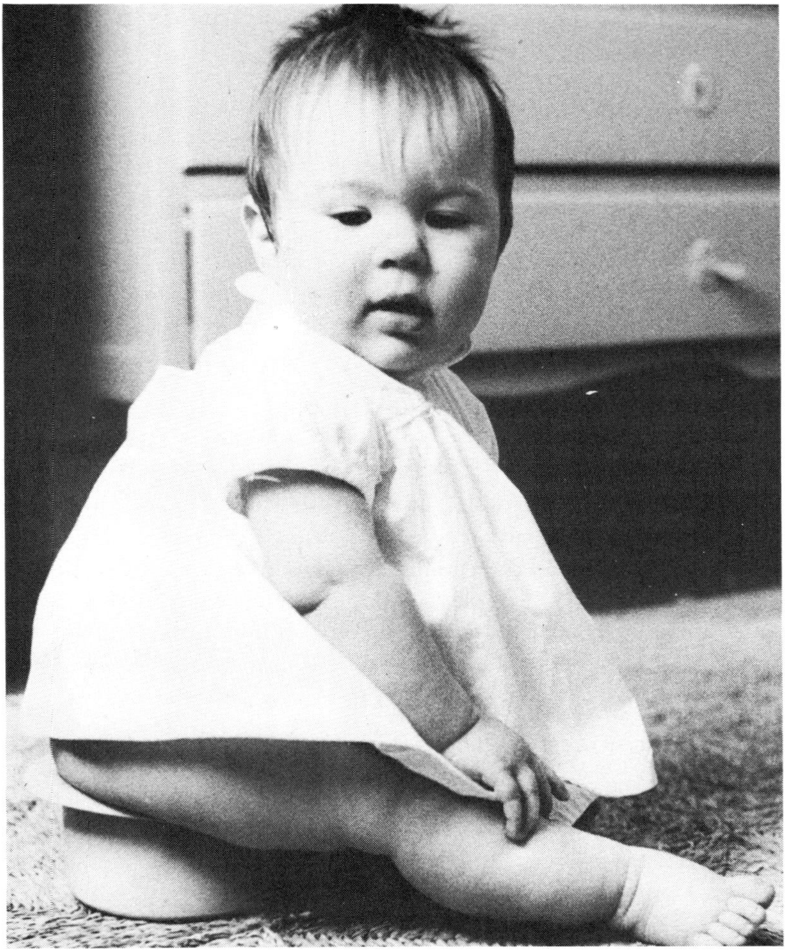

Figure 3.4 Toilet training can be commenced only when the child's nerves and muscles have developed sufficiently to allow control.

sounds are possible. At this stage, children will imitate others and, when encouraged, will repeat words they hear used often. They will have an understanding of the meanings of some words. Meaningful speech usually occurs between 18 and 28 months; by age 3, children can talk in simple phrases and sentences. For the development of communication skills, it is necessary for other people to talk to a child and provide encouragement in his or her attempts to speak and communicate.

Learning to control the elimination of body wastes

Children are considered to be toilet-trained when they are able to recognise and control the need to urinate and defecate. This can only be achieved when the nerves and muscles have developed sufficiently, which is usually achieved between 18 and 24 months. Between the age of 2 and $2\frac{1}{2}$ years children can usually control urination during the day, but may not be able to do so at night. Even when a child has reached a state of readiness for the task of toilet-training, it requires a great deal of patience and encouragement on the part of the parents for it to be mastered without frustration and unhappiness. Children also need to be dressed in clothing which is easy to manipulate.

Learning sex differences and sexual modesty

Children become aware of sex differences at about 3 years of age when they recognise and are curious about physical sex differences. It is at this age that children tend to become more selective concerning the toys with which they choose to play. Children often become more attached to sex-linked toys, which may be the result of imitation of parents and other people.

Achieving physiological stability

It can take up to five years for a child's body to settle down and achieve relative stability. Many children have allergies to certain types of foods while they are young, but these are often outgrown as metabolism becomes more stable.

Forming simple concepts of social and physical reality

Young children need opportunities to lift, touch and play with objects of different shapes, sizes, textures and colours. As their attention span is short, children need a variety of things to play with in order to develop concepts of the physical and social world. Stimulation, through experiences with their environment, and opportunities to explore and satisfy curiosity, helps children distinguish fantasy from reality. Children also learn to cope with new problems and tasks by making use of past experiences. The development of intellectual skills which enable children to understand their social world continues.

Learning to relate emotionally to other people

A child's first social relationships are with parents or parent substitutes, and during the early years the bonds of love and affection between child and parents develop. This emotional attachment becomes more obvious when a child is about 8 months old. Children develop a sense of independence between 1 and 4 years, but are still dependent upon parents. This is evident in the behaviour of children who run away from parents and 'hide', but become very anxious if the parent disappears. At about 2 years of age, children will play beside, but not with other children; it is not until the age of 3 or 4 years that children will play cooperatively with each other.

Learning to distinguish between right and wrong, and developing a conscience

Children generally develop a sense of right and wrong through the teachings, warnings and punishments of parents and other people with whom they have contact.

Developmental tasks during middle childhood

Many of the tasks that have to be accomplished during childhood are continuous: they are part of a developmental sequence that starts in infancy and childhood, continues into adolescence, and often extends into adulthood.

Learning physical skills necessary for everyday activities

As children grow in height and increase in weight, body fat is replaced by muscle and coordination improves. Improvement in physical coordination allows children to acquire the skills required for playing physical games and sports.

Building positive attitudes towards personal care

This is achieved as children become more aware of the need for personal hygiene, cleanliness and safety. Between the ages of 3 and 4 years, children usually develop such skills as brushing their teeth.

Learning to get along with age mates

Through interaction with playmates, children learn how to get along with others. When the behaviour of a child is not acceptable to other members of the peer group, he or she may be punished by rejection. It is a necessary part of development that children learn to identify with, and are able to relate to social groups outside the family unit.

Adopting a male or female social role

Sex-linked roles have already been discussed, as has the concern regarding the socialisation of children into traditional male and female roles. Nevertheless, as children grow and develop they usually begin to adopt sex-linked roles. This may not be a negative development for children if they are socialised in a family or social group which promotes equal opportunities and encourages the full development of children, regardless of sex.

Developing basic skills in reading and writing

The body is not biologically ready for writing until about 5 or 6 years of age although children usually show a preference for the use of the right or left hand before this age. When children first start to write, coordination is poor and the letters of the words are usually large and irregular.

Developing concepts for everyday living

In order to mature and achieve independence, children must develop intellectually so they can communicate, reason and solve problems.

Developing a conscience and set of values

Although this is initially developed within the family situation, it is usually reinforced through interaction with other people and groups outside the family unit.

Achieving a degree of personal independence

A child's approach to maturity entails finding a balance between dependence and independence. This involves developing a sense of competence, usefulness and responsibility, and sharing in the decision making processes within the family.

Children and Play

Play is any activity done for the enjoyment it provides. Play is essential for the physical, social and emotional development of children: it assists in the socialisation process and the development of competence. Play provides an outlet for a child's energy; it assists in the development of bones and muscles, and in the development of basic skills including language and communication; it helps a child learn to control his or her body; it encourages creativity and provides opportunities to get rid of feelings of anger and frustration. Play helps children to learn to get along with other children and to participate in society.

Play can include any activity a child enjoys doing, and it is through play that children learn about their environment and other people. Children require enough toys and equipment to play with, as well as space for play. At different ages, children and babies play in different ways. The older a child is, the more complicated play becomes. Small families cannot always provide enough play experiences for children, particularly social play. This is one of the reasons why many parents wish their children to attend a pre-school or day-care centre. Play is not merely an activity used to fill in time. It is essential for the total development of children.

Play can be classified as solitary, parallel or cooperative. Children of all ages play by themselves. This is called solitary play. However, children under 18 months of age are more involved in this type of play, as they have not developed sufficiently to play socially with other children. At about 2 years of age, children are happy to play alongside other children, but are still unable to share toys and cooperate in games with other children. This is called parallel play. While children enjoy playing games with their parents it is largely the parent who initiates the game and keeps it going. It is not until the child is about 3 years of age and sometimes older that he or she can play socially with other children. This is called cooperative play and provides children with the opportunity to learn about sharing, helping and being tolerant.

Types of Play

Play can be classified as *active play* or *passive play*. In active play, children are actually involved in some kind of activity, e.g. painting, drawing or climbing. In passive play, children watch or listen to someone else, e.g. listening to a parent or teacher read a story. Children need a balance of both active and passive play, otherwise they can become bored.

Play can also be classified as *discovery play*, *creative play*, *imaginative play* and *physical play*.

- *Discovery play* Children discover and learn about the environment by handling different objects and materials. This helps a child to develop concepts about the world and learn about reality. A one-year-old child is doing this when he or she fills up a container of water in the bath and then pours the water out again.
- *Creative play* This is any kind of play which involves a child making something, e.g. building with blocks, putting things together or making shapes out of playdough. This type of play improves hand–eye coordination and further develops his or her understanding of concepts.
- *Imaginative or dramatic play* This type of play usually involves pretend or fantasy play. Children can dress up and make believe they

Figure 3.5 As children develop socially, they learn to play and interact cooperatively with other children. (Photo: Herald & Weekly Times Ltd)

are someone else, or they can play with toys in a pretend way, e.g. talking to dolls as their mother may talk to them. This often involves role-play where children imitate the role of a parent. For example, a child may act out his or her inner feelings by punishing his or her dolls or teddy bear. By the age of 3 years, children are very involved in this type of play and will pretend to be shopkeepers, bus drivers, doctors, nurses etc.

- *Physical play* Through physical play, such as climbing, running, jumping, catching and throwing, children develop greater control of their muscles and become more skilled in coordinating the different parts of the body. Self-esteem is enhanced when children learn and master certain skills.

Opportunities for play

While play is an essential part of socialisation and certainly enhances the development of children, not all children have the same opportunities for a variety of play experiences. With smaller family sizes, the opportunities for children to play with siblings may be limited and families may look to other resources to provide this. For families who can afford the costs of child care or pre-school or kindergartens this need can be met. Also, economic resources are necessary for children to be able to participate in the same play experiences as other children. For low-income families this may not be possible. Some housing types, e.g. flats and units may not allow for outdoor activities, for noisy activities or for supervised play. It may be inappropriate in certain areas for children to play outside, unsupervised. Play provides children with the opportunity to interact with other children and to learn socially appropriate behaviour. This learning contributes to the development of competence and thus self-esteem.

Development during adolescence

During childhood the emphasis is upon mastery of basic skills and on social adjustment to the world beyond the family. While the first five years of a child's life are crucial for later development, the years during adolescence are also very important. It is during the period of adolescence that many important choices are made regarding courses of study and career options. During adolescence, an individual is expected to become physically, sexually, socially, and intellectually mature. This stage of the life cycle usually commences at about 12 years of age for girls and 14 years for boys, and usually ends at about 20 years of age. However, many children are involved in adolescent behaviour, including styles of dress and music, before puberty.

Adolescence is a time of change not just for the individual but also for the parents. As adolescence is a period where an individual is regarded as neither child nor adult, conflict within the adolescent and between adolescents and parents is inevitable. Conflict is one of the steps necessary for the achievement of independence: without tension, conflict, frustration and confusion there would be little development of personality. Adolescence is a period where the values and attitudes of parents and adolescents are tested and sometimes modified. For this reason it is essential that an atmosphere is created within the family where communication is fostered and encouraged. In recent years the potential for conflict between parents and adolescent children may have increased. Many adults are unemployed or facing the possibility of unemployment, as well has having real concerns about employment prospects for their children. Youth are remaining at home for longer as they are usually financially dependent on the family while they are completing education and trying to find employment. This can cause a strain on family relationships, physically, economically, psychologically and socially. The period of adolescence has been drawn out as a result of the longer period of time that adolescents are economically independent on their parents.

THE GENERATION GAP

A feature of adolescence that has been given much attention by social scientists is the generation gap. It has been suggested that prior to industrialisation, a generation gap as we know it did not exist. As children started productive work—either in the home or factory—at an early age, they moved from the status of a child to that of an adult. They did not have time to experience an adolescent period, as they had to contribute to the family's economic resources from a young age. Margaret Mead, in her research of primitive societies and other cultures, has found that while a period of youth may exist, the period of adolescence as we know it has not always existed. In primitive societies, children are given responsibility for family and work tasks at a younger age than in industrialised societies. In these societies children and parents do not experience the stress and conflict of adolescence.

In recent years some psychologists and sociologists have suggested that the generation gap is a 'myth'. Gay Ochiltree suggests there is little evidence for the existence of a generation gap and the idea of such may exist in the minds of the parents, rather than exist in reality'.[3] Further, research indicates that values held by adolescents are usually not in great conflict with those held by parents and that adolescents have a more positive view of adults than adults do of adolescents. Ochiltree also proposes that while a 'generation gap' may appear to exist on the basis of everyday arguments and conflicts, these arguments usually focus on minor issues rather than on life-long value differences, and most adolescents turn to parents for guidance over major concerns.[4]

Most studies of adolescence during the past few decades have shown that while a conflict of values may occur during the teenage years, most adolescents are likely in adulthood to have similar values to those of their parents. Adolescents of migrant parents may experience greater conflict if their parents are committed to the values of their 'home' country. Adolescents may be torn between the values of their peer group and those of their parents. It is interesting to note that migrant parents may be concerned about maintaining the norms, values and customs of their birth country, yet fail to recognise that these norms, values and customs may no longer be as relevant as they also have been subject to change over time.

Developmental tasks during adolescence

Developing mature relationships with age mates

The family is usually the first group in which an individual learns to interact. However, it is essential for the development of the adolescent that he or she learn to interact in other social groups. Peer groups are a valuable training ground for adolescents and at various stages during adolescence, an individual may appear to reject the family group in favour of the peer group. It is very important during this stage of the life span for adolescents to feel accepted by others of their own age.

Accepting a male or female social role

As discussed previously, the degree to which adolescents adopt and even reject traditional male and female roles is dependent upon many influences. However, it is necessary for adolescents to establish a sexual identity if they are to feel comfortable with themselves.

3 G. Ochiltree, *Children in Australian Families*, Longman Cheshire, Melbourne, 1990, p. 89.
4 Ochiltree, *Children in Australian Families*.

Accepting physical appearance

The age at which an individual reaches puberty varies widely, although sexual maturity is strongly hereditary. Adolescence is a time of rapid growth and development of the body: size and proportions alter; secondary sex characteristics appear; for the female, the menstrual cycle begins, and for males, the voice changes. Adolescents are often very sensitive during this period of physical change and may have feelings of rejection and inadequacy. As the adolescent reaches the later part of this developmental stage and the body stops growing and changing as quickly, he or she has to learn to accept the end result and realise his or her limitations. This may be a difficult adjustment for some adolescents, particularly when appearance does not meet ideals promoted in society.

Achieving emotional independence

Although adolescents still need and want acceptance and affection from members of their family, a shift away from emotional dependence upon parents towards emotional equality with parents is usual. The age at which an adolescent achieves this will depend on the individual and the family.

Achieving economic independence

Many adolescents show a desire to obtain part-time work while they are still attending school and when opportunities for this are available the first step towards economic independence has been taken. Many families rely on children obtaining part-time work in order to ease the economic burden. Economic conditions vary over time, but in times of recession, achieving complete economic independence can be very difficult for many young people. High youth unemployment rates of the late 1980s and early 1990s has prolonged the period of economic dependency.

Preparing for employment

It is important for young people to recognise the extent of their abilities and accept personal limitations if they are to set realistic goals regarding courses of study and employment choices. In periods of economic prosperity and full employment it is usually possible for a young person to choose a realistic particular career pathway, and after completing an appropriate course of study, expect to obtain a job. However, economic conditions are such that young people may experience great difficulties in obtaining any type of employment, despite abilities and qualifications. This can be very demoralising for young people who have spent many years in education preparing for future employment.

Preparing for relationships with other adults

While the adolescent may not be conscious of this task, emotional development and the achievement of independence are necessary for long-lasting relationships with other people. As the norms and values of society change, young adults may form relationships with the opposite sex that do not necessarily involve marriage. Nevertheless, such relationships still require a level of social and emotional maturity if they are to be beneficial for both partners.

Developing intellectual skills

Through intellectual development, the adolescent acquires the ability to consider what could be, as well as what is. Intellectual skills are a resource for both the individual and community, enabling the individual to participate in and contribute to the society in which he or she lives.

Achieving socially responsible behaviour

An adult's behaviour is strongly influenced by his or her previous socialisation and by the values internalised during this process. Adolescence is a critical period, as many of the experiences during this stage are important in shaping future behaviour. Thus, adolescents require opportunities to make their own decisions and accept responsibility for them, even though they may experience conflict and frustration during this process.

Acquiring a set of values

Adolescents often examine very closely the values taught by the family, and as a result they may accept or reject these values, in part or in full. It is unlikely that any adolescent will pass through this stage without at some time challenging the authority, values, attitudes and beliefs of his or her parents. It is a period in which adolescents must make decisions regarding social, sexual and moral behaviour. These decisions often have long-term consequences.

All individuals have the right to have basic needs satisfied and to have the opportunity to develop socially, intellectually, physically and emotionally. If the basic needs of children and adolescents are not met it is likely that development will be hindered and wellbeing will be threatened. This may have consequences later in life if an individual finds it difficult to form relationships with other people and to participate effectively in society.

REVIEW QUESTIONS

1 Define socialisation.
2 When does the most intensive socialisation occur?
3 What may be the consequences of inadequate socialisation?
4 Socialisation may be described in stages. Outline the stages of socialisation.
5 Describe the role of the school in socialisation.
6 Explain how the community can be used as a resource to supplement the role of families in socialisation.
7 Explain how socialisation practices may be different for children in migrant families.
8 Explain the term *gender*.
9 From birth, how are males and females often differentiated?
10 Why is it difficult in our society to avoid socialising children into sex-linked roles?
11 List steps that have been taken to avoid socialising children into traditional sex-linked roles.
12 Explain the difference between growth and development.
13 What is a developmental task?
14 Why do children master developmental tasks at different ages?
15 Outline the developmental tasks of early childhood.
16 Explain why some developmental tasks may continue throughout life.
17 Explain the value of play in the socialisation of children.
18 What may be the reason for the existence of a 'generation gap' in our society?
19 Outline the developmental tasks of adolescence.
20 Why has it become difficult for adolescents to achieve economic independence?

Case Study 3.1
'X':A Fabulous Child's Story

By Lois Gould

Once upon a time, a baby named X was born. This baby was named X so that nobody could tell whether it was a boy or a girl. Its parents could tell, of course, but they couldn't tell anybody else. They couldn't even tell Baby X at first.

You see, it was all part of a very important Secret Scientific Xperiment, known officially as Project Baby X. The smartest scientists had set up this Xperiment at a cost of Xactly 23 billion dollars and 72 cents, which might seem like a lot for just one baby, even a very important Xperimental baby. But when you remember the prices of things like strained carrots and stuffed bunnies, and popcorn for the movies and booster shots for camp, let alone 28 shiny quarters from the tooth fairy, you begin to see how it adds up.

Also, long before Baby X was born, all those scientists had to be paid to work out the details of the Xperiment, and to write the *Official Instruction Manual* for Baby X's parents and, most important of all, to find the right set of parents to bring up Baby X. These parents had to be selected very carefully. Thousands of volunteers had to take thousands of tests and answer thousands of tricky questions. Almost everybody failed because, it turned out, almost everybody really wanted either a baby boy or a baby girl, and not Baby X at all. Also, almost everybody was afraid that a Baby X would be a lot more trouble than a boy or a girl. (They were probably right, the scientists admitted, but Baby X needed parents who wouldn't *mind* the Xtra trouble.)

There were families with grandparents named Milton and Agatha, who didn't see why the baby couldn't be named Milton or Agatha instead of X, even if it *was* an X. There were families with aunts who insisted on knitting tiny dresses and uncles who insisted on sending tiny baseball mitts. Worst of all, there were families that already had other children who couldn't be trusted to keep the secret. Certainly not if they knew the secret was worth 23 billion dollars and 72 cents—and all you had to do was take one little peek at Baby X in the bathtub to know if it was a boy or girl.

But, finally, the scientists found the Joneses, who really wanted to raise an X more than any other kind of baby—no matter how much trouble it would be. Ms and Mr Jones had to promise they would take equal turns caring for X, and feeding it, and singing it lullabies. And they had to promise never to hire any baby-sitters. The government scientists knew perfectly well that a baby-sitter would probably peek at X in the bathtub, too.

The day the Joneses brought their baby home, lots of friends and relatives came over to see it. None of them knew about the secret Xperiment, though. So the first thing they asked was what kind of a baby X was. When the Joneses smiled and said, 'It's an X!' nobody knew what to say. They couldn't say, 'Look at her cute little dimples!' And they couldn't say, 'Look at his husky little biceps!' And they couldn't even say just plain 'kitchycoo.' In fact, they all thought the Joneses were playing some kind of rude joke.

But of course, the Joneses were not joking. 'It's an X' was absolutely all they would say. And that made the friends and relatives very angry. The relatives all felt embarrassed about having an X in the family. 'People will think there's something wrong with it!' some of them whispered. 'There *is* something wrong with it!' others whispered back.

'Nonsense!' the Joneses told them all cheerfully. 'What could possibly be wrong with this perfectly adorable X?'

Nobody could answer that, except Baby X, who had just finished its bottle. Baby X's answer was a loud, satisfied burp.

Clearly, nothing at all was wrong. Nevertheless, none of the relatives felt comfortable about buying a present for a Baby X. The cousins who sent the baby a tiny football helmet would not come and visit any more. And the neighbors who sent a pink-flowered romper suit pulled their shades down when the Joneses passed their house.

The *Official Instruction Manual* had warned the new parents that this would happen, so they didn't fret about it. Besides, they were too busy with Baby X and the hundreds of different Xercises for treating it properly.

Ms and Mr Jones had to be Xtra careful about how they played with little X. They knew that if they kept bouncing it up in the air and saying how *strong* and *active* it was, they'd be treating it more like a boy than an X. But if all they did was cuddle it and kiss it and tell it how *sweet* and *dainty* it was, they'd be treating it more like a girl than an X.

On page 1654 of the *Official Instruction Manual*, the scientists prescribed: 'plenty of bouncing and plenty of cuddling, *both*, X ought to be strong and sweet and active. Forget about *dainty* altogether.'

Meanwhile, the Joneses were worrying about other problems. Toys, for instance. And clothes. On his first shopping trip, Mr Jones told the store clerk, 'I need some clothes and toys for my new baby.' The clerk smiled and said, 'Well, now, is it a boy or a girl?' 'It's an X', Mr Jones said, smiling back. But the clerk got all red in the face and said huffily, 'In *that* case, I'm afraid I can't help you, sir'. So Mr Jones wandered helplessly up and down the aisles trying to find out what X needed. But everything in the store was piled up in sections marked 'Boys' or 'Girls.'

There were 'Boys' Pyjamas' and 'Girls' Underwear' and 'Boys' Fire Engines' and 'Girls' Housekeeping Sets'. Mr Jones went home without buying anything for X. That night he and Ms Jones consulted page 2326 of the *Official Instruction Manual*. 'Buy plenty of everything', it said firmly.

So they bought plenty of sturdy blue pyjamas in the Boys' Department and cheerful flowered underwear in the Girls' Department. And they bought all kinds of toys. A boy doll that made pee-pee and cried, 'Pa-pa'. And a 'girl doll that talked in three languages and said 'I am the Pres-i-dent of Gen-er-al Mo-tors.' They also bought a story-book about a brave princess who rescued a handsome prince from his ivory tower, and another one about a sister and brother who grew up to be a baseball star and a ballet star, and you had to guess which was which.

The head scientists of Project Baby X checked all their purchases and told them to keep up the good work. They also reminded the Joneses to see page 4629 of the *Manual*, where it said: 'Never make Baby X feel *embarrassed or ashamed* about what it wants to play with. And if X gets dirty climbing rocks, never say "Nice little Xes don't get dirty climbing rocks".'

Likewise, it said: 'If X falls down and cries, never say "Brave little Xes don't cry". Because, of course, nice little Xes *do* get dirty, and brave little Xes *do* cry. No matter how dirty X gets, or how hard it cries, don't worry. It's all part of the Xperiment.'

Whenever the Joneses pushed Baby X's stroller in the park, smiling strangers would come over and coo: 'Is that a boy or a girl?' The Joneses would smile back and say, 'It's an X'. The strangers would stop smiling then, and often snarl something nasty—as if the Joneses had snarled at *them*.

By the time X grew big enough to play with other children, the Joneses' troubles had grown bigger, too. Once a little girl grabbed X's shovel in the sandbox, and zonked X on the head with it. 'Now, now, Tracy,' the little girl's mother began to scold, 'little girls mustn't hit little—' and she turned to ask X, 'Are you a little boy or a little girl, dear?'

Mr Jones, who was sitting near the sandbox, held his breath and crossed his fingers.

X smiled politely at the lady, even though X's head had never been zonked so hard in its life. 'I'm a little X', X replied.

'You're a *what?*' the lady exclaimed angrily. 'You're a little b-r-a-t, you mean!'

'But little girls mustn't hit little Xes, either!' said X, retrieving the shovel with another polite smile. 'What good does hitting do, anyway?'

X's father, who was still holding his breath, finally let it out, uncrossed his fingers, and grinned back at X.

And at their next secret Project Baby X meeting, the scientists grinned, too. Baby X was doing fine.

But then it was time for X to start school. The Joneses were really worried about this, because school was even more full of rules for boys and girls, and there were no rules for Xes. The teachers would tell boys to form one line, and girls to form another line. There would be boys' games and girls' games, and boys' secrets and girls' secrets. The school library would have a list of recommended books for girls, and a different list of recommended books for boys. There would even be a bathroom marked BOYS and another one marked GIRLS. Pretty soon boys and girls would hardly talk to each other. What would happen to poor little X?

The Joneses spent weeks consulting their *Instruction Manual* (there were 249½ pages of advice under 'First Day of School'), and attending urgent special conferences with the smart scientists of Project Baby X.

The scientists had to make sure that X's mother had taught X how to throw and catch a ball properly, and that X's father had been sure to teach X what to serve at a doll's tea party. X had to know how to shoot marbles and how to jump rope and, most of all, what to say when the Other Children asked whether X was a boy or a girl.

Finally, X was ready. The Joneses helped X button on a nice new pair of red-and-white checked overalls, and sharpened six pencils for X's nice new pencilbox, and marked X's name clearly on all the books in its nice new bookbag. X brushed its teeth and combed its hair, which just about covered its ears, and remembered to put a napkin in its lunchbox.

The Joneses had asked X's teacher if the class could line up alphabetically, instead of forming separate lines for boys and girls. And they had asked if X could use the principal's bathroom, because it wasn't marked anything except BATHROOM. X's teacher promised to take care of all those problems. But nobody could help X with the biggest problem of all—Other Children.

Nobody in X's class had ever known an X before. What would they think? How would X make friends?

You couldn't tell what X was by studying its clothes—overalls don't even button right-to-left, like girls' clothes, or left-to-right, like boys' clothes. And you couldn't guess whether X had a girl's short haircut or a boy's long hair-cut. And it was very hard to tell by the games X liked to play. Either X played ball very well for a girl, or else X played house very well for a boy.

Some of the children tried to find out by asking X tricky questions, like 'Who's your favorite sports star?' That was easy. X had two favorite sports stars: a girl jockey named Robyn Smith and a boy archery champion named Robin Hood. Then they asked, 'What's your favorite TV programme?' And that was even easier. X's favorite TV programme was 'Lassie,' which stars a girl dog played by a boy dog.

When X said that its favorite toy was a doll, everyone decided that X must be a girl. But then X said that the doll was really a robot, and that X had computerised it, and that it was programmed to bake fudge brownies and then clean up the kitchen. After X told them that, the other children gave up guessing what X was. All they knew was they'd sure like to see X's doll.

After School, X wanted to play with the other children. 'How about shooting some baskets in the gym?' X asked the girls. But all they did was make faces and giggle behind X's back.

'How about weaving some baskets in the arts and crafts room?' X asked the boys. But they all made faces and giggled behind X's back, too.

That night, Ms and Mr Jones asked X how things had gone at school. X told them sadly that the lessons were okay, but otherwise school was a terrible place for an X. It seemed as if Other Children would never want an X for a friend.

Once more, the Joneses reached for their *Instruction Manual.* Under '*Other Children*', they found the following message: 'What did you Xpect? Other Children have to obey all the silly boy–girl rules, because their parents taught them to. Lucky X—you don't have to stick to the rules at all! All you have to do is be yourself. PS: We're not saying it'll be easy.'

X liked being itself. But X cried a lot that night, partly because it felt afraid. So X's father held X tight, and cuddled it, and couldn't help crying a little, too. And X's mother cheered them both up by reading an Xciting story about an enchanted prince called Sleeping Handsome, who woke up when Princess Charming kissed him.

The next morning, they all felt much better, and little X went back to school with a brave smile and a clean pair of red-and-white-checked overalls.

There was a seven-letter-word spelling bee in class that day. And a seven-lap boys' relay race in the gym. And a seven-layer-cake baking contest in the girls' kitchen corner. X won the spelling bee. X also won the relay race. And X almost won the baking contest, except it forgot to light the oven. Which only proves that nobody's perfect.

One of the Other Children noticed something else, too. He said: 'Winning or losing doesn't seem to count to X. X seems to have fun being good at boys' skills *and* girls' skills.'

'Come to think of it,' said another one of the Other Children, 'maybe X is having twice as much fun as we are'.

So after school that day, the girl who beat X at the baking contests gave X a big slice of her prizewinning cake. And the boy X beat in the relay race asked X to race him home.

From then on, some really funny things began to happen. Susie, who sat next to X in class, suddenly refused to wear pink dresses to school any more. She insisted on wearing red-and-white-checked overalls — just like X's. Overalls, she told her parents, were much better for climbing monkey bars.

Then Jim, the class football nut, started wheeling his little sister's doll carriage around the football field. He'd put on his entire football uniform, except for the helmet. Then he'd put the helmet *in* the carriage, lovingly tucked under an old set of shoulder pads. Then he'd start jogging around the field, pushing the carriage and singing 'Rockabye Baby' to his football helmet. He told his family that X did the same thing, so it must be okay. After all, X was now the team's star quarter-back.

Susie's parents were horrified by her behavior, and Jim's parents were worried sick about his. But the worst came when the twins, Joe and Peggy, decided to share everything with each other. Peggy used Joe's hockey skates, and his microscope, and took half his newspaper route. Joe used Peggy's needlepoint kit, Peggy started running the lawn mower, and Joe started running the vacuum cleaner.

Their parents weren't one bit pleased with Peggy's wonderful biology experiments, or with Joe's terrific needlepoint pillows. They didn't care that Peggy mowed the lawn better, and that Joe vacuumed the carpet better. In fact, they were furious. It's all that little X's fault, they agreed. Just because X doesn't know what it is, or what it's supposed to be, it wants to get everybody *else* mixed up, too!

Peggy and Joe were forbidden to play with X any more. So was Susie, and then Jim, and then *all* the Other Children. But it was too late; the Other Children stayed mixed up and happy and free, and refused to go back to the way they'd been before X.

Finally, Joe and Peggy's parents decided to call an emergency meeting of the school's Parents' Association, to discuss 'The X Problem'. They sent a report to the principal stating that X was a 'disruptive influence'. They demanded immediate action. The Joneses, they said, should be forced to tell whether X was a boy or a girl. And then X should be *forced* to behave like whichever it was. If the Joneses refused to tell, the Parents' Association said, then X must take an Xamination. The school psychiatrist must xamine it physically and mentally, and issue a full report. If X's test showed it was a boy, it would have to obey all the boys' rules. If it proved to be a girl, X would have to obey all the girls' rules.

And if X turned out to be some kind of mixed-up misfit, then X should be Xpelled from the school. Immediately!

The principal was very upset. Disruptive influence? Mixed-up misfit? But X was an Xcellent student. All the teachers said it was a delight to have X in their classes. X was president of the student council, X had won first prize in the talent show, and second prize in the art show, and honorable mention in the science fair, and six athletic events on field day, including the potato race.

Nevertheless, insisted the Parent's Association, X is a Problem Child. X is the Biggest Problem Child we have ever seen!

So the principal reluctantly notified X's parents that numerous complaints about X's behavior had come to the school's attention. And that after the psychiatrist's Xamination, the school would decide what to do about X.

The Joneses reported this at once to the scientists, who referred them to page 85 759 of the *Instruction Manual.* 'Sooner or later,' it said, 'X will have to be Xamined by a psychiatrist. This may be the only way any of us will know for sure whether X is mixed up — or whether everyone else is'.

The night before X was to be Xamined, the Joneses tried not to let X see how worried they were. 'What if?' Mr Jones would say. And Ms Jones would reply, 'No use worrying.' Then a few minutes later, Ms Jones would say, 'What if?' and Mr Jones would reply, 'No use worrying'.

X just smiled at them both, and hugged them hard and didn't say much of anything. X was thinking. What if — ? And then X thought: No use worrying.

At Xactly 9 o'clock the next day, X reported to the school psychiatrist's office. The principal, along with a committee from the Parents' Association, X's teacher, X's classmates and Ms and Mr Jones waited in the hall outside. Nobody knew the details of the tests X was to be given, but everybody knew they'd be very hard, and that they'd reveal Xactly what everyone wanted to know about X, but was afraid to ask.

It was terribly quiet in the hall. Almost spooky. Once in a while, they would hear a strange noise inside the room. There were buzzes. And a beep or two. And several bells. An occasional light would flash under the door. The Joneses thought it was a white light, but the principal thought it was blue. Two or three children swore it was either yellow or green. And the Parent's Committee missed it completely.

Through it all, you could hear the psychiatrist's low voice, asking hundreds of questions, and X's higher voice, answering hundreds of answers.

The whole thing took so long that everyone knew it must be the most complete Xamination anyone had ever had to take. Poor X, the Joneses thought. Serves X right, the Parents' Committee thought. I wouldn't like to be in X's overalls right now, the children thought.

At last, the door opened. Everyone crowded around to hear the results. X didn't look any different; in fact, X was smiling. But the psychiatrist looked terrible. He looked as if he was crying! 'What happened?' everyone began shouting. Had X done something disgraceful? 'I wouldn't be a bit surprised!' muttered Peggy and Joe's parents. 'Did X flunk the *whole* test?' cried Susie's parents. 'Or just the most important part?' yelled Jim's parents.

'Oh, dear', sighed Mr Jones.

'Oh, dear', sighed Ms Jones.

'*Sssh*', ssshed the principal. 'The psychiatrist is trying to speak.'

Wiping his eyes and clearing his throat, the psychiatrist began, in a hoarse whisper. 'In my opinion,' he whispered — you could tell he must be very upset — 'in my opinion, young X here — '

'Yes? Yes?' shouted a parent impatiently.

'*Sssh*!' ssshed the principal.

'Young *Sssh* here, I mean young X', said the doctor, frowning, 'is just about — '

'Just about *what*? Let's have it!' shouted another parent.

'Just about the *least* mixed-up child I've ever Xamined!' said the psychiatrist.

'Yah for X!' yelled one of the children. And then the others began yelling, too. Clapping and cheering and jumping up and down.

'SSSH!' SSShed the principal, but nobody did.

The Parents' Committee was angry and bewildered. How *could* X have passed the whole Xamination? Didn't X have an *identity* problem? Wasn't X mixed up at *all*? Wasn't X *any* kind of a misfit? How could it *not* be, when it didn't even *know* what it was? And why was the psychiatrist crying?

Actually, he had stopped crying and was smiling politely through his tears. 'Don't you see?' he said, 'I'm crying because it's wonderful! X has absolutely no identity problem! X isn't one bit mixed up! As for being a misfit — ridiculous! X knows perfectly well what it is! Don't you, X? The doctor winked. X winked back.

'But what *is* X?' shrieked Peggy and Joe's parents. 'We still want to know what it is!'

'Ah, yes', said the doctor, winking again. 'Well, don't worry. You'll all know one of these days. And you won't need me to tell you.'

'What? What does he mean?' some of the parents grumbled suspiciously.

Susie and Peggy and Joe all answered all once. 'He means that by the time X's sex matters, it won't be a secret any more!'

With that, the doctor began to push through the crowd toward X's parents. 'How do you do', he said, somewhat stiffly. And then he reached out to hug them both. 'If I ever have an X of my own,' he whispered, 'I sure hope you'll lend me your instruction manual.'

Needless to say, the Joneses were very happy. The Project Baby X scientists were rather pleased, too. So were Susie, Jim, Peggy, Joe, and all the Other Children. The Parents' Association wasn't, but they had promised to accept the psychiatrist's report and not make any more trouble. .They even invited Ms and Mr Jones to become honorary members, which they did.

Later that day, X's friends put on their red-and-white-checked overalls and went over to see X. They found X in the back yard, playing with a very tiny baby that none of them had ever seen before. The baby was wearing very tiny red-and-white-checked overalls.

'How do you like our new baby?' X asked the Other Children proudly.

'It's got cute dimples, said Jim.

'It's got husky biceps, too', said Susie.

'What kind of baby is it?' asked Joe and Peggy.

X frowned at them, 'Can't you tell? Then X broke into a big, mischievous grin, '*It's a* Y!'

4

Children and Youth

Australia's children

Of Australia's total population, approximately 22 per cent is comprised of children under 15 years of age. During the 1940s and 1950s when Australia's population was increasing rapidly, this figure was around 30 per cent. While the proportion of children under the age of 15 years has declined over the past few decades, children and youth under the age of 19 years comprise just under one-third of Australia's population. Of Australia's children, approximately 7 per cent were born overseas and 36 per cent have at least one parent born overseas. Half of all children live in urban centres of 100 000 people or more, and 75 per cent of children live in the eastern mainland states of New South Wales, Victoria and Queensland.[1]

---

1 Australian Bureau of Statistics, *Australia's Children, 1989*, Canberra, 1990, pp. 1–4.

Changes in Families

Approximately 80 per cent of dependent children live in couple families where both adults are their natural parents; 12 per cent of dependent children live in single-parent families; and 5 per cent of dependent children live in blended or stepfamilies. Of children living in single-parent families, approximately 70 per cent live with a parent who is either separated or divorced, 20 per cent live with a parent who has not married and less than 10 per cent live with a widowed parent.

During the past few decades the social institution of the family has undergone considerable changes, not only in terms of structure, but also in terms of roles and relationships. The increase in the workforce participation of women with dependent children has necessitated an expansion in both the availability and types of child-care facilities and support services. Children are more likely to be exposed to a wide range of role models and caregivers than when the majority of mothers remained in the home. Similarly, the increase in the divorce rate has meant that many children will experience and live in a variety of family formations during their period of dependency on the family. Larger numbers of children will move from a two-parent family to a single-parent family and possibly to a blended family or stepfamily. Such changes increase the complexity of a child's life; some parents will have the social and economic resources to help their children adjust to these changes, while other parents will require the assistance of support networks in order to meet the basic needs of their families.

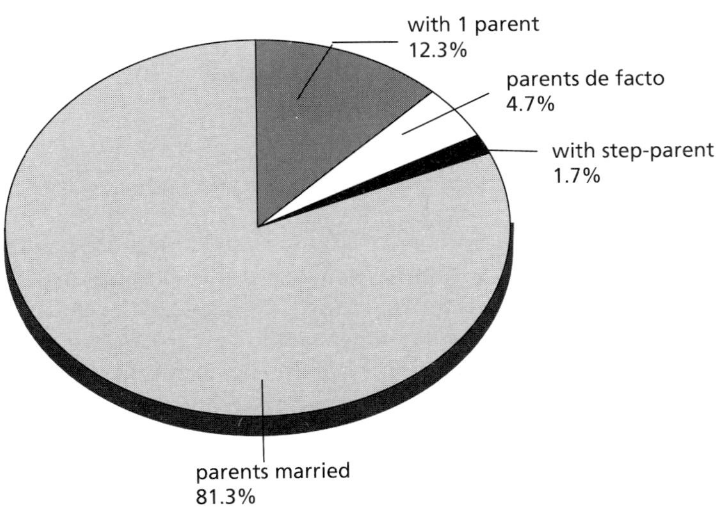

Figure 4.1 Living arrangements of dependent children, Australia, 1986.

THE WELFARE OF CHILDREN

Historical evidence shows that until last century, families were usually very parent-centred; children were totally subordinate to their parents and unless they could be used to enhance a family's economic resources they were not looked upon very favourably. Throughout the Middle Ages and until the eighteenth century, there existed a general belief that children were born evil and needed to be subjected to severe mental and physical discipline, and punishment in order to control sinful impulses. There has been considerable documentation concerning the manner in which children have been treated throughout history. Research in Britain has revealed that infanticide was common, children were often left to die at birth, they were neglected and abandoned, subjected to severe physical punishment which sometimes resulted in their death, as well as being imprisoned and executed for petty offences. The conditions in which children worked in factories were so appalling that many children were permanently maimed, and a large number were killed in the workplace.

The fact that many children were transported from Britain to Australia during the early part of last century for such trivial offences as stealing a handkerchief is evidence of how children were thought of prior to this century. While the situation of children in Australia last century may not have been as bad as it was in Britain, considerable evidence exists to suggest that a significant number of children died as a result of neglect, ignorance and maltreatment. Following European settlement of Australia, Aboriginal children suffered particularly as their traditional way of life was eroded. Aboriginal babies were frequently taken from their families and placed in institutions or in foster care, and in some cases they were adopted by white families. This practice continued until the 1960s.

CHILDREN IN THE TWENTIETH CENTURY

Contemporary families are more child-centred and more concerned with meeting all the needs of the child, not just the physical needs. The twentieth century is often referred to as 'the century of the child' as this century has witnessed a greater understanding of the needs of children. There has been a greater recognition of the rights of children, including the right to love and emotional support, to an education, to adequate nutrition and health care, to opportunities for play and recreation, and to protection from injury and exploitation.

Throughout the latter half of the nineteenth century there was a gradual introduction of laws concerning the protection and welfare of children, including laws which made elementary education compulsory and laws limiting the use of child labour. In addition, legislation was enacted in the late nineteenth century concerning the abuse of children by parents and other adults.

Developments this century

In Australia this century there have been major developments in welfare programs for families and children. Welfare programs have been directed at the maintenance of the family unit and the protection and promotion of the welfare of children. These programs have been subject to some criticism, and it has been claimed that some of these programs are inconsistent and have been developed without any real philosophy or direction. A primary concern in the past has been that only the welfare of the child or children has been addressed and not the total family situation, which may include problems of unemployment, poverty, inadequate housing, poor health, family violence etc.

Until the 1960s, state welfare authorities were concerned primarily with the welfare of children from lower-socioeconomic-status families, including working-class families and Aboriginal families. Child welfare was often typified by the removal of children from their natural families, as it was often believed that their families did not have the right attitudes or suitable environment for the rearing of children. It was believed that removal from the family would allow children to be resocialised in a more suitable environment to ensure they became productive members of society.

Inevitably, this meant that children were placed in some type of care where they were taught skills of manual labour and instilled with virtues of hard work, obedience to authority and acceptance of their lower status. In Australia last century many children who were in the care of child welfare authorities, as well as orphaned children from Britain, were sent to rural areas to serve as cheap sources of household and farm labour.

In recent decades, priority has been given to maintaining children within their natural family, and to establishing services aimed at prevention rather than protection. Services have been directed at providing facilities and support networks in communities in an attempt to reduce both the number of children and families in need or at risk. In situations where children can no longer remain with their natural families, every effort is made to place them in substitute care, such as foster care or in a family group home, rather than in institutional care.

WHAT IS CHILD WELFARE?

The term child welfare is very broad and difficult to define, and in the general sense it refers to the protection and promotion of the wellbeing of children. Government departments at both federal and state level have responsibilities for child welfare, although historically the main responsibility for child and family welfare has rested with each state or territory.

At the federal level, the responsibility has been mainly financial, through the provision of income support including social welfare benefits, family allowance and the provision of financial resources for special projects such as the construction of early childhood centres. At a state level, responsibility for welfare often rests with government departments which have such names as the Department of Community Welfare, Department of Community Services, Department of Children's Services etc.

Generally, state welfare departments have a number of functions: they promote the welfare of children, families and communities, as well as taking responsibility for the social control and correction of children. During the past two decades the activities of these departments have expanded to include community welfare, as it has been recognised that children and families operate within a community and need the resources a supportive community can provide. There has been a change in focus from child and family welfare to community welfare, as it is now recognised that the provision of community support services can prevent many problems for both children and families.

The functions of state welfare departments are wide and diverse and some of these are outlined below. It is important to note that while there are some functions which are common to all state government departments, these functions do vary among the states and territories and are always subject to change and review.

Functions and responsibilities of state welfare departments may include:

- promoting the welfare of individuals and families in the community through the provision of support services and facilities;
- coordinating available social welfare services for children, youth, families, handicapped people and elderly people;
- rehabilitation of young offenders, adoption of children, care of immigrant children, child employment, early childhood services and emergency assistance;
- support of community groups by providing services such as women's refuges and youth crisis centres;

- providing new and additional welfare services for groups who are disadvantaged or who have special needs;
- care and maintenance of children under state guardianship;
- supervision of children in foster homes, family group homes and child-care centres;
- protection of children from ill treatment and neglect;
- protecting and caring for neglected and homeless individuals and families;
- providing counselling services for individuals and families
- licensing of foster parents, children's homes, family daycare and baby sitting agencies.

While state welfare departments have widened the scope of their activities over the past two decades, their primary focus remains on providing child protection and services to dependent individuals and families.

Child Neglect and Child Abuse

From the mid-1970s there has been a growing concern about the incidence of child maltreatment or child abuse. During the 1980s most states amended their provisions concerning notifications of children known or suspected to be at risk to abuse or neglect. New legislation means that most professions and occupations involved with children, e.g. medical practitioners, teachers, welfare employees etc., are obliged to report any suspected cases of abuse and neglect. Since the mid-1970s there has been a dramatic increase in the number of confirmed cases of child abuse. It is difficult to say whether actual child abuse has increased or whether there is an increased community awareness of the problem and recognition of the responsibility to report suspected cases.

Babies and children have been abused and neglected throughout history, and non-accidental injury is not new. However, there is now an understanding that aggressive feelings towards a baby or a child are not unique. Many parents experience these feelings and may feel guilty about them but they can control these feelings. The difference is between *feeling* aggressive and actually *being* aggressive towards a child. Welfare services are aimed at the prevention of child abuse and neglect through the provision of support services, as well as counselling for parents who are charged with child abuse and neglect. Often, when a charge is made against a parent, it is usually the parent and not the child who is removed from the household. Even after counselling it cannot always be guaranteed that it will not happen again, and family breakdown often occurs.

The terms *child abuse* and *child neglect* are often used together as they may occur together. However, there is a difference between these two terms. Child *neglect* really refers to the situation where children are denied some or all of their basic physical, social, psychological and emotional needs. This can affect and hinder the development of children. Child *abuse* refers to the intentional behaviour by an adult which causes physical injury to the child. Child abuse is often referred to as *non-accidental injury*.

CHILD NEGLECT

When a child has been physically neglected it often means that he or she has not achieved normal height and weight for age yet there is no medical reason for this to occur. Children may be neglected if there is a lack of resources, or as a result of ignorance or incompetence of the primary caregiver, or because they never were or are not wanted.

Emotional neglect is often harder to diagnose because the child may have no physical signs of neglect. It may occur when the mother/father does not recognise the emotional needs of the child or cannot bond to the child. The parent or parents may believe that too much affection through cuddling and holding may spoil the child. Prior to this century, emotional neglect was very common in orphanages where children were fed and changed but there was very little holding, talking, touching, cuddling, affection and interaction. The importance of emotional bonding is now recognised in hospitals where mothers are encouraged to hold and cuddle their babies as soon as they are born. This is even more important for premature babies who may spend a considerable time in a humidicrib, and physical contact with the mother and/or father and other caregivers is actively encouraged.

Many authorities in the area of child abuse and neglect suggest that there are not enough post-natal (after birth) courses available for parents. Much of the antenatal (before birth) education available for parents concentrates on pregnancy and labour and not enough time is spent preparing parents for the problems that may occur after the child is born and brought home from hospital. Most parents would admit to sometimes feeling stressed about their baby or child, yet the norms of society are such that parents should not have these feelings and if they do they should be suppressed. Parents are normal people with normal feelings and faults—they lose their tempers and make unwise decisions. Problems of child abuse and child neglect may occur if caregivers are not aware of their feelings and do not know how to control them.

Child abuse

Many studies show that parents who neglect or abuse their child/children were themselves abused or neglected as children. For most parents who abuse children it is not that they do not want the child/children but rather that they cannot cope with crises or pressure, and often have little confidence in their ability to handle stressful and demanding situations. Parents in this situation do not know how to get rid of their aggressions through some other means. In some families the problems may be so great that there are few outlets for their aggression and feelings about their situation. The incidence of child abuse is higher among children of drug addicts, alcoholics and prostitutes.

In Australia, the law requires that welfare agencies, police, medical personnel, teachers etc. must report any cases of suspected child abuse to the appropriate government department. Medical assessment is necessary to prove child abuse and in most cases of child abuse medical experts can prove if the injury was non-accidental. Non-accidental injuries including burns, bruises, cuts, fractured limbs and internal injuries are recognised by trained medical personnel as the shape, size and nature of the injury is usually different from those which are accidental. Evidence suggests that when a child under the age of 3 years has sustained serious injury, he or she runs the risk of dying or having permanent damage particularly if he or she returns home to the same family situation. Sexual abuse is possibly more frequent than statistics suggest and it does not only occur in violent families. The abuser is most likely to be a relative or close friend of the family.

Substitute care

Substitute care refers to the provision of care for children which replaces existing parental care. This usually occurs over an extended period of time where the day-to-day care of a child is assumed by persons other than the child's natural parents. It does not include care provided to children in child-care centres or boarding schools. Substitute care may be protective or corrective or a combination of both. The main forms of protective care are adoption, foster care and institutional care, while corrective care is usually provided through institutional care in juvenile correction institutions. The current policy of the Department of Community Services is to provide alternative care to institutional care. Many childrens' institutions are being closed down and children are being placed in foster homes or group family homes.

Children may be placed in substitute care as a result of such factors as family breakdown, poverty, illness, inability to cope or because particular treatment, programs or facilities are required, e.g. for emotionally disturbed children or physically and intellectually disabled children. A child may also be placed in the care of the State if he or she is found guilty of committing an offence against the law, or because the child's physical, mental, emotional or moral welfare is at risk.

Over the last two decades there has been a decline in the number of children in substitute care and several reasons for this trend are outlined below:[2]

- The introduction in 1973 of income benefits for single parents and the increased availability of Commonwealth and State-funded community child-care facilities and other programs and services have assisted many parents to keep their children rather than relinquish them to the care of others.
- There has been an increased reluctance by welfare authorities to remove children from their parents. This has largely been due to a change in social attitudes regarding child welfare and a growing belief that substitute care should only occur when all possibilities of maintaining a child in the family are exhausted.
- There has been a decline in fertility rates since the mid-1960s as a result of the increased availability of contraception and abortion and a preference for smaller families.

Early childhood services

Historical development of child-care services

Until the late nineteenth century the aim of children's services was to protect children from abandonment, vice and destitution. Children's services did not provide assistance or support for families requiring child-care services. The assumption that the family should protect and care for its members existed until the twentieth century. This assumption was founded in the belief that government support would undermine the family's self-reliance and initiative, and that it was the responsibility of women to remain at home and look after children.

Prior to the Second World War the main child-care services available were in the private sector, including informal private daycare and neighbourhood care. These were often unsatisfactory as no government controls were exercised and many children were cared for

2 ABS, *Australia's Children*, p. 50.

in substandard conditions. During the Second World War the Commonwealth government provided funding for 'long-day' child-care centres. These were established to allow women to work whilst men were at the war. However, most of these centres were closed at the end of the war as it was assumed that the men returning home would resume their place in the workforce and women would return to the home. Women often had little choice but to drop out of the workforce because of lack of child-care facilities.

The revived feminist movement of the 1960s drew the public's attention to the lack of child-care facilities. During this period there was much controversy over the provision of child care. The prevailing attitudes in society were that a woman's place was in the home, particularly if she had small children. In 1969, less than 10 per cent of pre-school children of working mothers were in recognised child-care centres. The other 90 per cent were in private care and therefore without government support or supervision. Public argument concerning child care has continued up to the present day.

In 1972 the Whitlam Labour Government introduced the Child Care Act. This act provided for $5 million in the 1972–73 Budget to finance non-profit child-care centres for families with financial and other special needs, such as working parents, single parents, and migrant and Aboriginal families. In the 1973–74 Budget an additional $8 million was provided towards the cost of construction and operation of child-care services. It was about this time that the Family Day Care scheme was introduced through many local councils. In the 1974–75 Budget, $75 million was allocated to child-care services to provide a range of diversified and integrated services. These included early childhood education, long-daycare, short-daycare, family daycare, playgroup facilities, occasional care, before- and after-school care, holiday care and emergency care.

The Fraser Liberal Government (1975–83) was characterised by an overall reduction in expenditure on child-care services. Access to subsidised child care was restricted to those regarded as being in need. This did not necessarily include the need to work. Child-care places during this period of time were very limited. In 1984, the incoming Hawke Labor Government initiated changes to child-care provisions and promised an expansion in child-care places. Significant cuts to subsidies for child-care occurred in 1986 and this effectively raised the fees in most centres.

With the introduction of the National Child-Care Strategy by the federal government in 1988, priority has been given to increasing the number of child-care centres, family daycare schemes, occasional-care centres and outside-school-hours care services. Between 1989–92,

30 000 new places were to be established. At the time of the 1992 Federal Budget, there were 193 000 federally funded child-care places, compared to 46 000 places in 1983. The federal government's target in 1992 was to reach 250 000 places by 1995–96.

ATTITUDES TO CHILD CARE

Prior to the 1970s, child-care services were seen by society as child-minding services and not as a support system for the family. Nor were they seen as assisting in the physical, social and emotional development of children.

Since the 1970s there has been a large increase in the number of child-care facilities and thus the number of places available. However, there are still not enough places available and the waiting lists are very long. Also, many parents choose informal private child care as it is more available and often cheaper. Parents of children under the age of 3 years often prefer their child to be cared for by a relative or friend in an environment that is more like a family and one in which there is more time for individual care and attention.

Many child-care facilities are subsidised to some extent by various government bodies at federal, state and local government levels. However, the amount of these subsidies has varied considerably over the past two decades, and the cost of long-daycare in an approved child-care centre may be too high for many parents. While fee relief is available to low-income families, including single-parent families, the income cut-off point is not low enough for many families to qualify for fee relief. For a woman with two children in a child-care centre paying approximately $260 per week (non-tax-deductible), participation in the workforce may not be feasible, particularly when other work-related costs are added.

Whilst the needs of children with respect to child care may be very similar, the needs of parents may vary considerably. Community-based child-care facilities aim to assist and support families in satisfying basic social, physical and psychological needs of children. Depending on the age of the child, different services may be considered more appropriate by a parent or parents. Working parents may feel that family daycare or private minding satisfies the needs of a two-year-old child more than long-daycare will. On the other hand, a single parent with one child may feel that a daycare centre will provide the child with more interaction with other children as well as different role models. Many factors are important to parents when choosing a child-care facility, assuming such choice is available, and often it is not. If the flexibility of choice is available, parents often consider such factors as the environment of the facility or private home, attitudes of the staff or caregivers, operating hours, proximity to home and employment, and cost.

Types of child-care facilities

Long-daycare centres

Daycare centres were formerly seen as places where children were minded, and there was little attention paid to the social and emotional development of the child. Today, these centres are organised on a similar basis to pre-school centres: personnel are qualified in child care, teaching and nursing, and children are provided with facilities for indoor and outdoor play, sleep, rest, meals etc. Through group interaction, children develop skills and master tasks that are a necessary part of development and socialisation.

The majority of long-daycare centres are community based. They are usually funded by federal and state governments or local councils and they usually operate through local councils. Initial government funding is often allocated for the construction of the centre and an operational subsidy is paid to the centre for each of the available places. In addition to this subsidy, fee relief is available for low-income families. There are some privately owned long-daycare centres but low-income families are not eligible for fee subsidies and the fees may be higher than in a subsidised centre.

Figure 4.2 A pre-school or daycare centre can provide valuable socialising experiences for children as they learn to interact with others.

Long-daycare centres are usually open 50 weeks of the year from the hours of 7.30 a.m. to 5.30 p.m., although some have longer hours. Most government-supervised or subsidised centres take children from 6 weeks to 6 years. Privately operated centres often take children from 2 years to 6 years. This is because the regulations concerning the care of children under the age of 3 years require a higher staff ratio for the number of children. This of course increases the costs. Most government-operated or supervised centres give preference to families with special needs, for example those with both parents working, single-parent working families and migrant families. These centres must operate within guidelines set by the Department of Community Services or other relevant government authority.

Research shows that higher-income families are the main users of formal child-care facilities. The costs of full-time child care can be very high and for many parents it may not be viable to work, particularly if there is more than one child in child care. While fee relief is available for middle to lower-income earners, the costs of care plus work-related costs may mean that workforce participation is not worthwhile, given the extra stresses that are present when a mother undertakes two full-time roles.

Work-based child-care centres

There are few work-based child-care centres in Australia although the federal government is encouraging more employers to provide this service. Some large employer groups are considering this service, recognising that the provision of such a service means the skills and expertise of many valuable employees may be retained. Work-based child care allows mothers the opportunity to continue to breastfeed their babies, and for parents to spend more time with their children. Studies of work-based child care by the Office of the Status of Women has shown that this type of care reduces staff turnover in the workplace and reduces absenteeism which may occur when an informal child-care arrangement falls through.

As a result of extending government fee relief to middle and low-income earners using work-based child care, it has been estimated that an additional 28 000 new places will be created between 1990–95 in the commercial and employer sector. The government is emphasising the links between child care, workforce participation and productivity. The federal government will also assist in providing some funds for the establishment of centres and related resources.

Short-daycare centres

Short-daycare is a term used to include pre-schools and kindergartens; their operating hours are shorter than a long-daycare centre. These centres may be privately owned, managed by the local council or community-based. Short-daycare centres generally take children from 3 to 6 years of age. Depending on the centre, children attend from one to five days a week, usually from 9.00 a.m. to 3.00 p.m., although some centres have an extended licence and operate from 8.30 a.m. to 3.45 p.m. These centres are usually not suitable if the parent or parents are working because the hours are not long enough, unless someone else can care for the children before and after opening hours.

Like long-daycare centres, pre-schools and kindergartens provide an opportunity for children to mix with others their own age and to take part in activities which the family unit may not be able to provide. These centres have an educational focus and are usually staffed with trained early-childhood teachers and child-care assistants.

Family daycare system

This system is usually organised and supervised through the local council and some financial support is available from the federal government. Under this scheme, home-based mothers care for up to four pre-school children (including their own) during the day, and up to three children after school. Fee relief is available for low-income families. The program provides for occasional care, emergency care, regular part-time care, full-day care, before- and after-school care and holiday care. Family daycare homes are regularly visited by a scheme coordinator to provide assistance and advice, and to ensure that the needs of children are being satisfied.

Over the last decade family daycare has been used more than centre-based care for care of children under the age of 3 years. The most common form of child care for the 'under threes' is informal care, that is care by relatives, friends and neighbours. There have been some moves to encourage the use of family daycare rather than centre-based care as it is cheaper to provide this type of care. Centre-based care is more expensive as it requires the initial costs of construction and the ongoing costs of maintenance and staff salaries. Family daycare provides some advantages for the caregivers in that they can supplement family income by caring for children. This appeals to many women who have young children and wish to remain at home while their children are young.

The child-care system in Australia can only cater for approximately half the children whose parents have applied for a place. Over the past few years this deficiency has been acknowledged by the federal government and more child-care places have been allocated in budgets. However, the demand for quality child care still exceeds the supply.

Playgroups

Many community organisations provide facilities for children's playgroups. These are not childminding centres, as one parent is expected to attend with the child. Playgroups provide children with the opportunity to play and interact with other children, as well as offering parents the chance to interact with other adults.

Baby health or early childhood centres

These centres do not provide a child-care service, but rather a support system which aids and assists in the healthy development of children. The focus on community welfare has meant that such centres are providing a wider range of services for children and families.

The child-care debate

Some families see child care as necessary for the socialisation of children. Some regard it as necessary to enable both parents to work. Others see it as a combination of both these factors. Many parents believe that the modern family is too small and isolated to fulfil the social needs of adults and children, and that pre-school children need to interact on a regular basis with other children. Others, however, believe that the development of the mother–child bond is only achieved when the child and mother remain together, at home. Many mothers are confused by the debate and do not know what is the right choice to make, if a choice is available. Because of financial pressures many mothers of young children have no choice and must return to the workforce and many of these mothers feel guilty about leaving their children in the care of others.

The cost of child care

In recent years child care has received a lot of attention. The cost of child care has been questioned—some people maintain that child care should be tax-deductible, while others maintain it is a right for all families and should attract greater government subsidies. Some community groups are concerned about allowing child care as a tax deduction as they claim it would provide the greatest benefit to the higher-income earners. Another important issue for child care is the high staff turnover, which would appear to be increasing. This is difficult for children who often form strong attachments to staff and need the stability of permanent staff. Staff in child-care centres work long hours in a demanding environment, often under stressful conditions, for inadequate wages.

BONDING BETWEEN MOTHER/CAREGIVER AND CHILD

It was widely believed for many years that the mother's continual presence for the first years of a child's life is critical for his or her social and emotional development. Many early-childhood experts maintained that young children would suffer permanent psychological damage and future delinquency if they were not cared for solely by their mother during the first five years of life. In the 1960s this become a controversial issue as many women challenged traditional beliefs and chose to re-enter the workforce while their children were young. Obviously the need for women to remain in or re-enter the workforce for whatever reasons is reflected in the rapid increase in child-care facilities. This controversy seems to have settled down in recent years, perhaps as a result of the economic recession and the acceptance that two incomes in a family is often needed to maintain a fairly basic standard of living.

Research concerning the emotional bonds between mother and child suggests there is little difference in the mother–child relationship, whether the child spends the day with the mother, another caregiver or at a daycare centre.

It appears that the quality of care is as important as the quantity of care. Separation of child from primary caregiver does not cause distress when it is regular, predictable and familiar, that is, in the same place such as a child-care centre, a relative or a family-daycare mother. A study in Boston (USA) in 1976 compared two groups of children: the members of one group attended a daycare centre for five days a week from the age of $3\frac{1}{2}$ months to $2\frac{1}{2}$ years, and the other group stayed at home with their mother.[3] When the children were 20 months old, they were placed in an unfamiliar setting with the mother, another woman

3 J. Kagan, 'The child in the family', in A.S. Rossi et al., *The Family*, New York, 1978, p. 36.

and a friend of the family; the daycare children were placed in the same setting with the mother, another woman and the daycare teacher. During the 45 minutes of observation, all the children went to their mother when they were bored or needed reassurance. This did not mean that the children were not attached to others, but rather that they identified more closely with their mother.

EARLY CHILDHOOD PROGRAMS

Evidence suggests that the most important period for learning and physical, social and intellectual development is between birth and 6 years of age. If the appropriate development does not occur during this time it is virtually impossible to make up for it later in a child's life. The Australian Institute of Family Studies maintains that early childhood education should be available for all families, to provide environments where children develop confidence, social skills, problem-solving skills, language concepts, mathematical and spatial concepts, and physical skills. The investment in early childhood education is important for the future of our children and our nation. Competent children are more likely to grow up to be competent adults and able to participate effectively in society.

Children who are denied opportunities during the early part of their life to develop fully, as a result of a lack of stimulating experiences, are less likely to develop into competent members of society. Overseas evidence shows a relationship between poverty and poor health of children. Poor health can inhibit development of children during the early years of life and in the future. Studies in the United States of America over a twenty-year period show that children enrolled in good quality child-care centres for at least two years have fewer school absences, higher levels of post-secondary education and higher levels of earnings than children who did not have access to pre-school experiences.[4]

Significant attempts have been made in Australia to assist schools which have a high proportion of students from disadvantaged home backgrounds. Schools have received assistance to set up a variety of programs aimed at overcoming the disadvantage that many children and youth experience.

However, the same effort has not been made to set up programs for very young children. In the USA, a program called 'Headstart' has been operating for several years. This program aims at enriching the lives of

4 D. Edgar, 'Family problems: The cost–benefits of prevention', *Family Matters*, Australian Institute of Family Studies, no. 25, December 1989, p. 43.

Take twelve girls...

Girls now at school will be likely to work in paid employment for at least 30 years. Yet many schoolgirls still regard work as something to fill in the gap between getting married and having children. These facts from the Australian Bureau of Statistics may be enlightening.

Of twelve girls:

- three will need to work alongside their partner to keep the family going;
- three will get married and divorced soon after;
- one will have a partner who is physically violent and/or an alcoholic who can't hold a steady job;
- one will need to work because her husband is unemployed;
- one will never marry;
- one will be widowed;
- one will never have a child; and
- one will be supported by her husband all her adult life.

Figure 4.3 'Take twelve girls ... '

Source: *The Gen*, Women's Bureau, Department of Employment, Education and Training.

children socially, educationally and nutritionally before they commence school. The earlier a disadvantage can be eliminated by providing appropriate programs for both children and parents, the greater the chance that those skills which are required for effective social participation will be acquired. It is in early childhood where the development of literacy and numeracy begins, and many people believe that it is at this stage where the educational disadvantage most often associated with poverty can be minimised.

It is sometimes assumed that a young child is better off in the environment of his or her own home. However, not all parents do or can provide a stimulating environment that will encourage development. Research shows that the mothers who can provide an enriched environment and spend time with children in reading and playing are those who have the money, time, energy and education or inclination to do so. Not all parents have the resources to provide a stimulating environment. It may be that early childhood centres can assist in this way, regardless of whether the parents are in the workforce.

Programs for families with children

The Children's Service Program (CSP) assists families with dependent children to participate more fully in the community through the provision of financial assistance to the states and territories and other providers of quality child care, and other children's and family services. The main objective of the CSP is to support workforce participation by giving families with dependent children, especially low-income and single-parent families, access to affordable child-care services. Other programs which are designed to assist families in child care include Jobs, Education and Training (JET) for single parents. This scheme has been discussed in more detail in Chapter 5.

Development of competence

In recent years much attention has been paid to the need for children to develop the knowledge, skills and abilities which will provide them with the competence to earn a living, to take care of themselves, to form relationships and to participate effectively in society. Competence refers to the ability to acquire and perform those social roles that are valued and considered important in a particular society. It also refers to the ability to interact effectively with the environment: to control and adapt to the environment, to solve problems and reach goals. Forms of competence include reading ability, living skills, self-esteem, self-control and independence. At certain stages of a child's or young person's life, the achievement of different forms of competence will be

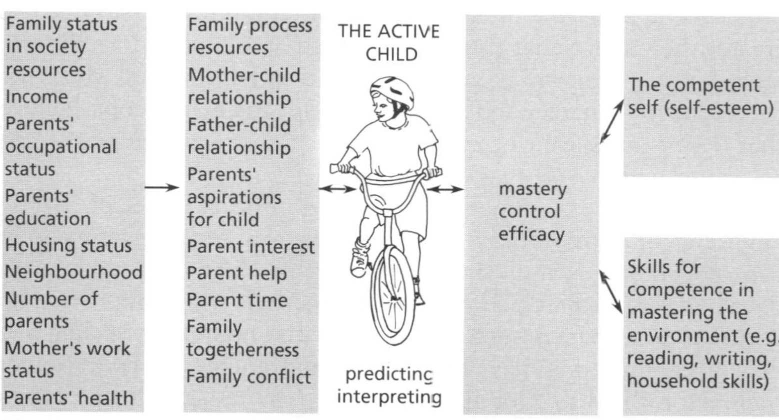

Figure 4.4 Development of competence in children

Source: Australian Institute of Family Studies.

considered important, and indeed necessary for future development.

To acquire an overall competence, children need to develop a set of competencies. Children need the opportunities which will enable them to develop those competencies required both now and in the future. While we may be aware of those competencies that were considered important in the past and those that are considered important now, it is difficult to determine which competencies will be important ten years from now.

As Gay Ochiltree notes in her book *Children in Australian Families*, in our society certain competencies are more highly valued than others, and these competencies include intelligence, formal educational qualifications, social skills, leadership skills, confidence and competitiveness.[5] People who possess those competencies that are valued by society are more likely to achieve the rewards that the majority of the population consider to be important, e.g. higher-status job, respect, financial security, independence etc. Further, children who develop competencies in one area, e.g. language skills, can transfer this learning to other areas in order to learn other competencies.

Certain types of competence may be regarded as more or less important in different societies. For example, obedience may be given a high priority in one society, but in another society priority may be placed on aggressiveness. Participation and survival in particular societies may require particular competencies, as well as competencies that are common to most industrialised societies.

Children who have access to those resources which assist in the development of competence have an advantage over those children whose families do not have the resources to do so. As has been discussed above and will be further discussed in Chapter 7, poverty and the lack of development of competence for both parents and children is closely related. However, it is important to recognise that the economic situation of families is not the only factor in determining the competencies that children may acquire. Yet, if there are insufficient economic resources to provide for basic needs it is unlikely that the potential of children will be realised. Children who are born into poverty and live in poverty do not have the same opportunities to develop or achieve those competencies that are required to participate effectively in our society. These children have less chance of obtaining the social and economic resources that are considered desirable for a satisfying and comfortable lifestyle.

5 Edgar, 'Family problems', *Family Matters* no. 25 p. 20.

Self-esteem

Competence refers not just to the skills, abilities and knowledge needed to master and live within the environment, but also to self-esteem and feelings of self-worth and proficiency. Self-esteem and potential will not be enhanced if children are not provided with the opportunity to acquire the knowledge, skills and abilities appropriate to the society in which they live. Children who have a good self-esteem regard themselves as competent and will act accordingly. At the same time, children who have negative feelings and a poor self-image are unlikely to be motivated to strive to acquire desirable skills and will not regard themselves as competent.

The competence and self-esteem of children is also influenced by family relationships, experiences provided, the environment in which they live, and the attitudes and values of parents, as well as parenting practices. Children who are encouraged to contribute to family discussions and express opinions are more likely to have higher self-esteem than children who are 'put down' constantly, or who live in an authoritarian-style family. Competence of children is developed when there is a high level of positive interaction between parents and children, and children are rewarded for competent behaviour. A stimulating, warm and supportive environment is as important as an abundance of economic resources. While an abundance of economic resources cannot compensate for the lack of a supportive environment, for children who have access to neither the future would appear to be bleak.

Issues for youth

The age at which childhood ends and adulthood begins is not clear. While young people reach political and legal adulthood at 18 years of age, they are often not regarded as having adult status. There are no clear age boundaries distinguishing youth from other groups in society, although that part of the population aged between 15 and 25 years is often referred to as youth. Obviously, such a wide age-span will mean that the resources, achievements, economic situation, needs, interests and activities of individuals within this age group will vary greatly.

The needs of a 15-year-old, and the issues that he or she may have to confront, will differ from those of a 23-year-old. Similarly, a significant number of individuals are still undertaking education at 24 years of age, while many others may have finished their education and have been fortunate enough to obtain employment. An 18-year-old youth who is unemployed is likely to have less options than a 22-year-old youth who is unemployed but has finished secondary education and undertaken some post-secondary education or training.

In the 1960s concerns about young people focused on their attitudes in relation to dress, music, sexual behaviour and alternative lifestyles. While some of these concerns may be relevant in the 1990s, new concerns relating to education and employment prospects have received greater attention. However, there are different views regarding youth: some people see youth as a disadvantaged group who are unable to obtain a place in the workforce and participate fully in society, while others see youth as enjoying a good life and expecting society to provide more than they deserve at their stage in life.

Employment

The number of full-time jobs available for youth has declined rapidly, while the number of part-time jobs has increased. Two decades ago, school leavers experienced few difficulties in obtaining full-time employment—employment which often had career potential and allowed financial and personal independence. In 1966, 58 per cent of 15 to 19-year-olds held a full-time job (58 per cent for males and 57 per cent for females). In 1991 it was 20 per cent (24 per cent for males and 17 per cent for females).

The decline in the number of full-time jobs and the need to obtain further educational qualifications has prolonged the period of financial dependency on the family. Youth employment is now concentrated in occupations requiring little training and few skills, and attracting low wages. Many jobs are part-time jobs and in the service industries. In 1991, of the total youth employed:

- 33 per cent of 15 to 19-year-olds were employed in the wholesale and retail industry—young males in wholesale and young females in retail;
- 50 per cent of young males were employed as tradespersons;
- 25 per cent of young males were employed as labourers;
- 42 per cent of young females were employed as clerks;
- 35 per cent of young females were employed as sales and personal services employees;
- 5 per cent of young males were employed as clerks;
- 10 per cent of young males were employed as sales and personal service employees.

These figures also show the segmentation of the youth workforce into traditional male and female occupations. Current trends in employment and unemployment clearly show that post-secondary education is essential in order to increase an individual's chances of finding employment which requires certain skills and will attract higher pay rates.

Unemployment

The unemployment rate for the 15–19 year age group is approximately 20 per cent, compared to 3.3 per cent in 1967. For the 20–24 year age group the unemployment rate is approximately 14 per cent. Youth unemployment has been recognised as being a structural problem in most industrial nations since the beginning of the 1980s. Unemployment for this age group is a complex issue. Some youth leave school early and are either employed or unemployed, others continue with their education while working full-time or part-time, and others continue with education, seeking or not seeking employment. The large majority of unemployed youth have left school early and often have no formal educational qualifications.

Education

Most research shows that the higher the level of education gained, the greater the chance of obtaining and maintaining employment. Youth from higher socio-economic backgrounds are more likely to have completed secondary education and to have undertaken some post-secondary education.

Education is a resource which is unevenly distributed in most societies, including Australia. Long-term unemployed youth are more likely to have been born into, and raised in, low-income families, often in poverty. This cycle of poverty is often perpetuated as children in this situation are more likely to leave school early and work in unskilled occupations which attract low wages.

Since the 1970s many programs have been initiated at both federal and state levels in an attempt to increase retention rates in secondary schools and increase employment opportunities for youth. Indeed, retention rates have increased significantly, with approximately 66 per cent of young men and 77 per cent of young women completing secondary education. Many young people stay at school not because they particularly value education, but because there are few employment opportunities. Despite financial assistance to low-income families for education, it is still distributed unequally in society. Some individuals have greater access to the resource of education than others.

Figure 4.5 Homeless youth: Many have experienced family breakdown as a result of low income and unemployment. (Photo: Salvation Army)

As education is a resource which is used to acquire other resources, lack of education can assist in perpetuating inequality.

FAMILY RELATIONSHIPS

Youth and adolescence is a time of increasing autonomy and a lessening of ties with the family. Increased physical, intellectual and emotional maturity may cause adolescents to question their concept of themselves and self-image may change. This period of transition from childhood to adulthood requires a family environment which is supportive and sets some limits, yet allows adolescents the freedom to make decisions, to accept new responsibilities and to form new relationships. Young people who live in supportive environments have high levels of self-esteem and competence are far more likely to survive the problems they encounter.

For whatever reasons, when young people cannot find employment, self-esteem is usually affected and parent–child relationships are often strained. Relationships are more likely to be strained when family income is low. If relationships become too strained and breakdown occurs, young people may be forced to leave home without any parental support.

For teenagers, junior wage rates and social welfare benefits are very low, and to survive without family support is very difficult, if not impossible. The costs of establishing and renting even the most modest accommodation is very high, and young people who are unable to live with their families may be living in poverty. Social welfare benefits available for young people include Job Search Allowance, Young Homeless Allowance and unemployment benefits. These allowances do not provide sufficient income support for independent living. The assumption still exists that all young people have access to supportive family networks, which have the resources to provide assistance if and when needed.

Many young people living at home are physically, emotionally and intellectually mature yet are still economically dependent on their family. Twenty years ago young people of the same age were usually employed and economically independent, and many were married with their own families. Youth who have access to the economic and social support of a family may experience less stresses than youth who do not have family support. However, in even the most supportive family situations, it is likely that conflicts will arise.

It can be very difficult for young people to achieve autonomy and independence if they are reliant solely on their family for income support. Such reliance on families may be a source of financial stress for both parents and youth and may contribute to other family tensions. In some families the tensions are too great and young people leave home. While social welfare benefits are available to young people, they are insufficient to provide for independence and autonomy.

HOMELESS YOUTH

While there are many young people who may desire to move out of the family home and live independently, it is not a necessity if their families continue to provide for and support them. However, for a small group in our society, remaining at home is not an option: survival means leaving home.

The reasons for young people leaving home early are complex and interrelated. The main reasons are family conflict, abusive family relationships, desire for independence, and family economic hardship and unemployment.[6] Also, evidence suggests that homeless young people may be more likely to have come from family situations where separation and divorce of parents, or repartnering of parents, had occurred. It is important to note that some degree of conflict occurs in all families: it is only when the conflict is constant and severe that

6 F. Maas & R. Hartley, *On the Outside: The Needs of Unsupported, Homeless Youth*, Australian Institute of Family Studies, Melbourne, 1988, p. 1.

family stability is threatened. Similarly, we cannot assume that families who are in a situation of dissolving and reforming will have a higher level of conflict which will cause young people to leave home. The evidence appears to be that the additional pressures that families may experience as a result of structural change may create stresses and pressures for young people. Young people may find the readjustment to a new situation too great to tolerate and may not be prepared to accept a new adult in the family. Conflicts may arise with repartnering, particularly if there are other stresses present such as inadequate income and unemployment.

Young adults who are financially dependent upon their family may rebel by leaving home if they have not been given some degree of autonomy and independence as well as responsibility. Some young people may experience conflicts between the values of their parents and the values they have formed through an upbringing in Australia. This may occur if their parents hold strongly to values of another culture. If the differences in values are great, there may be high levels of family conflict.

While individual and family factors are important contributing factors to youth homelessness, there are other macro factors which impinge. As discussed above, youth unemployment can generate conflict within a family that may have been avoided if the young person was employed and able to contribute financially to the family.

The small amount of money paid under the Job Search Allowance or Austudy assumes the family of the recipient is willing and able to provide other physical and financial support. The amount paid by these benefits is insufficient to make any substantial difference to the financial circumstances of a low-income family. Youth living in low-income families may leave the family unit in order to ease some of the financial burden, as well as to avoid the conflict over money that may be ever-present.

While it is difficult to estimate the number of homeless and unsupported youth living in Australia, over the last decade there has been an increased awareness of this problem. Greater attention has been paid to providing income support, to providing opportunities for acquiring education, training and work skills, and to providing short-term and long-term accommodation.

Equality of opportunity

Although the general standard of living has improved in Australia throughout this century, a significant number of Australian children and youth live in poverty. Growing up in a low-income family means that children have fewer opportunities than those whose families have a higher income. Children and youth at greatest risk to poverty are those living in single-parent families and large families, particularly when they are dependent upon social security for income support. Twenty per cent of Australian children are living in families who are dependent on social security benefits, including unemployment, supporting parent or sickness benefit.[7]

Children living in poverty are more likely to live in inadequate housing and to change residence more frequently. They are less likely to complete secondary education or obtain post-school qualifications. Such a situation is often the beginning of a poverty cycle for children which is very difficult to break. This poverty cycle means less education, fewer skills, low-paid jobs and a greater chance of long periods of unemployment. It is necessary to break into this cycle and provide children with the resources to participate in society and to become competent members of society. Children living in poverty often do not have access to opportunities to acquire the skills and competence required for effective participation in society. Poverty and the effects on children and youth have been discussed in greater detail in Chapter 7.

Review questions

1 What is the proportion of children in Australia under the age of 19 years?
2 Why do a significant proportion of Australian children experience different family formations?
3 Describe how children were generally treated by adults prior to the nineteenth century.
4 How has the focus of welfare services for children changed this century?
5 Why is attention now paid to the welfare of communities as well as to the welfare of children and families?
6 Distinguish between child *abuse* and child *neglect*.
7 Outline some of the major factors contributing to child abuse.
8 Why has there been a decline in the number of children in substitute care?
9 Until the last two decades there has been a resistance to expansion of child-care facilities. Why?

---

7 G. Ochiltree, *Children in Australian Families*, Longman Cheshire, Melbourne, 1990, p.12.

10 Why do parents often use informal care in preference to formal child care?
11 Distinguish between long-daycare centres and short-daycare centres.
12 Identify the advantages of family daycare.
13 Suggest some advantages of work-based child care.
14 Outline the nature of the controversies which surround the provision of child care.
15 Why is child care considered desirable for all children, regardless of whether parents are working outside the home?
16 Explain what is meant by the term *competency*.
17 How is competency developed by children and young people?
18 Why have youth unemployment rates increased over the last decade?
19 In what situations is family conflict likely to have negative consequences for young people?
20 Explain how a lack of educational opportunities can contribute to poverty.

SURVEY

PRE-SCHOOL CENTRE OR DAYCARE CENTRE?

A Staff

Name of staff	Position on staff	Training and qualifications

B Hours and enrolments

1 Days of week open ______________________________

2 Daily hours ______________________________

3 Total number enrolled ______________________________

How many attend full day? __________ half day? __________

4 How many children attend:

Five days per week? ______________________________

Four days per week? ______________________________

Three days per week? ______________________________

Two days per week? ______________________________

One day per week? ______________________________

5 How many children attend because one or both parents are working?

C Cost

1 Daily ______________________________

2 Weekly ______________________________

Are there any fee concessions given when more than one child from the same family attends? ______________________________

D Parents

Number of children from:

1 One-parent families ______________________________

2 Two-parent families ______________________________

3 Families of migrant origins ______________________________

E Age and sex of children

1 Attend from __________ to __________ years

Are there any exceptions made? ______________________________

2 Number of children aged:

less than 1 year ______________________________

1 year ______________________________

2 years ______________________________

3 years ______________________________

4 years ______________________________

5 years ______________________________

3 Number of boys ______

4 Number of girls ______

5 Twins ______

F Outline of daily activities and organisation

Times	Activities (indoors or outdoors)

G Food

1 Are full meals provided? ______

2 Are there any special request made by parents? ______

______

3 Where do children eat? ______

Time	Type of food given

H Health and hygiene rules

What specific rules or practices are adopted in relation to care of the sick, meals, personal hygiene, etc.?

______

______

______

______

______

I Teaching

1 Are children organised into groups? If so, on what basis?

___

___

___

2 Do any of the children require special attention, e.g. in relating to other children and adults?

___

___

3 Which aspects of the child's socialisation are bing reinforced? ___

___

___

___

4 What forms of discipline (punishment) are used, if any? ___

___

___

5 Are children taken on any outing? Give examples

___

___

6 What types of lessons are taught? What skills are developed?

___

___

___

___

___

___

7 What atmosphere is created for the children?

___

___

___

5

Single-parent families and blended families

Formation of single-parent families

Since the mid-1970s there has been a dramatic increase in the proportion of single-parent families. This has been mainly due to changes in family law which has provided for easier access to divorce. Single-parent families may be permanent or temporary formations. They result from different situations; and individual families will have access to differing types and amounts of resources. Many single-parent families are able to satisfy the needs and wants of their members reasonably independently, while others must rely to a greater extent on community and government support.

The discussion of single-parent families and blended families in this chapter is not meant to portray them as atypical or deviant, but rather as significant family formations in Australian society. As with other family formations, single-parent families and blended families will have particular problems and challenges to face as a result of their organisation and reorganisation.

Single-parent families may arise as a result of:

- Death of one parent from accident, sickness, disease, age, war, suicide, murder etc.
- Separation of parents, which may be permanent or temporary. The work of one parent may take him or her away from the family for long periods of time during the year, as with the armed forces. In the case of a temporary separation, roles and tasks within a family may only have to be re-allocated for a short period of time. It may also be a permanent separation, where neither partner wants a divorce.
- Illness of one parent may mean that he or she can no longer support the family.
- Desertion, i.e. where one partner has left the family group.
- Imprisonment, where one partner is permanently or temporarily absent from the family.
- Single mother or father, where one parent has a child or children in their care. Most commonly this situation occurs when a woman chooses to have and raise a child by herself.
- Breakdown of a relationship, in that parents and children live together in one household but there is little or no communication or interaction between parents.
- Divorce, i.e. where the parents have legally dissolved the marriage. This is probably the major contributing factor in the formation of single-parent families.

Throughout this chapter as well as in other chapters statistics regarding single-parent families have been presented. The figures which indicate the number of single-parent families in Australia often vary. This variation is due to how the number of single-parent families is measured. The following information indicates some of the characteristics of single-parent families:

- Of all families, approximately 10 per cent are single-parent families.
- Of all families with dependent children, 15 per cent are single-parent families. In 1973, only about 7.3 per cent of families with dependent children were single-parent families.
- Approximately 12 per cent of dependent children live in single-parent families.
- For children living in single-parent families, approximately 70 per cent live with a parent who is either separated or divorced, 20 per cent live with a parent who has never married and less than 10 per cent live with a widowed parent.
- On average, single-parent families have 1.3 children, compared to 1.9 for couple families. Children in single-parent families tend to be older than children in couple families.

Figure 5.1 Lone mothers with children form the largest proportion of single-parent families in Australia.

- Of all single-parent families, approximately 87 per cent are headed by a female and 13 per cent are headed by a male. During the 1980s there was a slight increase in the number of male-headed single-parent families and a corresponding decrease in the number of female-headed single-parent families. However, in the 1990s this trend was reversed.
- There are more single-parent families living in urban areas than in rural areas.
- Female single parents are more likely to be dependent upon social security for income support than male single parents. However, during the last few years there has been an increase in the workforce participation of female single parents. Some of this increase has been due to the introduction of employment assistance schemes, and child care provisions to allow single mothers to undertake re-training or further education, in order to increase workforce skills. In 1991 over half of lone mothers were in the labour force.

Divorce patterns in Australia

As a result of the higher divorce rate over the last two decades, it has often been claimed that the family unit is breaking down. As shown in Table 5.1 there was a large increase in the divorce rate in the years following the Family Law Act of 1975–76, but since this initial increase, divorce rates have fluctuated and since stabilised. At the beginning of this century, 4 per cent of Australian marriages ended in divorce, in 1971, the rate was 14 per cent, and by 1987 the divorce rate appeared to have stabilised, with about 35 to 38 per cent of marriages ending in divorce. Since 1990 the rate of divorce appears to have increased again.

While the increase in the divorce rate between 1971 and 1988 is very significant, it does not necessarily indicate that marriage as an institution is no longer considered viable. Prior to 1976, it is likely that

Table 5.1 Marriage and divorce rates 1961–91

Year/Period	Number of marriages	Number of divorces	Average duration of marriage (years)
Annual averages			
1961–65	83 250	7 542	13.60
1966–70	106 185	10 681	13.40
1971–75	111 802	17 348	11.90
1976–80	106 297	45 220	10.60
Annual totals			
1978	102 958	40 608	10.50
1979	104 396	37 854	10.30
1980	109 240	39 258	10.20
1981	113 905	41 412	10.20
1982	117 275	44 088	10.40
1983	114 860	43 525	10.60
1984	108 655	43 124	10.60
1985	115 493	39 830	10.60
1986	114 913	39 417	10.60
1987	114 113	39 725	10.20
1988	116 816	41 007	10.10
1990	116 959	42 635	10.10
1991	113 869	45 630	10.30

Source: Australian Bureau of Statistics data

as many couples were unhappy in marriage, but only those from the higher socioeconomic groups could afford the economic cost of divorce. Further, social attitudes towards divorce were less tolerant then than they are now.

Prior to 1976 many couples preferred to remain separated rather than to obtain a divorce, as it was both difficult and expensive to obtain. The Family Law Act of 1975–76 provided for 'no fault' divorce, with the only grounds being the 'irretrievable breakdown' of marriage. Provided the court is satisfied that the partners in the marriage have lived separately and apart for 12 months, that the marriage has no chance of working, and that both partners will be responsible for the maintenance of children, a couple can obtain a divorce with minimal legal expenses. All matters relating to division of property, maintenance of the other partner and children, and custody of the children, have to be settled by the partners before they can apply for a divorce. If the partners cannot agree on these matters, they must attend the Family Court of Australia, which makes the relevant decisions. Under these conditions, divorce proceedings can be lengthy and expensive.

Cultural origin

Divorce rates in Australia also vary with ethnic origin. The proportion of women who are separated or divorced is smaller at almost all ages for overseas-born women than for Australian-born women. Southern European-born women, especially Italian and Greek, and Asian-born women are much less likely than Australian-born women to be separated or divorced. In contrast, women born in New Zealand and Germany and younger women born in the United Kingdom and Ireland are more likely than Australian-born women to be separated or divorced.

Divorce, length of marriage and children

The largest increases in divorce rates have occurred in the 25–29 year age group, and therefore there has been an increase in the proportion of divorces involving marriages of less than five years. Divorce is more likely for people marrying at younger ages. The proportion of divorces involving marriages of less than five years duration has increased from around 10 per cent in the early 1970s to over 20 per cent in the early 1990s. However, the greatest proportion of divorces occur 5–9 years after marriage. Consequently, the average duration of marriage prior to divorce has decreased over the past two decades. This is shown in Table 6.1.

There has been a general decline in the proportion of divorces involving children. This may be due to the trend to have children later in marriage and the trend to shorter duration of marriage prior to divorce. In 1967, 66.5 per cent of divorces involved children; in 1988, 57.5 per cent of divorces involved children who were less than 18 years of age. It is expected that around 18 per cent of children will experience the divorce of their parents by the age of 18 years.

In the future

While there has been some stabilisation of divorce rates, it has been suggested that as future generations of married women become attached to the workforce, they may become less concerned about the economic consequences of divorce. Higher rates of divorce are a distinct possibility in the 1990s and it has been widely suggested that during this decade approximately 40 per cent of marriages will end in divorce.[1]

Indeed, evidence from the 1980s suggests that it is becoming increasingly common for women to initiate separation and divorce in situations where men perceive few problems with the marriage and do not want a divorce. It may be that more women are rejecting the traditional roles of wife and mother; and if they are not economically dependent on their male partner, divorce may be increasingly seen as a viable option.

Families are dynamic, not static: statistics relating to marriage, divorce and fertility rates do not always convey the actual dynamics of family formation, dissolution and re-formation.

Factors contributing to the increase in single-parent families

Within each family there may be specific factors contributing to the separation and/or divorce of the partners. These factors include:

- ill health of either partner;
- economic stresses which may force one partner to move away in order to obtain employment;

1 P. McDonald, 'Families in the pursuit of personal autonomy', *Family Matters*, no. 22, December 1988, p.41.

- particular personal problems including drug addiction, alcoholism etc.;
- interests outside the home which may be incompatible with family life, including religious, sporting or political activities;
- incompatible roles, where partners cannot agree on the roles that each should undertake.

While the above factors may play a significant part in the breakdown of existing relationships they do not explain the increasing number of females who choose to become single parents. It is necessary to look at the broader trends which have contributed to the increase in the number of single-parent families.

General trends

Despite the considerable increase in the proportion of single-parent families over the past two decades there has actually been a decline in the growth rate of single-parent families. Figures from the Australian Bureau of Statistics show that between 1976 and 1981 there was a 43 per cent increase in the number of single-parent families, but between 1981 and 1986 there was only a 10 per cent increase.

There is no one factor that can be identified as being the cause of the increase in the number of single-parent families. The factors outlined in the following discussion are interrelated and all have contributed in some way to the increase in the number of single-parent families. Certainly, legal changes were required in order to make divorce a more viable proposition, but at the same time, changes in social attitudes were necessary to make divorce more acceptable within the community. Income support in the form of social welfare benefits were required to allow single parents to be economically independent. The availability of these benefits was a result of political and legal changes.

Social factors

- Attitudes towards divorce and having children outside of marriage have changed over the last two decades and there is a greater acceptance of single-parent families.
- Social pressures from friends and relatives to stay married when the marriage is not satisfactory are far less than they were half a century ago.
- The campaign of equal opportunity for women and the emphasis on independence and personal fulfilment achieved through working

outside the home have allowed women to see themselves in a role other than that of wife.

- The growth of the mass media has helped make individuals more aware of the alternatives available and has provided information about help that can be obtained by individuals and families.
- Support systems provided by governments and local communities are available to assist single-parent families in a variety of ways. Such support systems were non-existent a few decades ago.
- During the 1980s there was a significant increase in the number of ex-nuptial births. Ex-nuptial births accounted for 8.8 per cent of all births in 1971, 12.1 per cent in 1980 and 23 per cent in 1991. Evidence from national surveys suggests that approximately half of these births are to de facto couples and about half to single women.[2] Ex-nuptial births are more likely to be to older women, and more likely to be acknowledged by the father.
- There has been a large decrease in the number of teenage marriages as a result of pregnancy. Marriage is no longer seen as the only course of action when an ex-nuptial pregnancy occurs.

Economic and educational factors

- Throughout this century there has been an increase in the real standard of living for most families. This allows individuals to be less dependent on their families and relatives and makes it possible for one parent to provide for family needs. (However, in times of high inflation and economic recession, this may be very difficult, and indeed single-parent families form the largest group living in poverty.)
- Higher educational qualifications have contributed to increased job opportunities for women and higher income levels. Thus, it is often feasible for women to support a family alone, although more and more two-parent families find that two incomes are essential in order to provide for needs and wants.
- The trend to a smaller number of children in each family means that many women remain in the workforce during the childbearing period, and thus retain workforce skills and maintain careers. This provides many women with the economic independence to support themselves and their children if they wish. Women are no longer tied to a marriage or relationship because they are economically dependent upon a man.

2 McDonald, 'Families in pursuit of personal autonomy', p. 18.

Technological factors

- Reliable methods of contraception have enabled women to choose if and when to have children, as well as how many to have. The trend for women to remain in the workforce during the childbearing years is related to the tendency to have smaller families. Women who remain in the workforce do not lose workforce skills and therefore retain a degree of economic independence, which can provide them with greater options.
- The increase in the number and type of labour saving devices, and convenience and take-away foods has allowed women greater freedom from the home and thus the opportunities to explore other options including participation in the paid labour force.
- Advances in medical technology have contributed to increased life expectancy for both males and females. We may encounter a situation where people change marriage partners more often during their lifetime. It has been suggested that it is unrealistic to expect people to remain married to each other throughout a long lifespan, where needs and interests may change dramatically.

Political and legal factors

- The Family Law Act of 1975–76 provided for no-fault and less expensive divorce, and replaced the term 'illegitimate child' with 'ex-nuptial child.'
- Social services for single-parent families have increased since the Second World War, although the economic benefit is not large enough to act as an incentive for a woman or a man to choose to become a single parent. However, the provision of social service benefits may mean than more women choose to keep children rather than adopt or foster them out. Also, these provisions provide an option for women who cannot join the workforce, but are living in an intolerable marriage or relationship.
- The increased availability of family supports such as child-care facilities and fee relief for low-income earners provides a further option for single parents.
- Prior to the Second World War it was very difficult for a woman to join the workforce and support herself and two or three children. The money she may have earnt in the workforce was unlikely to be enough, and if she *could* find a job, it would have been very difficult to obtain good-quality child care.

Religious factors

- Although divorce is not actively encouraged by the Church it is more accepted now than it was a few decades ago. Certainly, it is unlikely that members are excluded from a religious faith if they have divorced and/or chosen to be a single parent.

Consequences for parents and children

Parents and children in single-parent families have the same needs as individuals in two-parent families. Generally, single-parent families have the same functions and tasks to perform as two-parent families, but it may be more difficult to do so, as more responsibility falls to one parent. In single-parent families there is often less flexibility if a crisis arises: if a parent becomes sick and unable to undertake the necessary tasks, there may be no other adult family member who can take over.

While the following discussion tends to focus on problems that single-parent families may face, it is not intended that only negative images of these families be conveyed. For many single-parent families, the difficulties that may be encountered following marital dissolution may be minor compared to those faced prior to it. That is, the advantages of divorce and becoming a single-parent family may far outweigh the disadvantages.

Among single-parent families, considerable differences do exist. Variables including income, assets, educational qualifications, ages of both children and parents, and cause of family formation means that it is difficult to form generalisations about single-parent families. The following discussion highlights those problems and difficulties that are relevant for a significant proportion of single-parent families.

Household organisation and division of labour

The large majority of tasks which have to be undertaken in a two-parent family comprise a full-time job for both adults. The single parent may find that he or she does not have sufficient time, energy, money or skills to undertake all tasks in a satisfactory manner. In order to do so, he or she may have to reduce the quantity of the tasks undertaken, or the quality of what is done, or be forced to rely on outside resources for assistance.

In doing the work of two parents, the single parent may find he or she has less time to spend with children and may feel that their needs are not being satisfied. If a parent does manage to undertake the necessary household tasks and meet the needs of the children, it is likely that he or she will have little time left for personal leisure or satisfaction of his or her her own needs. If a single parent is working outside the home, the hours away from work may be taken up with household tasks, leaving little time for leisure. At the same time, if the parent is not working outside the home and is relying on social welfare income support, there may be few resources for those leisure activities which require money. Lack of personal time is possibly a greater problem when children are young and require considerable physical care and attention.

Single-parent families who have the support of an extended family network may be able to cope with crises and unexpected events with less stress than those who do not have access to such support systems.

Development of children's competence

Participation in household tasks and activities is an important part of childhood socialisation and problems may arise if the parent wishes to accomplish tasks quickly and efficiently but does not give some responsibility for tasks to older children. On the other hand, single parents must take care not to overload children with too many tasks and responsibilities.

Some studies of single-parent families and stepfamilies have shown that while children may experience some difficulties in development as compared to children in 'intact' families, in other areas they may be ahead. For example, children in disrupted families often take on additional responsibilities and may have higher levels of life skills competence.[3] Generally, in single-parent households, adolescents appear to have greater responsibilities for household tasks and this is usually accompanied by a higher level of autonomy.

Decision making

In two-parent families, both parents usually exert some authority and make decisions. This may be a joint activity, or each parent may assume authority and decision making in different areas.

In single-parent families, the lone parent is usually forced to make

3 P. Amato, *Children in Australian Families: The Growth of Competence*, Prentice-Hall, Sydney, 1987, p. 141.

all major decisions, without the support, influence or assistance of another adult. This can be very difficult as the lone parent has no-one to consult when difficult decisions have to be made. Also, older children who have spent time in a two-parent family may resent the fact that only one parent makes the decisions and there is no one else to turn to if they feel the decision is unfair.

When a family has become a single-parent family as a result of separation or divorce, the loss of one parent can intensify the influence of the remaining parent. The lone parent must be careful not to exercise absolute authority, or children may see authority and power as something which can never be challenged.

Emotional support and interpersonal relationships

During the period following marital separation, interpersonal relationships are often marked by tension and disruption. Paul Amato suggests that during the period of initial separation three major problems emerge.

1 Everyday family life tends to become disorganised and less cohesive.
2 Relations between custodial parents and children tend to deteriorate.

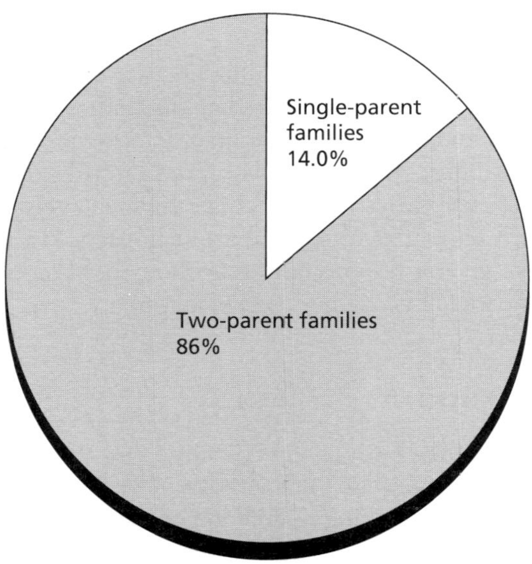

Figure 5.3 Proportions of single-parent and two-parent families in Australia
Source: Australian Bureau of Statistics

3 Contacts between non-custodial parents and children become less frequent.[4]

Family life becomes more organised after the first year and routines and relationships are re-established. In the long term, a harmonious single-parent family is likely to offer more satisfying relationships for all members than a two-parent family where conflict was ever-present.

In the case of divorce, children have to make major adjustments, particularly if they are old enough to understand what is happening. This can increase the stress for both parents, who are trying to adjust to the changed situation themselves as well as assisting in their children's adjustment. Children will be further affected if there is a high degree of conflict between parents either during or after the breakup of the marriage.

Most studies show that the quality of family relationships both before and after divorce or separation will influence the adjustment of children to the changed family situation. Also, the degree to which interaction occurs between the children and the grandparents and relatives of the non-custodial parent is significant in the adjustment of children.

Interaction with non-custodial parents

When one parent leaves the family, children have to adjust to a new relationship with the non-custodial parent. The type of relationship maintained with the non-custodial parent will be affected by the amount of contact the child/children have with him or her. While it is difficult to generalise, there is some evidence to suggest that in the majority of cases, the bond between non-custodial parents and children becomes weaker over time. However, it appears that fathers who live alone and have not formed other family relationships are more likely to maintain contact with their children. Non-custodial parents may establish other relationships and may also lose touch with the everyday lives of their children. This can place a strain on parent–child interaction and the relationship may be difficult to maintain.

Some studies suggest that if the father–child relationship was not good prior to the marriage breakdown, then it will weaken considerably after divorce. Other studies suggest that the quality of the father–child relationship prior to marriage breakdown has little to do with future relationships with children. Further research is needed in this area to draw any firm conclusions.

---

4 Amato, *Children in Australian Families*, p. 104.

Effects on adolescents

Early studies of divorce in the period following the Second World War reported that a high proportion of juvenile delinquents came from 'broken homes'. Since this time, studies of children in divorcing families both in Australia and overseas have arrived at differing conclusions. However, the accumulating body of research suggests that separation or divorce does not necessarily produce problem children or contribute to juvenile delinquency. Given a caring and autonomous relationship with at least one parent, adolescents can cope with separation and divorce of parents, provided they are not subjected to prolonged family conflicts.[5] It would appear that the social behaviour of adolescents is more directly related to the interpersonal relationships that exist within their family, rather than to the type of family in which they live.

Needs of adults

Adults, like children, have certain needs. They also require emotional security and love and affection from other people. The lone parent may experience reduced social relationships, as old friendships that both partners shared may be lost with divorce or separation—this is more likely to be so with divorce, rather than widowhood. As many social occasions involve couples, the lone parent may feel isolated from social activities, and in any case, the cost of babysitting may be outside the budget. There is a danger that when emotional needs are not satisfied, a lone parent may take his or her frustration out on the child, and parent–child relationships may suffer during this adjustment period.

Interaction with grandparents

For some grandparents, the effects of divorce may be positive as they may develop a closer relationship with their grandchildren and assume greater caregiving and supportive roles. For other grandparents, divorce within the family network may mean being denied access to children and losing contact with grandchildren. Research undertaken by the Australian Institute of Family Studies (AIFS) reveals a variety of outcomes for grandparents when marital separation and divorce occurs within a family.[6] The amount of contact that children have with

---

5 R. Dunlop & A. Burns, *'Don't Feel the World is Caving In': Adolescents in Divorcing Families*, Australian Instituten of Family Studies, Melbourne, 1988, p. 9.

6 Specific reference is made to the research study *Economic Consequences of Marriage Breakdown, 1984 and 1987*.

maternal and paternal grandparents is strongly influenced by the living arrangements of children.

Maternal grandparents appear more likely to maintain relationships with grandchildren, because children usually live with their mothers following marital separation and because mothers are more likely than fathers to initiate contact with relatives.

Interaction with paternal grandparents often declines unless the children live with the father, in which case there is a greater frequency of contact. However, while frequency of contact is higher for grandparents on the custodial parent's side, the research by the AIFS found that at least monthly contact was reported for many grandparents on the non-custodial parent's side. In families where non-custodial fathers have little contact with children, it is also likely that there will be little contact with paternal grandparents. Lack of contact with paternal grandparents is usually not due to denial of access to children, but rather to the non-custodial parent not arranging or providing for access.

SOCIALISATION

One of the major functions that families undertake is the socialisation of children. There is some concern that in single-parent families, children may not be exposed to role models of both sexes. At the same time, much attention has been paid to the negative aspects of socialising children into traditional male and female roles. Nevertheless, it would appear to be beneficial for children of both sexes to be exposed to both male and female role models.

Research suggests that, provided children are exposed to role models of both sexes and have opportunities to develop positive interpersonal relationships with both sexes, there should be few problems for children who have spent a large amount of time in a single-parent family situation. As the majority of single-parent families are headed by a female, consideration needs to be given to providing an equal balance of male and female role behaviour, interests, activities and skills.

While it has been suggested that children raised from birth in single-parent families may experience problems with role identification, the mass media alone, to which most children are exposed, provides a wide range of role models. Also, children encounter a wide range of role models outside the home, through education and other activities in which they are involved.

Child development and divorce

Gay Ochiltree, in her book *Children in Australian Families*, has proposed that children whose parents separate and/or divorce have a number of tasks in addition to their normal developmental tasks. These are:

- acknowledging the reality of the separation
- regaining a sense of direction
- dealing with feelings of loss or rejection
- forgiving parents
- accepting the permanence of divorce.[7]

Some of these tasks are more relevant to older children, but for some younger children in divorcing families, adjustments to divorce may be difficult and the achievement of some of these tasks may take a considerable length of time. On the other hand, babies may not be affected at all if they continue to receive the same care and attention from the primary caregiver.

Economic resources

Single-parent families are now the largest group living in poverty, and female-headed single-parent families are more at risk to poverty than male-headed single-parent families. In general, single parents and their children will be more financially secure and less at risk to poverty if the parent can find paid work.

However, the demands of the care of children can be so great that workforce participation is not a viable option. Also, work-related costs may mean there is little financial advantage over social security income support. It should be remembered that many mothers in two-parent families find the demands of home and work roles too great, even with the support provided from the other partner. Nevertheless, over the past decade there has been an increase in the workforce participation rates of female single parents.

Use of social welfare

Marriage breakdown accounts for approximately 65 per cent of individuals using the sole parent's benefit, and the majority of people relying on this benefit for income support are females.

Almost four out of five single female parents rely on the Sole Parent

7 G. Ochiltree, *Children in Australian Families*, Longman Cheshire, Melbourne, 1990, p. 60.

Pension at some time, but it would appear that this pension is seen by many single parents as a temporary measure of income support. During the period following marital separation many single parents use this pension as a 'safety net' form of income support. Most women want financial independence, and within a few years income is usually gained from workforce participation rather than social welfare. The average length of time that single mothers spend on this benefit is about 3.5 years. Long-term recipients of this benefit are usually females who are physically unable to work, lack skills and access to employment and/or have children with special needs.

Many women receiving the sole parent's benefit would like to be able to work part-time to supplement this benefit. However, the amount that can be earnt before the pension is reduced is fairly small and the costs of working to earn a small amount of money may mean that workforce participation is not worthwhile. Over the past ten years there has been some relaxation in the guidelines regarding the amount of other income that can be earnt before the pension is reduced. However, it would appear that there needs to be greater consideration given to women in this situation, as part-time and casual work can often lead to full-time work, thus reducing dependency on social security benefits.

Living standards

Many parents and children experience a change in living standards following the breakup of a marriage. Reduction in the amount of available economic resources often means that not only is there a change in housing situation, but often a cut-back in the amount of money spent on food, clothing, and leisure and recreational activities. Children are likely to experience difficulties adjusting to changed economic circumstances. It may mean not being involved in activities they once took for granted, including membership of sporting teams and other social activities.

When financial strain occurs in single-parent families, it is often necessary for children to become part of the workforce as early as possible in order to supplement family finances. While low-income families are entitled to financial assistance for education of children, this assistance is often inadequate for family needs. Most research indicates that children who spend a substantial part of their childhood living in poverty have a greater chance of living in poverty when they are adults.

WORKFORCE PARTICIPATION

The workforce participation rates of male single parents are much greater than those for female single parents, even when the children are young. Male single parents are also more likely to work full-time, while female single parents are more likely to work part-time. Further, female single parents who are in the workforce are more likely to have been working outside the home prior to separation and divorce. At the same time, female single parents who are not in the workforce are less likely to have been working outside the home at the time of separation and divorce.

In the situation of a marriage breakup where the parent with the primary care for the children is the female, she may find she has to take on the role of breadwinner. If she did not work prior to the marriage breakup, difficulties may be experienced in re-entering the workforce. Lack of workforce skills and workforce experience, and the lack of affordable child care may force the female single parent to rely primarily on social services and child support for income.

Also, assuming that a job can be obtained, it may not be an economically viable proposition to work outside the home. If the parent has few workforce skills, the type of job that can be obtained may not attract enough income to cover all work-related costs including transport, clothing and child care. Financially, it may offer little advantage over social security income support, particularly if there is considerable stress associated with working outside the home.

A common problem for many adults seeking employment is lack of education and/or appropriate training. While re-training is in theory a good idea, for many people, including single parents, the cost of courses and associated books and materials, often in addition to child care, means that re-training or further training is not feasible.

The breakup of a marriage has economic implications for all concerned, and often involves a significant decline in standard of living, as assets are usually divided. Single parents who wish to remain at home may find it is impossible to provide the family with adequate housing, food, clothing and other needs, and may be forced to seek employment. Many single parents who are in the workforce experience a considerable amount of role conflict, as they often would like to be at home, particularly if their children are young.

While for many female single parents workforce participation is stressful and does not offer significant benefits, for others, the benefits of workforce participation are substantial. It enables parents to develop relationships with other adults, to enhance personal self-esteem and develop workforce skills. Single parents who have access to family and friends to help out with child care and when the children are sick are more likely to be able to maintain workforce participation.

More and more single females who have established careers and own or are paying off their own housing, are choosing to have a child and become a single parent before they are too old to do so. For these women, the economic costs may not be a problem as they have jobs which attract sufficient income to make working outside the home worthwhile. It is important to remember that while these women may not endure the same economic stresses, they will encounter many other stresses that are common to parents in single-parent families.

Housing

Like any family, the housing needs of single-parent families will be influenced by the specific needs and priorities of the group, and the composition of the family. The type of housing, the amount of living space available and the external environment are important factors in reducing stress and tension within families. Housing helps satisfy basic human needs. Physically, housing should provide adequate shelter and protection, and space for individual and family activities, relaxation, recreation, peace, quiet, privacy and comfort. Psychologically, housing should provide an environment where individuals feel safe and secure and can express their independence. Socially, housing should provide an atmosphere which fosters self-expression, interaction and communication.

One of the greatest problems for many single-parent families is finding a reasonable place in which to live on a fairly limited income. It has been generally accepted that 25–30 per cent of income be spent on housing. In single-parent families where there are no other assets or income apart from social security payments, the proportion of income spent on housing often exceeds 30 per cent, particularly in urban areas. The cost of housing, whether mortgage repayments or rental costs, can place a family in relative poverty and force mothers of young children into the workforce, when they may wish to stay at home with young children.

With the breakdown of a marriage, the family home is often sold to divide property between the two partners and often neither partner can afford to purchase the family home alone, i.e. buy the other partner's share in the house. Many problems of adjustment may result if a family has to move away from a familiar neighbourhood to an area in which they can afford to live. This may involve children changing schools and losing friends at a time when they need stability. Single-parent families may have to tolerate a lower standard of housing because it is cheaper, closer to the parent's place of work, or closer to child care.

In relation to housing:

- Single-parent families are far more likely to be renting accommodation than are two-parent families, which often have the resources of two incomes.
- A significant number of single-parent families share accommodation with other people.
- Widowed mothers are more likely to own their own home, or to be paying it off, than are divorced or deserted mothers.
- Female single parents are more likely than male single parents to be renting housing in both the private and public sector.
- Male single parents are more likely to be paying off their own home than are female single parents.

Renting and buying

For single-parent families who own their own housing, there is a much greater chance of economic security, as housing costs are a major contributing factor to poverty. The family home usually has to be sold, and changing residence, often to a lower standard or in a different area, can cause more upheaval and stress for children, as well as for the parents. Following marital breakdown, the majority of female single parents have no option but to rent accommodation. This is in contrast to custodial male single parents who are more likely to be purchasing their own homes, while custodial female single parents are more likely to be in the public and private rental sector.[8] The high number of female-headed single-parent families renting in the private sector is a major contributing factor to the large number of female single parents and their children living in poverty.

Rents often differ little from weekly repayments on a housing mortgage, but home ownership is often restricted for low-income families because of the necessity of saving the initial deposit. It is very difficult to save for a deposit and pay rent at the same time, therefore many single-parent families are forced to rent accommodation. Rentals for houses are often beyond the economic resources of most single-parent families, and these families often have little choice in the type of accommodation they can afford. Accommodation may be unsatisfactory for young children if there is not sufficient external and

8 M. Wulff, 'Divorce and the family home: Housing problems and policy directions', *Family Matters*, no. 22, December, 1988, p. 36.

internal space for safe play. Also, renting is not always secure and families may have to move after the lease has expired.

Public housing

While many single-parent families may qualify for public housing, waiting lists are long and housing may not be available in the area in which they have family and social support. Public housing can often provide a higher standard of accommodation than private rental accommodation, but families may not be prepared to move to an area in which they do not know anyone.

Over the last decade there has been a movement away from the placement of public housing in certain areas. The trend now is to integrate public housing into established and establishing areas. This provides for a mix of people and there is a greater chance that the necessary community resources will be available. It is important to note that without access to public housing greater numbers of single-parent families would be living in poverty.

Single-parent families should have the same housing opportunities as two-parent families, if they are to meet individual needs and maintain a satisfactory standard of living. A single-parent family with two children will require the same space and facilities as a couple family with two children. The increased divorce rate, the higher number of single women choosing to have children and the economic recession has had implications for public housing.

Purchasing housing

Single mothers are at a great disadvantage in acquiring adequate shelter. Many single mothers have been out of the workforce for a period of time sufficiently long enough to make returning to the workforce very difficult. This decreases the chance of securing employment which would attract a high enough income to allow for the purchase of housing. This situation is made worse by high housing prices and high mortgage interest rates.

Single fathers have usually not experienced disruption to their working life as a result of childrearing and have thus maintained workforce skills and experience. This makes them more employable and more likely to obtain employment which attracts a higher income. A higher income allows a greater opportunity to purchase housing. Also, wages for males still tend to be higher than wages for females. Further, single female parents may be regarded by lending institutions as a risk, and while discrimination on the basis of marital status is illegal, an affordable housing loan may be difficult to obtain. This is an unfortunate situation as the opportunity to purchase housing can often provide single-parent families security in the future and far less risk of relative poverty.

Financial stress and housing difficulties are less likely to be experienced when a single-parent family occurs as a result of death of a spouse. Often the remaining spouse and children collect benefits from insurance or superannuation and this usually means the family home can be retained. When this happens, children are not subjected to the same types of stresses as often occur in a divorce.

SUPPORTS FOR SINGLE-PARENT FAMILIES

SOLE PARENT'S BENEFIT

The development of this benefit has been discussed in Chapter 2 (see pp.53–4). Depending upon the amount of other income, single parents receiving this pension may be entitled to a Pensioner Health Benefits card. This card entitles the beneficiary to fringe benefits which may include travel concessions, health-care benefits, electricity and gas rebates, telephone rental reduction, rebate on water and council rates, and assistance for education.

Pension rebates are adjusted twice each year, in line with the consumer price index. Pensions may also be adjusted with federal government budgets. You will need to check with your local office of the Department of Social Security to obtain the most recent rates.

CHILD SUPPORT SCHEME

This scheme was introduced in 1988 with the establishment of the Child Support Agency (CSA) within the Australian Taxation Office. The Agency collects child support from liable parents and these payments are distributed to custodial parents on a monthly basis by the Department of Social Security. The collection of child support is by automatic withholding of payments by employers in the case of the PAYE tax payers and, in the case of self-employed people, by direct monthly payments to the CSA.

In 1989, Stage 2 of this scheme was introduced, replacing the system of court-ordered child maintenance. If the parents cannot agree on the amount of child maintenance to be paid, the CSA will determine an amount using a formula set out in legislation. Stage 2 of this scheme only applies to people who separate or have a child born on or after 1 October 1989.

Jobs, Education and Training program (JET)

This program is administered by the Department of Employment, Education and Training, the Department of Social Security and the Department of Community Services and Health. JET was introduced in 1989, and it provides an integrated program of assistance for sole parents. Assistance includes access to education, job search assistance and child care support. Participation in the program is voluntary. For example, a single parent may wish to undertake education and/or training in order to obtain workforce skills. During the period he or she is undertaking this education a place in a child-care centre may be made available by placing additional staff in a centre.

Other benefits

Depending upon financial circumstances, single-parent families may be eligible for benefits payable to low-income families. Refer to Chapter 7 for more information about these benefits.

Community supports

A number of voluntary agencies in the community provide emergency help, food and clothing and temporary accommodation. As government agencies tend to provide financial and specific forms of support, many families rely heavily on non-government organisations for other forms of assistance. Non-government organisations which provide considerable assistance include St. Vincent de Paul Society, Smith Family, Red Cross, Salvation Army and the Brotherhood of St. Laurence. Within the local community there is often access to crisis and refuge centres, counselling services and temporary accommodation.

There are many community organisations with branches at state, city or local level which provide help and support for children and adults in single-parent families. These organisations enable lone parents to meet other adults in similar situations and enjoy adult relationships, as well as providing children with the opportunities to experience other adult role models. Information on these organisations can be obtained by contacting your local council. These organisations include Parents without Partners, Lone Fathers Association, Lone Parent Family Support Service, Supporting Mothers groups, Prisoners Aid Association, etc.

Child care

Child care facilities, including family daycare, child-care centres, before- and after-school care, holiday care, occasional care and emergency care have been discussed in greater detail in Chapter 4. Single parents who are working outside the home are often given priority for child care and may be eligible for fee relief, depending upon the amount of income earnt. Single parents may also qualify for fee relief if children attend community-based pre-schools. Unfortunately, there are not enough community-based child-care facilities or pre-schools, and single parents may experience difficulties in obtaining access to child care or early childhood education. Private daycare and pre-school centres are often expensive and may not have sufficiently long hours for parents to leave their children whilst they are at work.

Management decisions

The needs and wants of single-parent families will vary according to the interests and values of each particular family. Each single-parent family will have different resources at its disposal, different goals to reach, and different decisions to make. Many single-parent families will not have the resources to satisfy needs and wants and achieve their goals. Listed below are some decisions and choices that single-parent families may have to consider and make.

- How to provide the basic needs of adequate clothing and nutritious food for all family members.
- Where to live will be one of the major decisions that has to be made, as housing consumes significant economic resources. How much families can afford to spend on housing will determine both the type of housing and the area in which it is located. To live in a certain area may mean that more money has to be spent on housing, transport and child care. The alternative may be another area, or public housing. While the alternatives may cost less and may allow more economic resources to be allocated to satisfy other needs and wants, it may also mean the loss of support networks including family and friends.
- Whether to work outside the home and have less time and energy for household activities but more income or to stay at home and have more time and energy for home and leisure activities, but fewer economic resources. Working outside the home may not provide additional income if it means spending more money on transport, child care, clothing, convenience foods and other work-related

expenses. However, it may be beneficial to the emotional health of the parent if a job can be obtained. Workforce participation may also provide more opportunities for social interaction with other adults.
- Whether to use other community resources, e.g. child-care services, for help or rely on one's own resources and thus save money. The use of available resources may, however, be beneficial for both parents and children.
- How to allocate tasks in the household so that neither the children nor the parents undertake more work than is necessary, and so that tension and conflict does not result.
- How to provide the children with other adult models, so that they will identify with both sexes.

All these decisions are interrelated, and for most families economic resources are limited, so decision making can never be a simple matter. Making one decision will involve many smaller decisions, and may at the same time affect the outcome of other decisions that have to be made.

Blended Families and Stepfamilies

Remarriage

In one of three marriages today, one or both of the partners have been married before; this compares to only one in seven marriages in 1971. The rise in the number of people having been married previously is due to the large increase in divorce rates following the Family Law Act of 1975–76.

While a large number of people remarry following divorce, remarriage rates in 1986 were considerably lower than they were in 1971, indicating a declining interest in remarriage. The chance of remarriage decreases as age increases: men and women in the age group of 40–44 years are less likely to remarry than men and women in the age group of 25–29 years. It would appear that some individuals who have experienced marriage and divorce are reluctant to remarry, wishing to retain some degree of independence. This trend may also be related to the greater acceptability of non-marital relationships.

It is important to note that men are more likely to remarry than women. Also, divorce rates are higher for remarriages of divorced persons than for persons in their first marriage. In 1988, about 15 per cent of both men and women divorcing were doing so for the second time.

CHARACTERISTICS OF BLENDED FAMILIES AND STEPFAMILIES

Of all families with dependent children, blended families comprise 7 per cent and approximately 5 per cent of dependent children live in blended families or stepfamilies. With the increase in divorce rates since 1975–76 the number of blended families or stepfamilies has increased. A significant number of children may move from a two-parent family to a single-parent family and then back to a two-parent family situation. Even with high divorce rates and decreasing remarriage rates, separated parents tend to gravitate towards forming nuclear families.

Blended families have varying characteristics. They may consist of children of both partners, children of only one partner and/or children of the new union. Families with a stepmother are different to families with a stepfather and different to families where both partners bring children into the new relationship. However, as mothers usually have the custody of children following a divorce it is more common for children to live with a stepfather rather than a stepmother. In Australia, almost half the children whose parents divorce have a stepfather living in the household within the next six years. It is also needs to be noted that the partners in a blended family may be legally married or living in a de facto relationship.

Stepfamilies or blended families are usually more complicated than single-parent families or two-parent families, as the introduction of a new adult and/or stepsiblings and half-siblings gives rise to very different family dynamics.

The creation of a blended family or a stepfamily may create problems for some children. At the time of divorce, children have usually experienced emotional upheaval over the separation of parents and may have had to adjust to a change of residence, school and friends. Children often have strong ties with the original family network, including the other natural parent, relatives and grandparents. In the single-parent family situation, children may exert considerable influence in the decision making of the family and the introduction of a new adult into the family may be seen as a threat by the children. Older children who were included in decision making in the single-parent situation may resent their loss of power in this area, particularly if children are no longer consulted regarding significant decisions.

Role of step-parents

The role of a step-parent is perhaps the most difficult parental role. Children often resent step-parents, and step-parents find this situation difficult to cope with. The introduction of a step-parent into a family can cause upheaval, and children may resent the intrusion into the relationship they have established with their parent. This can create conflict with the children and with both the step-parent and the natural parent, as well as between the adult partners. Children may be jealous of step-parents and see them as a rival for the attention and time of their custodial parent. Girls have been reported to have more difficulty in accepting stepfathers, probably because it intrudes on the close relationship they have developed with their mother during the single-parent family stage.

It may take some time to establish new routines, organisation and customs within a family and to minimise the conflicts that have arisen from the change in the family situation. Children are more likely to adjust to a step-parent when they are very young and similarly, step-parents are also likely to adjust more easily to the situation at this time. When children are older, step-parents may be more uncertain about their role in relation to stepchildren and children may resent the role of a step-parent as a disciplinarian. At the same time, natural parents are not always sure about the role that step-parents should play in relation to their children.

Most studies of stepfamilies have found that problems occur when a step-parent assumes a role of disciplinarian to older children. Children may resent receiving discipline from someone they virtually regard as a stranger, and it would appear that for older children, discipline is better left to the natural parent. Older children may suffer feelings of guilt and conflict if they come to like their step-parent and form some type of attachment to him or her. They may think they are being disloyal to their non-custodial parent.

While children are likely to experience significant problems with the change in family situation, step-parents will also experience difficulties. Apart from having responsibilities to the new family, step-parents often have obligations to their own children who may or may not be living with them. These obligations are financial as well as psychological and social. Apart from contributing to the financial support of children from a previous marriage, step-parents usually need to spend time with children. Conflicts may arise as the step-parent attempts to meet all obligations.

Step-parents often provide a supportive role for the other parent. Rather than providing direct assistance with the supervision and care of the children, the new partner may merely provide support for the parent. This alone can ease the burden for the parent, as it is someone else from whom to seek advice and guidance and with whom to discuss problems. A new adult in the family can increase the range of social contacts and activities available to a family. Generally younger children have a higher involvement with step-fathers than older children. Younger children are possibly more responsive to step-fathers initiating interaction and organising activities.

CHILDREN LEAVING HOME

Recent studies have shown that children in stepfamilies may be more likely to have lower self-esteem, to leave home early because of conflict, and to cut short their education. Lack of resources may decrease opportunities for children to participate in educational and social activities, thus children are not provided with opportunities to develop competence. There also appears to be an over-representation of children from stepfamilies among homeless children.[9] If there is a high level of conflict in the family, children may leave home early to escape the conflict. Leaving home early has been found to be related to early sexual experiences and early childbearing, which are in turn associated with lower attainments in adult life and a greater risk of living in poverty.[10]

POSITIVE CONSEQUENCES FOR BLENDED FAMILIES

While the blending of families may give rise to specific problems and conflicts, for many of these families, the positive consequences outweigh the negative, particularly when the children have a satisfactory degree of interaction with their other parent and related kin. Stepchildren may actually benefit by being exposed to a wider range of social contacts and role models and by living with a parent who is happier as a result of re-partnering. Further, the addition of another adult may raise the household's standard of living and reduce financial stress. For many single mothers this provides a relief from reliance on social security benefits and living in poverty. It may also allow a return

9 K. Funder et. al., 'Stepfathers in children's lives', *Family Matters*, no. 31, April 1992, p. 14.

10 K. Funder & S. Kinsella, 'Divorce, change and children: Effects of changing family structure and income on children', *Family Matters*, no. 30, December 1991, 21.

to a standard of living enjoyed before the dissolution of the first marriage.

In general, children in stepfamilies live in households with higher average incomes than those in female-headed single-parent families. Higher household income appears to be associated with higher self-esteem in children and generally higher levels of competence. This has long-term effects for children, as self-esteem and competence will influence what they achieve in their lives.

'Living in a stepfamily' program

This program was developed by Ruth Webber and is published by the Australian Council for Educational Research. It has been used by many community and welfare organisations interested in assisting stepfamilies. The program gives information, provides support and helps develop parenting strategies that are appropriate to the special needs of stepfamilies. The program presents a positive approach to stepfamilies, yet recognises the difficulties that stepfamilies encounter. Emphasis is placed upon improving interpersonal relationships, and suggestions are provided as to how problems can be tackled.

Review questions

1. Single-parent families do not always result from divorce. How else may single-parent families form?
2. Of all family groups with dependent children, what proportion are single-parent families?
3. What proportion of children in Australia are living in single-parent families?
4. Why are the majority of single-parent families headed by a female rather than a male?
5. Why did the divorce rate increase dramatically after 1976?
6. Why has the proportion of divorces which involve children decreased over the last decade?
7. Outline the factors that have contributed to the higher divorce rates during the last two decades.
8. What particular problems may children encounter in single-parent families?
9. Outline the challenges that lone parents may encounter?
10. How may the problems of a single-parent family headed by a male be different from those families headed by a female?

11 Describe the positive consequences of single-parent family formation.
12 In single-parent families, the life skills competence of children is often very good. Why?
13 List the resources that are available in your local community to assist single-parent families. Note, local councils often have a directory of the resources that are available.
14 Outline the decisions a single parent may have to make regarding workforce participation. What may be the consequences of these decisions?
15 When children experience the divorce of their parents, they may have to undertake additional developmental tasks. List these tasks.
16 In what ways may decisions made by single-parent families differ from decisions made by blended families?
17 How may resource utilisation differ in a blended family compared to a single-parent family?
18 When single-parent families and blended families form, relationships with the extended family network may change. What are the implications of these changes for grandparents and grandchildren?
19 Outline the controversy surrounding juvenile delinquency and family dissolution and formation.
20 For children living in blended families or stepfamilies, what may be the positive consequences?

Case study 5.1

The deserted wife

Joan and Bill have been married for 15 years. They have four children: Steven, 14, Lynette, 13, Felicity, 10, and Peter, aged 7. Three months ago, Bill was involved in a robbery and is now serving a seven-year sentence in a state prison.

Joan and the children are renting the same house as they were prior to Bill's imprisonment. In addition to rent payments, Joan has to meet other commitments including credit card payments, electricity, gas, telephone, etc. Joan has not worked outside the home for many years, but now she has used the little savings that had accumulated and she is finding it difficult to make ends meet on social welfare benefits. Joan would like to stay in the present house, as her children are happy in the area and attend the local school. She feels that to move from the house may cause the children to become even more unsettled.

QUESTIONS

1 What conflict is Joan facing?
2 What values are affecting this conflict?
3 As the wife of a prisoner, to what social security benefits is Joan entitled? What would Joan's income be from social security, including family allowance? Do you think this would be sufficient to meet her current needs of housing, food and shelter, as well as other commitments?
4 List the decisions that Joan may make.
5 Joan's goal is to provide a stable environment for the children. What resources may she have access to in order to achieve this goal?
6 Outline the problems the children may face while their father is in prison.
7 What emotional problems may Joan face while her husband is in prison?
8 How could Joan utilise the children as a resource during this period?
9 If the family were to move from the familiar area in which they live, what problems may they face?
10 What type of housing assistance is Joan entitled to? How would Joan obtain this assistance?

CASE STUDY 5.2
THE DIVORCÉE

Cheryl is 26 years of age and has recently been divorced. She has two children: Narelle, 3, and John, 5. Cheryl's ex-husband pays $50 per week towards the maintenance of the children and is entitled to see them every second weekend. Cheryl has not worked outside the home since John was born, as she felt she wanted to be with the children while they were young. She did, however, work as a legal secretary for two years prior to John's birth.

Cheryl is entitled to a sole parent's pension, but this is subject to an income and assets test. She does not feel that her total income and savings are sufficient to meet the needs and wants of her family. Cheryl has $10 000 in a building society—the settlement from her divorce—but does not like drawing on this for everyday living expenses, as she would like to use it as a part deposit on a house or unit. As she is currently paying rent on a two-bedroom unit, she has little chance of saving more money for a larger deposit.

Cheryl could save more if she went back to work, but she would see the children less and would have to arrange for Narelle to be minded during the day and for John to be minded before and after school. A part-time job would be ideal as she would see the children more, but part-time work is difficult to obtain and she may not earn any more than she currently receives from social security benefits.

QUESTIONS

1 What is the major decision that Cheryl has to make? What are her alternatives?
2 What are Cheryl's goals?
3 What values may influence Cheryl's decisions?
4 List the resources Cheryl may have to help her make this decision?
5 If Cheryl decides not to seek work outside the home, what further decisions might she make?
6 If Cheryl does decide to seek employment, what other decisions might she have to make?
7 Check with your local office of the Department of Social Security to determine the current rate of pension for a sole parent. Also check to see how much other income can be earnt before the pension is reduced.
8 Will Cheryl's savings affect the income received from her pension? (This information is usually available in pamphlet form from the Department of Social Security.)
9 If Cheryl could obtain employment, how may her resources change? Which resources may be more limited? Which resources may be in greater supply?
10 How may Cheryl experience role conflict if she returns to the workforce?
11 If Cheryl were to stay at home, a strict budget would be necessary. Devise a budget for Cheryl.
12 Are there any problems that Cheryl's children may experience in a single-parent family situation?

Case study 5.3

The blended family

Angela and Sean have been married for four years. They have one child, Chris, aged 3. This is a second marriage for both partners. From her first marriage, of eight years, to Paul, Angela had one child, Mark, now aged 15. Sean and his first wife, Judy had two children, Kylie and Rodney, now aged 14 and 16 years respectively.

Prior to the birth of her second son, Chris, Angela worked in the public service sector as a clerk/typist. Angela returned to the workforce when Mark started school. She separated from her first husband when Mark was 8 years old, and divorced one year later. Sean was divorced from his wife, Judy, when he met Angela. Angela and Sean subsequently married, although they lived in a de facto relationship for about a year. Angela wanted to have more children although Sean did not really want to do so. Angela resigned from her job prior to the birth of Chris and returned to the workforce when he was 6 months old. Kylie and Rodney live with their mother but regularly visit Angela and Sean's home. Judy, who has a professional career, has not at this stage formed another long-term relationship.

Two years after he and Angela were divorced, Paul married Sally, who had not been married previously. Sally and Paul have one child, Julie, who is 4 years old. Sally and Paul, and Angela and Sean live fairly close to each other and are often involved together in family celebrations and other activities which involve the children.

Questions

1. For each individual included in this case study, list the life cycle stage he or she is experiencing.
2. For each individual, list particular needs that each individual may have.
3. Explain why, and how, the needs of these individuals may be different.
4. Explain how the relationships in this case study may form an extended family network.
5. What types of conflicts may blended families experience?

Case study 5.4

The deserted husband

Kevin and Janette have been married for 10 years and have experienced conflict in their marriage for the past three years. They have three children: Sharon, 9, Susan, 7, and Christopher aged 5. Kevin returned home from work two weeks ago to find a letter from Janette stating that she had left him and the children and wanted a divorce as soon as was possible. Janette did not want to leave the children, but she was unemployed and untrained and did not see how at the present time that she could afford to support herself and the children. However, she informed Kevin that when she is financially more secure she wants the children to live with her, as she feels a mother is more capable than a father of caring for children. Kevin, however, feels that a mother who deserts her family should not have the responsibility for care of the children.

Janette did not leave a forwarding address, and although Kevin has tried to locate her through friends he has had no success. Kevin is a builder, leaving home at 7 a.m. in the morning and not returning home until 5 p.m. The next-door neighbour has agreed to mind the children before and after school, but this is only a temporary solution and Kevin must make alternative arrangements.

Questions

1 Why was it necessary for Janette to inform Kevin in writing of her wish for a divorce?
2 How long must they be separated before they can obtain a divorce?
3 Under what conditions is a divorce granted?
4 Which tasks (that may previously have been performed by Janette) will Kevin have to accomplish during the week?
5 What new role will Kevin have to undertake?
6 If Kevin does not want to assume responsibility for the care of the children, what steps could he take?
7 Is Kevin entitled to social security? Under what conditions?
8 What difficulties may the children experience in this changed family situation?
9 What management problems may Kevin encounter?
10 Are there any community resources available that Kevin may be able to use to assist in meeting the needs of his family?
11 Who do you think should have the responsibility for the rearing of the children, Kevin or Janette? What arguments can you provide to support your choice.

6

DUAL-INCOME AND WORKING FAMILIES

'DUAL-CAREER' AND 'DUAL-WORKER' FAMILIES

In this book, the term 'dual-income families' has been used to refer to both 'dual-career' families and 'dual-worker' families. The terms 'dual-career families' and 'dual-worker families' are often used differently. A dual-career family may be defined as one where both partners work outside the home, usually earning a higher-than-average income and with a high commitment to careers which are personally fulfilling and satisfying. In dual-career families it is likely that work commitments require long hours and often work is brought home at nights and on weekends. A dual-worker family may be defined as one where both partners are employed in work outside the home but their respective jobs cannot really be regarded as careers because they are often not personally satisfying and promotion prospects are limited.

There are sometimes problems with distinguishing between dual-career families and dual-worker families. In families where both partners work, one partner may have more demanding work commitments than the other partner, whose job may be part-time, or may have set hours, or of the type where work is not taken home. In this situation, it could be said that one partner has a career while the other partner has a job. To which classification does a family such as this belong: dual-career or dual-worker?

Also, families may experience cycles—they may change from being a single-income family to being a dual-income family and then back to being a single-income family. This is more likely to happen in times of high unemployment. During the recession of recent years many families have also experienced a situation where both partners have become unemployed.

Much of the mass media treatment of dual-working families concentrates on 'successful' women who have jobs which attract higher than average salaries and cope with the demands of two full-time roles. Equal media space or time is not usually allocated to how 'successful' working fathers can juggle the demands of home and work roles. This can give a distorted picture of women in the workforce, for when higher salaries are earnt by both partners more domestic supports can be utilised. For the majority of working families, this is not the reality. Two average salaries in one family are usually required to meet basic living expenses and are often not sufficient to pay for supports such as extensive home help and nanny services.

While it is important to be aware of the distinction between dual-career and dual-worker families, many of the issues and problems that confront these families are common to all working families, particularly such issues as time spent with children. The major difference is that some families have greater access to economic resources to ease some of the burdens of household work and maintenance.

With young people staying at home for longer periods of time, many families may have children as well as parents participating in the workforce. This means a variety of tasks have to be juggled. Also, for many single-parent families where the sole parent is in the workforce many of the issues outlined in this chapter are relevant.

PARTICIPATION OF MOTHERS IN THE WORKFORCE

The dramatic rise in the number of females in the workforce this century has been due not only to the increasing proportion of women remaining in the workforce after marriage but more import antly to the proportion of women returning to the workforce after childbearing. The workforce participation of females in general was discussed in

Chapter 2. This chapter will therefore concentrate on the tendency for women with children to remain in the workforce and to pursue a career.

The dual role of women in the twentieth century—at home and at work—is not new to our society. Prior to industrialisation, as discussed in Chapter 2, women usually always performed two roles, although the productive work role may have been undertaken in the home in conjunction with household work. As industrialisation accelerated and men left home to work in factories and offices, it was taken for granted that a woman's place was in the home. A married woman tended to take a job only if the husband's income was inadequate to support a family. It was also very difficult for married women to obtain a job as social attitudes did not really support married women working. Prior to the Second World War, remaining at home was the norm. This is not the case now, and involvement in the workforce is the norm rather than the exception.

Table 6.1 shows the dramatically increased participation of married women in the workforce since the Second World War. However, it is necessary to examine this table carefully to see exactly what it is illustrating. The figures are referring to the proportion of married women who were in the workforce in a given year. In 1954, only 12.6 per cent of married women were in the workforce; in 1993, of all women who were married, more than 50 per cent were in the workforce in either a full-time or part-time capacity.

Table 6.2 also illustrates the increasing participation of married women in the workforce, but it shows the proportion of married women in the total female workforce. As shown, in 1933, of the total female workforce, only 11 per cent were married females; by 1990 approximately 61 per cent of the female workforce consisted of married women. However, Australia still lags behind many other countries in terms of the proportion of married females in the workforce. The workforce participation rate for married women in Australia in 1991 is comparable to that in many other countries two decades previously. For example in Sweden, over 80 per cent of married women are currently in the workforce. Sweden provides more family supports to enable women and men to undertake two full-time roles.

Economic changes

A feature of the employment of married women has been that a significant proportion tend to move in and out of the workforce at various times. Traditionally, married women have often joined the workforce for a short period of time in order to achieve a family goal or meet short-term financial obligations.

Table 6.1 Percentage of married women in the workforce, 1911–93

Year	Percentage
1911	6.1
1921	4.0
1933	5.4
1947	8.6
1954	12.6
1961	17.3
1966*	27.4
1967	30.5
1972	37.5
1977	42.6
1980	42.8
1982	42.0
1984	43.5
1986	47.1
1988	49.0
1991	50.0
1993	51.0

* *From 1966 the census definition of the workforce changed to include part-time work*
Source: Australian Bureau of Statistics data

Table 6.2 Percentage of married women in the female workforce, 1911–90

Year	Percentage
1911	11.1
1921	9.2
1933	11.0
1947	15.3
1954	30.5
1961	38.3
1966	47.8
1971	56.8
1981	59.0
1984	59.2
1986	59.5
1990	61.0

Source: Australian Bureau of Statistics data

It is likely that this movement in and out of the workforce may have declined with the economic recession. Despite home and family pressures, women who maintain jobs during periods of high unemployment may be reluctant to give them up, as it may not be possible to obtain another job when they wish to return to the workforce. At the same time, during periods of economic recession, it is difficult for women to obtain employment when opportunities and jobs are limited and competition high. This is particularly so for women with limited educational qualifications and few workforce skills. Further, economic conditions are now such that many families require two permanent incomes to satisfy needs and maintain an acceptable standard of living.

Sections of business, government and the media have often blamed the increased workforce participation of married women for the unemployment situation. Even in the past few years there have been murmurs from some sections of society proposing that married women should be the first to be retrenched during periods of unemployment, and that males and single females should have preference in employment. This is despite anti-discrimination and equal employment opportunity legislation. Statements regarding this subject are possibly no longer as blatant as in 1978, when one headline of the *Weekend Australian* (14 January) read 'If Mum Quit Work, There'd Be Jobs for The Boys (and Girls)'[1] This belief may still exist in some sections of society, but to express it publicly today would incur the anger of many individuals and groups in society.

Social changes

Workforce participation rates of married females vary markedly among different groups in society, according to age, educational qualifications, the number and age of dependent children and elderly relatives, and family income. Over the last decade, the age at marriage has increased, as has the age at which women have their first child. Thus women are in the workforce for a longer period before childbearing than they were 20 years ago. Statistics show that the more children a woman has, the less chance there is that she will work outside the home. The organisation required and the costs of child care for three pre-school children may not make paid employment worthwhile—financially or otherwise.

The relative increase in the workforce participation of married

---

1 Quoted in K. Windschuttle, *Unemployment*, Penguin, Melbourne, 1979, p. 140.

females with dependent children is much greater than for married females without dependent children. However, the age of dependent children is a major factor in determining workforce participation. As the age of dependent children increases so too does the workforce participation of married females. This is discussed in greater detail later in the chapter.

It is now common in Australia for most women to work until the birth of the first child, and many women re-enter the workforce when their children go to school. There is a growing trend, however, for women to re-enter the workforce before children reach school age, with a significant number of women taking only the minimum amount of necessary leave, e.g. 12 weeks. Many women choose only to take a minimum period of leave in order to retain their job and future employment prospects. It can no longer be assumed that all mothers with pre-school-aged children remain at home.

Societal expectations

Despite the increasing workforce participation of married women with children, the decision to remain in the workforce or re-enter the workforce when children are young creates conflict for many women. Old expectations concerning the wife/mother role still exist to some extent, and many people in our society still expect a woman to cease work with the birth of a child and remain at home while the child is young. Even for women who can afford to take time out of the workforce this could mean loss of job or career and future employment opportunities.

A man is socialised from birth to expect that he will work outside the home, regardless of whether he has children. While there has been a far greater social acceptance of 'working mothers', there has not really been a corresponding recognition of 'working fathers'. It is still assumed by many people that there is someone at home looking after the children, and basically the responsibilities for child care or arranging child care still remains with the woman.

Educational changes

Married women with higher educational qualifications are more likely to be in the workforce in full-time positions than less well-educated or qualified married women. Higher educational levels mean that married women face a more favourable job market and a higher opportunity cost if they choose not to work outside the home. Opportunity cost means the income that would be foregone if a person chooses to leave the workforce and remain at home. When working out this cost it is also necessary to consider work-related costs such as child care, transport, clothing etc. These costs can often offset the cost of working outside the home.

Part-time and casual work

Part-time workforce participation has been a constant feature of female employment in Australia. Only 9 per cent of males in the labour force work part-time, compared to 37 per cent of females in the labour force; and of the proportion of married females in employment, nearly half work part-time. Studies carried out by the Institute of Family Studies have shown that about three-quarters of women in full-time or part-time employment would prefer to work part-time.[2]

The availability of part-time employment is related to prevailing economic conditions. In periods of full employment, employers are more willing to take part-time workers; and conversely, in periods of high unemployment and economic recession, part-time employment is likely to be reduced. While part-time employment offers many advantages to married women, it also has many disadvantages. The main advantages of part-time employment are the shorter and often flexible hours which allow more time with children, as well as more time for home-related tasks. The time available for other home-related activities may mean that stress and tension is reduced. On the other side, part-time employment often involves jobs which are less satisfying and stimulating; opportunities for promotion are limited and there is little provision for holiday and sick pay. Also, it may mean loss of future career prospects, because a career may not be regained when full-time employment is possible.

Part-time employment for married women can be a 'Catch 22' situation—it may allow women to meet family obligations, but it may not satisfy their own needs for a satisfying career. Part-time employment can also be seen as a mechanism to support traditional home and work roles. It allows women to participate in the workforce but does not really threaten traditional family roles or increase the household workload for the husband/father. Permanent part-time work for women is preferable to casual work as casual work tends to be low-paid, low-status, non-unionised, with few or no career prospects. In

---

2 H. Glezer, 'Mothers in the workforce', *Family Matters*, Australian Institute of Family Studies, no. 21, August 1988, p. 34.

recent years, moves have been made towards increasing the availability of permanent part-time work and job sharing, particularly in government departments.

Factors contributing to the workforce participation of mothers

In the eighteenth and nineteenth centuries, industrialisation segregated masculine and feminine roles, and it was assumed that there was a natural division of functions between the sexes. Throughout this century and particularly over the past few decades there has been progress towards equality of females and males in society and, in particular, in the workforce. However, full equality has not yet been achieved, and it is unlikely to happen for some time. A report by the International Labour Organisation (ILO) released in 1993 proposed that if present trends continue, it would take nearly 1000 years for women to gain the same economic and political power as men.[3]

The increase in the workforce participation of women has been almost entirely due to the workforce participation of married females. There are many reasons for the large increase in the labour force participation of married women. No one factor can be singled out—they are all interrelated. These factors are outlined below.

Marriage bar

Early this century, females employed in the public service and banks were required to resign when they married unless special permission was granted. Also, married women were often excluded from training schemes and promotion. This rule was eventually removed in most states, although it was not until 1947 in New South Wales that the marriage bar for female teachers was relaxed. Prior to this date, female teachers had to resign upon marriage and reapply for appointment as temporary employees. The marriage bar in the Commonwealth Public Service was not lifted until 1967, and it was not until 1972 that the three major airlines—Qantas, Ansett and Australian Airlines (TAA)—agreed to remove the marriage bar.

---

3 *Sydney Morning Herald*, 6 Feb, 1993, p. 1.

Equal pay

Behind the controversy surrounding equal pay for women lay the belief that if women were paid the same wage for the same work as men, they might be tempted to ignore domestic responsibilities and join the workforce. Many sections of business and industry were opposed to equal pay for women because they knew it would take away a cheap source of labour. It took nearly 70 years for the principle of equal pay to be legally established, and until the mid-1970s for it to be put into practice on a universal basis. The fact that women can in theory earn as much as men is an incentive to remain in the workforce. In practice, women on average earn less than men.

Maternity leave

Shortly after the marriage bar was discontinued by the public service, maternity leave provisions for permanent female employees were introduced. Women employed in the public service were granted a maximum of 26 weeks leave, 12 of which were compulsory. This was initially granted without pay, but in 1973 the regulation was changed to allow women 12 weeks with pay, although this was not necessarily full pay for the entire period. Also at this time, men were granted one week's paid paternity leave, although this paid leave was later discontinued.

While provisions for maternity leave exist in the private sector, in general it is unpaid and has not been very successful. Unpaid maternity leave returns women to economic dependency on men and, for some, to social welfare. Parental leave is discussed in more detail later in this chapter.

Fertility rates

The decline in the number of children per family has been a factor enabling women to remain in the paid workforce. While it is certainly not easy for women with one or two young children to combine motherhood and a career, it is even more difficult for women with three and four children. It is usually not viable for a mother of three or four children to remain in or re-enter the paid workforce on a full-time basis, as the organisation and work-related costs are often too great. Statistics show that the more children a woman has, the less chance there is that she will work outside the home. As the majority of couples are now choosing only to have two children, there is a greater chance that more women will remain in or re-enter the workforce.

Age of children

Married women with dependent children under five years of age are less likely to be in the workforce compared to married women with children over five years of age. However, during the last decade there has been a significant increase in the number of women with children under five years of age remaining in the workforce, often taking only a short period of maternity leave. The reasons for this include the desire to maintain a career, economic necessity and increased availability of child care.

In 1989, the rate of workforce participation of mothers with children in the 0–4 years age group had reached 44 per cent; of which 27.3 per cent were working part-time, 13.5 per cent full-time and 3.2 per cent unemployed. However, as children get older, workforce participation rates increase and in 1989, approximately 68 per cent of mothers with children in the 5–14 years age group were working, with 29.4 per cent working full-time, 34.7 per cent part-time and 3.8 per cent unemployed.[4]

Educational qualifications

As discussed earlier in this chapter, the general increase in educational qualifications for females has played a significant part in raising their social status, as well as in providing more employment opportunities. Married females with higher educational qualifications are more likely to be in the workforce full-time than females without post-school qualifications. Higher educational attainments provide greater employment opportunities, higher income and increased job satisfaction. Many women with post-school qualifications are reluctant to abandon careers, and associated social and economic rewards, in order to pursue motherhood on a full-time basis.

Employment opportunities

Although females are still concentrated in certain occupations, including clerical work, sales, nursing, teaching etc.—more females are entering occupations that were once reserved for males. This trend is likely to increase as females continue to attain higher educational qualifications. However, it is more conducive for females to enter traditional male occupations when the economy is buoyant, rather than in recession.

---

4 G. Ochiltree, 'The place of children in society', *Family Matters*, Australian Institute of Family Studies, no, 26, April 1990, p. 53.

Economic motives

In order to acquire and maintain a certain standard of living, it is often considered necessary in many families for both partners to work outside the home. Whether two incomes are essential to satisfy basic needs has been a widely debated issue, although less so during times of economic recessions and high housing prices. Two incomes are often necessary for families to maintain a certain lifestyle; but for many families, two incomes are necessary for survival.

Opportunity cost

Opportunity cost refers to the income that would be foregone if a married women chooses to leave the paid labour force. It is the income that would have been earnt in the workforce, less the work-related costs of child care, clothing, transport etc. For females with higher educational qualifications and good employment opportunities, it is very difficult to give up the potential rewards that may be available if they remain in the workforce. A full-time home role may not be economically viable.

Social attitudes

As the age at marriage has increased, so too has the age at which women have their first child. Women are now in the workforce for a longer period of time before marriage and childbearing than they were twenty years ago. It is more socially acceptable now to delay childbearing, and for many females it is difficult to give up the financial independence they enjoyed before having children; thus many women choose to remain in the workforce. Further, to give up a career for even a few years while children are young can mean a career is lost and never regained. Encouragement and support given by the husband/partner is usually a major factor influencing the satisfaction or dissatisfaction experienced by women when combining home and work roles.

A National Survey conducted in 1984–85 revealed that 62 per cent of men and 61 per cent of women approved of women working outside the home, even if their husbands were capable of supporting them. However, the results also showed that more men than women believed that women should devote all their time to their families. Overall, there were only a small percentage of both men and women who believed strongly that married women should not work outside the home, or that they should work outside the home.[5] Similar results were found in the National Social Science Survey of 1989, which surveyed approximately 4500 people. Tables 6.3 and 6.4 indicate male and female attitudes regarding the employment of women.

In general, attitudes towards mothers working outside the home have become more positive. Changing social attitudes are also reflected in the increased number of child-care facilities that are available to enable women to participate in the workforce.

SOCIAL AND INTELLECTUAL STIMULATION

For a few decades now, the idea that housework and child care is the sole responsibility of women has been increasingly challenged by women. Many women find that child care and household activities do

Table 6.3 The effects of women's employment on the family: Men's and women's views

A pre-school child is likely to suffer if his or her mother works	agree	47% females
		56% males
	disagree	36% females
		27% males
A working mother can establish just as warm and secure a relationship with her children	agree	64% females
		51% males
	disagree	28% females
		39% males
Family life suffers when the woman has a full-time job	agree	46% females
		51% males
	disagree	38% females
		31% males
It is more difficult to raise children successfully when both parents work full time	agree	62% females
		69% males
	disagree	23% females
		18% males

Note: The percentage who 'neither agree nor disagree' makes up the difference between 100 per cent and those who agreed and disagreed.
Source: Based on National Social Science Survey data, Australian National University, 1989

5 B. Graetz & I. McAllister, *Dimensions of Australian Society*, Macmillan, Sydney, 1988, p. 34.

Table 6.4 Should women be employed and do they really want to be? Men's and women's views

A job is all right, but what most women really want is a home and children	agree	36% females
		42% males
	disagree	39% females
		28% males
Being a housewife is just as fulfilling as working for pay	agree	52% females
		43% males
	disagree	30% females
		27% males
A husband's job is to earn money; a wife's job is to look after the home and family	agree	26% females
		32% males
	disagree	55% females
		46% males
A woman should devote almost all her time to a family	agree	29% females
		30% males
	disagree	51% females
		46% males
A married woman should not attach much importance to a career	agree	18% females
		21% males
	disagree	55% females
		52% males

Note: The percentage who 'neither agree nor disagree' makes up the difference between 100 per cent and those who agreed and disagreed.
Source: Based on National Social Science Survey data, Australian National University, 1989

not offer sufficient stimulation or social interaction, and work outside the home is often seen as a way of satisfying these needs. Many women are no longer convinced that motherhood represents the greatest achievement in life.

Women's movement

During the 1960s and 1970s many women's organisations were formed, often focusing on specific issues, such as law reform, child care, equal pay, family planning and refuges for women and children. This movement has challenged many of the assumptions that have existed concerning the roles of women in the home and workplace. Also, from this movement have emerged many women who have been able to articulate the needs and concerns of women and to highlight the inequalities sustained by women.

Technology

It is difficult to say whether the increased number of labour-saving devices and convenience foods available on the market have allowed women to work outside the home, or whether the demand for these goods was created by the increased employment of married women. Most studies of domestic technology have concluded that there has been little change over the past two decades in the amount of time spent in household work. The average time spent in food preparation and laundry has remained fairly constant, and while there has been some saving of time in cleaning and gardening, it appears that shopping, child care and 'other house' activities require more labour now than they did in the early 1970s.[6]

If labour-saving devices have reduced the amount of time and energy expended in household activities, although this is doubtful, time and energy is still required for the operation, care and maintenance of such appliances. The desire to obtain such appliances and other consumer goods has been one of the motives for women returning to the workforce.

Factors hindering the workforce participation of mothers

As the majority of women work, the choice to remain at home has both economic and social disadvantages. Our economy is geared to two-income families, and many families could not provide for basic needs without two incomes. Secondly, because of the increasing number of women in the workforce, friendships are often formed as a result of social interaction in the workplace, rather than as a result of social interaction in the neighbourhood. A woman who has chosen not to return to the workforce may find few opportunities for social interaction in the neighbourhood, as many of the women may be in the workforce. While, for many women, paid employment may offer social and economic advantages, there are many factors discussed below which may not actually prevent workforce participation, but they can certainly make it more difficult. Indeed, some of the factors that encourage workforce participation also hinder it.

6 M. Bittman, *Juggling Time: How Australian Families Use Time*, Office of the Status of Women, Department of the Prime Minister and Cabinet, Canberra, 1991, p. 30.

SOCIAL ATTITUDES

While attitudes towards women working outside the home have changed, the old expectations concerning the wife/mother role still persist to some extent. For this reason, women often experience feelings of guilt if they remain in the workforce, particularly when the children are young. People are often more sympathetic to a mother working because of financial necessity, rather than for motives of career and self-fulfilment.

Some people maintain that if a woman chooses to have children, she should be prepared to remain at home for a number of years, and if she is not prepared to do this, then she should not have children. A married woman is often asked if she works; a man is rarely asked the same question. A father who spends long hours away from young children while working is rarely accused of ignoring home responsibilities—indeed, he is often applauded for being a hard worker and a good provider. Women who spend a large amount of time away from home and children do not often enjoy the same praise.

ECONOMIC CONDITIONS

Traditionally, females have always been accepted more readily into the workforce when the economy has been prosperous. While it has not been apparent in the recession of the late 1980s and early 1990s, there has been a trend in earlier recessions to hire males and single females in preference to married females. There has existed a belief that married females should be first to be retrenched during periods of economic downturns. Indeed, during these periods the workforce participation of married females has sometimes been cited as a cause for high unemployment levels.

LACK OF CHILD-CARE FACILITIES AND FAMILY SUPPORTS

Despite significant improvements in this area since 1972 and a federal government commitment to increase the number of child-care places, there are still insufficient child-care facilities in Australia; this is apparent in the very long waiting lists.

The cost of care for one child at a council or community child-care centre ranges from $100 to $140 per week. This high cost, particularly if there is more than one child in care, can remove the incentive to work, because it may not be economically feasible to do so. While the costs of family daycare or private child care may not be as high, the cost is often sufficiently high in proportion to income to make working outside the home unfeasible. While fee assistance for child care is available for low-income families, it is primarily single-income families that are eligible for this assistance.

Child-care services (discussed in more detail in Chapter 4) are one of the most important domestic supports for working families. The cost and availability of child care can limit its usefulness for many parents. Combined with the organisation required to get children ready for child care or school, drop them off and pick them up in the afternoon, many women may decide it is not worthwhile to work when children are young. Many women feel more comfortable if their children are minded by a relative or member of the immediate family, and for this reason many working families use informal child care or private arrangements for child care. The Institute of Family Studies has found there is a high use of informal, unpaid child care, that is, care by relatives and friends. Approximately 45 per cent of working mothers rely on this type of care. For mothers who do use formal child-care facilities, approximately 20–25 per cent of income is spent on child care costs.[7]

While there has been some increase in the number of child-care centres for children aged between six weeks and five years, there is still a lack of facilities for before- and after-school care, although there has been a significant increase over the past decade. Families who have been fortunate enough to obtain a place in a child-care centre often find that when their child goes to school, there is no formal system of before- and after-school care in the area in which they live, and they are often forced to rely on private arrangements which may be unsatisfactory and temporary.

DOMESTIC TECHNOLOGY AND DOMESTIC SUPPORTS

There is a tendency for Australian women to regard domestic help as an extravagance and many working mothers feel guilty about using such help, believing they ought to be able to manage alone. Professional women tend to use domestic services much more than women on lower incomes, which may in part be because those with lower incomes feel that spending money on household help reduces income and does not make it financially worthwhile to work outside the home. In addition,

7 H. Glezer, 'Mothers in the workforce', p. 31.

some time must be spent in the organisation and arrangement of domestic help.

Labour-saving devices are a domestic support for dual-income families, but they do not free women from all household tasks. The resources of convenience foods, take-away meals and restaurants are used more by dual-income families, but not just to save time—for many women, working is the means by which a family can enjoy more leisure activities such as eating out.

Parental leave and flexible hours

For many mothers, working full-time may mean spending less time with children and having to arrange before- and after-school care and holiday care. The 'normal' working day and working week appears to be based on the assumption that all workers have a 'wife' who does the shopping, cooking and cleaning, delivers and collects the children from school, and attends to all home-related tasks and domestic emergencies. There is a need for greater flexibility of hours for both men and women if men are to become more involved in fathering and in household activities. Perhaps it is unlikely that men will campaign for greater flexibility of hours if it means they will have to spend time undertaking tasks that may not be as challenging and satisfying as the workplace can provide.

During the last two decades Australia has addressed the issue of maternity and paternity leave in relation to unpaid leave following the birth or adoption of a child. However, parental leave, that is, leave to look after sick children or to attend to their specific needs is almost non-existent. When children are sick and cannot attend child care or school, or parents wish to attend a school activity in which their children are involved, adults are often forced to take sick leave or holiday leave, as there are usually no other leave provisions available to cover these contingencies.

In Australia as in many other countries, when children are sick it is usually the mother who takes time off work to look after the children. Since there exist virtually no leave provisions for parents when children are sick, parents are often forced to use their own sick leave. If the illness of a child is prolonged and the parent is forced to take substantial or regular time off work, his or her job may be at risk. Some families have the resources of friends and grandparents who will assist in the care of sick children, but this is not a universal arrangement.

Employers rarely offer the flexibility of parental leave or the option to make up lost time at a later time or, when possible, to complete work at home. Further, there are virtually no emergency child-care facilities for sick children—facilities that would provide care for children who are not extremely ill but are not quite well enough for child care, pre-school or school.

Many families find that when children attend community child-care centres they are very susceptible to minor illnesses as a result of the close contact they have with the other children. The fact that children play together means that children are likely to 'pick up' any illness or disease present in the centre. Centre policies usually prohibit children attending when they are sick. In some instances when the illness is minor it would be possible for children to attend the centre and be confined to a special care section, thus minimising cross infection. Obviously, for this to occur extra staffing and funding is required. If all the additional costs for this were to be met by parents it is unlikely to be satisfactory, as it would be cheaper for parents to use their personal sick leave. However, in terms of lost worker productivity it may be cost-productive in the long run to provide this type of care.

While governments have recognised the importance of child care, many large employers have not yet seen child care as an investment in the future of this country. There still appears to exist the widespread assumption that all families have two adult partners, with one partner at home who can take care of all children's needs, and increasingly, also, aged parents.

Although provisions for maternity leave have improved since the Second World War, Australia still lags behind some other countries in this area. For example, in Sweden, both parents get 15 months of shared paid leave after a child's birth, 60 shared paid days off per year to look after sick children; two days off per year to visit day-care centres and schools; and the right to reduce the working day to six hours for child-care purposes. Swedish economists claim that the national cost of child care and parental leave is compensated twice over by the economic benefit of having women in the paid workforce. Belgium and Germany also have generous parental leave allowances.[8] Most maternal and parental leave in Australia is unpaid, and when some payment is made it is only for a short period of time.

Many employers are realising the value of parental leave, as well as work-based child-care centres. The provision of maternity leave increases the retention of skilled women employees and saves money, as retraining of another employee is avoided. Work-based child care can decrease absenteeism, lateness and leaving early, and increase worker productivity.

---

8 M. Bittman, *Juggling Time*, p 15.

Lack of part-time work

Many women would prefer part-time work on a permanent basis, but are locked into full-time work because of a lack of permanent part-time employment opportunities. The National Social Science Survey of 1989 found that for those women with pre-school-aged children who wanted employment, part-time rather than full-time work was desired. Part-time work is often at the lower end of the job market, in jobs requiring less skill and where wages are lower. There are greater numbers of women with higher educational qualifications and specialised training who would like to use these skills in a part-time capacity or through job sharing. Many employers do not believe that flexible and part-time work is economically productive, and there has been an unwillingness until recently to make concessions for working mothers. However, job sharing schemes and permanent part-time work in other countries have demonstrated that productivity is not reduced.

Proximity of employment to home

Women are often limited in employment opportunities if they wish to work relatively close to home, in order to reduce travelling time and increase the time spent in the home and with children. Women may forgo job and career opportunities which offer more challenging and stimulating work but involve more travelling time, and thus more time away from home.

Employment and promotion opportunities

Women who wish to re-enter the workforce after leaving it in order to have children may find they no longer possess the skills required in the workforce. Technology in a particular field can advance so rapidly that skills learnt some years earlier are no longer applicable. Women who have lost experience or seniority through absence from the workforce are often forced to take jobs where few skills are required.

While opportunities do exist for re-training through TAFE colleges and private institutions, this often involves costs such as fees and child care. It may be difficult to afford this with only one household income. It may also be impossible for women to work, undertake courses of study at night, and provide the care and attention that children require.

For the above reasons, the occupational distribution of married women is different from that of single women. More married women than single women are working in the unskilled workforce sector, where promotion opportunities are limited.

This trend is changing as more women remain in the workforce for a longer period of time before childbearing, and often re-enter the workforce following a period of maternity leave. Some employers are reluctant to promote married women, believing that they may leave the workforce at some time to assume home responsibilities.

It is also sometimes assumed that married women will not have the time to commit to the demands of a higher-level job. For many women, this is a reality—while they may like to develop their career, their home and family commitments may not allow it. Some employers do not like employing women with young children, as they maintain the absentee rate is much higher, as women have to take time off work in order to care for children if they are sick. If the absentee rate is higher, it may be alleviated by the introduction of more flexible hours and leave conditions for both men and women.

Women have often been criticised for their lack of involvement in trade unions and campaigns for better work opportunities for females, including flexible hours, re-training courses and child-care facilities. However, few male workers with the same family responsibilities have campaigned seriously for these improvements so they could spend more time with their children.

Aged relatives

For many women in the workforce who may have 'survived' while working with children and reached a stage where their children are older and independent, a new problem may arise—the care of aged relatives. With increased life expectancy and the tendency for elderly people to remain living in an independent situation, for many women the role of providing support for elderly relatives falls to them and not to men. Women may have raised their children, but then are often obligated to take over the care of aged relatives.

Role conflict and role strain

In the nineteenth century, women did not have to make the choice between a career and motherhood, nor did they have to decide whether they would combine a work and home role. Today women can choose to remain at home, if economic circumstances permit this, or they can choose to combine motherhood and paid employment. Whatever decision is made, it would appear that women experience guilt. Mothers of young children who are in full-time employment may question whether they have made the right decision, as may women who have chosen to withdraw from the workforce and remain at home with young children.

Over the last two decades norms have become confused: the old idea of mothers remaining at home has been challenged, but at the same time there is not yet complete acceptance of mothers or young children working outside the home. It is for this reason that many women work or desire to work part-time, which is often seen by both men and women as an acceptable compromise.

When women do work outside the home, they are likely to experience role strain. There may be times when the demands of one role conflict with the demands of the other role, for example when a child is sick and a woman has to choose between going to work and staying home with the child. It may also occur when the demands of both roles are so great that stress and tension result, and the woman may not be able to complete the tasks of either role in a manner that she and/or others around her find satisfactory.

The extract on page 182 is taken from a booklet called *Occupation: Housewife*, produced by the New South Wales Women's Advisory Council. It illustrates the role of a housewife. Many women in Australia combine this full-time role with a full-time role outside the home.

WORK AND ROLE ALLOCATION WITHIN FAMILIES

In Chapter 2 the division of labour in the household in the pre-industrial era and the effects of industrialisation and technology on the division of labour in the home and workplace were discussed in detail. It may be necessary to review the appropriate section in Chapter 2, in order to be aware of the contribution that women have made to productive work in the home and how the status of women has changed as a result of the differentiation of work in the home and workplace.

The greater the time required for household labour, the more limited the opportunities for workforce participation by married females, particularly when males do not participate in household labour. This may be a mechanism used to keep women in the home and out of the workforce. Indeed it has been argued by many people that the family unit and the unpaid household worker assists in maintaining our capitalist economy.

Position Vacant: Housewife

Applications are invited for the position of manager of a lively team of four demanding individuals of differing needs and personalities. The successful applicant will be required to perform and co-ordinate the following functions: companion, counsellor, financial manager, buying officer, teacher, nurse, chef, nutritionist, decorator, cleaner, driver, child care supervisor, social secretary and recreation officer.

Qualifications: Applicants must have unlimited drive and the strongest sense of responsibility if they are to succeed in this job. They must be independent and self-motivated, and be able to work in isolation and without supervision. They must be skilled in the management of people of all ages. They must be able to work under stress, for long periods of time if necessary. They must have flexibility to perform a number of conflicting tasks at the one time without tiring. They must have the adaptability to handle all new developments in the life of the team, including emergencies and serious crises. They must be able to communicate on a range of issues with people of all ages, including public servants, school teachers, doctors, dentists, tradespeople, businesspeople, teenagers and children. They must be competent in the practical skills listed above. They must be healthy, creative, active and outgoing, to encourage the physical and social development of the team members. They must have imagination, sensitivity, warmth, love and understanding, since they are responsible for the mental and emotional well-being of the team.

Hours of work: All waking hours and a 24-hour shift when necessary.

Pay: No salary or wage. Allowances by arrangement, from time to time, with the income-earning member of the team. The successful applicant may be required to hold a second job, in addition to the one advertised here.

Benefits: No guaranteed holidays. No guaranteed sick leave, maternity leave or long service leave. No guaranteed life or accident insurance. No worker's compensation. No superannuation.

Source: NSW Women's Advisory Council

Figure 6.1 Generally, males are participating more in household activities. However, the male partner often perceives his household role as one of a 'helping hand' and not a sharing role.

The unpaid household worker, usually the female, not only provides the necessary support required for the male to participate in the workforce, but she also produces the children who will become the workers in the future, and who and are essential for economic activity and growth. Also, she carries out many other services such as care for the sick and the aged, which would otherwise have to be paid for by the

State. Unpaid household work is largely invisible and society does not tend to give recognition to work not undertaken for pay. As long as women continue to undertake most of household work they will be limited in the extent to which they can participate equally in the labour force with men.

The following discussion includes results of studies over the past few decades. These studies have focused on the division of labour in the home. It is during this period of time that women's involvement in the paid workforce has increased dramatically. However, there does not appear to have been a significant corresponding decrease in the proportion of unpaid household work undertaken by women. Women are undertaking a dual role, with little or no time for leisure; men are enjoying the benefits of the dual incomes but not contributing significantly to household work.

THE 1950S

In 1957–58 Adler surveyed 1313 primary school children, aged 12, in five capital cities in Australia to determine which parent made most of the decisions within the family, and which parent undertook the majority of household activities within the family.[9] Adler used a technique called 'Day at Home', whereby children were asked 45 different questions related to activities at home and in the family. The questions were in the following format, and the children were instructed on how to answer the questions.

1 Who decides what is to be done?
  e.g. who decides when the windows will be washed?
2 Who does what is to be done?
  e.g. who washes the windows?
3 Do mother and father disagree about what is to be done?
  e.g. do they disagree about washing the windows?

The results obtained by Adler indicated that the mother decides upon and carries out the majority of activities, even in areas not associated with housework and child care. Adler concluded that the Australian family was mother-dominated, and he suggested the term *matriduxy* to describe this phenomenon. The method of research used by Adler has been used for the survey 'Role and work allocation within the Australian family', which is included later in this chapter.

9 S. Encel, 'The family', in A.F. Davies & S. Encel (eds), Australian Society: *An Introduction*, 2nd. edn., Cheshire, Melbourne, 1970, pp. 279–81.

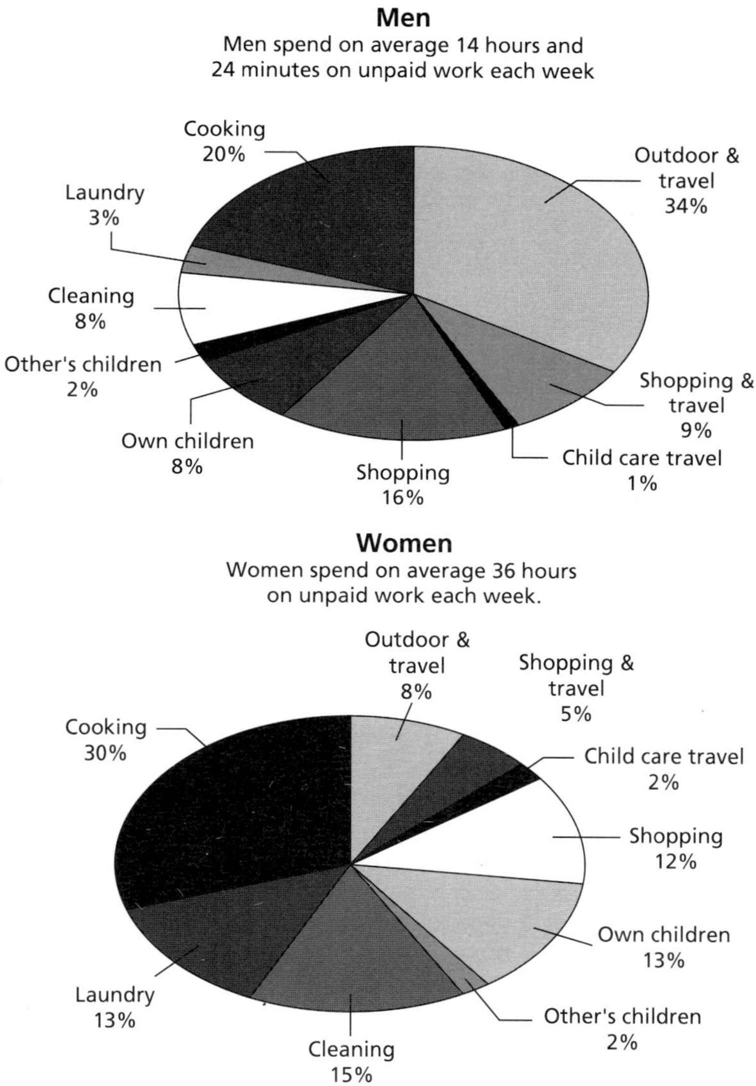

Figure 6.2 Proportion of time spent on unpaid tasks.

Source: ABS, Pilot Time Use Survey: Selected findings adapted from M. Bittman (ed.), *Juggling Time: How Australians Use Time*, Office of the Status of Women, 1991, p. 15

THE 1970S

Although more than 30 years have passed since Adler's survey, and more women are now in the workforce, recent results of similar surveys suggest that role and work allocation within the family have not changed a great deal. A general social survey of Australian families in 1975, approximately two decades after Adler's survey, suggested that household tasks were still traditionally divided, regardless of whether the wife/mother worked outside the home.[10]

The increased participation of married women in the workforce has not significantly increased the involvement of men in household activities and child care. That is, the participation of men in household activities has not increased at a rate which corresponds to the increased involvement of married women in the workforce. A general social survey of Australian families in 1975 found that household tasks were traditionally divided, regardless of whether the wife/mother worked outside the home. The majority of mothers did the household shopping and household tasks, while household repairs, mowing the lawns and taking out the garbage were primarily undertaken by men.

In the studies 'Two Options' and 'Having Families', which were undertaken during the late 1970s and looked at both single-income and dual-income families, the following observations were made.[11]

- Generally, if a wife worked outside the home, it was more or less taken for granted that she would carry out both roles at the same time. For this reason many women said they would prefer to work part-time so they had more time to undertake household tasks.
- It would appear that the higher the income of the husband, the less likely he was to be involved in household tasks.
- When husbands did participate in household tasks, they generally undertook fewer tasks than wives and were more involved in child care than in housework.
- Many women reported that it was often easier to do household tasks themselves than to try and involve husbands.
- When husbands do become involved in household activities it is more on the basis of 'helping out', when requested, rather than assuming voluntary responsibility for certain tasks.

THE 1980S AND 1990S

In 1987 the Australian Bureau of Statistics undertook a survey called 'Pilot Survey of Time Use', the intention of which was to provide detailed information about the diverse range of activities that occupy

10 *Facts on Women at Work in Australia*, Canberra, 1979, pp. 40–1.
11 Results of studies 'Two Options', by J. Harper & D. Worrell; and 'Having Families', by L. Richards; outlined in J. Harper & L. Richards, *Mothers and Working Mothers*, Penguin, Melbourne, 1979, pp. 182–96.

people outside the paid work force.[12] The survey sampled 1000 Sydney households and yielded the following results:

- Regardless of income, education, social background, employment or age, women do more unpaid work than men. On average, women do approximately 36 hours a week of unpaid work while men on average do less than half that amount. Unpaid work is done mostly in the household—things like cleaning, cooking, shopping, gardening and child care.

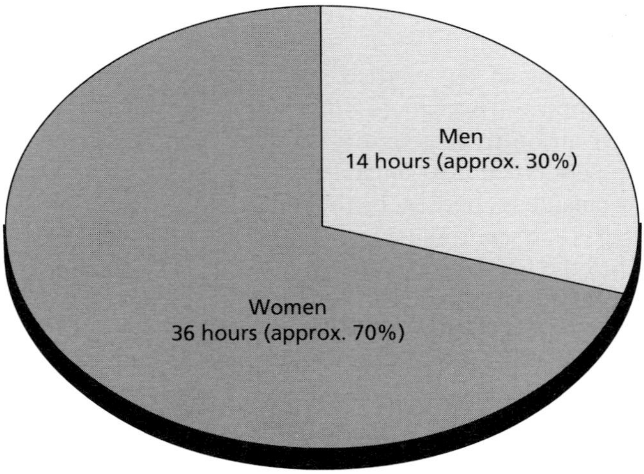

Figure 6.3 Unpaid work: Average hours per week for men and women.

Source: ABS, Pilot Time Use Survey: Selected findings adapted from M. Bittman (ed.), *Juggling Time: How Australians Use Time*, Office of the Status of Women, 1991, p. 13

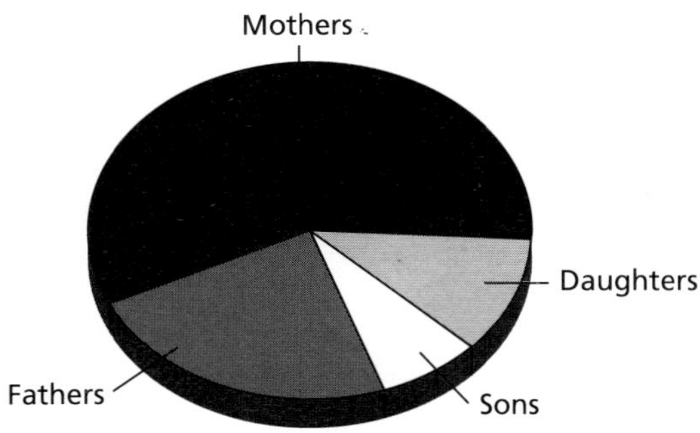

Figure 6.4 Unpaid work within the family. For every hour of unpaid work done by a son, a daughter does 1 hour and 20 minutes, a father does 2 hours and 45 minutes, and a mother does 6 hours and 20 minutes.

Source: ABS, Pilot Time Use Survey: Selected findings adapted from M. Bittman (ed.), *Juggling Time: How Australians Use Time*, Office of the Status of Women, 1991, p. 19

12 M. Bittman, *Juggling Time*, p. 4.

- No matter how many hours of paid work a wife does, her husband's contribution to the unpaid household work remains relatively constant.
- Despite the increasing use of labour-saving devices in the home, Australians spend about the same time in the kitchen and the laundry as they did in 1974. Two-thirds of women's unpaid work is still done indoors. Men spend on average one-third of their unpaid work in outdoor tasks like maintaining the pool, the car and the yard. For men, a high proportion of unpaid work is devoted to play or travel.
- When a woman gets married, she increases the time spent on food preparation and household work. Her spouse reduces the amount of time spent on these activities; he slightly increases the amount of time spent on outdoor unpaid work.
- If a woman has children, by the time children reach school age, the average time spent in paid work increases by 70 per cent.
- Within the family, for every hour of unpaid work done by a son, a daughter does 1 hour and 20 minutes, a father does 2 hours and 45 minutes, and a mother does 6 hours and 30 minutes.

In 1990, the Institute of Family Studies surveyed approximately one thousand families concerning the division of labour in household tasks. The results of this survey indicate that it is still primarily the woman's role to do the housework and cook the meals. Even when both partners are in full-time employment, the majority of housework is still undertaken by women. For example, in families where the wife worked full-time, 81 per cent of women cooked the evening meal, 88 per cent of women did the housework and 60 per cent of women took children to activities and appointments. While men participated more in household activities when the wife worked full-time, their participation was not significantly greater than when the wife did not work outside the home. In families where the wife did not work outside the home 5 per cent of husbands vacuumed the carpets; in families where the wife worked full-time, 7 per cent of husbands vacuumed the carpets—not a very significant difference.

It may not be difficult to work out the reasons as to why men are not participating to any greater degree in household activities—they possibly just don't like it. The main characteristics of housework established in a British Survey in 1985 by Ann Oakley would support this.[13] Housework was found to be lonely, monotonous and boring, with repetitive and fragmented tasks that had to be completed within a

---

13 M. Waters & R. Crook, *Sociology One* (2nd edn.), Longman Cheshire, Melbourne, 1987, p. 122.

limited time. This study found that the hours spent in housework were long, with an average of 77 hours per week being involved. Housework does not attract any monetary compensation and there is very little satisfaction gained from work which is never finished. Men often say they believe in sharing housework and child care but research shows that it does not always happen in practice. Thus, what men say and what they do is usually quite different.

In developed societies such as Australia, unpaid work attracts little recognition, despite the fact that the cost of employing someone to do all the unpaid work in a household would be very high. In our society status, economic rewards and personal identity usually come from work in the paid labour force. Women, who carry out the majority of unpaid work in the household are not regarded as economically productive, and if they do not undertake paid work outside the home they are classified as dependants.

WORKERS WITH FAMILY RESPONSIBILITIES

During the past few years there has been a greater recognition that most workers have family responsibilities and it is wrong to place all the burden for juggling work and family commitments onto the female. Governments and other community groups have recognised that work and family responsibilities are often difficult to balance, and that the dual role for the majority of women is likely to affect their health, employment opportunities and the quality of family life.

In March 1990, Australia ratified the International Labour Organisation Convention 156 on Workers with Family Responsibilities. (However, at the time of writing it was unclear whether the Commonwealth government was able to ratify this Convention legally.) This convention recognises that male workers as well as female workers have family responsibilities, and that these responsibilities go beyond the years of early child care: they extend across the life cycle. It is now an aim of national policy to enable workers with family responsibilities to meet those responsibilities without discrimination and, as far as possible, without conflict between their employment and family commitments.[14] Further, The Office of the Status of Women in the Department of the Prime Minister and Cabinet is co-ordinating a community education program which seeks to assist women and men to successfully combine family and work responsibilities.

While a more equitable sharing of domestic responsibilities is required to enable women to participate and progress in the labour

---

14 M. Bittman, *Juggling Time*, p.4.

force, a re-education of many employers is also required, so that family responsibilities are seen as belonging to men as well as women. This may be difficult, because many employers find it convenient to assume there is a woman at home attending to domestic responsibilities, rather than have to address the issue of workers with family responsibilities.

Society still assumes that women will take primary responsibility for child care and household work and that men should put their jobs first. In a two-income family the income of the wife is often seen as secondary or supplementary and the job of less importance. This is compounded by the fact that on average women's wages are still lower than men's wages. Men are still under the same pressure to be the main breadwinner of the family and this pressure can mean they are deprived of sharing family responsibilities and contributing equally. The expectation that men should put jobs before family still exists, and when the amount of unpaid work to be undertaken in a family is at its greatest, that is when children are very young, this is the time when men usually spend the most hours in the workplace.

Flexible work structures

Many employers have opposed the idea of unpaid leave for both male and female workers to attend to domestic responsibilities, claiming that such leave will erode profits. Children and aged relatives requiring care when sick are a major domestic responsibility that many workers face, but there are few provisions to allow workers to meet these obligations. Also, different cultural factors can influence family obligations but these may not be recognised by employers. Leave provisions do not usually acknowledge extended family obligations or periods of mourning following the death of a relative.

Studies suggest that greater parental leave provisions would provide for more flexibility for the employer and the employee as well as improve employee morale. Flexibility of hours, for example, may mean that employees can take time off for home responsibilities when required and the work can be undertaken at another time. Apart from reducing employee stress, flexibility in the workplace can increase job productivity. Many workers, particularly women, are at risk of losing their jobs if they request time off work to meet family obligations and they are therefore more inclined to take sick leave in order to avoid this possibility. Also, women tend to go to work when they are sick as they know they may need the leave at a later date to look after sick children or aged relatives. Women from non-English speaking backgrounds are at a greater disadvantage, particularly if their English language skills are limited. These women tend to work in less skilled occupations where they know they can be easily replaced, and they lack the language skills and the power to negotiate with their employer.

Australian society is still structured to a large extent around the stay-at-home wife and the traditional family structure of male breadwinner and dependent wife and children, yet this traditional family structure accounts for less than one-quarter of Australian households. While there have been changes in shopping hours, many other services and business continue to operate within traditional 'office hours'. This can mean that workers have to take time off work to access these services. Some businesses have introduced or trialled more flexible hours to take account of this change in society, but these are in the minority.

Not only is it children that need care by adults, many aged people also require care. Australia's population is ageing and will continue to do so as the 'baby boomer' generation reaches retirement age. The proportion of older persons is getting bigger while the proportion of people in the workforce is getting smaller. There is a trend for elderly people to remain in their home, but this often requires a relative to provide support and assistance when required. It is less costly for society to maintain elderly people in their own homes, but this requires a recognition by society that the people caring for the elderly are often workers who need time off work to carry out these duties.

Juggling work and family commitments is a major cause of stress in working families. When there is a balance between home and work life for both men and women, adults and children benefit. Women benefit physically and emotionally and this can increase opportunities with employment; men are able to develop the relationships they have with their partner and children; and children are brought up in a family where they observe parents with both work and family roles. Children are also provided with the opportunity to contribute more to the workload of the family and to acquire those skills required for the development of social competence.

In Australia, as in many other countries, the demands of family life are seen as the sole responsibility of the family. Many employers are unaware or do not want to know that family responsibilities have an effect in the workplace. It is believed and promoted by many government bodies and community organisations that a more flexible workplace which acknowledges that both male and female workers have family responsibilities would increase worker productivity. The costs to society of marriage breakdown, child poverty, ill health, domestic violence etc. could be reduced through a more enlightened approach to work and family commitments. The costs of parental leave provision and flexibility in the workplace would be far less than the costs to society of poverty and abuse, and family breakdown.

Responsibility to ensure a better balance of tasks within the home and the workplace rests not only with the individual; it needs to be addressed by all involved—workers, employers, community groups and governments. It is also necessary to examine existing work structures and to develop more flexible work arrangements, so the needs of all groups, children, employees and aged people can be satisfied.

MANAGEMENT DECISIONS

Following are some of the management decisions a family will have to consider in regard to the work roles of partners:

- The first decision a woman will have to make is whether she will leave the workforce for a few months, a few years, or permanently, if the decision is taken to have children. Will staying at home with children provide sufficient stimulation? Can wants and needs be satisfied with one income?
- Will a break from the workforce for either partner affect future employment and career prospects?
- If workforce participation of both partners is considered a desirable option, will it be full-time or part-time? Is a choice possible? Are two incomes required to meet living expenses, costs of raising children, housing costs and higher material expectations?
- Is workforce participation of both partners financially viable when work-related expenses are calculated?
- How will household tasks be allocated within the family? Who will attend to the cleaning, laundry, food preparation, maintenance and payment of accounts?
- What child-care facilities are available? Are these satisfactory for both parents and child/children?
- What domestic supports, if any, will be utilised? Will someone be employed to do some of the household tasks, or will these be undertaken by family members? Can the family budget meet existing financial commitments as well as the added costs of child care and domestic help?
- Will working outside the home allow sufficient time for interaction, development of relationships and leisure time?
- How will the family cope with emergencies such as illness of children? Will there be flexibility in the workplace to allow for this?
- Will job satisfaction and financial rewards outweigh role conflict and strain that may be incurred?
- What individual and family values and goals are influencing choices being considered?

CONCLUSION

While in theory, the barriers to equality in the workplace for women have been progressively reduced, there are significant difficulties for women who combine work and motherhood. Society has expected women to cope with the increased workload they undertake, little has been done in Australia to provide the assistance and support that families require, in order to successfully integrate family and work responsibilities. There is a greater need for alternative and flexible work schedules for men and women, parental leave provisions, flexible child-care provisions, outside-school and holiday-care facilities, sick-child-care facilities and centres for the aged.

In 1990, 43 per cent of women and 41 per cent of all men in the labour force had dependent children; 45 per cent of married women with children aged 4 years or under were in the labour force and 57 per cent of all employed married women had dependent children.[15] As women continue to increase educational attainments, their commitment to the workforce will also increase, particularly as the proportion of women in the professional, managerial and skilled workforce also increases. It is unlikely that women with higher education qualifications and training are going to opt to leave the workforce if they have children. It would appear that most families will require two incomes in order to raise children, meet housing costs and live in a consumer society. The growth of Australia's economy requires a future population. Natural population growth is not likely to increase if people cannot afford to have children or choose not to have children because the demands of work and family life cannot be met simultaneously.

If more equal relationships between women and men are to emerge, significant changes to the nature and structure of paid employment are required since men still earn more than women. This preserves the status of men as primary breadwinners and women as supplementary breadwinners. To achieve a balance between the work and home roles of both men and women, a flexible restructuring of work is needed to take account of the needs of parents, children and aged relatives.

15 Australian Bureau of Statistics, *The Labour Force Australia, 1990*, Canberra, 1991.

REVIEW QUESTIONS

1 Why is a distinction often drawn between *dual-worker* families and *dual-career* families?
2 Is the dual role of women a new phenomenon? Explain your answer.
3 What major event this century gave married women the incentive to enter and remain in the workforce?
4 Of all married women, what proportion are now in the workforce?
5 What proportion of the female workforce consists of married females?
6 What does the term 'opportunity cost' mean?
7 Why are women less likely to participate in the workforce when they have three or more children?
8 Why do many women prefer to work part-time rather than full-time?
9 What factors have contributed to the increasing workforce participation of married women?
10 What does the term *marriage bar* mean?
11 How can parental leave help families meet work and family commitments?
12 What effects have labour-saving devices had on the workforce participation of married women?
13 Outline the factors that make it difficult for women to combine two full-time roles at home and at work?
14 What does the term *matriduxy* mean?
15 Discuss the effects of the workforce participation of married women on work and role allocation within the home.
16 Discuss how Australian society can assist families in balancing the demands of family and work.
17 Why do women who work outside the home often experience role conflict? What types of conflicts may they experience?
18 What domestic supports can dual-income families use to decrease the household work load?
19 Why may a working mother with pre-school children experience more role conflict than a mother with teenage children?
20 List some of the management decisions that a dual-income family may have to consider?

CASE STUDY 6.1

THE CAREER COUPLE

Marina, aged 32, and Allan, aged 36, have been married for eight years. Throughout this time they have had no real desire to have children, as they have been involved in their respective careers, courses of studies and social activities. They believe they have now reached a point in their lives where they should decide whether or not to have children. They have virtually decided to do so, but both still have some doubts.

Marina and Allan realise that such a decision will dramatically alter their lifestyle. However, Marina feels that having children will ultimately affect her life more in the immediate future than it will Allan's. Both partners agree that Marina should remain at home with the child for the first few months, but this means that Marina may have to resign from her job, unless she can negotiate unpaid leave.

Marina works in an advertising agency and finds the work stimulating and enjoyable. She has been offered a higher position within the company and has decided to accept the promotion. It will however, involve more time spent in the workplace. If Marina chooses to have a child and resigns from her job she may have difficulty in finding a similar position at a later date. On the other hand, if the agency agrees to give her leave of absence she feels she may not be able to meet the demands of the new position plus the demands of motherhood when she returns to the job.

QUESTIONS

1 Why does Marina feel that a child will affect her lifestyle more than it will her husband's?
2 What conflicts is Marina facing in making a decision about whether or not to have children?
3 Why do Marina and Allan have some doubts about the decision?
4 What conflict is Marina facing in her decision to accept the promotion?
5 Assuming Marina and Allan do have a baby, when Marina returns to the workforce what type of role conflict is she likely to experience?
6 Why does it appear that Marina will experience more conflict than Allan? Is it possible to change this situation so that conflicts and strains can be shared more equally?
7 What type of management decisions will Marina and Allan have

to make if they have a child and Marina resumes work outside the home?
8 How would Marina's and Allan's lifestyle be different if they found they were unable to have children?
9 How will the utilisation of human and non-human resources change if Marina and Allan have a child/children? Which resources will be more limited?
10 When reading this case study, what assumptions are evident?

CASE STUDY 6.2

THE DUAL-INCOME FAMILY

Sophie and Angelo have been married for 15 years and have three children: Mary, 14, George, 12, and Janice aged 9. Angelo is a pastrycook and therefore starts work very early in the morning, usually at about 4.00 a.m., generally returning home by 1.00 p.m. Sophie worked part-time as a nursing sister after Janice turned 2, and then two years ago she obtained a position as a full-time nursing sister at a private hospital close to home. Sophie does shift work and her hours vary each week. For example, during one week she may have to work two day shifts, two night shifts and one afternoon shift. She has to work two weekends in every month, but receives time off during the week each time she does so. Sophie is hoping to find a position elsewhere, so she can work a set shift everyday and have the same two days off every week.

Sophie and Angelo believe it is necessary for Sophie to work set hours every week, as there are many times when neither parent is at home with the children. Sophie enjoys her work, but would feel more relaxed if she could work an afternoon or evening shift. This arrangement would mean that one partner was always at home with the children, but at the same time it may mean that Sophie and Angelo have little time to spend together.

QUESTIONS

1 What problem is this family facing?
2 What adjustments may Angelo have had to make when Sophie returned to full-time work outside the home?

3 How may the irregular work hours of the parents affect family harmony and communication?
4 In this family, the children may be given added responsibilities and more tasks to perform. Why? What tasks do you think the children could undertake when both parents are at work?
5 What tasks could Angelo undertake within the household?
6 What tasks could Sophie undertake within the household?
7 Why does Sophie wish to change her working hours? What values are influencing this action? What priorities may be associated with these values?
8 In this family, which resources may be limited? Which resources may be in greater supply?
9 How could this family use domestic supports to ease the household work load?
10 What management decisions may Sophie and Angelo have to make concerning the household and family?

Survey

Role and work allocation within the Australian family

This survey may be used as a guide for interviewing two-parent families where either or both partners work outside the home. The aim of the survey is to determine:

1 Who makes the decisions in the family about what tasks have to be completed?
2 Who actually completes the task after the decision has been made?

It would be interesting to compare the results for dual-income families with those for families where only one partner works outside the home. It must be remembered that, in order to obtain data from which you can draw generalisations about Australian society in the 1980s, a large number of families would have to be surveyed. Thus, if this is carried out as a class survey with only a small number of families interviewed, it could not be concluded that the findings apply to the majority of families living in Australia.

SURVEY GUIDE

A Work roles outside the home

For both parents (if applicable), list the number of hours worked outside the home per week.

a Parent 1 ____________________

b Parent 2 ____________________

B Composition of the household

1 Number, sex and age of children

____

____

____

2 Any relatives (grandparents, etc.) living in the household

____

____

3 Total number of people living in the household

____

C Decision-making and task allocation

The following list of questions could be extended to include other decisions that are made within the family and other activities that are part of family life.

1 a Who decides what food will be purchased for family meals?

____

b Who does the shopping for the food?

____

2 a Who decides what food will be eaten for dinner at night?

____

b Who does the preparation and cooking?

____

c Who cleans up after the meal?

____

3 a Who decides on the amount of pocket money or allowance the children will receive?

____

b Who gives the money to the children?

____

4 a Who decides on when the ironing will be done?

____

b Who does the ironing?

____

5 a Who decides when the gardening will be done, or when the lawn will be mowed?

____

b Who does the gardening and/or mows the lawn?

____

6 a Who decides where the family will go for holidays?

____

b Who makes the arrangements for the holiday?

____

7 a Who decides when the car needs cleaning and washing?

____

b Who cleans and washes the car?

____

8 a Who decides when the vacuuming will be done?

____

b Who does the vacuuming?

____

9 a Who decides when minor repairs need to be made around the home, e.g. replacing a washer in a tap, changing a light-globe?

____

b Who does these repairs?

____

10 **a** Who decides on the allocation of economic resources for the family budget?

____

b Who pays the bills and takes care of the accounts?

____

11 **a** Who decides when major family expenditures will be made, e.g. buying a new refrigerator?

____

b Who buys the refrigerator or organises the purchase?

____

12 **a** Who decides who will drive the car on family outings?

____

b Who drives the car?

____

13 **a** Who decides when the children will go to bed?

____

b Who puts the children to bed (if they are young) or checks on them?

____

14 **a** Who decides when the family will visit relatives?

____

b Who organises the visit?

____

15 **a** If the children are young, who decides what they will wear?

____

b Who dresses the children?

____

When the survey has been completed, conclusions can be drawn for the following questions:

- Which partner makes most of the decisions within the family? Is one partner dominant in the decision-making process or is it a shared operation?
- Which partner undertakes most of the activities or organisation? Is

it the same partner who makes most of the decisions, or are household tasks and organisation equally shared?

- Is one partner more involved in the overall running of the household? Is there a difference when both partners work outside the home?
- Are the decisions made by either partner related to traditional sex-linked roles?
- Are the tasks and activities that the partners undertake within the household related to traditional sex-linked roles?

7

Low-income families and poverty

A sufficient income is necessary for a person's independence, security, psychological, social and physical well-being. It enables individuals and families to provide food, clothing, housing, education, transport and health care. Sufficient income allows families to maintain a standard of living considered acceptable by the community; a standard of living that supplies not only essentials, but also the flexibility to provide for other needs and wants. An adequate income allows access to the resources of freedom of choice and freedom of opportunity. Individuals and families in poverty do not have access to such resources.

Types of poverty

Absolute or primary poverty

There is no doubt, when looking at developing countries such as India, Asia, Africa and some South American countries, that poverty exists on a large scale. Poverty in these countries usually means a lack of food, clothing, shelter, education, knowledge, health services and medical care. It means susceptibility to disease, malnutrition, physical and mental retardation, and—for many children and adults alike—death.

Poverty in developing countries is often referred to as *primary* or *absolute poverty*. This type of poverty occurs when *the amount of income is insufficient to meet basic needs*—clothing, food and shelter—even when managed efficiently. For many people in developing countries there is often no income at all.

Poverty perpetuates poverty. Individuals and families in developing countries are often caught in a cycle that can rarely be escaped. Living in less-than-subsistence conditions, people are often malnourished; with little money, little food, lack of medical care and with a lowered resistance, they are subject to communicable diseases and infection. When people are sick and unable to afford medical treatment and food, malnutrition worsens. When this condition is combined with an inability to produce or buy food, the cycle perpetuates itself unless death intervenes. As indicated in Figure 7.1, primary poverty is a vicious cycle.

In the last few years however, with more attention being paid to poverty and related issues, many social scientists are maintaining that absolute poverty does exist in Australia and is increasing. That is, there is a growing number of people who cannot provide for even very basic needs, because social welfare is inadequate and/or because of ignorance of the social welfare assistance that is available. Alcoholism and drug

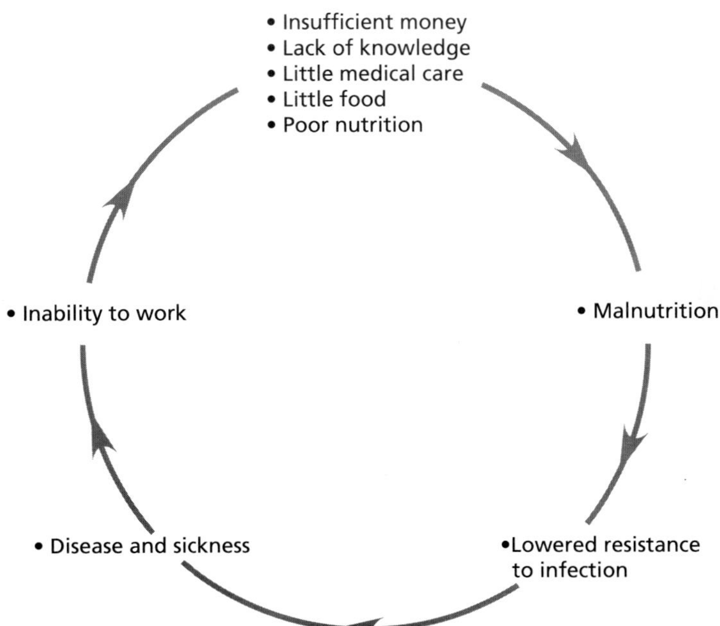

Figure 7.1 The absolute poverty cycle

dependency may be the cause of some Australians living in absolute poverty.

Often it is difficult to determine if poverty has resulted from insufficient income or the inability to manage it. Also, it may be difficult to distinguish between *primary* and *relative* poverty, as they may overlap.

Relative or secondary poverty

Many Australians who are considered poor by our standards would be regarded as affluent if compared to the poor in developing countries. Poverty is relative to the overall living standard of the country in which it exists, and therefore it is necessary to clarify the concept when discussing it in relation to developed countries such as Australia. Townsend, a social scientist who has undertaken many studies on poverty in the United Kingdom, defines relative poverty in the following manner:

> Individuals, families and groups can be said to be in poverty when they lack the resources to obtain the type of diet, participate in the activities and have the living conditions and amenities which are customary, or at least widely encouraged or approved, in the

Figure 7.2 Inadequate housing tends to go hand in hand with poverty. During the 1930s depression, many families experienced poverty. (Photo: M. Deliopoulos/Housing Commission of Victoria)

societies to which they belong. Their resources are so seriously below those commanded by the average individual or family that they are, in effect, excluded from ordinary living patterns, customs and activities.[1]

Like all other countries, Australia has always had a proportion of the population living in poverty, and until this century few social welfare services were available to assist people living in poverty. Industrialisation, technological advances and rises in real standards of living have, in many countries, reduced the extent of poverty. This has meant not only that basic needs have been satisfied but increases in the real value of wages have enabled the satisfaction of less-than-basic needs.

When individuals and/or families have an adequate income to satisfy basic needs but their income falls markedly below that of the rest of the community, they may be said to be in poverty *relative* to the rest of the community. This definition of poverty, like the definition given above, refers to relative poverty. Individuals and families living in relative poverty are unable to obtain what the majority of the population consider essential for comfortable living at that particular time.

For example, what was regarded as a reasonable standard of living in 1940 is unacceptable by today's standards: goods and services that may have been considered luxuries then are now regarded as essential. Many of the goods and services that are available now were not necessary to function in society in 1940, but they are necessary to function and participate in society in the 1990s. Many individuals and families in the 1940s survived without washing machines and motor cars and higher education; in the 1990s it is very difficult to function and participate in our society without access to these goods and services.

Relative poverty may also occur when, as a result of poor management or unwise spending, the income is insufficient to provide for basic needs. Poor management often results from lack of knowledge or skills to budget income. Many people are quick to criticise those in relative poverty as being bad money-managers, lacking in self-control, and capable of a better living standard if they budgeted more carefully, worked harder and were more thrifty.

It is very easy to criticise and blame the victims of poverty, and while the incomes of these individuals and families can often be managed in theory, in practice it is almost impossible. A low income allows little room for flexibility or for the satisfaction of other needs and wants: the

1 P. Townsend, quoted in D.Edgar, D. Keane & P. McDonald (eds), *Child Poverty*, Australian Institute of Family Studies, Allen & Unwin, Melbourne, 1989, p. 25.

lower the income, the less the flexibility. This lack of flexibility of income means that individuals and families with low incomes cannot participate in society to anywhere near the same extent as the majority of the population. People who have the flexibility to participate in society have a much greater chance of becoming competent members of society than do individuals born and raised in relative poverty.

Poverty in developed countries is often hidden. We may be aware of the homeless adults and youth who tend to congregate in inner-city areas but we are often not aware of the many other individuals and families whose standard of living is well below that considered acceptable by the rest of society. As will be discussed later in the chapter, it is often unsatisfactory to define people in poverty as those living on less than a certain income. This does not always take into account factors such as housing costs, size and composition of the family or specific needs. These and other factors influence the amount of income required to maintain a satisfactory standard of living.

THE RELATIVE POVERTY CYCLE

Like primary poverty, relative poverty also perpetuates poverty, as shown in Figure 7.2. Many studies have shown that parents with low-paid employment, inadequate housing and often poor physical health give birth to infants with a high risk of illness and death. Living in deprived conditions, these children often do not have basic needs satisfied and education is often given a low priority. Lack of educational qualifications leads to low-paid and low-status jobs with little opportunity for improvement and thus little opportunity for higher wages. As marriage often occurs between individuals of similar socioeconomic backgrounds, the cycle is perpetuated.

Unfortunately, poverty has been entrenched in the social structure since settlement of Australia, and just giving more money does not eliminate poverty or the social inequality that accompanies it. There is a need to ensure that all children and young people have not just the access to educational facilities, but the opportunities and support to obtain the education as well as the work and living skills required to participate fully in our society. In addition, access to the resources of health, housing and welfare are also required to reduce and eliminate poverty.

It is easier for society to provide income support to alleviate a degree of poverty than to develop mechanisms to break the poverty cycle. For example, non-English speaking migrants have a better chance of obtaining more highly skilled jobs and thus higher incomes if they can speak English. However, they often do not have the time to do this if

Figure 7.3 The psychological, social and physical wellbeing of individuals and families can be seriously affected if they do not achieve a standard of living accepted by society.

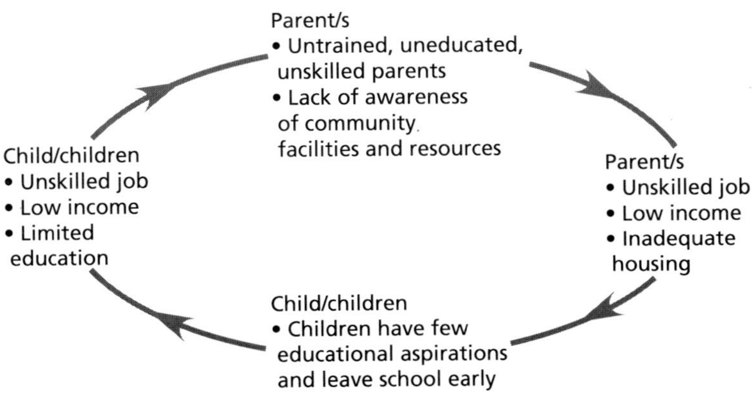

Figure 7.4 The relative poverty cycle

they are working long hours during the day and attending to family commitments during the night and at weekends.

The Brotherhood of St. Laurence in Melbourne has proposed for some time that poverty is characterised by, and perpetuated by a lack of:

- power over resources
- power over relationships
- power over information
- power over decision making.

FACTORS CONTRIBUTING TO POVERTY

For most individuals and families, poverty is a result of complex, interrelated, economic, social and psychological factors, not just a lack of income. Some of the major factors contributing to poverty are outlined below.

LACK OF INCOME

A low income, no matter how well managed, may barely provide basic needs of food clothing and shelter. Certainly, the income provided by social security benefits alone does not enable all the recipients to maintain a standard of living considered acceptable in our society. This is particularly so for those people who do not own their own housing but are paying rent, such as single-parent families, aged pensioners and the unemployed.

LACK OF EDUCATION

An individual who is unskilled, untrained and lacking in educational qualifications can usually only obtain a job that commands a low income. As this income may be barely sufficient to meet basic family needs, children, if present, may be encouraged to leave school at the earliest possible age to assist the family's earning capacity and relieve some of the financial strain. As children of low-income earners often lack educational qualifications, they too can usually only obtain unskilled jobs with low incomes.

When parents have had little education, they are often less likely to encourage children to study while they are at school, let alone seek higher education. In many families, students may be eligible for educational assistance, for example Austudy, but this assistance is often not used due to ignorance of such assistance, or lack of interest in pursuing an education.

Housing

The high costs of housing can be a major contributing factor to the poverty of many individuals and families. If the proportion of income spent on housing leaves insufficient funds to spend on food, clothing and other needs, then social, psychological and physical welfare can be adversely affected.

A housing survey conducted by the Australian Bureau of Statistics in 1988 found that relative housing costs were higher for single-parent families renting privately than for any other family group. On average they spent 37 per cent of gross weekly income on rent.[2] If more than 30 per cent of income is spent on housing, individuals and families are said to be in financial housing stress. Individuals and families who are forced to live in substandard accommodation because of lack of money will also have their wellbeing affected.

Traditionally, housing costs have risen more quickly than wages or pensions and benefits. High inflation rates and high mortgage interest rates have increased the costs of purchasing and renting housing. For many individuals and families, the cost of housing in relation to income is disproportionately high. Further, a low-income family living in Adelaide and renting private accommodation is likely to be better off than a family earning the same income but living in Sydney, where housing costs are higher. Housing costs vary markedly throughout Australia, but low-income earners generally have little choice in where they live as they need to live close to employment opportunities.

Housing costs vary considerably throughout the life cycle. Families with young children tend to pay very high housing costs when their income is low in relation to needs.[3] Further, those who rent housing tend to have housing costs which are higher than those of owner–purchasers. Often, private rental rates are more than mortgage repayments on a housing loan but low-income earners often have little choice but to rent as it is impossible to pay rent and save for a housing deposit at the same time. Low-income earners who rent in the private sector, despite government rent assistance, still have higher housing

2 J. Vipond, 'Child poverty and housing', in D. Edgar, D. Keane & P. P. McDonald (eds), *Child Poverty*, p. 78.

3 Australian Bureau of Statistics, *Australia's Children 1989: A Statistical Profile*, Canberra, 1989, p. 19.

costs than those who are able to rent public housing. However, public housing waiting lists are very long and there is no guarantee that public housing, when offered, will be in an area close to present or potential employment.

UNEMPLOYMENT

Since 1975 there has been a significant increase in the unemployment rate. Young people have been particularly affected by unemployment as developments in technology have meant many traditional jobs have disappeared or have been reduced in number as a result of automation. The average length of time spent unemployed has increased and this can have adverse implications. Generally, the longer the period of unemployment, the less likelihood there is of obtaining employment and the greater the risk of relative poverty.

The economic recession in Australia has meant a decrease in employment opportunities and an increase in retrenchments and redundancies. When there is an unexpected reduction in income, so that commitments and fixed expenses cannot be met, relative poverty may result. It is likely that for an individual who is retrenched and cannot find immediate employment, unemployment benefits will probably be inadequate to cover the commitments that were budgeted for on a higher income. This same situation can arise in a two-income family where the family was dependent on both incomes to meet expenses. Unemployment of one adult partner usually does not allow application for unemployment benefits as this benefit is income-tested and the other partner's income is taken into account.

INFLATION AND ECONOMIC RECESSION

Inflation can contribute to poverty because it essentially reduces purchasing power. During times of high inflation, middle-income and high-income families may have to make some adjustments to living standards, but they generally have the resources to provide for such flexibility. For low-income earners, income is never sufficient to allow flexibility for rising costs of basic needs of food, clothing and accommodation, whether rental increases or mortgage interest-rate increases. When inflation erodes the living standards of middle and higher-income earners, basic needs can still be provided for; this is not the case for low-income earners. High inflation and increased mortgage interest rates can create relative poverty for many people. Low-income families may not have the flexibility to pay increased mortgage repayments. During the late 1980s and early 1990s many families had no choice but to sell their homes when interest rates increased so markedly that they could not afford the repayments.

Although the wage-indexation scheme was designed to provide for inflation, when applied on a percentage basis, the poor are even more disadvantaged. A national wage rise of 3 per cent per week obviously gives more flexibility to an employee earning $600 per week than it does to an employee earning $400 per week. Similarly, taxation cuts applied to employees on a percentage basis rather than a flat-rate basis does the same thing, that is, it advantages higher income-earners.

Inflation generally favours those who have equity in land and houses, which rise in value, but inflation makes it more difficult for low-income earners to meet rental increases and to purchase housing. Inflation and economic downturns can contribute to unemployment, particularly for less skilled and less educated people who are made redundant. Employees with more education and skills have a better chance of finding employment if they are retrenched than those with limited education, training and skills.

THE 'CONSUMER-CREDIT' SOCIETY

The mass media is an inherent part of developed societies, whereby people are informed and persuaded of what they need and want. Advertising and marketing makes individuals not only aware of what is available but also of their need to acquire it. An affluent country requires individuals and families to consume goods and services if the economy is to survive. The mass media tempts us to buy even when we cannot afford to do so. Television, found in almost every home, is the major mechanism by which we become aware of what we should have in order to maintain an acceptable standard of living. Children also place tremendous pressure on parents to provide those things presented by the media as important and desirable. Most parents find it hard to refuse children the toys, goods and entertainment that a large percentage of other children enjoy.

Advertising shows us what we need, and credit provides the opportunity for us to have it. A 'consumer-credit society' brings even the lowest income earner within reach of his/her wants. Low-income earners cannot always afford to buy goods outright—the cheapest method of purchase—as they do not have the cash to pay the full price initially. Credit enables people to participate in our society and to purchase those things that the majority of the population believe contribute to a desirable standard of living. Unfortunately, the high costs of credit can create large debts that can never be paid off and put many families into even greater poverty.

To blame the victim for their poverty is still common, and it is usually done by those who have the resources to purchase the goods and services promoted by the media and considered necessary by a large proportion of the population. It is too easy to criticise the poor for using credit and amassing never-ending debts when they are continually confronted by a standard of living they can never enjoy.

Anxiety-reducing behaviour

Frustration with a life of poverty may lead to income being spent on things other than basic needs, to the extent that often basic needs are not satisfied or other commitments are not met. Low-income families may use credit to purchase goods even when they know they have little chance of meeting credit repayments. This is commonly referred to as 'anxiety-reducing behaviour', that is, doing something enjoyable in order to reduce stress or make life more enjoyable and thus escape from reality for at least a short period of time. The majority of people participate in some form of 'anxiety-reducing behaviour', and many of us can afford to do so. Spending money is enjoyable for many people, yet those individuals and families living in relative poverty are often denied the flexibility to do so and thus the flexibility to escape temporarily from a monotonous and often stressful existence.

Orientation towards the present

Middle and higher socioeconomic groups tend to be future-oriented in their approach to life. They are concerned with higher education as a means of ensuring adequate income; health insurance as a means of meeting medical expenses, superannuation or life insurance to provide for retirement and savings to meet unexpected emergencies.

For those in poverty, to be future-oriented can be depressing and futile as the future often holds nothing better. The poor cannot usually afford to take out insurance or put money aside for an emergency, as all available money must be used for present expenses. In the event of an emergency, the poor are often plunged into even deeper debt as there are no savings to cover the expenses. Some people adopt the attitude that there will be someone to help if and when a crisis occurs e.g. money is not put aside to pay expenses of gas and electricity and when threatened with disconnection of services, no action is taken. Such actions often lead to more expense, e.g. paying additional money to have the electricity reconnected.

Unexpected expense, illness or handicap

Poverty may result if large amounts of money have to be paid for unexpected illness or other debts, thus reducing the amount available for basic needs and commitments. Long periods of illness may mean that sickness benefits from place of employment cease or are exhausted, and social service benefits are not enough to cover living expenses.

Emotions

In our society money is associated with many emotions: lack of money can lower an individual's self-esteem; money can be used to convey feelings of love, fear, hate, anger etc. For example, people may equate money with love and insist on excessive amounts being spent on them, thus placing the family further in debt. Partners may retaliate against each other by spending large amounts of money as a form of punishment. Money can be used to buy the affection of children, particularly in families where there is conflict. Thus, people can overcompensate for lack of love and affection by overspending. Unfortunately, in some families this can have not only psychological and social effects but also severe economic consequences as well.

Extent of poverty in Australia

During the 1950s and 1960s Australia, like many developed nations, experienced a period of great economic growth and poverty appeared to be a thing of the past. In the late 1960s and early 1970s, public awareness of poverty increased as it became apparent that poverty did exist in Australia and the extent was increasing. Since this period of time considerable research has been done to determine the extent of poverty in Australia.

The Commission of Inquiry into Poverty

The first attempt to determine the extent of poverty in Australia was through a study undertaken in the late 1960s by the Institute of Applied Economic and Social Research at the University of Melbourne. The findings of this study generated public debate and in response to this debate the Commonwealth government established a Committee of Inquiry into Poverty. The Commission was chaired by Professor Ronald Henderson and the report on poverty which was published in 1975 as a result of the Commission's findings became known as the Henderson Report.

The Commission of Inquiry into Poverty determined that approximately 8–10 per cent of the population were 'very poor', that is, living below the level of income which could provide basic needs. A further 7 per cent of the population was classified as 'rather poor', that is, their level of income was not sufficient to provide an acceptable standard of living.[4] Many social scientists have since proposed that these figures are conservative by today's standards and that the extent of poverty is far greater than was initially believed. It has been proposed that approximately 12 per cent or more of the population are now 'very poor', or that between two and three million Australians are living in poverty.

The Poverty Commission determined that for a family consisting of two adults and two or three children, the poverty line could be taken as an income of approximately 60 per cent of the average weekly wage. During the last 15 years much debate has occurred about this poverty line and whether it really can be used to determine if families are living in poverty. Despite much criticism, no alternative has been found and the Henderson poverty line is still used as a basic measurement for poverty and in formulating social policy and social welfare reforms. Nevertheless, it must be remembered that the poverty line is effectively a measure of minimum physical survival, not of minimum social functioning.[5] That is, a family with an income marginally above the poverty line may just be able to satisfy basic needs but they will be unable to function effectively or actively participate in society, and enjoy the standard of living enjoyed by a greater majority of the population.

THE POVERTY LINE AND HOUSING

When establishing whether individuals and families are living in poverty, most researchers use two types of poverty lines: the *before-housing* poverty line and the *after-housing* poverty line. The before-housing poverty line determines if an income is adequate to meet all costs including housing. The after-housing poverty line determines if an income is adequate to meet all costs after housing costs have been paid.

This distinction between before-housing costs and after-housing

4 *Poverty in Australia*, First main Report of the Australian Commission of Inquiry into Poverty, AGPS, Canberra, 1975, pp. 14–16.

5 A. Graycar & A. Jamrozik, *How Australians Live: Social Policy in Theory and Practice*, Macmillan, Melbourne, 1989, p. 29.

costs is made because it takes into account the substantial variation in housing costs that individuals and families face.[6] For example, two families may have identical incomes yet one family may have housing costs significantly greater than another family. For this reason, researchers in poverty consider the after-housing measure more useful. The costs of housing as a contributing factor in poverty were recognised by the Commonwealth government in their Family Assistance Package with the extension of rent assistance to low-income earners renting in the private sector.

Groups at risk to poverty

The groups of people who can be identified as having a high chance of living in relative poverty are not a homogeneous group—they represent a broad cross section of the population, have different needs and wants, access to different resources and live in different conditions and situations. Since the Commission of Inquiry into Poverty nearly twenty years ago, the groups at risk to poverty have changed. Twenty years ago, the aged were the largest group in poverty, now single-parent families are the largest group living in poverty.

Establishing whether certain individuals and families are living in poverty is very difficult as many variables need to be taken into account. These variables include:

- housing costs—one of the main factors contributing to poverty;
- renting, owning, or purchasing accommodation;
- assets, if any;
- short-term or long-term employment;
- employment prospects;
- existing expenses and commitments;
- composition of family;
- number and ages of children.

Unemployed adults

The most important determinant of low income is whether the major breadwinner in a family is employed or unemployed. The incidence of unemployment has certainly increased during the last few decades; in 1967, 1.7 per cent of people in the labour force were unemployed but by 1993 the figure was over 11 per cent.

6 H. Brownlee & A. King, 'The estimated impact of the family package on child poverty', in D. Edgar, D. Keane & P. McDonald (eds), *Child Poverty*, pp.126–27.

To meet basic needs, to participate in society and to maintain an acceptable standard of living often require that both adult partners in a family are employed. In two-income families where one of the breadwinners loses employment, the family is usually not entitled to employment benefits as a spouse's income is regarded as 'other income'. When family income is suddenly reduced and there is insufficient money to meet expenses and commitments, relative poverty may result. Similarly, in one-income families, where the sole earner loses employment, unemployment benefits will probably not be sufficient to meet commitments or to maintain the present standard of living.

Certain groups of people are more prone to unemployment, including uneducated, unskilled, rural and itinerant, overseas-born and older workers. These groups of people tend to experience longer periods of unemployment. Also, females tend to experience higher unemployment rates than males. Many individuals and families living in relative poverty are not able to obtain work even though they are actively seeking it.

Older workers

Data collected by the Australian Bureau of Statistics indicate that employees in the 35 years plus age group experience more difficulties in obtaining employment than employees in younger age groups. Difficulties in finding employment increase with age, and people over the age of 55 years who are retrenched or made redundant are likely to remain unemployed until they are eligible for an aged pension. It would appear that there is a trend towards the employment of younger employees with more formal qualifications rather than the experience of older employees. Many older employees have found that while they may attempt to retrain or acquire other workforce skills, employers still opt for younger employees.

Overseas-born workers

Migrants who have limited English language skills and little training, or qualifications not recognised in Australia, are more likely to experience relative poverty. In many migrant families, both parents are employed, and often in jobs where wages are not particularly high. Migrants have traditionally been employed in jobs which involve shift work. When both partners are involved in shift work, families are more subject to stress. However shift work is often essential in order to satisfy basic needs. Non-English speaking migrants who have arrived in Australia within the last five years experience much higher unemployment rates than migrants who have been in Australia for more than five years.

CHILDREN

As the value of real wages and social security benefits have declined, and levels of unemployment have increased, the number of single-parent families have increased as have the number of children living in poverty. It has been estimated that the number of children living in poverty has increased from 6 per cent of all children in 1972–73 to 21 per cent of all children in 1985–86.[7] As the economic recession extended into the 1990s, it is expected that the number of children living in poverty has also increased.

As poverty perpetuates poverty, it is necessary to intervene in the cycle of poverty to improve the life chances of children living in poverty. While the economic costs of doing this may be high now, the social and economic costs will be larger in the future. Children living in poverty are likely to have fewer educational qualifications and fewer work skills than children from higher socioeconomic backgrounds. The poverty cycle means less education, fewer skills, low-paid jobs and a greater chance of long periods of unemployment. It is necessary to break

Figure 7.5 Voluntary agencies often provide support for children and young people. (Photo: Salvation Army)

7 H. Brownlee & A. King, op. cit., p. 123.

into this poverty cycle and provide children with the resources to participate in society and to become competent members of society. To do this means that the adults of the future will be less dependent upon society for social and financial support.

The first six years of life is the most rapid stage of development physically, socially and intellectually. Children during this stage, who are denied the opportunities to develop fully through a lack of stimulating experiences and participation in society, are less likely to develop into competent members of society. Overseas evidence shows a relationship between poverty and poor health of children. Poor health can inhibit development of children during the early years of life and in the future.

Studies in the USA over a twenty year period show that children enrolled in good quality child-care centres for at least two years, have fewer school absences and less grade repetitions, higher levels of post-secondary education and higher levels of earnings, than children who did not have access to pre-school experiences.[8] There is a great need to expand early childhood services so all children have access to pre-schools, kindergartens or child-care centres. Unfortunately there are insufficient places in early childhood organisations for all children to attend. For low-income families, the costs of child-care centres or pre-schools may be too high and if government centres or pre-schools are available in the area the waiting lists may be very long.

Apart from expansion of early childhood services, many social scientists have also stressed the need for parent education programs and the expansion of employment re-training programs, in order to allow parents living in poverty the opportunity to obtain workforce skills and be able to re-enter the workforce. While some schemes have been initiated in the past, and lately expanded, there is still a great need for intervention in the poverty cycle.

Children, unlike adults, cannot be blamed for their poverty, yet these same children now living in poverty are likely to be the adults living in poverty a generation from now. Poverty carries a cost for all of society, not just for the poor. These costs are both economic and social. Economically, the costs are great to those experiencing the poverty as well as to society, which has to support social welfare expenditure. Secondly, children living in poverty sustain a social disadvantage in that they do not acquire the skills and competence for social functioning in society.

It is for this reason that the focus on poverty has transferred from

---

8 D. Edgar, 'Family problems: The cost–benefits of Prevention', in *Family Matters*, Australian Institute of Family Studies, no. 25, December 1989, p.43.

adults living in poverty to children living in poverty. It is easy to blame adults for their own poverty, but it is impossible to blame children for the poverty in which they live.

YOUTH

The incidence of unemployment is greater for youth than for adults. In August 1967, 3.3 per cent of youth aged 15–19 years in the labour force were unemployed; by 1990 the figure was over 20 per cent.[9] The number of full-time jobs available for teenagers has decreased, yet there has been a dramatic increase in the number of part-time jobs.

Family circumstances, including family disharmony and family breakdown, may mean it is not possible for young people to remain in the family home. Youth unemployment itself can be a cause of family disharmony as it can create conflict and tension. Further, in order to obtain employment, young people may have to leave home. Youth with limited education and few skills are unlikely to find employment during an economic recession.

Long-term unemployed youth are more likely to have been born into, and raised in, low-income families. A major contributing factor to poverty is lack of education and training and consequent low income. This cycle of poverty is perpetuated as children in low-income families are less likely to complete school and obtain post-school qualifications, and are more likely to be in unskilled occupations, which attract low wages.

Unemployed youth are effectively dependent on their families, because Job Search Allowance (introduced in 1988) does not provide enough income for youth to live independently. Job Search Allowance is also subject to a parental income and assets test. While youth between the ages of 16 and 18 years of age who are not living with their families are entitled to the Young Homeless Allowance, in addition to the Job Search Allowance, many young people in this situation would be living in relative poverty as a result of housing costs.

Unemployment for young people has implications not just for the individuals themselves but also for their families. Many young unemployed people leave home because of economic stress in the family but even if they qualify for the Young Homeless Allowance, they too are likely to experience economic stress.

---

9 Australian Bureau of Statistics, *Social Indicators* no. 4, Canberra, 1984, p.189.

Single-parent families

The Poverty Commission found that single-parent families ranked high in the groups of people living in poverty. Since the Commission's original findings, the Family Law Act was introduced and the number of single-parent families has increased dramatically. It must be noted that the increase was not due solely to the Family Law Act but rather to interrelated social, economic, political and legal factors. While the number of single-parent families has stabilised in the last few years, they are now the largest group of people living in poverty. As the majority of single-parent families are headed by a female, a very large number of women and their dependent children are living in poverty. The increase in the number of female-headed single-parent families has contributed to the feminisation of poverty.

The number of single-parent families living in poverty increased from 33.8 per cent in 1972–73 to 46.2 per cent by 1981–82, and by 1990 the number had increased to approximately 50 per cent. Further, the number of female-headed single-parent families living in poverty has increased from 37.5 per cent to over 50 per cent, while the number of male-headed single-parent families living in poverty has increased from 16 per cent to 19 per cent.[10] This difference is due in part to the fact that there are more female-headed single-parent families and, despite equal pay, women earn less than men. Secondly, a greater proportion of female-headed single parents rely on social welfare for income support than do male-headed single-parent families.

In 1986, 14.6 per cent of all families with dependent children were single-parent families and of all single-parent families, 83.9 per cent were receiving income support from social security payments. However, by 1990, 46 per cent of mothers in single-parent families were in the workforce, either full-time or part-time.

The majority of single-parent families are headed by females yet many do not have the resources to participate in the workforce. Child care is often not available and if it is, the costs may not make it worthwhile to work. Further, work-related costs and the physical and emotional energy required to undertake two full-time roles alone may not make paid employment feasible. Money earned in the workforce may not be a lot more than would be received from social security income support. This is compounded by the reality that females, despite equal pay, earn less than males.

---

10 B. Cass, 'Children's poverty and labour market issues: Confronting the causes', in D. Edgar, D. Keane & P. McDonald (eds), *Child Poverty*, pp. 159–160.

Large families

Large families are subject to relative poverty, especially if they are dependent on a single or low income. The more children in a family, the greater the amount of income required to feed, clothe and house a family. As the number of children in a family increases there is less chance of the children acquiring higher education and other opportunities available in society. After single-parent families, the next largest group in poverty are large families. Between 1975 and 1986 the proportion of families with four or more children living in poverty increased from 7 per cent to 40.7 per cent.[11] Research also indicates that there are more two-parent families with two and three children living in poverty.

Large families are also more likely to be single-income families as the financial costs of child care and the organisation required for both adult partners to work in a family where the children are young does not make workforce participation a viable proposition, particularly if the potential earnings are not high.

The Aged

In 1975 the Australian Commission of Inquiry into Poverty determined that the largest group of people living in poverty were those over 65 years of age. The aged have been replaced by single-parent families as the largest group living on or below the poverty line. However, the aged are still at risk to poverty, particularly those who rely on social welfare benefits and who are renting housing. Pensioners who own their own accommodation are far less likely to experience relative poverty. Also, the increasing trend to contribute to superannuation means that more aged people will have retirement incomes higher than pensions paid by social security. Income security for the aged is discussed in more detail in the next chapter.

Aborigines

This group is probably the most disadvantaged in our society, having the worst health and housing, and the lowest educational, occupational, economic, social and legal status of any group in Australia. There is no easy solution to the problem and there has been much discussion and argument concerning the preferences and needs of Aborigines.

11 B. Cass, ' Children's poverty and labour market issues', in Edgar, Keane & McDonald, p.101

Generally, Aborigines are poorly paid, have high unemployment rates, and often fail to receive the benefits to which they are entitled. As a result of lack of money, knowledge, education and skills, many Aborigines are living in relative poverty.

It is difficult to make generalisations regarding the housing of Aborigines, as they live in a diverse range of situations and conditions throughout Australia, from major urban areas to settlements on the outskirts of country towns to remote rural areas. Existing evidence indicates that housing occupied by most Aborigines is overcrowded and often substandard. While discrimination against Aborigines is illegal, many people are reluctant to rent accommodation to Aborigines. Dwellings occupied by Aborigines in rural areas are less likely to have gas or electricity, sewerage and water, and bathroom facilities. The housing situation appears to be worse in rural areas than it is in urban areas.

Many Aborigines have been ambivalent about the value of a European-style education for their children, as education has often been seen as a mechanism to remove any remaining Aboriginal culture. School retention rates for Aboriginal children are significantly lower than they are for non-Aboriginal children. In the past two decades considerable attention has been paid to increasing the educational attainments of Aboriginal children. Increasing educational and training attainments is one strategy which can assist in breaking the poverty cycle.

Rural and farm workers

It is difficult to estimate the extent of poverty amongst rural families, particularly those who farm as a means of living. Farmers are subject to both environmental changes and economic changes, both of which can cause great variations in income. In times of world economic recessions and lack of world markets for produce, farmers can be particularly affected. If there is no produce to sell, or a general surplus of produce to sell, income can be very low. During such times it is not easy to sell property and move elsewhere, and in any event the farmer may not have those skills necessary to obtain other employment.

Employment opportunities are more limited in rural areas and for many individuals and families the cost of relocating is too high. Farm workers who do not own properties but work on farms are often retrenched during periods of economic recessions as farmers cannot afford to pay their wages. Both farmers and rural workers are prone to relative poverty.

Disabled and chronically ill

Poverty is frequently associated with an inability to work because of sickness, handicap or chronic illness. While government benefits have increased for disabled people, housing costs can mean living in relative poverty. Handicapped and disabled people are often denied the opportunity to work, or depending upon the degree of handicap, employment options may be very limited. Many handicapped people must take-part-time work, and therefore are more likely to suffer relative poverty. For some people, sudden injury or illness means they can no longer work in the job for which they were trained or qualified. A sudden reduction in income and subsequent difficulties in meeting fixed commitments can cause relative poverty.

Effects of low income and poverty

Poverty does not simply refer to a lack of income, but also to lack of education, employment, power, opportunities and resources, poor health and little access to social and community resources. Poverty means an inequality of access to resources.

Being poor can mean:

- To live in unsuitable accommodation and surroundings.
- To be caught in a poverty cycle from which there is no escape.
- To have low self-esteem.
- To be deprived of the resources and opportunities to realise one's potential.
- To be criticised for being a poor manager.
- To be denied educational opportunities, which in turn may lead to better job prospects and more income.
- To be unable to participate in society.
- To be suffering from malnutrition.
- To be denied access to the best health services available.
- To have few resources for legal assistance.
- To feel constant anxiety about how to make ends meet.
- To be unable to provide opportunities for children.
- To have no savings to use in the event of crisis such as unemployment or illness.
- To have to make choices between alternatives which are all necessary for individual and family wellbeing.
- To live in a constant state of anxiety.

- Having no flexibility in the budget.
- Not being able to provide for the wants and needs of children, e.g. birthdays and Christmas.
- Living in social isolation.
- Not being able to plan for the future.
- Having little choice in the time of purchase, place of purchase, quality of purchase and method of purchase:
  - **a** The poor consumer often cannot take advantage of sales, even though these may offer goods that are needed in a few month's time. The poor consumer has to spend all income on what is presently needed.
  - **b** The poor consumer often has little choice of where to shop. Although groceries may be cheaper at the supermarket two suburbs away, the consumer may not have the transport or the money to get there and bring the groceries home, nor may he or she have anywhere to leave the children while this is done.
  - **c** The poor consumer is often forced to buy inferior goods and foods simply because that is all that can be afforded. It may at times be good management to buy better quality goods, as they last longer, but low income may prevent this practice.
  - **d** It may be good management to buy in quantity if better value is obtained this way, but the poor can usually only afford to provide for immediate needs.
  - **e** When individuals and families in poverty require an item and there is no income available, the only alternative is credit. Credit means paying off the account, plus more in the form of interest.

Housing

Low-income families have the same housing needs as other families, but they often do not have the economic resources required to obtain adequate shelter. For many low-income families, acquiring their own home may never be realised. It is difficult to save for a deposit on a home and the money to cover the costs associated with home purchase because a large proportion of income must be allocated to rent. Often monthly mortgage repayments are comparable to monthly rental payments but saving the initial deposit is difficult when other living expenses have to be met. Families who own or are paying off their homes sustain an advantage during inflation, as values of properties also rise and equity in property is realised. High rentals may mean families are forced to rent cheaper accommodation which may not provide sufficient space for family and individual activities. To live in affordable accommodation may mean a family has to move to an area away from their extended family and social network. This can involve loss of friendships and support networks for both adults and children.

In recent years schemes have been introduced to assist first home buyers and more low-deposit loans are available from many lending authorities, However, in times of high inflation many low-income families have found themselves in a situation where they can no longer afford to pay mortgage repayments as rising interest rates have increased the minimum repayment so much that it is not possible to meet obligations. While low-deposit loans can make housing an affordable alternative, it only does so when families are not overextended in repaying the loan.

Over the past two decades public housing authorities have more seriously addressed the problem of housing for low-income families. Rather than provide public housing in only certain locations, attempts have been made to geographically spread public housing in order to provide an age mix and social mix of residents. This often enables individuals and families to remain in familiar areas, close to family and friends and the community resources with which they are familiar. It also allows for a variety of housing types which is more likely to meet the needs of different families. Rental assistance is now available not only to families who rent in the public sector but to low-income families who rent in the private sector.

CHILDREN AND HOUSING

Housing which provides protection from the environment and has sufficient living space and basic amenities such as heating, lighting, clean water supply and hygienic cooking, washing, and toilet facilities is essential for good health and wellbeing. Many children live in accommodation which does not provide these facilities. Most of these children are in low-income families. Further, many children in low-income families do not have security of accommodation. Moving house requires a child to make considerable adjustments to new surroundings, new friends and a new school. While moving house may not necessarily be stressful it can be if it happens frequently. Frequent moving can also have negative effects on a child's educational progress.

The Australian Bureau of Statistics *Internal Migration Survey, 1987* found that children in single-parent families were twice as likely to have changed residence in the past twelve months.[12] Further, the 1986 *Income Distribution Survey* found that 94 per cent of children in couple-families lived in a separate house compared to only 70 per cent of

12 *Australia's Children 1989*, p.18.

children in single-parent families. Only 2 per cent of children in couple-families lived in high rise accommodation whereas 12 per cent of children in single-parent families lived in high rise accommodation.[13] On the basis of these figures it is likely that many children in single-parent families have limited space for playing and for outdoor activities.

SOCIAL SERVICES AND PROGRAMS FOR FAMILIES

Over two and a half million people are living almost entirely on social security benefits and, as a result, are living on or near the poverty line. If the number of people who are living on very low incomes is added to this figure, the number of people living in or near poverty is probably over three million. While social welfare benefits have increased significantly in the past ten years, these benefits are still inadequate and the large majority of pensioners and beneficiaries are at risk to poverty.

PENSIONS AND BENEFITS

Most pensions and benefits are subject to an income and/or assets test. Income does not just include wages. It also includes interest, dividends, profits, superannuation and rent. Assets do not include the pensioner's home and surrounding land but do include savings, investments, cars, caravans, boats, businesses, farms, household contents and personal effects. Pensioners can have assets to a certain value before the pension rate is affected.

Pensions and benefits are fairly standardised, thus rates for unemployment, aged, special and sickness benefits are fairly similar. Certain conditions including waiting periods apply for all these benefits. Payment rates for these benefits are adjusted during the year, so it is necessary to contact an office of the Department of Social Security to obtain exact details of income support. Also, recipients of these benefits are often entitled to additional benefits, including Family Allowance Supplement and rent assistance. In 1987, the amount of income was increased that could be earnt before a reduction in pension or benefit occurred. This allows pensioners and social welfare beneficiaries to undertake some part-time or casual work without sustaining a significant reduction in pension or benefit.

Pensioner health benefits cards and transport concession cards are issued to all age, sickness and special benefit pensioners, disability

---

13 *1986 Income Distribution Survey*

support pensioners, sole pensioners as well as people receiving Job Search Allowance and Newstart Allowance. These concession cards allow pensioners to obtain discounts on many services including transport, telephone, health, council rates, electricity, gas, water and sewerage rates and entertainment. Concessions may vary from state to state. It is expected by the end of 1993 that these cards be replaced by a new pensioner concession card.

Job Search Allowance

This was introduced in 1988 and replaced junior unemployment benefits. This allowance is payable thirteen weeks after a young person leaves school and is payable to young people aged 16 and 17 years. The payment rate is based on the assumption that a young person will receive some form of financial support from his family.

Young Homeless Allowance

This allowance is paid to 16 and 17 year olds who receive Job Search Allowance or Sickness or Special Benefits, and to full-time students above the minimum school-leaving age provided they satisfy the strict definition of homelessness.

Family Assistance Package

During the late 1980s the Commonwealth Government made a number of changes to social welfare in an attempt to reduce poverty, and in particular child poverty. These changes have occurred within the framework of the Family Assistance Package and have affected Family Allowance and Family Allowance Supplement.

In 1987 the Family Allowance became income-tested, although the Social Security Review had recommended that it be retained as a universal payment to all families. The Australian Institute of Family Studies maintains that the Family Allowance should be a universal payment made to all children as it is a universal responsibility of all taxpayers to provide for the future adults of this country. At the same time as the Commonwealth Government income-tested the Family Allowance, the Family Allowance Supplement was introduced to replace the Family Income Supplement. The Family Allowance Supplement provides assistance to both working and non-working low-income families with children. The allowance is income-tested.

Prior to 1989 the Family Allowance had only been increased on an ad hoc basis whereas other pensions and benefits had been indexed in accordance with movements in the Consumer Price Index since the mid-1970s. Prior to 1989, families receiving the Family Allowance had effectively sustained a reduction in real income as the allowance had only been increased once between 1976 and 1989 despite high inflation rates. Since 1989 the Family Allowance has been indexed and is adjusted twice a year in accordance with movements in the Consumer Price Index.

Rent assistance

Rent assistance has been paid to pensioners and social welfare beneficiaries for some time, and in 1987 the scheme was expanded to include assistance to low-income families who are renting private accommodation. Expansion of rent assistance indicated a recognition by the government of the insufficient stock of public housing.

Children's Services Program

The Children's Services Program has also been extended to support workforce participation by providing families with dependent children, especially low-income families, access to a wider range of child-care services which are affordable. Priority has been given to increasing the number of child-care places in child-care centres, family daycare, occasional-care centres and outside-school-hours care services. Fee relief is provided to assist in the costs of child care. A further 30 000 child-care places were established between 1989 and 1992.

Child Support Agency

In 1988 the Commonwealth Government introduced the Child Support Agency to ensure that following the breakdown of marriage, non-custodial parents continue to provide support for their children. This agency has been set up under the control of the Commissioner of Taxation with the aim of providing a more reliable method of child maintenance collection. The amount of money paid by the non-custodial parent to the custodial parent depends upon the income of both parents, number of children and ages of children. The collection of child support is by automatic withholding of salary or wages by the employer in the case of PAYE taxpayers, or in the case of self-employed people by direct payments to the Child Support Agency.

Sole parents

The Commonwealth Government has also introduced programs aimed at enhancing education, training and employment opportunities for lone parents. These programs include JET—Job Education Training—and New Start aimed at the long-term unemployed aged 21 to 54 years. These programs aim at improving the economic wellbeing of their children through a shift from dependence on government pensions or benefits to paid employment. From 1987, sole parents have also been paid an additional allowance for dependent children as part of the Family Assistance Package.

Educational and training assistance

Austudy is the Commonwealth Department of Employment, Education and Training's main student assistance scheme. It is a means-tested allowance payable to students aged 16 years and over, and helps full-time students from low-income families. Abstudy is means-tested assistance available to Aboriginal and Torres Strait Islander students who are studying full-time at any approved secondary school, approved primary, special school or tertiary institution.

Programs such as Jobtrain, Skillshare and Job Placement and Employment Training Program (JPET) are initiatives which have been funded by the Federal Government to assist individuals to acquire skills and training appropriate for the workforce. Details of these schemes are available through CES offices.

Voluntary organisations

Voluntary organisations play an important role in assisting individuals and families living in poverty, as well as raising awareness of the extent of poverty and lobbying governments to take further initiatives to reduce poverty. These organisations include the Smith Family, Red Cross, Legacy, St Vincent de Paul Society and the Brotherhood of St. Laurence. Apart from providing income supplementation, these organisations also assist in providing food, clothing and often, emergency shelter.

Other initiatives

While much has been done to eliminate poverty, the elimination of poverty cannot occur solely through income support. The poor are not a fixed group of people that must exist in society or a group of people that society must always support. Many social scientists argue that there is a need to restructure society in order to increase the quality of life for those currently living in poverty, and thus narrow the gap between the rich and poor. Individuals and families living in poverty need to have greater access to the resources provided by society in order to reduce social isolation, increase competence, be able to participate in society and break out of the poverty cycle. The poverty cycle must be intercepted during childhood and youth.

One initiative which is gaining strength is the DEET (Department of Employment, Education and Training) proposal of 1990. DEET has proposed along with many other individuals and groups that all youth need some post-compulsory school training and/or education. DEET argues for a comprehensive work and training program for all young people under the age of 20 years. Such a program would ensure that every young person would be in full-time training or in a job which provided skills training.

Don Edgar, founding director of the Australian Institute of Family Studies, maintains there is a need to focus on the underlying causes of poverty and develop strategies for eliminating poverty other than through direct income support. These strategies need to include greater assistance with the costs required to raise and educate children, expanded adult training and retraining programs, increased child-care facilities and services, and family support services. Edgar maintains that we must move away from describing how poor people are, to discussions of how poverty can be eliminated. Society cannot afford poverty as it carries a cost for everyone, not just for those living in poverty.[14]

MANAGEMENT DECISIONS

While it is obvious that many families in Australia do not have sufficient income, no matter how well it is managed, there are some families who are living in relative poverty even though they earn an income sufficient to cover more than basic needs. This may occur as a result of short-term or long-term mismanagement and/or lack of knowledge and skills. Also, some low-income families may not be aware of consumer rights, sound consumer practices and budgeting techniques. Sound consumer practices and management skills outlined

---

14 D. Edgar, 'Social costs of poverty', in D. Edgar, D. Keane & P. McDonald (eds), *Child Poverty*, p.3.

in this section cannot be applied to those families living in poverty through no fault of their own.

For a budget to be workable, it must be flexible. It must allocate money to fixed needs and expenses, it must allow for incidental expenses and it must provide for savings to cover unexpected expenses such as replacement of and repairs to equipment and appliances.

In a household budget or financial plan, money has to be allocated for the following:

- Housing, whether mortgage repayments or rent.
- Food and expendable household items.
- Clothing and laundry.
- Transport, including fares and/or petrol, plus maintenance, insurance and registration of car if owned.
- Repayments for loans, e.g. for car or other purchases.
- Medical expenses and insurances.
- Entertainment, recreation and leisure activities.
- Council and water rates, if accommodation is owned.
- Telephone account and rental, if connected.
- Incidentals, e.g. newspapers, stationery.
- Savings for unexpected expenses, household insurance, replacement and repair of appliances etc.

The proportion spent on each of the above will vary with the size and composition of a family, as well as resources and values. The majority of families in Australia do not have unlimited financial resources and many difficult decisions are necessary in order for families to maintain a standard of living within a budget. Decisions are influenced not only by the availability of resources, but also by the values and goals of the individual and the group. Decisions about utilising income include:

- How much income to allocate to needs and wants?
- Which method of payment to use? How much credit to use and from what source?
- Where to shop to ensure best dollar value? Is transport available?
- How much reliance to be placed on advertising as a source of information?
- How much extra to pay to ensure good quality? Is this always important? Will the extra money spent really ensure good quality?
- When to buy? Will it be cheaper at a later date or at a sale? Will it still be available?
- If food is purchased in bulk, is there sufficient storage space? What quantity of food to buy to ensure money is saved but not wasted?

Poverty is a value-laden social issue. People who have not experienced poverty or a sudden drop in income may find it difficult to perceive living a day-to-day existence. Some people believe poverty to be an essential part of a technological society; some see it as the fault of the people in poverty; others believe such an unequal distribution of resources within a society to be wrong.

Most Australians rank family life as one of the most important aspects of their lives, but for families to remain intact an adequate income must be available to provide for those needs and wants considered appropriate in our society.

REVIEW QUESTIONS

1 Distinguish between relative poverty and absolute poverty.
2 How is relative poverty often defined?
3 Explain the differences between the relative poverty cycle and the absolute poverty cycle.
4 Describe the effects that relative poverty may have on children.
5 Why is it difficult to break out of the poverty cycle?
6 Why may living in poverty contribute to low self-esteem?
7 Outline the factors which may contribute to relative poverty in Australia.
8 Why are lack of education and training major contributing factors to poverty?
9 Why is housing a major cause of poverty for some families?
10 How have inflation and the economic recession contributed to poverty?
11 What is meant by the 'poverty line'?
12 Explain the difference between the before-housing poverty line and the after-housing poverty line.
13 List the groups at risk to poverty in Australian society.
14 In Australia, which is the largest group of people living in poverty? Explain why this is so.
15 For aged people, what is the biggest determinant of poverty?
16 Why has youth unemployment increased during the last decade? What recommendations have been made to reduce youth unemployment?
17 Why has there been a change in focus from people living in poverty to children living in poverty?

18 When unemployment happens to older workers, what may be the short-term and long-term implications?
19 Outline the decisions that may have to be made when developing a budget or financial plan.
20 Outline the initiatives that have been implemented as part of the Family Package in order to reduce child poverty.
21 Why is it important to eliminate child poverty?

Case study 7.1
A family in relative poverty

Paul and Jill Smith have been married for five years. They have three children aged 4 years, 2 years, and 6 months respectively. Paul left school at 15 and currently works as a labourer at a factory about 8 kilometres from home. Jill is at home with the children, having been married at 18 and giving up work for the birth of her first child. Jill worked as a cashier after leaving school at 15 years of age, and Paul has worked in unskilled trades since leaving school at 16. Paul's net income (i.e. after tax) per week is $380. He rarely has the opportunity to work overtime, so this can not be taken into account in the family's budget.

Paul and Jill rent a two-bedroom unit for $140 per week but find it far too small for five people. They would like to get something larger, but cannot afford a higher rent. Paul and Jill can barely cover costs of rent and other basic needs and have little chance for saving for a housing deposit. They have applied for public housing accommodation but have been told they may have to wait up to three years if they wish to remain relatively close to their family and friends, and to Paul's employment. Paul and Jill have had to use credit to purchase and replace household items. They have credit card debts over $4000 and are experiencing difficulties in paying these off as they can barely afford to meet the minimum monthly repayments of $200.

Paul would like to retrain to improve his employment prospects but could only do so at night. He is concerned about being at home less and not being able to share with Jill some of the burden of caring for the young children. Paul and Jill cannot afford to send their eldest child to pre-school. Their nearest community pre-school, where they would be eligible for fee relief, is too far away. Jill would have to take all children on public transport to use this service. Jill feels anxious and discouraged much of the time, as she finds the physical environment in which they live is not suitable for children to play, either inside or outside their unit. Finances do not allow Jill to go out much and without private transport it is difficult to manage the children on outings by herself.

QUESTIONS

1 Underneath is a framework for a budget or financial plan. Complete a budget for this family. To do so you will need to contact your local office of the Department of Social Security to obtain the most recent rates for available social services.

Net income: $380
Plus social welfare:
Family Allowance _______
Family Allowance Supplement _______
Rent Assistance _______
Total income _______

Weekly expenses:
Housing _______
Food and household items _______
Transport _______
Clothing _______
Repayments for loans _______
Medical expenses/insurance _______
Electricity and/or gas _______
Replacement and maintenance of household items _______
Telephone _______
Incidentals _______
Savings _______
Total expenses _______

2 Do you think the budget you have devised is realistic? Justify your answer.

3 Does this income provide a standard of living considered acceptable in our society?

4 In late 1993 the average weekly wage, for males, was approximately $614 (before tax). First, determine the net income of this wage and then determine the 'poverty line' based on 60 per cent of the average equal wage. Considering the housing costs for Paul and Jill, are they living in relative poverty?

5 For this family to have an acceptable standard of living, what level of income would they need?

6 What strategies could be developed by governments and community organisations to assist this family to break out of the poverty cycle?
7 If this family continues to live in poverty what may be the long-term outcomes for the children?
8 Explain why poverty perpetuates poverty?
9 Which community resources could assist this family?
10 Contact the Australian Bureau of Statistics—they can provide recent information on average weekly earnings. Using the current average weekly wage, establish the current 'poverty line'. Try and devise a budget for a family of four living on the 'poverty line'.

CASE STUDY 7.2

THE SINGLE MOTHER

Elizabeth is 20 and has a 6-month-old son, David. David's father and Elizabeth decided not to get married when Elizabeth found she was pregnant, as neither was certain of the chance of a stable marriage. Against her parent's wishes, Elizabeth decided to have and keep her child, although she realised she would encounter many problems in doing so.

Elizabeth completed an office skills course when she left school at 16 years and worked in a clerical job before David was born. Although she misses work, financially and socially, she is unable to find a way to have the baby minded and resume employment. She would like to return to the workforce when David goes to school. She feels very lonely, as she does not have much in common with her friends now, nor does she have the money to go out with them. She spends most of her time watching television when she is not caring for David. She has to budget very carefully to pay rent on her one-bedroom flat and to provide the necessities for herself and her son.

QUESTIONS

1 What government benefits is Elizabeth entitled to? What would her total income be? Compare this to the average weekly wage for all employees. And for females?
2 What personal resources does Elizabeth have?

3 What community resources may be available to Elizabeth of which she is unaware? How can she find out about these?
4 When Elizabeth decided to have and keep the baby, do you think she was aware of the full implications?
5 Are there any alternative courses of action available to Elizabeth which may increase her economic resources?
6 How may Elizabeth use community resources to reduce her loneliness, and provide greater opportunities for social interaction with other people?
7 If Elizabeth decides not to return to the workforce for some time, what problems may arise?
8 As David grows up, what decisions will Elizabeth have to make?

Case study 7.3
The unemployed family

Kathy and Rod have four children—three boys and one girl—whose ages range from 3–12 years. Until six months ago Rod was employed as a supervisor with a company that produced plastic products, but the firm has now gone out of business. Rod has tried to find work and is willing to take any job. He has applied for many jobs through the newspapers and the CES. While he has had quite a few interviews he has not yet secured a job. Rod completed high school but has very few formal qualifications and experience in only one industry.

Kathy and Rod and the children live in the home they purchased 10 years ago; they are still paying this off and their monthly housing repayments are $700. They are also paying off the family car and must meet monthly repayments of $200. Financial commitments nearly exceed the money they are entitled to from social welfare.

Kathy has not worked for some years, but since Rod's retrenchment she has managed to obtain some private housecleaning for two days a week to help ease some of the financial burdens. Rod received very little redundancy money when he was retrenched, as the company he had worked for was bankrupt. All of the accumulated savings have been used and Rod is fairly despondent and worried about the future. In this family the situation has caused stress and disharmony as Kathy and Rod realise they may have to sell their housing in order to meet financial obligations.

QUESTIONS

1 Why has relative poverty occurred in this family?
2 Contact your local office of the Department of Social Security to determine all the social welfare benefits available to this family.
3 With social welfare benefits, what is the total family income?
4 How much income can Kathy earn before the unemployment benefit would be reduced?
5 Try and devise a budget for this family. Is it possible to do this? Why or why not?
6 How can Kathy and Rod continue to manage on their present income?
7 What problems may this family face if Rod's unemployment is long-term?
8 What community resources are available to assist this family?

8

THE AGED

THE AGED POPULATION

The first issue to be addressed when discussing the group of people in society known as 'the aged' is at what age a person becomes old or elderly and therefore a member of the group often referred to as the aged.

In setting a general retirement age of 65 for men and 60 for women, society sets this group of people apart from the rest of the community. Does this mean when a person reaches the age of 65 or 60 he or she is of no productive use to society and is thus classified as 'old'? Does an individual become old not when he or she reaches a certain age, but when there is some loss of physical and/or mental abilities? Does an individual become old when he or she retires from the workforce and becomes financially dependent upon the age pension or superannuation?

Although some companies no longer insist on a fixed retirement age and allow some employees to work beyond 65 years of age, the majority adhere to a fixed retirement age. In recent years in Australia, some state governments have modified regulations regarding the mandatory retirement age and have allowed employees to continue working past the age of 65 years. At the same time however, many employees in both state and private work sectors have been retrenched or made redundant well before 65 years of age. For many people who may wish to work until they are 65, their goal may not be realised, as it has become difficult for older employees to find employment during an economic recession. Workers who are unemployed in their 50s may face a situation where they never work again. Many economists have argued that raising the retirement age would cause even greater unemployment, as it would mean fewer jobs would be available for younger members of the workforce.

Indeed, during the economic recession of the 1980s and 1990s it became apparent that younger workers have been valued more than older workers, and the experience and skills of older employees have been devalued. It would appear that innovation is valued more than wisdom and experience. This is a situation which does not occur in all developed societies.

The retirement ages for men and women were determined in 1871 when life expectancy at birth was approximately 42 years of age. Retirement as we know it would not have existed last century for many people. At the time the retirement age for males was set at 65 years of age and the retirement age for females was set five years lower, at 60 years of age, female life expectancy was, as it is now, greater.

For some individuals, old age may occur at 50 years; for others it may not occur until 80 years of age. It is obviously impossible to find a definition for that group of people which society regards as aged or elderly. The aged are not a homogeneous group—they will have varying physical and mental capabilities, differing amounts of resources at their disposal, different problems with which to cope, and many will have access to a wide range of social and family support systems, whereas others will not.

Our society tends to determine whether people are old on the basis of chronological age, and we are often not very sensitive to the individual differences that exist among the aged population. Ageing is a very personal adjustment: for some people the adjustment to growing old is very minor while for others it may be major. The aged are often defined as those in the last one-third to one-quarter of the life span. Given that people may now spend more time in retirement than they did in the workforce, this may be an inappropriate definition. Neugarten proposes categories for the aged population which combine chronological and functional criteria. These categories are *young–old* (55–65 years), *middle–old* (65–75), and old–old (over 75 years). Thus, the stigma of age is transferred to the oldest, usually physically weakest group, and the young–old and middle-old are more likely to retain status and prestige.[1]

Australia's aged population is spread across an age span of thirty to forty years, consisting of people with differing needs and wants. Further, the aged population is differentiated by age, sex, socioeconomic status, ethnicity and health status. Socioeconomic status is an important determinant of wellbeing in old age, as it is at any stage of the life cycle. It is thus very difficult to generalise about the characteristics of the aged population.

STATUS AND PRESTIGE

Some societies such as Japan and Thailand value the experience and wisdom of older employees, and in traditional Chinese society, old age is highly honoured. In traditional Aboriginal society it is the older men who exercise authority and transmit the culture to younger generations. While many Aboriginal aged people live with families, they are not necessarily those of their own children or grandchildren. There is also concern that as young Aboriginal people enter the mainstream culture the status of Aboriginal elders may diminish. In the societies referred to above, respect and affection for the elderly are shown in such ways as honorific language and priority in seating and serving.

In Australian society old age is often seen as a problem: the aged are regarded as a burden for society. Also, in societies where extended residential households have not been common, the aged are unlikely to be seen as heads of households. In Japan, about three-quarters of the aged continue to live with their families.

Perhaps in earlier times when life expectancy was lower and the proportion of people who survived past 65 years of age was far smaller, it may have been regarded as a special achievement to reach old age, and status and prestige were conferred on old people. The rapid growth in computer and information technology may have assisted in eroding the value once placed upon the expertise, knowledge and experience of older people.

Through restricted access to social and economic resources, physical wellbeing and political power, the social status of elderly people is often less than that of younger generations. Aged people who have a financially comfortable retirement are more likely to retain social status and prestige because they have the economic resources to continue to participate in society. For aged people who lose significant economic

---

1 V.J. Callan, *Australian Minority Groups*, Sydney, 1986, p. 97.

power when they retire from the workforce, loss of social status and prestige may be very significant.

LIFE EXPECTANCY

Life expectancy refers to the average number of years a person of a given age and sex might expect to live. Table 8.1 shows the life expectancy for males and females in Australia from 1881 to 1991. This table shows life expectancy for males and females at birth and at 65 years of age.

Throughout this century life expectancy has continued to increase. Males and females born in 1991 can expect to live until they are 74.4 years and 80.3 years old respectively. The difference in expectation of life between males and females is gradually reducing. In 1986 females at birth were expected to live 6.3 years longer than males, while in 1991 the difference has reduced to 5.9 years. This gap between the life expectancies of males and females is expected to continue to narrow. The Australian Bureau of Statistics has projected that by 2031 life expectancy at birth will have increased to 77 years for males and to 84 years for females.

Due to advances in medical science and technology, increased public awareness of health issues, better living conditions and improvements in diet and community health care, life expectancy in most developed countries has passed the 70-year mark for males, and for females the 80-year mark. One hundred years ago both males and females would have little time left after leaving the workforce to spend in retirement; now they may have thirty to forty years, or even longer.

Table 8.1 Life expectancy in Australia, 1881–1981

	At Birth		At 65 years of age	
Year	**Males**	**Females**	**Males**	**Females**
1881–90	47.2	50.8	11.1	12.3
1901–10	55.2	58.8	11.3	12.9
1932–34	63.5	67.1	12.4	14.2
1953–55	67.1	72.8	12.3	15.0
1965–67	67.6	74.2	12.2	15.7
1975–77	69.6	75.6	13.1	17.1
1983	72.1	78.7	14.2	18.3
1990	73.9	80.0	15.2	19.0
1991	74.4	80.3	15.5	19.2

Source: Australian Bureau of Statistics data

AGEING POPULATION

A major finding of the 1991 census is the increase in the proportion of people aged 65 years and over. This proportion increased from 8.5 per cent of the total population in 1971 to 10.6 per cent in 1986 and to 11.3 per cent in 1991. In contrast, the proportion of children (under 15 years of age) in the population fell from 28 per cent in 1971, to 23.3 per cent in 1986 and to 22.3 per cent in 1991. The ageing of Australia's population is not significantly due to increased life expectancy. It is a result of the increase in the proportion of the population aged 65 years

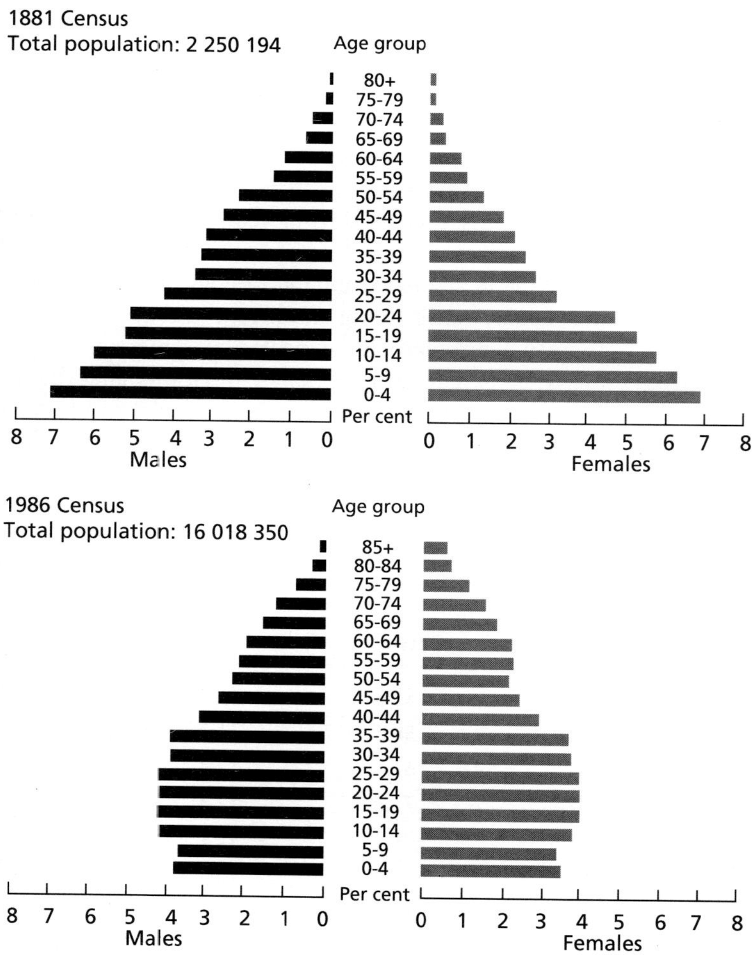

Figure 8.1 Population age pyramids, 1881 and 1985.
Source: Australian Bureau of Statistics

and over and the decrease in the proportion of the population aged 15 years and less.

Australia's population has been ageing for the past one hundred years, as shown in Figure 8.1. By 1980, the aged population had doubled since the Second World War and is expected to double again by the year 2001. The increase in the aged population is a result of high fertility levels in earlier decades, lower mortality rates and previous high migration rates which also assisted in increasing fertility levels. The aged population will accelerate in the year 2012 when the children born in the post-Second World War 'baby boom' reach retirement age.

CHARACTERISTICS OF THE AGED POPULATION

- Decreases in mortality this century have meant that the number of people surviving to the age of 75 years has doubled, the number of people surviving to the age of 85 years or more has tripled, and those surviving to the age of 95 years has increased eight times. This very significant increase in those living past 80 years of age has implications for health care and community services as the number of people who suffer from diseases such as Alzheimer's is expected to increase.
- During the next twenty years the population aged 65 years and over will rise by about 48 per cent, the population aged 75 years and over by 118 per cent and that aged 85 years and over by 145 per cent.[2]
- In the period between 1976 and 1981 about 75 per cent of the aged population were dependent upon the age pension for income. In 1986 this figure had fallen to 65 per cent. It is expected that the number of aged people dependent on pensions is likely to decrease. At the same time, however, the economic recession has meant that the value of superannuation benefits for many have been eroded. Financial security for many retired people is uncertain as they wonder how they will survive on a limited income for an unknown number of years. At the same time, however, more aged people own their housing and more have invested in retirement income than was the case in the past.
- Current government policy is to encourage both male and female employees to prepare for their retirement by contributing to superannuation while they are in the workforce. Also, industry-wide superannuation is being phased in to ensure that by the end of the century all employees will be contributing to superannuation.
- Over the last century there have been significant increases in the

2 A. Graycar &A. Jamrozik, *How Australians Live*, Melbourne, 1989, p. 248.

proportion of men and women who have married and an increase in the average time span between marriage and widowhood. While a greater number of marriages end in divorce now than at the beginning of this century, remarriage is still popular, particularly for men. There will therefore be more married couples than widows and widowers surviving into old age. Spouses can provide mutual support, enhancing quality of life and contributing to increased life expectancy.

- There has been a tendency in the last two decades for older people to stay in independent and separate households much longer after the death of a spouse. It has often been suggested that the care of the aged was not a problem when extended families were common. However, it must be noted that Australia has never had a history of extended families living in the one household. At the same time, there are more older people in Australia who live with their adult children than live in nursing homes and hostels.
- About 10 per cent of the aged live in extended family situations and as the population ages there will be implications for the public and private costs of caring for the aged. While residential extended families are not really common in Australia, extended family networks are readily apparent. Families develop and share kinship networks, communicating with each other in person or by telephone, celebrating family occasions together and helping and assisting each other. With increased life expectancy, four-generation families are likely to become more common resulting in even more emphasis on reciprocal relations between generations.
- Approximately 80 per cent of aged people are owner–purchasers of their housing and about 18.5 per cent rent housing. Of aged persons living in rented dwellings about half live in public housing. As the age of a person increases there is more chance that he or she will live in a non-private dwelling such as a nursing home. Approximately 40 per cent of those over the age of 85 years live in non-private dwellings.
- Women are currently the overwhelming majority of the aged population. At age 65 years, there are 100 men for every 108 women. At age 75 years, there are 100 men for every 137 women and at the age of 85 years there are 268 women for every 100 men.[3] These male–female ratios are likely to decrease as the gap between life expectancy for males and females narrows.
- There are more aged women living alone than men living alone. The number of people over the age of 75 years living alone is increasing

3 Graycar & Jamrozik, *How Australians Live*, p. 254.

and this has implications for the health and welfare services that must be provided in order to assist the aged living alone. Approximately 8 per cent of elderly people live in non-private dwellings, including nursing homes, hostels and hospitals. The majority of these people are over 75 years of age and there are significantly more women than men living in nursing homes and hostels. The health and medical factors which are most likely to contribute to an elderly person over the age of 75 years entering a hostel or nursing home are immobility, dementia and incontinence.

- Women are more disadvantaged in terms of income and housing. While 78 per cent of men over the age of 65 years are home owners, only 69 per cent of women over the same age are homeowners.[4] It has been estimated that about 20 per cent of the aged population are poor or very poor. More women than men are in this category.
- In 1966, 23.3 per cent of men aged 65 years and over were in the paid labour force. By 1986 this had dropped to 8.7 per cent. For women the corresponding figures are 4.4 per cent to 2.4 per cent.
- There is a growing number of aged from non-English speaking backgrounds who may be in need of special services as a consequence of language barriers and cultural differences. With the ageing of the post-war migrant population there is a greater proportion of people from non-English speaking backgrounds. Currently, the ethnic groups with the highest proportion of older persons are those from Eastern Europe, the ageing survivors of the post-Second World War immigrants. Such people make up 11 per cent of the aged but by early next century they will comprise approximately 25 per cent.
- Socioeconomic status is an important determinant of wellbeing in old age. Aged people from higher socioeconomic groups retain their capacity to participate in society because of their ability to exercise economic, social and political power. As with all groups in society, the aged also experience unequal access to the resources of society. Access to economic resources, health resources and social resources has an important bearing on the lifestyle and 'quality of life' experienced by the aged.

Needs of the Aged

For the aged to maintain their dignity, independence and individuality, it is the responsibility of society to ensure that their needs are met. For the aged, some needs will diminish in importance, but at the same

4 Graycar & Jamrozik, *How Australians Live*, p. 256.

time new needs will arise. All people have certain physical, social and psychological needs which must be satisfied to achieve a state of wellbeing.

Physical needs include:

- Adequate warmth and shelter are basic needs for all people. Many elderly people have poor blood circulation, and often need more clothing and more warmth. This can mean an increase in heating costs.
- A diet which satisfies both hunger and nutritional requirements.
- Good health; a state of complete mental, social and physical wellbeing.
- Access to health and medical care.
- Satisfaction of sexual needs, needs which society often tends to believe cease in old age.
- Mobility, and the provision of transport to allow people to participate in society and use the available resources.
- Adequate income to provide for these needs.

Figure 8.2 Most elderly people can play a useful and satisfying role in our society. Knitting of garments for grandchildren is a common example. (Photo: M. Lowe)

Psychological needs include:

- Goal-directed activities within an individual's physical and mental capacity, e.g. part-time work, new interests.
- Love and affection from family members and friends.
- Respect from members of the community.
- A sense of belonging and contributing to society by involvement in productive activities.
- Positive attitude toward life.
- Maintenance of individuality and independence.

Social needs include:

- The opportunity to exercise some of the rights and privileges, e.g. authority and prestige, formerly held in the family or workforce. This enhances feelings of being needed and useful.
- The opportunity to perform social roles in the family and community, e.g. mother, father, grandparent, child carer.
- Participation in the overall planning of society, e.g. citizens' groups.
- Social contact and interaction with family members and the rest of society.

Issues for the aged and for society

Increased life expectancy has created many difficulties for the aged relating to retirement, recreation, income, loneliness, health, medical care, dependency and housing. As individuals have different needs and varying amounts of human and non-human resources, there can be no single solutions to the problems that many aged people face. Rather than regard these difficulties as problems it is perhaps more appropriate to regard them as issues which need to be addressed. It cannot be left to the aged alone to solve their economic, social, physical and political problems; society as a whole also has a responsibility to address these problems. Elderly people are no different from younger people in that they need to have an interest and purpose in life to give it meaning.

Retirement and recreation

Upon retirement the aged person faces one of the greatest adjustments in his or her life. Job satisfaction and responsibilities, and financial rewards, may be missed; family routines change; personal associations from work may cease; status which accompanies the work role is lost; and there may be difficulties in finding interests to fill leisure time. Many aged face a 'Catch 22' situation: they have more time for leisure and recreational pursuits, but may not have the money nor the physical capabilities to enjoy it. Although senior citizens' centres do provide for social interaction and for a variety of activities, these cannot always fill the gap that retirement has created.

Many people feel that only work—either full-time or part-time, can provide a feeling of being wanted and useful. Some aged persons do continue working past retirement age, but part-time work for the aged is very scarce. During the past two decades there has been a decline in the labour-force participation of older people. During economic recessions, people may be forced into earlier retirement, when jobs are scarce and re-employment is unlikely. In this situation, people approaching the category of 'aged' may be unable to obtain employment even if they are still competent and capable of working.

Educating the community to have a more positive view of old age, so that it is regarded as a natural part of the life cycle and not a separate phase, may help the aged adjust more easily to retirement and increased leisure time.

INCOME AND HOUSING

It has been suggested that a comfortable retirement requires an income of two-thirds to three-quarters of pre-retirement income. The aged pension does not provide this and even those people who have invested in superannuation schemes may find they have insufficient income to maintain an acceptable standard of living. While some expenses may decrease in old age, such as insurance premiums and mortgage repayments, income is still required to cover expenditure on food, clothing, health, housing-related costs, heating and cooling, and leisure. A satisfactory level of income is required to make retirement comfortable and dignified, and allow for participation in activities in the community.

Aged people who own their own homes are more likely to have a far more comfortable retirement than those who must pay rent for accommodation. Housing costs can take up a significant proportion of income, whether income is obtained from social service benefits, investments or superannuation. Fortunately, aged people have high rates of home ownership in Australia. Results from the 1991 census show that a greater proportion of older people own their housing than was the case some decades ago. Aged people who are dependent on social service benefits and paying rent are more likely to be living in poverty.

Since the Second World War, an increasing number of people have invested in insurance and superannuation schemes in order to have a comfortable life following retirement. Indeed, the federal government has for some time been promoting this, for as Australia's population continues to age, the economy may not be able to afford the costs of income support for an increased aged population.

Younger generations are being encouraged to make provision now

Figure 8.3 Loneliness and social isolation are serious problems for many elderly people in our society.

for their old age. However, 40 per cent of men currently in the workforce are not contributing to superannuation, and many are not contributing a sufficient amount for retirement. A significant amount of money must be allocated to superannuation each week in order to provide for a comfortable retirement income; and many individuals cannot afford to pay anything into a superannuation scheme. For many individuals and families, it is difficult enough to provide for present needs, let alone future needs.

A source of concern is women and superannuation. Many women have had breaks in their workforce participation and have thus ceased contributing to superannuation schemes. While their spouses may belong to a superannuation scheme, if a divorce should occur, a woman may face a severely reduced standard of living in retirement.

LONELINESS AND ISOLATION

Many aged people who live alone are not lonely, because they have opportunities for interaction within their neighbourhood and community, as well as with their family. Loneliness can result, however, when physical incapacity, poor health, or insufficient income reduces mobility and opportunities for interaction. Aged people with no family, or with no family living close by, perhaps face the greatest risk of social isolation. This situation may be exacerbated when a spouse dies, leaving the other partner with many years to spend by themselves.

Many elderly people who become hypochondriacs are really only reaching out for someone, such as a doctor or nurse, to talk to or perhaps to alleviate their loneliness. Some mental disorders may be attributed to loneliness and social isolation. Programs have been initiated whereby younger people of all ages visit the aged in the community in order to interact with them, to understand their problems more fully and to find out about the past.

HEALTH AND NUTRITION

Although the extent differs with each individual, certain physical and mental changes do occur as age increases. Physically, there is a decline in appearance; sight and hearing problems may develop; a general reduction in strength and endurance is evident; there is a decline in sexual potency; and there is greater difficulty in stooping, bending, stretching, lifting etc. Because people now live longer, there is a greater chance they will become chronically ill or physically handicapped.

The aged are subject to strokes, neurological disorders, arthritis, fractured hips, osteoporosis and arteriosclerosis, incontinence and senile dementia. Medical care and technology often mean that the lifespan of aged people suffering from these disabling diseases is prolonged. Many of the aged do not wish to admit to being old or sick, which places a strain on those who live near or with them and many are reluctant to seek medical advice because of the cost. Perhaps the most disabling disease and the one that places the greatest strains upon relatives, nursing staff and the health care system is senile dementia, a condition which is more prevalent in the 85-plus age group. Possibly more than half of nursing home residents suffer from some form of dementia. Incontinence is also a problem which is costly for individuals, families and communities.

If the cost of health care in an ageing population becomes unmanageable, rationing of access could become a reality, particularly when quality of life is considered. Thus, certain treatments and medical technology may only be available for people who are expected to benefit substantially in terms of quality of life, rather than just length of life. Some countries already confine expensive procedures such as organ transplants and kidney dialysis to younger sections of the population.

The aged have certain nutritional needs which, if not satisfied, can lead to more serious health problems. Decreased physical capabilities in some cases may mean that some aged people are not able to prepare adequate meals, and some aged people have little interest in preparing meals for themselves. Low income can mean that some aged people cannot afford to buy foods which will satisfy nutritional requirements. Lack of knowledge, particularly in the case of widowers, whose wives formerly prepared all the meals, may also prevent the elderly person from preparing nutritious meals.

DEPENDENCY AND MOBILITY

Alan Walker, a British social scientist, has identified four types of dependency.[5] These are:

- *life cycle dependency*, which means exclusion from paid work;
- *physical and mental dependency*, which relates to physical, social and psychological incapacity;
- *political dependency*, which is a restriction of the freedom of an individual to determine his or own course of action;

---

5 Graycar & Jamrozik, *How Australians Live*, p. 263.

- *financial and economic dependency*, which involves reliance wholly or partly upon the state for support.

Perhaps one of the greatest needs of the aged is for independence. At the same time, however, the aged also want to feel that they are useful and needed, and can contribute to the wellbeing of other people. Aged people have a greater chance of maintaining independence if they have low housing costs, access to transport, and friendship and family networks in the area in which they live.

Lack of mobility, whether as a result of health or other reasons, can be a major cause of social isolation. Elderly people often cannot negotiate public transport and many cannot afford to use taxis. If they are able to use public transport but live in an area poorly serviced by it, problems of isolation and dependency may be further complicated. It has been estimated that approximately 10 per cent of the elderly are incapacitated to the extent that they cannot look after themselves, and a further 10–20 per cent have some limitations, for example they cannot walk long distances or have difficulties climbing stairs.

Over the last decade much attention has been paid to the dependency of the aged. Concerns about the current and future dependency of the aged upon the social, medical and financial resources of a society are often expressed. While the 75-plus age group accounts for over one-quarter of all health expenditure in Australia, the contribution that the aged make to others in society is often ignored. The Australian Institute of Family Studies has found that aged people are more likely to be the providers rather than the recipients of support; they are likely to give money to their families when it is needed; to provide accommodation in the case of separating families, and to mind and care for grandchildren.

Since industrialisation most developed countries have experienced a greater emphasis on individualism and personal autonomy, and less on the role of the family as a source of financial security and support in old age. Individualism has been given as one of the reasons for the decrease in marriage rates over the past few decades, and it may be one of the reasons why aged people wish to maintain their independence and not become a burden on younger relatives.

Aged migrants

Australia has always placed a strong emphasis on the migration of entire families and although migration to Australia has included a relatively small number of elderly persons, our population now includes a sizeable and increasing number of overseas-born ageing people. This group has specific needs apart from income and housing needs. Aged ethnic people who have lived in Australia for many years who have well-developed family and social networks and who speak English, are unlikely to experience the isolation and loneliness in old age that recently arrived non-English speaking migrants may experience. It is important to remember that the majority of ethnic aged in Australia have spent a substantial part of their lives in Australia and are likely to have developed strong social and family networks.

For many migrants the usual pattern has been for younger members of family groups to come to Australia and send for elderly parents once they are established. Elderly migrants are not eligible for financial assistance for travel and their welfare after arrival is seen as the responsibility of their sponsors if they come from countries with which Australia does not have reciprocal social security arrangements.

Eligibility for aged pensions generally requires ten years residency, although as outlined later there are exceptions. In some families, older relatives stay at home and mind the grandchildren so both parents can participate in the labour force. Often, the elderly grandparent may not assume his or her traditional role of patriarch or matriarch. Communication may be difficult, particularly if grandchildren do not speak the native language of their grandparents. This situation may intensify the loneliness experienced by the newly arrived immigrants. Many elderly immigrants are financially dependent upon their children and to leave their children's home may increase financial, linguistic and cultural difficulties.

However, while many newly arrived migrants may take up residence with their children, census and survey data dispel the popular belief that migrants, particularly from non-English speaking countries, are more likely to live in extended-family and multiple-family households. Only a small proportion of migrants from non-English speaking countries are living in extended-family situations. Statistics show that individuals in certain migrant groups, particularly Vietnamese and southern Europeans, are far less likely to live alone when compared with Australian-born people. Thus, when an elderly parent in a southern European family dies, and the spouse is the only remaining person in a household, it is more likely that he or she will move in with a related family unit rather than remain alone. For Australian-born aged people, individuals in this situation are more likely to remain living alone than to move in with related family.

While statistics may indicate that in general, overseas-born aged people are no more likely than Australian-born to reside in extended-family households, these statistics do not indicate the importance that overseas-born groups often place on extended-family networks.

Migrants may not form extended families in the sense that they share one household with many families or generations living together, as most residences in Australia are not large enough to accommodate large groups of people. The emphasis that migrants place upon family reunions, that is, relatives migrating to Australia to join families who are already settled here, and the tendency to live in the same neighbourhood as relatives, indicates the importance placed upon family and kinship.

However, not all migrant families have close relatives living in Australia, and this lack of family and kin networks can contribute to social isolation for some migrants. Opportunities to maintain the language and the lifestyles of the country of origin can be essential to quality of life in old age, especially for more recently arrived non-English-speaking aged people.

Community resources for migrants are often inadequate and resources for aged people such as senior citizens' centres may not be appropriate due to cultural and, particularly, language differences. Opportunities for cultural activities and social interaction need to be provided in the context of a community language. While there have been some aged people's housing and nursing homes built for ethnic groups, the demand is greater than the supply. For elderly migrants to go to a nursing home, they may experience many cultural differences as well as problems concerning diet and language. The lack of bilingual nursing staff, therapists and medical practitioners can hinder effective health care for a multilingual aged population.

Until recently, ethnic communities in Australia were reluctant to develop special accommodation for the aged because ethno-specific accommodation was suggestive of a lack of respect and interest in the aged.[6] However, migrant communities are now giving priority to the establishment of suitable accommodation for the aged. The development of specific facilities for ethnic aged is also more viable when there is a larger number of people who speak a community language.

Many ethnic aged live in isolation and even if they do live with their families, they can be alone for long periods when family members are at work. The ethnic aged may be more affected if language difficulties prevent them from using public transport and general community services. In response to many difficulties experienced by non-English-speaking ethnic aged, migrant resource centres have been established in areas of high migrant density. These centres provide support for all agencies, both government and voluntary, to assist migrants and to

---

6 Callan, *Australian Minority Groups*, p. 114.

provide a focus for community participation in order to meet the needs of migrants, both young and elderly.

Social Welfare and Community Resources

Aged people require a wide range of supports, especially income support, health services, housing support and social services.

Age Pension

During the period 1900–08, Victoria, New South Wales and Queensland introduced an old age pension; and in 1909 the Commonwealth government legislated for a Commonwealth-wide age and invalid pension scheme. Prior to the introduction of pensions, the aged were dependent on family and voluntary agencies for support. Entitlement to this pension has changed considerably throughout this century, but since 1985 payment of age pensions has been both income-tested and assets-tested. An age pension may be granted to a woman at 60 years of age and to a man at 65 years of age.

Normally, an aged person must have at some time lived in Australia continuously for ten years and be living in Australia at the time of application, but applicants who do not meet this requirement may be eligible for a special benefit. Australia has reciprocal social security agreements with the United Kingdom, New Zealand, Italy and Canada, which means the residence requirement of ten years in Australia does not normally have to be satisfied for migrants coming from these countries. Australia ia also negotiating with other migrant-source countries to establish similar agreements.

As pension rates are adjusted during the year it will be necessary to contact an office of the Department of Social Security to determine age pension rates as well as the amount of additional income that can be earnt without the pension being affected.

Special Benefit

This benefit can cover a variety of needs, although the recipient must be in 'financial hardship'. This means the recipient does not have enough money for absolute necessities such as rent and food and is not in a position to earn money because of age or illness or some other acceptable reason. This benefit may be paid to elderly migrants who do not meet residence requirements.

Concession cards

The Pensioner Health Benefits Card and Transport Concession Card are issued when a pension is granted. From April 1993 all pensioners were eligible for these cards and in November 1993 these two cards are to be replaced by a single plastic pensioner card. Social security concession cards may allow pensioners to obtain discounts on many services including transport, telephone, health, council rates, gas and electricity, and entertainment.

Carer's pension

A carer's pension is payable to a person providing constant care and attention for a severely disabled age or invalid pensioner. The person needing care must be living at home and have a physical, intellectual or psychiatric problem which means that help is required for ordinary tasks such as eating, dressing or taking a bath; or constant supervision is necessary to prevent injury to the person or to someone else. Anyone who is caring for someone who would otherwise be admitted to a nursing home may be entitled to receive the Domiciliary Nursing Care Benefit.

While care for a disabled person or aged person by a caring relative is obviously far more desirable for the person in need, it is also less costly for society. In 1989 the Carer's pension and Domiciliary Nursing Care Benefit totalled about $133 per week, whereas subsidies to nursing homes per resident were often as high as $460 per week.[7] Attention needs to be given to the strains—financial, physical, social and emotional—placed upon families who provide care to aged relatives.

Home and Community Care Program—HACC

This program was established in 1985–86 and is jointly funded by the Commonwealth government and the state and territory governments. HACC funds organisations and community groups which provide basic

7 R. Batten, W. Weeks & J. Wilson (eds), *Issues Facing Australian Families: Human Services Respond*, Melbourne, 1991, p. 305.

Figure 8.4 Senior citizens' and community centres provide many opportunities for retired people to take part in constructive and social activities.

maintenance and support services for the frail aged and people with disabilities, to enable them to remain living at home. The purpose of this program is to enhance the independence, security and quality of life of people in order for them to remain at home and avoid admission to long-term residential care.

Services receiving funding in this program include home help and personal care; respite care; home maintenance; food services such as delivered meals; community nursing and paramedical services, and education and training for service providers and users. Many of these programs and services are administered through local councils, hospitals and community centres. Domiciliary services such as these are provided within a strict budget, and while they may allow the time for personnel to carry out duties, there is often little time for social contact, something which aged people often need and appreciate. Some services, such as meals-on-wheels, are also dependent upon volunteer workers. Some services and facilities available for the aged are outlined below:

- *Senior citizens' centres* provide recreational and social opportunities for people who have retired from the workforce, and for the elderly.
- *Meals-on-wheels* provides nutritious lunches for aged and disabled people who are unable to prepare their own meals.
- *Home help* provides household assistance with cleaning, maintenance and small household repairs. Due to limited funding this caring and support system cannot provide for all those in need, and supervisors often have to make difficult decisions as to who is the most in need of assistance. There are problems in developing home care services that are efficient and well co-ordinated yet flexible enough to meet the diverse needs of the people for whom the program services.
- *Home and district nursing services* provide nursing and care services for pensioners in their own homes. This type of care may include assisting the frail aged in tasks such as bathing and dressing.
- *Day centres* provide a social facility which aged people can visit perhaps for one day a week to seek medical advice, talk to social workers, have a meal and talk to other people. What these centres offer vary among communities. Often a community bus will pick up elderly people and take them home at the end of the day. For carers looking after frail aged at home it can mean a well-earned break one day a week.
- *Councils on ageing* have been established in each state. These councils publish easy-to-understand pamphlets on all facets of ageing: health, diet, finance, accommodation, travel, retirement, social activities, as well as legal and financial matters. In addition to being information providers, these councils also have a political base, lobbying for the aged and promoting age-related issues. Other groups which represent the aged include the Australian Pensioners' Federation, the Voice of the Elderly and the newly founded Pensioners Party of Australia, which attempted to obtain a seat in the Senate in the 1993 Federal election.
- *Information centres*, sometimes known as community centres, were established during the 1960s by local councils. They offer a variety of services including information and referral services. Many form part of community health centres and/or local hospitals.
- *What's Age Got To Do With It?* is a volume published by the Commonwealth government. It focuses on issues such as self-esteem, constructive use of time, food and diet, exercise, and programs relating to transport, conducting meetings, recreational activities, holidays, arts and crafts and use of community centres. State governments, through the various bodies responsible for the welfare of the aged, have produced materials with the aim of enriching life

for the aged. Wellbeing is directly affected by the resources that are available to enrich life for all people, young and older. Governments, voluntary agencies, community members and families need to share the responsibility for the wellbeing of the aged.

SUPPORT SYSTEMS FOR THE AGED

As the number of aged increases, so too will the number of aged people requiring care. While family care (or rather, care by women) may be seen as a cheap alternative, and is already happening in many families, this notion is based on the assumption that women are available to carry out this task. As the workforce participation of married women increases, less and less women will be available to provide care for aged relatives.

For many years the Commonwealth government has provided resources for people living in institutional care, such as nursing homes and hostels. However, less has been done in the area of domiciliary services, that is, services which assist aged people to remain living in their own homes. Thus, a significant number of elderly people have to move to nursing homes or hostels due to a lack of domiciliary services. Since 1985, funding in this area has been increased in order to maintain and extend existing services and facilities. Such services and facilities include personal care services, home help, meals-on-wheels, day centre programs, senior citizen's centres and pensioner rebates for certain services. For individuals who wish to remain living independently and for families who wish to care for aged relatives in their own home, such support services are essential.

In the USA, programs have been initiated to encourage elderly people to take on new social roles, as volunteers in schools and in early childhood facilities. The aim is to maintain the connections between the generations and to provide a useful and productive role for senior citizens.

FAMILY CARE

One of the increasing concerns in the care of the aged is the workload and stresses experienced by carers. While government policies towards the care of the aged now emphasise the maintenance of independence and most people in society agree that this is the most appropriate manner in which to care for the aged, it assumes that family members are available to act as carers.

Most carers are women, that is, daughters who often have family and work responsibilities. With increased life expectancy, it is not uncommon to find situations where a woman is assisting an elderly parent to live independently by providing assistance, maintaining a job in the workforce, managing a household and providing assistance to children and perhaps even grandchildren. Some women who are not in the workforce or who have left the workforce may find themselves caring for aged relatives as well as grandchildren. Thus, carers are often less available to care, something which is often ignored, as it is more convenient to assume there is someone living close who is available to undertake this responsibility.

Feminist authors have recognised the 'gendered' nature of community care. Family care can be seen as a cheap alternative, as families, namely women, can provide care at little cost to the State. There is increasing concern that the role of carer, usually performed by a woman, is creating unrealistic demands on women who attempt to combine work and family responsibilities. This has created what Betty Friedan has termed the 'superwoman squeeze'.[8] Our society awards little status or prestige to those people who look after the aged; greater status and prestige is given to those who look after the younger generations.

Housing

It is essential when planning or providing housing for the aged, to create a physical environment that contributes to the social, psychological and physical wellbeing of the individual. Physically, such an environment should provide for privacy, protection, convenience, comfort and mobility. Socially, it should provide an environment where social interaction, self-expression and communication can be fostered, both inside and outside the physical area.

The physical environment comprises the internal design of the house or building, the external surroundings and the available community facilities. An appropriate physical environment can reduce stress and anxiety, motivate and stimulate the elderly to be involved in the community, and to remain independent and self-sufficient if they are capable of doing so. Housing can contribute to overall psychological and physical health.

A highly developed technological society demands that people adjust to a rapidly changing environment. Whilst young people are generally adaptable, the aged are often not so and in many cases do not

8 Quoted in D. Edgar, 'Ageing: Everybody's future', *Family Matters*, no. 80, Dec. 1991, p.18.

have the physical capacity to adjust. It is often necessary to modify the physical environment to suit the aged, and to help them cope with problems they may face—in failing hearing and sight, poor sense of balance, lowered mobility and agility, and declining physical strength. Approximately half of the physical accidents that happen to elderly people occur in the home, often because of inappropriate design. Listed below are some of the more common design features considered important in housing for the aged.[9]

- Use ramps instead of stairs. Where stairs are necessary, easily gripped rails should be installed on both sides (as they should with ramps) and be of a colour which is in contrast with the adjacent walls.
- Seats should be installed in shower recesses.
- Water and temperature controls should be placed so that they can be adjusted before entering the shower.
- Bench and shelf heights should be lower than normal and benches should be placed in corridors.
- Scatter rugs and mats that do not grip the floor should be avoided.
- Door-knobs and taps should be able to be gripped easily, i.e. they should not be rounded.
- Safety glass should be used, and clear glass should be marked to be visible.
- Hazards such as changing levels in floors and at doorways should be avoided.
- Visual and sound alarm systems should be installed.
- Doors and doorways should be wider than standard size and be easy to open.
- All signs, including floor numbers should be easy to read.
- Doors, ramps and stairways should have good lighting.
- An attractive atmosphere should be created through the use of plants and visual art.
- Rooms should provide for privacy as well as for interaction.
- Housing should be situated close to community facilities.

There is no one type of housing appropriate for all aged persons. Suitable housing will be determined by available resources, state of wellbeing and physical independence. Elderly people who are healthy and independent may be able to live in and maintain their homes, perhaps with some assistance. However, some elderly people who are semi-dependent may find a retirement village more appropriate; frail dependent elderly people may have no choice but to live in nursing home or hostel accommodation.

---

9 Based on M. H. Hoekstra, *The Aged and Housing in Perspective*, Sydney, 1976, pp. 19–21.

Figure 8.5 Retirement villages such as this are designed to meet the needs of the elderly, providing accommodation at a low cost and with opportunities for social interaction. (Photo: M. Deliopoulous, Housing Commission of Victoria)

TYPES OF ACCOMMODATION

OWN HOME OR STRATA TITLE ACCOMMODATION

Over the last decade there has been a growing recognition that many elderly people who have in the past been placed in hostels and nursing homes could, given the support of community services and modifications to their existing residence, remain in their own home. People become sentimentally attached to a home and neighbourhood in which they have often spent many years. Many elderly people often move from their family home when income becomes too small to pay for its maintenance, or when they are physically unable to care for it. It has been shown that relocation can contribute to psychological problems or ill health as it often means a significant adjustment to a new environment, new neighbours, shops, health care staff etc.

As a compromise between staying in their own home or moving to an aged persons' home, many elderly people often choose to purchase strata title accommodation in the form of a unit, villa or townhouse. This often means they can stay close to a familiar neighbourhood and to friends, retaining their independence but having a smaller area to care for and maintain. Such a move may mean that some familiar possessions have to be given up, and it may also mean the loss of daily contact with neighbours and friends. Living in medium-density accommodation can be impersonal and it may take some time to develop social contacts with people living in similar circumstances. Also, an elderly person may not be able to cope with the noise of young neighbours, or with climbing stairs when there is no lift available.

Aged persons' homes and hostels

It was not until 1954 that definite steps were taken to provide accommodation for the aged in the form of homes and hostels (often referred to as retirement villages). Often such communities are composed of separate unit accommodation, hostel accommodation and nursing home facilities. Figures 8.6 and 8.7 are two such examples.

Many of these retirement homes and villages have been built by church groups and voluntary agencies, often with the assistance of government subsidies. Units may be bought or rented, depending on each occupant's financial position, and residents are entitled to live there until death but cannot sell or lease the unit to their heirs. If they are 'founder donors'—that is, make a donation towards the cost of a

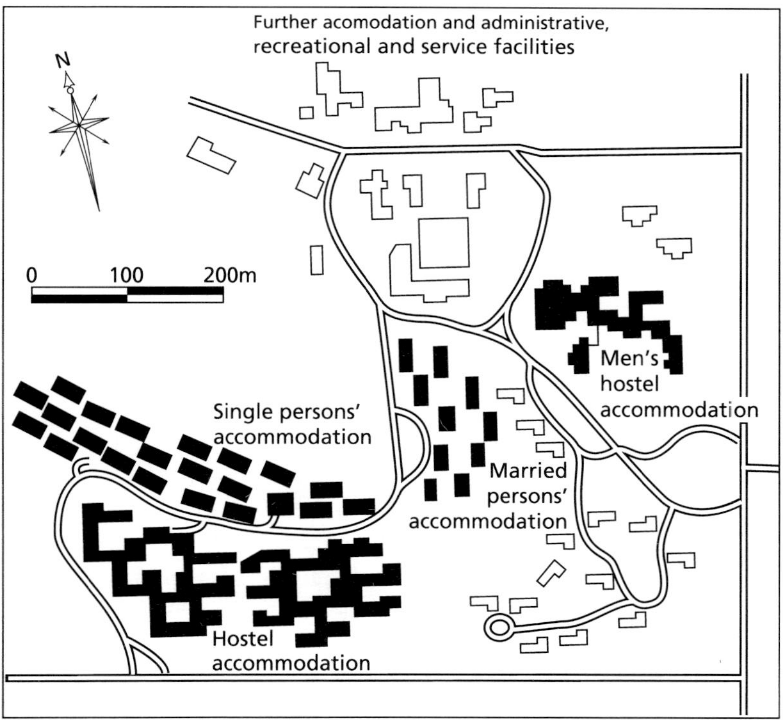

Figure 8.6 War veterans' home ground plan, Narrabeen, NSW.

Source: M.H. Hoekstra, *The Aged and Housing in Perspective*, Ian Buchan Fell Research Centre, University of Sydney, p. 51a.

unit, they will have had to pay their money before the unit was built, as the government requires proof that an organisation has a certain amount of money before a subsidy can be granted. If the family home has to be sold to provide this donation, there may be problems with temporary accommodation. Those who have not previously owned housing may not have sufficient money to obtain this type of accommodation unless they are assisted by community organisation such as the Lions clubs or Rotary.

This system has over the years favoured the more affluent elderly, and for those with little money, there is insufficient rental accommodation of this type. However, there are other types of aged accommodation available, including self-contained strata units which can be purchased and sold. Depending upon the facilities and location, the prices of these vary considerably. Also churches and other community groups often provide self-contained rental accommodation for aged pensioners.

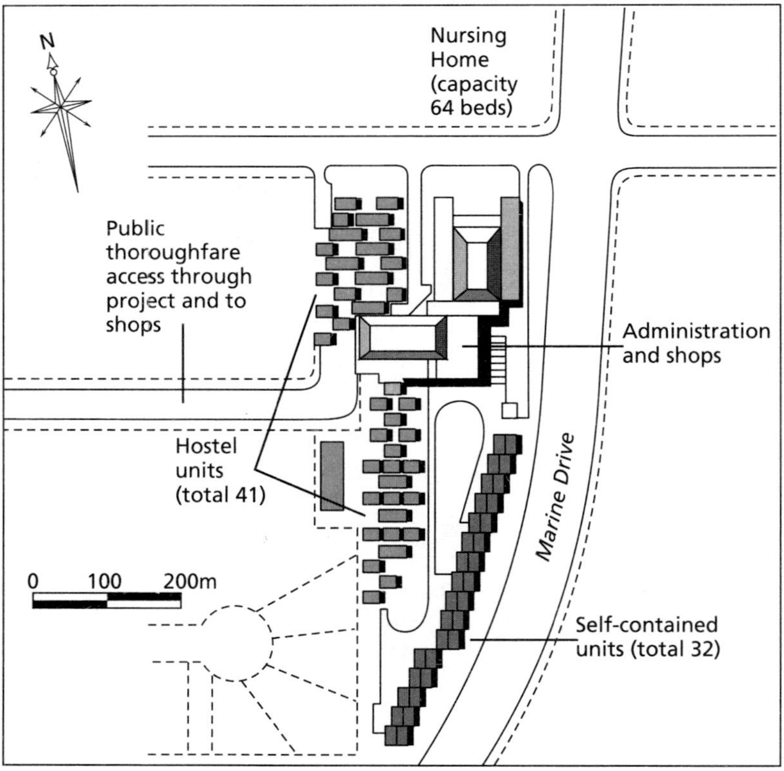

Figure 8.7 Towradgi Park, Wollongong, NSW (Architect: Leif Kristensen).
Source: M.H. Hoekstra, *The Aged and Housing in Perspective*, Ian Buchan Fell Research Centre, University of Sydney, p. 51a.

Aged persons' homes do provide many advantages for the aged: they are usually situated in pleasant surroundings, with a resident manager and staff, and suitable design features. They offer social interaction, but allow residents to maintain some independence, as they choose between the privacy of their unit or the interaction in a communal sitting-room or recreation room. Neighbours are also close by in case of an emergency and the buildings have been designed to allow for the comfort and safety of the aged.

Hostel accommodation usually consists of private bedroom and bathroom facilities with communal dining and recreation areas. This type of accommodation usually appeals to those elderly people who cannot cope with cleaning, shopping and meal preparation but are not sick enough to need nursing care. Full board is usually a little less than is received from the pension, but the money left over may not be sufficient to cover personal expenses. As there is insufficient hostel accommodation, many aged who need some care but are not completely dependent on other people may be forced to enter nursing homes.

Nursing homes

Nursing homes provide for people who need continuous nursing and professional care. Nursing-home care should only be provided when a person needs constant medical attention. One of the greatest criticisms of nursing homes is that many are built and operated solely for profit, and they deprive patients of dignity. With staff coming and going, and multi-bed rooms, there is often little opportunity for privacy. The nature of nursing homes is such that it is often impossible for patients to create a homely atmosphere.

No more than 4–5 per cent of people aged 65 years or over are residents of nursing homes in Australia. People in nursing homes are usually there because they have chronic multiple diseases, resulting in progressive disabilities and impairment.

As discussed below, the Commonwealth government has addressed many of the problems that have been traditionally associated with nursing homes and have initiated new guidelines for their organisation and operation. In the past, nursing homes were often characterised by overcrowding in wards, inappropriate grouping of patients in large dormitories, unsuitable rehabilitation environments and inadequate dining and sitting room space. There was also an observed tendency for nursing home patients to display physical and mental deterioration after a period of time.[10]

---

10 J.S. Western, *Social Inequality in Australian Society*, Melbourne, 1983, p. 317.

Over the past decade there has been a trend away from aged people living in nursing homes, with increased emphasis on the aged living independently with assistance. However, often there is no alternative than for aged people to enter a nursing home when they are unable to live without constant care and attention. Retirement villages which provide various forms of accommodation offer more flexibility for the aged. Co-ordinated communities of aged persons' units, hostels and nursing home accommodation can mean aged people move to different types of accommodation when it is necessary but they can still remain close to social networks they have developed.

'Granny flats'

'Granny flats' can sometimes be an ideal solution to the problem of housing the aged, providing privacy and independence but situated close enough to other family members to allow for social interaction and assistance when needed. For many years state governments and local councils did not allow granny flats to be built in backyards. However, in recent years there has been significant relaxation of these regulations, as housing has become increasingly expensive in urban areas and the trend to maintaining the independence of the aged has accelerated.

Segregated and integrated housing

There has been much debate as to the most satisfactory living arrangements for aged people. Some people have favoured age-segregated living, as in a retirement village, and some favour integrated or age-mixed housing. Integrated housing benefits society, as each individual comes in contact with a wide range of people in the local community. Aged people often feel younger if they have more contact with younger people and families. On the other hand, it can be argued that a segregated housing development provides security of social interaction, appropriate physical design features, and often, the availability of medical care, meals and cleaning services.

Perhaps the solution is to integrate the elderly with other social groups so that they retain the option of taking part in community activities but remain part of an aged community. For example, the placing of child-care centres close to aged persons' homes may provide opportunities for interaction between the young and the old.

Government responsibility in residential care for aged people

The aim of the Commonwealth government's aged residential care program is to ensure that frail, aged people who are assessed as being unable to live at home have access to residential support and care services appropriate to their needs. The Commonwealth government provides support in the form of nursing homes and hostels as well as providing significant subsidies to these facilities.

In 1986 the Commonwealth government initiated planning to ensure there were sufficient places available in nursing homes and hostels to meet the needs of the over-70 age group. Also, mechanisms have been established to ensure that only those people who really need nursing-home care are admitted. Teams have been set up by the Department of Community Services and Health to monitor nursing homes and hostels to ensure they meet government standards and provide quality of life and quality of care for the aged residents. These teams talk to residents, visitors and staff to learn how the facility meets the needs and wishes of the residents. These teams are concerned that these facilities operate to ensure social independence, freedom of choice, a homelike environment, privacy and dignity and safety.[11]

The needs of specific groups, including ethnic and Aboriginal communities, have also been addressed and steps have been taken to improve access of these groups to aged care. Also, care has been taken to ensure a wide geographical spread of nursing home and hostel accommodation and to ensure that financial disadvantage does not restrict entry to government-supported facilities. To allow for the development of different types of accommodation other than nursing homes, funding to hostel accommodation has been increased since the mid-1980s. Organisations who operate hostel accommodation for the aged have been allowed greater flexibility to raise funds from borrowings and from entry contributions by the occupants.

The amount of government subsidies received by hostels depends upon the proportion of financially disadvantaged residents; the higher the proportion, the higher the subsidy. This approach acknowledges the lower number of people who can make an adequate entry contribution.

Short-term care

While government programs for aged residential care focus on long-

11 Australian Bureau of Statistics, *Year Book Australia*, No. 75, Canberra, 1992, pp. 215–220.

term care, there are also provisions for short-term or respite care. Often aged people need more personal care if they are recovering from an illness or an operation and sometimes carers need a break from their responsibilities.

Rights of older people

In 1989 the Commonwealth government initiated the development of a charter in order to establish and protect the civil, human and legal rights of residents in nursing homes and hostels. The key initiatives include:

- The development of a Charter of Residents' Rights and Responsibilities between residents and proprietors which clearly establish the rights and responsibilities of residents and proprietors and establish the basis on which care and accommodation is provided.
- The establishment of a Community Visitors Scheme which aims to improve the quality of life of residents in nursing homes who have fairly limited social and family contact. Community visitors will provide companionship to residents and assist them to initiate or continue contact with the community if they wish.
- A comprehensive information strategy to enhance the awareness of the community of the types of services available for older people and the rights and entitlements of residents.
- The establishment of independent advocacy services to provide information, advice and support to residents and to take up grievance issues on their behalf.[12]

Multi-purpose centres

Many small communities in rural and remote areas do not have access to the range of services available in larger communities. In order to provide accessible health services to all Australians, the Commonwealth government is providing grants for the establishment of multi-purpose centres to be established in under-serviced rural areas. These centres provide many health and welfare services including hospital care, residential aged care, disability and home and community care services.

Rent assistance

Aged people who are receiving an age pension and are renting private accommodation are entitled to rent assistance. People who are lodging

12 *Year Book Australia*, no. 75, p. 219.

and paying board or living in a caravan or a boat that is moored are also entitled to rent assistance.

Public housing

During the past two decades public housing policies have changed considerably. Rather than locate public housing in particular locations, it is now policy to provide a geographical spread of public housing, as well as to provide different types of housing to suit individuals and families with different needs. This means that aged pensioners applying for public housing have a greater chance of remaining in an area with which they are familiar.

In most states, lone pensioners and pensioner couples are able to apply for special bedsitter or one and two-bedroom accommodation through the state department responsible for housing. In most states applicants for public housing who are over 80 years of age receive accelerated progression of their application for public housing. This applies even when only one member of the household is over 80 years of age, as in the case of an aged couple.

Management decisions

Although the physical, social and psychological needs of the aged community are fairly similar, it must be remembered that all aged people are individuals. Individuals have different priorities as regards their needs and wants, and different amounts and types of resources to utilise. Individuals alone cannot often satisfy all needs—others in society must help them do so. The major decisions an aged people confront may include:

- Where to live: This will be influenced greatly by the resources available to maintain the current home, including physical capabilities, health and income. An aged persons' home may be an alternative to staying in the family home as it may provide for more social interaction, but moving to a new area may mean the loss of a well-established community and social network. For many aged people, there may be little choice: financial resources will determine where they live and where they live may not necessarily satisfy physical, social and psychological needs.
- What to do upon retirement with increased time for leisure and recreation. It is important to be involved in goal-directed activities,

so that self-esteem and independence are maintained. For many aged people, income is limited so activities are required which allow for social interaction and creative expression but are not costly.

- How to provide the basic needs of food, clothing and health care. For the majority of the aged population, this will not be a problem as income and assets will be sufficient to cover these requirements. For some elderly people in the community, however, this can be a major problem, particularly for those who are receiving a pension and renting accommodation.
- How to avoid dependency and isolation.
- How to maintain social contacts by retaining mobility. In some instances these decisions may have to be made by other members of the family, as many elderly people continue to live in inappropriate situations, to the detriment of their health. Again, some elderly people may not have the resources to even consider alternatives; they may have no choice but to remain living in an inappropriate environment.

Despite illness and disabilities many aged people have positive attitudes towards good health and quality of life. Society creates negative images of the aged and often views them as inferior, weaker and dependent upon the working population. Like the rest of the population, it would appear that people as they age will continue to experience the unequal access to social and economic resources they experienced through all the earlier stages of the life span. However, with general levels of education increasing, it is expected that the aged will continue to become more politically aware and active. They will be more likely to challenge policies that affect them, as well as to lobby for more rights. As more and more women remain in the workforce and work in satisfying occupations they too will resent the changes associated with retirement.

In keeping with the massive social and technological changes which have occurred over the last few decades, expectations about the aged and what roles they should adopt may become less defined during the next few decades. Perhaps ageing in the next century will attract less negative images and stereotypes. As the 'baby boomers' age next century there may be a minor revolution against ageist attitudes. Perhaps, there will be a new vision of productive ageing and society will allow and provide more opportunities for the aged to contribute to community life. That is, aged people will cease to be separated from society, they will be integrated and will be regarded as a valuable human resource which should not be wasted.

REVIEW QUESTIONS

1 At what age do you think an individual becomes 'old'? Justify your answer.
2 Why has life expectancy increased during the past 100 years?
3 What is meant by an ageing population?
4 What may be the advantages of classifying the aged as 'young–old', 'middle–old' and 'old–old'?
5 Why are the aged not a homogeneous group?
6 Outline the needs of the aged.
7 What are the major issues that society must address in relation to the aged?
8 In relation to the aged, what is meant by *dependency*?
9 Which health problems are the aged most likely to encounter? Which problems are likely to lead to nursing home accommodation?
10 How may the skills and abilities of the aged be utilised in society?
11 In what ways does society take away the dignity of the aged?
12 Why may elderly people become isolated and lonely?
13 Which aged people are most likely to experience poverty?
14 What problems may the ethnic aged face? How can these be addressed?
15 Pensioners are often entitled to fringe benefits. How do these benefits assist pensioners?
16 What resources does Home and Community Care provide?
17 Explain why family care for the aged has become known as 'gendered care'?
18 Describe the adjustments elderly people may have to make when they move from their family home.
19 Outline the resources that are available in your community to assist the aged to live independently and yet have opportunities for social interaction?
20 If an elderly person wishes to remain living in his or her home, what design modifications could be made to assist in this?
21 Discuss how the environment in which an elderly person lives can affect wellbeing.
22 Discuss the advantages and disadvantages of 'social mix' housing.
23 Since the mid-1980s the Commonwealth government has taken many initiatives with regard to housing for the aged. Outline the developments that have taken place.
24 Identify the major management decisions that may have to be made by aged individuals and families.
25 Why are the aged becoming a more politically powerful group?

Case study 8.1

The widow

Mrs Richards is 84 years old and is house-bound because of arthritis. She lives in a high-rise public housing unit but has not been able to leave the unit for three months because of her disability. Mrs Richards can walk across the room, but has to have a rest before she can walk back again. Mrs Richards finds tasks such as opening bottles and peeling vegetables very hard to accomplish. A neighbour, Mrs Timms, calls in every day to see her and do any shopping she requires. Three times a week, meals-on-wheels volunteers deliver a hot lunch. A nursing sister from a community home-help service visits Mrs Richards three times a week to assist her in having a bath.

While Mrs Timms was on holidays at her daughter's home, Mrs Richards fell over and broke her hip. Even though she has a telephone, she was unable to reach it and lay on the floor for a whole day before the nursing sister from the community home-help service found her. When the ambulance came, Mrs Richards became very anxious as she did not want to leave her home and familiar surroundings. She was also distressed at leaving her savings which were hidden under her bed.

Following Mrs Richard's operation in which she had a hip replacement, she went to a nursing home for three months. During this period of time she underwent physiotherapy to assist her to walk as independently as possible, given that she suffers from arthritis. Mrs Richards is not disabled or ill enough to remain in a nursing home, yet she cannot really cope sufficiently well by herself to return to her unit. Mrs Richards daughter and her family live in another city and are not close enough to be able to help her in daily activities.

Questions

1 Could Mrs Richard's accident have been avoided? Justify your answer.
2 How could the design of housing be improved to allow people like Mrs Richards to remain in familiar surroundings?
3 Why may elderly people be reluctant to leave familiar surroundings?
4 What adjustments may Mrs Richards have to make if she were to move somewhere else?
5 Community programs are available to assist elderly people to remain in their own home. Apart from programs such as meals-on-wheels and home-help services what other resources and facilities could be developed to assist people such as Mrs Richards?

6 Why do elderly people often keep their savings in their home rather than in a financial institution?
7 Outline the alternative housing choices available to Mrs Richards. For each alternative list the advantages and the disadvantages.

Case study 8.2

The widower

Mr Lomas is a 75-year-old widower with no surviving children; his wife died two years ago. Mr and Mrs Lomas had always lived in an inner city area, usually in a rented house. When Mrs Lomas died, Mr Lomas moved to a smaller unit. After he has paid for his rent, food, electricity and gas, Mr Lomas has little money left from his pension to pay for anything else. All his savings are exhausted. Although he has a few friends, two of his close friends died recently and he has become very lonely.

Mrs Lomas always did the cooking and housekeeping, and since she died Mr Lomas has not really eaten properly nor taken good care of himself. He has few skills to prepare nutritious food, and his diet mainly consists of bread and the cheapest canned food he can buy. Mr Lomas finds his unit very noisy, as many of the families who live in the block have young children who play outside in the garden and courtyard. He spends his day going for walks in the park. He cannot afford to use the heater in winter as the electricity is too expensive. While he has a television set, it is broken and in need of major repair or replacement. Mr Lomas likes watching television as he finds it stops him from feeling as lonely, but he cannot afford the cost of repair or replacement.

Questions

1 Contact your local office of the Department of Social Security and establish the current single age-pension rate. If Mr Lomas is spending approximately half this amount on rent, how much income does he have left to pay for food, clothing, electricity, gas and other expenses?
2 Would this amount be sufficient to cover fixed expenses as well as provide for other needs?
3 Contact the Australian Bureau of Statistics and ascertain the

current average weekly wage. Take 60 per cent of this wage to determine the 'poverty line'. Given that Mr Lomas has to pay for housing, is he living below the 'poverty line'?

4 As a pensioner, to what fringe benefits is Mr Lomas eligible? Will any of these benefits assist him financially? Explain.
5 How could meals-on-wheels assist Mr Lomas? Why do you think he may not have investigated this scheme?
6 What may be the effects on Mr Lomas' psychological wellbeing if he continues living like this?
7 How may his poor diet affect his physical wellbeing?
8 To what alternative accommodation may Mr Lomas be entitled? If he could obtain public accommodation, what may be the benefits?
9 Why are widows often more self-sufficient than widowers?
10 What community resources may be available to enhance the social, physical and psychological wellbeing of Mr Lomas? Explain how.

CASE STUDY 8.3

THE AGED COUPLE

Mr and Mrs Barton have lived in Wollongong in their three-bedroom home for 40 years. Mr Barton is aged 70, and Mrs Barton is aged 64: both are receiving the age pension. They have two children and five grandchildren: their daughter Carol, and son-in-law Jim, live in Sydney (about 70 kilometres from Wollongong) with their two children; son Bruce and daughter-in-law Janine live in Wollongong.

Six months ago, Mr Barton had a stroke, and spent a considerable time in hospitals and nursing homes. Although he is slightly paralysed, he has now returned home and Mrs Barton is looking after him. However, as Mrs Barton has arthritis she is finding it increasingly difficult to tend to her husband, complete the household tasks and maintain the home and garden.

Mr and Mrs Barton talk to their children on the phone regularly, but now find it difficult to travel to Sydney to see their daughter. Bruce and Janine visit occasionally. Carol and Jim and their family visit about once a month, but they are finding that, as their children grow older and develop new interests, they have fewer free weekends.

Carol and Jim have suggested that her parents sell the home and buy a unit in a retirement village in Sydney, where medical facilities will be close at hand for Mr Barton. They have also offered to build a 'granny flat' in their backyard, where Mrs Barton could live if Mr Barton has to go to a nursing home. Mrs Barton is unsure of what to do. She feels that if she goes to live with her daughter, she will be a burden and might not like the noise of the children. She also realises that she will miss the friends she has made in Wollongong. However, she knows she can no longer look after herself, her husband, and the house without some form of assistance.[13]

QUESTIONS

1 What problems are the Bartons facing?
2 What conflicts are contributing to the problem?
3 Using the decision-making framework, outline this problem in terms of the four steps of the framework.
4 What may be the consequences of each of the alternatives the Bartons have available?
5 Are there any other alternatives that have not yet been thought of?
6 What may be the consequences of these alternatives?
7 What values may be influencing each of the alternatives that Mrs Barton is considering?
8 What human and non-human resources may the Bartons have available for use?
9 What may be the needs and wants of Mr and Mrs Barton?
10 For each alternative available to the Bartons, outline the related economic, social and technical decisions that may also have to be made. It may be helpful to present this in table form.

---

13 This survey was based on 'Survey of social life of old people', in T. Brennan, *New Community: Problems and Policies*, Sydney, 1973, pp. 328–41.

SURVEY
AGED PEOPLE

This survey could be used as a guide for interviewing aged people living in a variety of situations.[14] These may include aged people living alone, aged couples still living in their family home, aged widows or widowers living in aged persons' homes, hostels, nursing homes, Housing Commission units, etc.

A Personal details

1 Age ____________________

2 Sex ____________________

3 Marital status:

  a Married, living together ____________________

  b Single ____________________

  c Separated ____________________

  d Widowed ____________________

  e If widowed or separated, for how long? ____________________

4 Distance from son/daughter/other relatives ____________________

5 Distance from close friends ____________________

B Work

1 Occupation before retirement ____________________

2 Age at which stopped working ____________________

3 Reason for retirement:

  a Compulsory ____________________

  b Illness ____________________

  c Own choice ____________________

  d Other ____________________

4 Present part-time work, if any ____________________

  No. of hours per week ____________________

---

14 Based on 'Survey of social life of old people' in T. Brennan, *New Community: Problems and Policies*, Sydney, 1973, pp. 328–41.

C Income

1 Source:

a Pension (type) ______

b Wages ______

c Other, e.g. superannuation ______

2 Any extras which add to income, e.g. gifts, clothes, food, etc.

______

D Agency contact

Do you see any of the following? (Yes or No)

a Department of Social Security ______

b Department of Veterans' Affairs ______

c Meals-on-wheels ______

d Community aid or resource centre ______

e Ministers of religion ______

f Church societies ______

g Citizens' organisations, e.g. Apex, Rotary ______

h Home-help service ______

i Social worker ______

j Others ______

E Health

1 Any physical limitations, e.g. bedridden, chair-bound, difficulty in climbing stairs, difficulty in walking, restrictions in using hands, hearing or sight problems

______

______

______

2 Medical supervision

a Any visits from doctors, nurses, district nurses, etc. ______

b Distance from own doctor ______

c When was the last time you saw a doctor?

______

3 Food eaten today or yesterday

Breakfast ______________________

Lunch ______________________

Dinner ______________________

F Accommodation

1 **a** Type, e.g. house, unit, hostel, aged persons' home ____________

b Number of bedrooms ______________________

2 **a** Length of time in present accommodation ____________

b Length of time in previous accommodation if moved recently

____

c Reason for move ______________________

3 Housing Commission accommodation (if applicable)

a Length of time on waiting-list ______________________

b Did you have a choice of area? ______________________

c What was your reason for this choice? ______________________

4 Satisfaction with your present accommodation

Yes or No ____________ Reason ______________________

5 Heating

a Type of appliance ______________________

b Is it adequate for your needs? ______________________

G Household tasks

1 Who does the following around the house?

a Shopping ______________________

b Cooking ______________________

c Cleaning ______________________

d Laundry ______________________

e Gardening ______________________

f Odd jobs ______________________

2 Do you need more help around the home? ______________________

3 Where do you do your shopping? ______________________

a How long does it take you to get there? ______________________

b How do you get there, e.g. walk, bus, car? ______________________

9

HOUSING AND FAMILIES

HOUSING NEEDS OF INDIVIDUALS AND FAMILIES

The physical environment, including the internal design of housing and the external surroundings, can influence how well individuals and families satisfy their needs. While adequate housing is a basic need of all individuals and families, housing itself can help the family satisfy other physical, social and psychological needs.

Depending upon their interests, attitudes, cultural background and values, families will have varying perceptions of their needs and will place different priorities upon them. Some families may place a high value on internal living space, while others may place a high value on community and recreational facilities. The extent to which families can satisfy some of their needs through housing will depend primarily upon the economic resources they have available. At the same time, some families may place a higher value on holidays or entertainment and thus prefer to spend a higher proportion of their income on these commodities rather than on housing.

The needs of all families are not the same, nor are they static: they change as the composition and size of the family alters, and as the roles and activities of family members change. Individuals and families do not exist or function independently of the society in which they live. Society, to a large extent, determines the needs of a family and sets the standard of housing required to meet these needs. Achievement of the 'great Australian dream' of owning a separate house on its own block of land may appeal to families with dependent children, but may not be desirable for aged people who live alone, or for couples who choose not to have children.

Housing, like poverty, is relative to the standard of living of the society of which the family is a part. In areas of Asia, South America and Africa, families live in overcrowded huts without lights, water, sanitation or ventilation. These dwellings often house more than five people per room and provide little protection from the weather. What Australians may regard as substandard accommodation would be regarded as luxurious in some developing countries.

In Australia, many families have sufficient resources to be able to choose their physical environment and modify it to suit their needs. Unfortunately, not all families have the resources to be able to satisfy their needs. Families may place different priorities upon their housing requirements, but there are basic physical, psychological and social needs that are essential for the wellbeing of individuals and families. It is difficult to place needs into categories as they are all interrelated: in satisfying a physical need of a family, certain social and psychological needs will also be satisfied. For family harmony and wellbeing it is necessary to consider the needs of individual members as well as the needs of a family as a whole.

Physical needs

Protection and safety

Shelter must provide protection from the extremes of weather, e.g. heat and cold, if families are to feel secure and remain healthy. An environment that is subject to flooding, bushfires, strong winds, land slip, etc. can produce anxiety and stress for a family. A physical environment should be safe, providing protection from hazards, disease and infection. Parental anxiety is reduced when concerns about children falling down stairs, into swimming pools, off balconies or wandering into dangerous areas are minimised.

Comfort

The geographical aspects of a dwelling can contribute significantly to the comfort of individuals and families. A dwelling that faces west and catches the afternoon sun may not be a problem, but if a child's bedroom has this aspect the hot afternoon sun may be a hindrance to afternoon rest. A dwelling facing south will be subject to southerly winds and little sun in winter, whereas one that faces north-east will receive more sun throughout the year. The design of a dwelling and the internal arrangements of space can often overcome these problems—but many families do not have the flexibility of resources to ensure that the location and aspect of a dwelling is ideal in all aspects. Families have different standards and different requirements of physical comfort.

Health and rest

As adequate sleep and rest are essential for good health, bedrooms should provide privacy and adequate ventilation for comfort and relaxation. When, for example, bedrooms are not situated away from living areas, undisturbed rest can be difficult. Apart from poor physical health, insufficient sleep and relaxation can cause tension and irritability. Efficient sanitation facilities or services are also essential for the health of families.

Internal convenience

If a dwelling is designed so that is allows for efficient work with a minimum of fatigue, frustrations can be reduced. Adequate lighting, efficiently arranged work centres, sufficient storage space, ample power points, easily cleaned surfaces, and good heating and cooling, can all contribute to the comfort of the family. The degree and type of comfort and convenience required by families will vary with size and composition: a four-bedroom house may not be convenient for an aged widow, and a two-bedroom unit may not be convenient for a family with two pre-school children. On the other hand, a two-bedroom unit could be very convenient for a working couple who spend less time at home.

External convenience

Some families may place a higher priority on the convenience of a dwelling to place of employment, recreational facilities, health services and community resources than they do on the design of the house. Other people may be more concerned about being situated close to employment rather than recreational facilities and vice versa. Some areas have more community facilities for young single people and couples, whereas other areas have more facilities for expanding families.

Families who cannot afford to spend a large amount of income on housing may be limited in their choice of location and may be forced into areas where there are few opportunities for employment and limited community facilities. This can mean they are forced to spend more money on travelling and have fewer opportunities to pursue other interests. Access to public transport, shops, medical centres, leisure facilities, educational facilities and family support services can aid in the socialisation of all family members. When these community resources are not available to families, physical, social and psychological wellbeing may be affected.

Space

The amount of internal, external, closed and open space required by each family will depend upon its size and composition, activities and interests, and stage of family life cycle. Some families may need less internal space as they spend less time at home, whilst others will require more space if leisure and recreational activities are home-centred. Dwelling space costs money, thus many families have to compromise between their ideal requirements and what they can afford. Well-designed housing cannot only give the illusion of being larger but it can also provide more usable living space than can a poorly designed house of the same size. Unfortunately, well-designed housing usually costs more.

To maintain satisfying interpersonal relationships certain amounts of space are required when people live together. Space is required for sleeping, eating, meal preparation, grooming, cleaning, recreation, privacy, storage, individual activities and group activities. Ideally, space should be flexible so that it can be utilised differently as needs and interests change.

Overcrowding can limit the emotional and social development of all people living together in the same housing. Lack of space, both internal and external, can limit the activities of individuals and families and thus affect social development. It has been suggested that, as a lower limit of internal space requirements, one person needs one room, two people need two rooms, after which one bedroom is required for every three people plus two extra living spaces. As an upper limit of external space requirements, one person needs one room, two people need two rooms, three people need three rooms, and after that, one bedroom for each two people, with two extra living spaces. Both limits require that

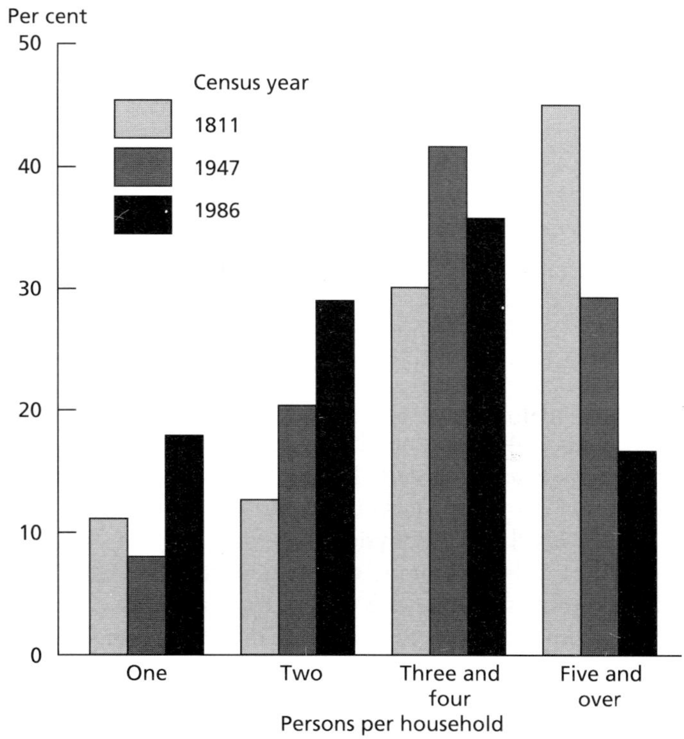

Figure 9.1 Household size: Number of persons in household, Australia 1811–1986.

Source: ABS, *Commonwealth Year Books 1988* and *1991*, pp. 266, 130 respectively.

the housing has a bathroom and a kitchen.[1] The average number of people living in a dwelling varies with the type of dwelling. In Australia, separate houses accommodate an average of three people, while medium-density and high-rise buildings tend to house an average of two people per dwelling. In 1986, there was an average of one person for each bedroom. Between 1981 and 1986 there was a decrease in the number of dwellings containing less than two bedrooms, and in 1986, three-bedroom dwellings still accounted for the majority of housing. However, during this period of time there was an increase of 21 per cent in the number of dwellings with four or more bedrooms.[2]

Demographic changes in fertility and mortality are contributing to smaller households, and there has been a continuing growth in one-person and two-person households. Figure 9.1 indicates the decline in the number of people per household dwelling between 1811 and 1986.

1 R. King, *The Dimensions of Housing Need in Australia*, Sydney, 1973, p. 22.
2 Australian Bureau of Statistics, *Australia in Profile*, Canberra, 1988, pp. 59–60.

The average number of people per household dwelling has decreased from 3.5 in 1954 to 2.9 in 1986. Early figures from the 1991 Census indicate that household growth will be greater than population growth and the number of people per dwelling will have further reduced.

Physical environment

> An essential ingredient of successful urban planning is the recognition that the physical environment bears directly upon the social and psychological environment. The planner has the responsibility to consider the implications of his physical design for the social and psychological wellbeing of its users.[3]

Although the majority of housing in Australia satisfies most of the physical needs described earlier, the degree to which each dwelling satisfies these needs varies widely. Even in Australia, not all families have physical needs of housing satisfied. Different families may have different ideas as to the ideal physical environment, but in Australia there does appear to be a common conception: real-estate advertising emphasises seclusion, water views, location, trees, gardens, quiet streets, proximity to shops, schools and recreational facilities. Inadequate or inappropriate housing can lead to ill health, family conflict, poor interaction, stress, tension, feelings of insecurity and the absence of normal interpersonal relationships.

For most individuals and families, housing is the major expenditure; for low-income families, this expenditure can perpetuate relative poverty. The physical environment must assist in satisfying social and psychological needs.

Psychological needs

Security

Housing provides a buffer between family and society. The dwelling and its location should be such that it provides psychological security for individuals within families. Families may feel insecure if they know they may have to move because of rezoning. Similarly, individuals and families who are renting may also experience insecurity if they know they can be told to leave their accommodation at short notice. In general, owner–purchasers of dwellings often feel more secure, both financially and psychologically.

3 M.H. Hoekstra, *The Aged and Housing in Perspective*, Sydney, 1976, p. 1.

Identity and self-esteem

Housing is often an extension of the people occupying it. It is part of their self-image, and allows them to identify with something that belongs to them. When housing is substandard, the self-esteem of those within a family can be affected. Tenants may sustain feelings of inferiority if they have not met the general Australian standard of owning or purchasing housing.

Independence

Housing should provide space for independent activities of both individuals and the group. Space or territory is required to develop individual interests and activities independently of others. Children also need space for activities that are an important part of socialisation.

Love and affection

Housing should provide an atmosphere whereby emotional needs can be satisfied through family interaction. When conflict and tension arise as a result of poor housing environment, the emotional needs of individuals in a family may not be fully met.

Stimulation

The physical environment should provide varied stimulation of the senses—sight, sound, smell and touch. A dwelling may be very functional, but have little aesthetic appeal to simulate the senses. Some people do not mind if a living area faces a brick wall of a nearby dwelling, provided the internal physical environment is satisfying and comfortable. For other families, the external physical environment—including garden, trees and outlook—is a more important medium of stimulation. As Australia becomes more urban in character, it is important for many people that housing provides sufficient stimulation. Stimulation is essential for the psychological health of individuals and families.

The greater the availability of economic resources, the more individuals and families can afford to pay for an environment which is pleasant and stimulating, e.g. bush and/or water views. Low-income families, who do not have these economic resources at their disposal and cannot afford to spend a large amount on entertainment or recreation, may lack stimulation within their environment.

Creativity and self-expression

Humans need to be able to make some imprint on their environment. For families, this need is often satisfied by decoration of the interior of housing: adding personal items and arranging furniture. Individuals also need some personal space, e.g. a bedroom, where self-expression is fostered. For families who rent accommodation, this need may not be well met: to re-decorate a dwelling and then move elsewhere can be costly as well as frustrating.

Quietness

Some people enjoy living in a noisy environment where there is much activity in preference to peaceful seclusion. For others, living in an area subject to traffic noise, plumbing noise and industrial noise can be disturbing. Families should have some choice as to where they live, but economic circumstances often limit this freedom.

Social needs

The need to belong

Most humans need to feel as though they belong to a particular group or community. This is usually achieved through membership of a family group, and housing provides a home base for this need to be satisfied.

Socialisation, interaction and companionship

Families remain the primary agency for the socialisation of individuals. The physical environment should provide for the growth and development of all members by providing a situation where interaction and communication are fostered and encouraged. Adequate space, stimulation, comfort, convenience and facilities for self-expression all assist in the socialisation process.

Although companionship is a basic human need, it is also necessary to have space for individual activities. When children have nowhere to play with their toys other than the living-room, and the parents want to use the area to entertain friends or listen to music, conflict and stress can result.

Privacy

The amount and type of privacy required by families will vary with the size, composition and activities of individual families. In addition to the space required for group activities, areas must be allocated to provide activities: parents need privacy from their children, and children need privacy from their parents. Private space—for study, sewing, reading, listening to music etc—is necessary to maintain family harmony.

Leisure, recreation and relaxation

Individuals and families vary greatly as regards both the type of leisure and recreation they enjoy. If a family utilises community recreational and leisure facilities, they may require little space in the home for leisure and recreational activities. A family may need more space to cater for the diverse activities of all individuals; a couple without children may be more concerned with using available space for entertainment. If leisure and recreational pursuits require equipment, e.g. golf clubs, bicycles, fishing rods, surfboards etc., storage space will also be required.

Status

For some people, housing simply means shelter; for others it is a status symbol. For many families, housing satisfies both these needs and enhances the prestige of individuals and families. Housing is often seen as an extension of self.

Low-density, medium-density and high-density housing

As 86 per cent of Australians now live in urban areas, and with rural–urban migration continuing, either the urban sprawl must extend further or the density of housing must increase. With rising land and house prices in urban areas, the great Australian dream of owning a free-standing house in the suburbs is becoming unobtainable for many people. A detached dwelling may have much to offer the family in satisfying social and psychological needs, but it is by no means the only form of housing that can do so.

As illustrated in Figure 9.2, at the 1986 Census 81 per cent of Australia's population lived in separate or detached dwellings, 11 per cent of the population lived in medium-density dwellings and 1 per cent in high-rise accommodation. When comparing the Australian-born population with the overseas-born population, the former are more likely to live in medium-density and high-rise housing. However,

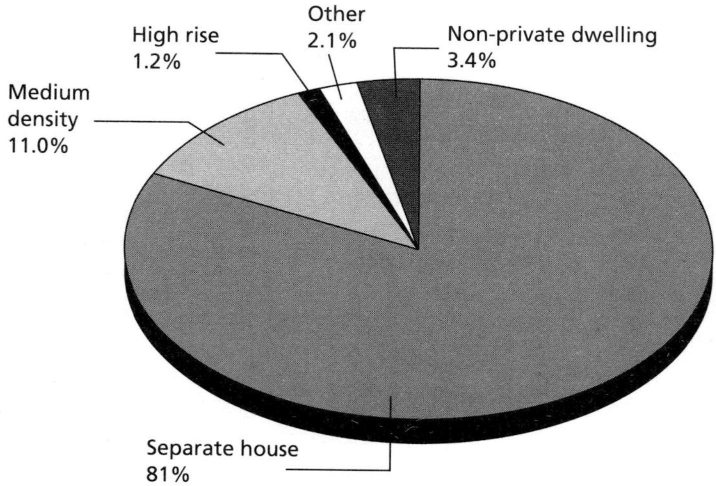

Figure 9.2 Type of dwelling, Australia 1986.
Source: Various ABS data

the majority of overseas-born still wish to live in detached dwellings; 75 per cent of overseas-born live in separate houses. It is apparent that most families with dependent children live in separate or semi-detached houses, but a comparatively high proportion of single-parent families live in medium-density housing. This is shown in Figure 9.3.

It has been generally believed that owning a separate or detached house gives a person respectability, status and pride. Low-density housing has been the community norm in Australia for many years. This form of housing has many advantages: it offers privacy and space and, unlike a unit, can be extended if the need arises.

However, this type of housing can also create problems of isolation and loneliness if there is little opportunity for interaction within the surrounding neighbourhood. For families where both partners work, there may not be time for the required upkeep and maintenance. Families without children, aged couples, and single pensioners may not require a free-standing house with three bedrooms. Low-density housing cannot therefore be regarded as the ideal form of housing.

There are more dwellings in Australia that are undercrowded rather than overcrowded. A high proportion of older people occupy housing designed for nuclear families and many have little interest in moving to a smaller dwelling. Thus, there is a significant under-utilisation of separate detached houses in Australia; this can create problems for young people who are trying to obtain housing in established areas and, for the aged, problems of maintaining homes and gardens.

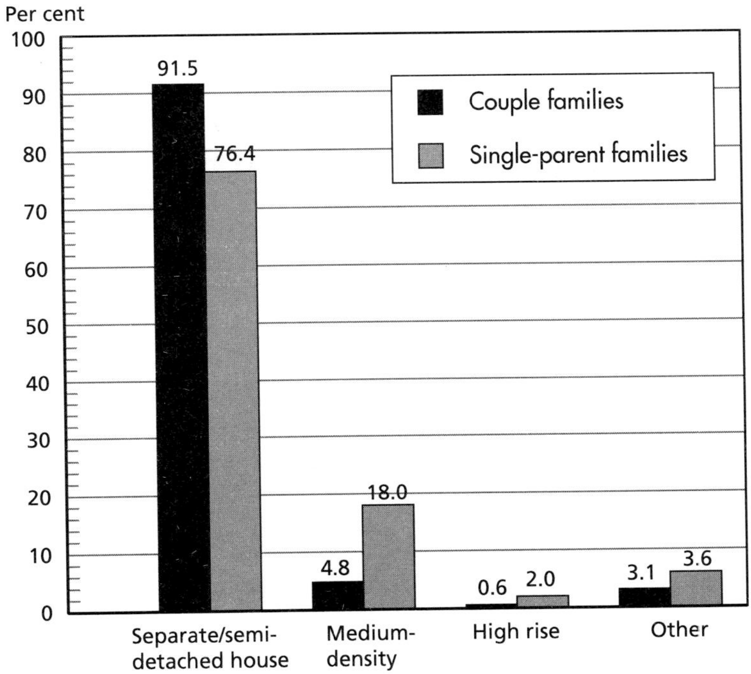

Figure 9.3 Housing arrangements for couple families and single-parent families, Australia 1986.

Source: Various ABS data

Current community values and standards are such that children should have a separate room from their parents, children of different sexes should have separate rooms, and each adolescent child should have a separate room; there must be external play-space for children, and adequate living and bathroom facilities. While these standards appear to relate to low-density housing, medium-density housing can satisfy the needs of many families.

Integration of low- and medium-density housing can provide variations of dwellings in one locality, so that families at different stages of their life cycle can find accommodation to suit their needs. Integration can provide a greater diversity of people, and allow those with lower incomes a greater choice of locality. When medium-density housing is built in established areas, there may be a greater availability of community facilities, including transport, employment, educational institutions, recreational opportunities and family support systems. The dispersal of medium-density housing throughout established areas may provide aged people with the incentive to move. Often elderly people do not wish to move away from familiar areas and remain living in unsuitable residential situations.

Medium-density housing has become more popular during the past decade as the cost of low-density housing has risen and the limitations of low-density housing have been recognised. Medium-density housing can include blocks of units no more than three storeys high, terraced houses, villas, townhouses, semi-detached houses and duplex houses. This type of housing is described as 'medium-density' because it occupies less land and there are more people per square hectare than in low-density housing, but not as many as in high-density accommodation. Medium-density housing is seen as a compromise between the under-utilisation of housing, as in low-density, and the overcrowding which is experienced in high-density housing. Medium-density housing is also seen as a way of stopping the urban sprawl—the building of housing on the urban fringes, where there is a lack of established community resources and support networks.

Medium-density housing was restricted in the past to certain areas by zoning laws, but in most states it is now built in the same areas as low-density housing. Units, townhouses, duplexes and villas are usually strata-title; owners have legal ownership of their accommodation but share responsibility and ownership of common property.

Homelessness

Census collectors have attempted to obtain data on the homeless—people who live in the open, in cars or truck cabins, or temporarily in tents and caravans (not caravan parks). Some people who are homeless may also be counted among the people who spent the Census night in shelters, refuges and hostels for the homeless. Because of the difficulty in locating homeless people, the number of homeless counted in the Census is likely to be understated.

Types of housing

Semi-detached houses

These are usually two houses of the same design, joined together and having a common middle wall. Although such dwellings have a fairly narrow frontage, some often have a small garden at the rear of the dwelling and a driveway at the side. The size varies with the design, but usually they have two bedrooms. This type of housing has less space than a fully detached house, thus it may be suitable for small families, couples or elderly people. Often these houses are built close to city centres and this appeals to many people who work in the city.

Figure 9.4 A detached home in the suburbs.

Figure 9.5 A semi-detached house in South Melbourne, renovated by the Victorian Housing Commission. (Photo: M. Deliopolous, Housing Commission of Victoria)

TERRACED HOUSES

These are an extension of semi-detached houses and may be one, two or three storeys high. Usually they are built in a row, having common

Figure 9.6 Three-storey terraced housing in Kings Cross, Sydney.

walls on both sides, but some have one common wall, with driveway access at one side. The size of the outdoor living area usually varies with the size of the house. If this area is small, it may have the advantage of little maintenance. The number of bedrooms ranges from two to four, thus making them suitable dwellings for a variety of family types. Terraced housing offers advantages over unit living, as it provides more external living space.

TOWNHOUSES

These are a modern version of terraced housing, often built around a courtyard rather than in a row. Some housing developments combine medium-density blocks of units with groups of townhouses. A well designed townhouse can offer as much privacy as a detached house if the courtyard is not overlooked by neighbours. Townhouses have less external space than detached houses, but there is usually sufficient outdoor living area for relaxation, entertainment and children's play. There is usually a common garden area.

While this type of dwelling may not be suitable for elderly people because of the stairs, it may be very suitable for other families. A townhouse can be sufficiently large enough to allow space for activities and privacy, yet small enough to reduce maintenance.

Figure 9.7 Townhouses in Melbourne built by the Victorian Housing Commission.

Villa units

Villa units are a compromise between detached houses and medium-density units. They are usually single-storey, with no common walls, and have a private lawn and garden. They have the appearance of smaller detached houses, yet offer similar advantages to townhouses. They can be a viable alternative for elderly people, as maintenance is reduced and there are no stairs. The space provided is often sufficient for a family with two children.

Duplexes

A duplex house is two storeys high, each level being a self-contained dwelling, that is, one house on top of another. Sometimes two adjoining identical dwellings are constructed on a single block of land. Duplex dwellings have the advantage of providing cheaper housing and are becoming more common in urban areas, particularly in the major cities where the land costs are high.

Dual occupancy

This is a provision by which additional dwellings could be added to a detached cottage or dwelling. This can take a variety of forms including conversion of one dwelling to two separate housing areas, adaptation

Figure 9.8 This housing development combines villa and units with townhouses. (Photo: M. Deliopolous, Housing Commission of Victoria)

and extension of an existing dwelling, or the building of a dwelling often known as a 'granny flat'. Some families with large houses have been able to let out part of their housing as self-contained units; this has been done to help pay off the mortgage or increase family income when economic resources have been limited. Dual occupancy may have become more common in frequent years as young couples live with parents, but effectively in separate households. This reduces housing costs for young couples as they save for their own housing.

Medium-rise units

As with townhouses and villas, the size and design of units varies enormously. They range from 'studio' units (bedsitter) to one-bedroom, two-bedroom, three-bedroom and large penthouse-type units. As the size and facilities increase, so too does the cost. The facilities inside each unit vary considerably: some have internal laundries, while others have external or communal laundries. In general, older units are less likely to have internal self-contained laundries or spacious kitchens.

The suitability of units for individual families will depend upon the size of sleeping and living areas, internal facilities, size of balconies, extent of soundproofing and maintenance costs. The viability of unit living at various stages of the family life cycle will be determined by the composition and needs of the family. There is no firm evidence to suggest that personal garden space is necessary for the socialisation of

Figure 9.9 Duplex housing built by the Victorian Housing Commission

children, but there should be adequate internal space for all family members. Some units are designed to offer large outdoor living areas on balconies, and provide buffer zones between family space and common property.

Units can be an ideal environment for couples or families who spend little time at home or do not wish to spend time on maintaining the extra space of a house and garden. The suitability of units for elderly people will be dependent on the availability of a lift, as stairs can present a problem: unit blocks three storeys high with garages built

Figure 9.10 Medium-density housing: This block of mixed double and single-storey units in North Geelong, Victoria was built for public housing. (Photo: R. Giesbers)

underneath are not, for example, required to provide a lift. Residents of unit blocks with a lift generally have higher maintenance costs.

High-rise housing

High-rise dwellings have come in for much criticism over the past two decades, and as a result most state housing departments have adopted a preferential policy of planned housing developments of low and medium density. While many of the criticisms of high-rise units are valid, there are also advantages in this type of living.

Low-income high rise has been criticised far more rigorously than upper-income high rise. High-rise dwellings in affluent suburbs may provide more space, better-quality amenities and facilities, and more desirable physical surroundings, but they do have some problems that are common to low-income high-rise dwellings. However, more affluent families can choose where to live; low-income families have less flexibility. Both groups have similar basic needs, but one socioeconomic group has a better chance of satisfying them. Lack of private space affects lower socioeconomic groups more than higher socioeconomic groups, as the latter have the resources to go out more and engage in activities outside the home. Low-income families are less likely to own a car and have fewer opportunities to visit areas away from their immediate physical environment. Higher income means the possibility of more space, and thus greater freedom in the choice of internal and external physical environment.

It is difficult to determine if the problems of families living in low-income high-rise accommodation are due to the physical environment itself, or rather to the lack of opportunities which result from the low

Figure 9.11a High-rise housing development built by the Victorian Housing Commission. (Photo: Stuart Pemberthy Pty Ltd)

Figure 9.11b Community centres in housing developments provide opportunities for social interaction between the inhabitants. (Photo: M. Deliopolous/Housing Commission of Victoria)

income. As it is more likely to be a combination of many factors, moving from a high-rise development to medium-density housing will not solve all problems or satisfy all needs. The benefits of low-income high-rise are listed below:

- With rising land prices, high-rise dwellings can provide more accommodation in a given area at a lower cost per dwelling.

- High-rise developments are usually situated close to transport, shops and other amenities.
- As a lift is provided, problems related to steps and stairs are avoided.
- This type of dwelling can provide for a social mix: combinations of young families, older families, single people and the aged.
- For some individuals and families, the location and design of this physical environment allows more mobility.
- Rental is usually lower than for detached housing.
- Little personal maintenance of external areas is required.
- High-rise dwellings can offer views that are unavailable in low-density housing.
- If there is adequate space, appropriate design and attractive surroundings, and suitable playgrounds, and if community facilities are nearby, high-rise dwellings may suit the needs of many individuals and families and promote their social and psychological wellbeing. It is important that people have a choice of the density of housing in which they want to live. High rise dwellings have limitations, some of which are listed below:
- Perhaps the greatest disadvantage of high-rise dwellings is overcrowding. Crowding may promote more interaction, but overcrowding can lead to stress and tension. There may also be a correlation between overcrowding and increased infection. When defining overcrowding, it must be done in relation to the society's standard of adequate space. For example, families in Hong Kong live in grossly overcrowded dwellings, yet studies have shown that this does not lead to anti-social behaviour. This has been attributed to traditional Chinese values of family cohesion, which are internalised by individuals through the socialisation process. Also, in Japan, particularly in Tokyo, space is so limited and expensive that families have no choice but to live in small apartments.
- Although high-rise residents often complain of isolation and loneliness, it is unclear whether this results from the physical environment per se or lack of a supportive family and social network. Lack of appropriate community facilities can certainly contribute to isolation and loneliness.
- Parents often feel unable to cope with emergencies that arise while children are playing in unsupervised playgrounds below the unit. They may therefore be reluctant to let children play by themselves and confine them indoors, which can inhibit interaction and hinder socialisation. Most parents feel a private backyard allows children security and freedom without upsetting the neighbours: children can leave toys unattended in their own backyard, but this is not possible in the communal playground of a high-rise dwelling.

- A Sydney study has shown that children in low-income high-rise units are more likely to play in nearby parks than in the unit playground area—possibly because the area does not provide enough intimacy or security. The playground area is often open and exposed, and visually uninteresting: there is a need to enclose these areas, and to provide toilets at ground level and some form of adult supervision. This study further discovered that children in low-income high rise did not identify with outdoor space, whereas children in upper-income high rise were more likely to include the external surroundings of the dwelling when asked to illustrate their home.[4]
- Communal facilities, including external laundries, can cause conflict over use, and frustration when the equipment malfunctions.
- Structural noise, e.g. plumbing, waste disposal, laundry use, stairway design and lift operation can all create problems for residents. Children who play in corridors may disrupt neighbours.
- The sway of high-rise buildings, and air currents that prevent windows from being opened fully, may affect some residents.
- Lack of privacy, storage space, and space for individual as well as family activities can create conflict and tension.
- Parents are often concerned and anxious about children riding alone in lifts. Frustration occurs when lifts continually malfunction, or when the waiting time is considered to be too long. While more affluent high-rise accommodation may have similar problems, services are usually of a higher standard as the residents can afford to pay more.
- Families who live in this type of public housing accommodation often do not identify with it as being home. There is a stigma attached to low-income high-rise housing, and such feelings can lower the self-esteem of individuals and families.

Other forms of housing

Over the last decade there has been a relaxation of the regulations regarding granny flats, modular homes and caravan accommodation. Granny flats and other forms of housing for aged people have been discussed in the previous chapter. Due to the economic recession and the high costs of housing there has been a significant increase in the number of people living in modular homes and caravans. There is perhaps a need for an increased use of forms of accommodation which can be utilised when the need arises. The use of temporary dwellings or

4 R. King, *The Dimensions of Housing Need in Australia*, p. 17.

backyard caravans to be used as flexible additions for children, teenagers or aged relatives needs more investigation.

TENANTS AND OWNERS

The majority of families in Australia place a great value on home ownership. Home ownership contributes to feelings of psychological, social and physical security, and a sense of control over one's lifestyle. Australia has traditionally been renowned as a nation of home owners with approximately 70 per cent of dwellings being occupied by the owner/s or purchaser/s.

Figure 9.12 shows the proportion of people who own, are purchasing or are renting accommodation. Early figures from the 1991 census show that more homes in Australia are now owned and the proportion may be closer to 40 per cent. This is a result of an ageing population and thus more people having paid off their mortgage. However, with rising prices, inflation and the high interest rates of the 1980s, the proportion of home purchasers may not have continued to increase, as census figures indicate that the number of properties purchased between 1981 and 1991 dropped dramatically—from 33 per cent in 1981 to 26.6 per cent in 1991. Approximately 24 per cent of people reside in rental accommodation and, of this, 5 to 6 per cent rent from public housing authorities.

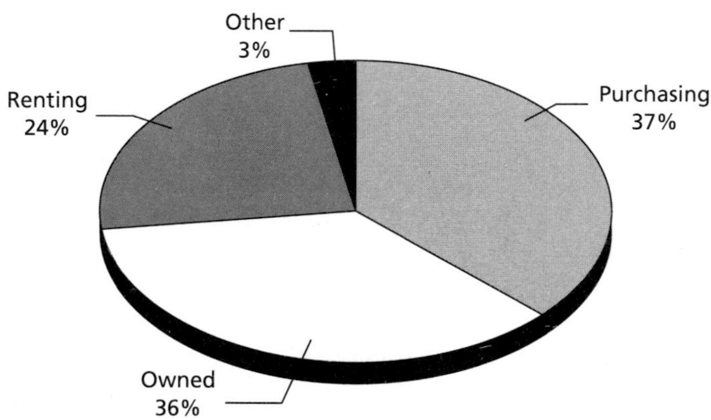

Figure 9.12 Owning, buying, renting, Australia 1986.
Source: Various ABS data

FAMILY STRUCTURE

Figure 9.13 shows the differences with regard to renting and owning that exist between couple families with dependent children and single-parent families. There is a higher proportion of single-parent families renting accommodation than the proportion of couple families with children. While more couple families with children own or are purchasing housing, the difference between the proportion of both family formations who own housing is not significant.

Single-parent families headed by a male are more likely to be purchasing accommodation, while those headed by a female are more likely to be renting accommodation. Many female single parents find home ownership out of their reach as a result of high housing costs and the fact that wages for women still tend to be lower than for males. It is important to note that many single-parent families are likely to change

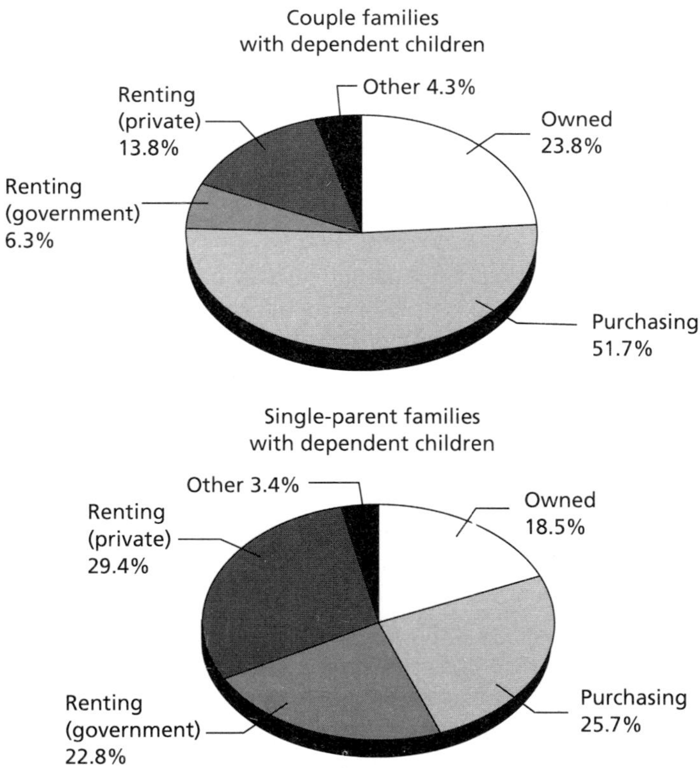

Figure 9.13 Housing occupancy by family type, Australia 1986.
Source: Various ABS data

their family formation and become a blended family. When there are two adult partners, families are more likely to be purchasing accommodation.

Overseas-born Australians

Home ownership and home purchasing among the overseas-born and the Australian-born are very similar, yet there are some significant differences. Home ownership rates for those born in Italy, Malta, Greece and Yugoslavia are virtually the same as the Australian-born population. However, in 1986 only 39 per cent of Vietnamese, 48 per cent of New Zealanders and 58 per cent of those born in Turkey and the United States of America owned or were purchasing housing. The differences are largely due to length of residence in Australia—the longer the period of time spent in Australia, the greater the likelihood of being an owner/purchaser. Vietnamese sustain a disadvantage in purchasing housing as they have tended to come to Australia under refugee and humanitarian programs and do not meet the usual economic criteria.

Aborigines

Prior to European settlement, Aborigines traditionally lived in shelters constructed from local and easily obtainable materials. They could be erected quickly and abandoned if necessary, or erected elsewhere. Some Aborigines who live in tribal areas continue to construct temporary shelters.

Most Aboriginal and Torres Strait Islander households are family households and very few Aboriginal people live alone. Ten per cent of the Aboriginal population live in multi-family households compared to 2 per cent for the total population. This can indicate two things: Aborigines prefer to reside together and there is a shortage of housing for Aborigines.

In rural areas, substandard housing seems to be a problem for many Aborigines. Housing is often lacking facilities for food storage and preparation as well as bathroom and laundry facilities. On many Aboriginal reserves, facilities are also inadequate and in country areas, residential blocks for Aboriginal housing are often grouped together and segregated from the rest of the town. While discrimination on the basis of race or ethnicity is illegal, Aborigines have been denied access to housing for this reason.

Aborigines have the least choice in the housing market. Approximately 10 per cent of Aborigines own or are purchasing accommodation, compared to over 70 per cent for the total Australian population. European-style housing is often not a solution for Aboriginal people. Attempts have been made to build more appropriate accommodation for Aborigines in the form of larger homes to cater for extended family and friend networks. However, European-style housing is not always the answer and does not really cater for the large diversity of Aboriginal lifestyles or for the difficulties often experienced by Aborigines in adapting to contemporary Australian life.

Housing costs

Housing costs can take up a large proportion of family income and can contribute to poverty in low-income families. (This has been discussed in greater detail in Chapter 7.) Housing, including running costs, is usually the greatest expense for families. It has been recommended that housing costs do not exceed 25 per cent of family income, yet this is often insufficient to meet mortgage repayments or pay rent. Low-income earners may spend up to 50 per cent of income on housing costs, particularly if they reside in major urban areas. A housing survey conducted by the Australian Bureau of Statistics in 1988 found that relative housing costs were higher for single-parent families renting in the private sector. On average they spent 37 per cent of gross weekly income on rent.[5] Many families have little choice but to spend a high proportion of income in order to secure very basic housing.

It is acknowledged that individuals and families who spend more than 30 per cent of income on housing are likely to suffer financial housing stress. Some families may choose to spend a high proportion of income on housing, as they place a high priority on home ownership, location, status etc.—also they may have sufficient flexibility of income to provide for other needs. Generally, couple-only families have the highest average mortgage repayments due to high housing prices and to higher repayments early in the life cycle.

From the mid-1970s onwards there has been a rapid escalation in housing prices. As housing prices increase, so too do rentals, as landlords have to reap a certain income from the investment to keep up with inflation. For individuals and families trying to purchase housing it can be very difficult to pay rent and save for a deposit on housing. The financial costs of changing residence—including legal

5 Australian Bureau of Statistics, *Australia's Children*, 1989, Canberra, 1990, p. 19.

fees, stamp duty and real-estate agent fees—may force families to remain in a dwelling that does not meet their needs. Families who rent dwellings also sustain costs in moving residence, although they are not as great as when buying and selling.

Home owners are financially better off than tenants. They can benefit from inflation as home prices rise and they accumulate more equity in their dwelling. Tenants, however, are forced to pay high rents, thus limiting their ability to save for a deposit on a home. Furthermore, rents may increase so much that low-income families can no longer afford to rent a dwelling of optimum size or live in the area of their choice. This may mean moving away from familiar areas and community facilities, and cause disruption to family life. Also, the quality of rental accommodation is often lower than that of owned accommodation.

During the economic recession of the 1980s and 1990s many families have faced unemployment and have not been able to meet mortgage repayments. When future employment prospects are bleak, for many families there is no choice but to sell the family home and buy less expensive accommodation. Even so, downgrading accommodation also requires a significant amount of money to be spent on legal fees and stamp duty costs. At a time when the family is sustaining considerable stress as a result of unemployment, change in housing can also produce more stress for adults and children.

WELLBEING

Families who own or are purchasing housing sustain some advantages in a society which places a high value on home ownership. Owner/purchasers have greater opportunities for self-expression. Families usually stay in one place for a longer period and may be able to develop friendships with neighbours. Studies have shown that stability and security of tenure can be as important to the wellbeing of children as the quality of the housing. Stability in housing is particularly important for children when they are experiencing other stressful circumstances or disruptions in their life, such as in the case of separation or divorce of parents or the blending of families.

Being restricted to one location for a long period of time may not be acceptable to everyone, as it might preclude living near the workplace or other amenities that a particular family may value. On the other hand, families who rent accommodation may be asked to leave at fairly short notice if the dwelling is sold and it may be difficult to find other accommodation quickly. It is often stated that tenants have an advantage over owners as they do not have to pay rates or insurance on the dwelling, but these expenses are in fact included in the rent. Most families rent housing at some stage during the life cycle, but not all have the same opportunities to purchase a home. Renting accommodation provides little financial security, and for this reason the aged who do not own their accommodation can be severely disadvantaged by high rentals.

When the advantages and disadvantages of renting and buying are analysed, it must be done in relation to the effect of the physical environment upon the social and psychological wellbeing of families. On the one hand, renting accommodation may contribute to feelings of insecurity. On the other hand, overcommitment to high mortgage repayments may create anxiety. Each state has a government agency which deals with tenant's rights and provides assistance to tenants in disputes with owners and real-estate agents.

HOUSING DECISIONS THROUGH THE LIFE CYCLE

As families move through the stages of the life cycle, different demands will be placed upon particular resources as individual and family needs change. Ideally, families would be able to change accommodation as housing needs change, but limited economic resources prevent this for most families. In discussing the needs of families through the life cycle, we must be realistic about what the average family can afford to pay for accommodation. Alternatives to a free-standing house must also be

Table 9.1 The family life cycle

Stage	Number of years	Sub-stage
1 Beginning or establishment	0–6±	
2 Expanding	31±	a) Child-bearing b) Primary-school children c) Secondary-school children d) Children leaving home
3 Contracting and retirement	20±	

considered, as this is not the only type of housing that can satisfy individual and family needs. Housing decisions throughout the family life cycle will be influenced by personal values, present and future needs and interests, amount of time spent at home, income, employment status of one or both partners, age, health, number of children (if any) and availability of housing.

Any framework used to illustrate the family life cycle must be flexible; not all families have children, and those that do will have varying numbers of children at different ages and sexes, and at different intervals. Families will spend varying amounts of times in the stages and substages of the life cycle: some families may repeat stages while other families may be in two stages at the same time. A family can change from being a single-parent family to a blended family to eventually a couple family. Blended families can experience a situation where they have very young dependent children and at the same time have older children who are in the process of leaving home.

BEGINNING FAMILIES

In addition to living space, a couple will often require a bedroom and another room which can be used as a study, workroom or storeroom. This room may become the first child's bedroom if the couple chooses to have a child or children. Couples may rent accommodation until they have sufficient money saved as a deposit for a housing loan. Loan repayments during this stage may be quite high in relation to wages, as both partners may not have reached their highest income-earning level. It may also be a consolidation period, in which high mortgage repayments are made in order to acquire some equity in property.

As the cost of housing is high, it is unlikely that many couples will be able to initially purchase housing. If the majority of both partners' interests are pursued outside the home, they may not require a large amount of internal housing space and they may opt for a unit, villa or semi-detached house. The accommodation may not be the most desired type, but it may be within the limits of their economic capacity.

There is little information available on the life cycle of childless families. As both partners usually work and have not felt the economic strain caused by having children, they will possibly have more flexibility in housing decisions. The type of dwelling chosen will be primarily dependent upon economic resources, interests and values.

Expanding families

With the birth of the first child there is usually no immediate need for a family to move to larger accommodation. As a child grows and becomes more mobile, the need for space will increase. Similarly, the number of children a family has will determine the total amount of space required for harmonious living.

The bearing of children usually brings major changes to a family's economic position as household costs rise. If the wife/mother stops working, there may have to be considerable adjustment because household income is reduced. However, as many women leave work only temporarily, this may be only a short-term problem. If both partners continue working it will obviously be financially easier to obtain and maintain accommodation, although the work-related costs of a family with children will be higher than the costs for a family without children. Also, even when both partners are working, they may prefer housing which is not so large as to require all non-working time to be spent in cleaning and maintenance.

A family with young children requires a dwelling that has space, whether internal or external, for children's play and activities. It is usually desirable that this area can be easily supervised by parents who may be involved in other household activities. When economic resources are limited it is not always possible to afford accommodation that provides this convenience, and so children's bedrooms often have to serve as play areas. If bedrooms are not large enough for play, children may be inhibited in their activities.

Family and housing expenditures are perhaps highest during the years when children are at secondary school, as this is the time when costs of education, clothing and leisure tend to increase. It is desirable that teenagers have separate bathroom facilities from parents, and that they have a room to themselves. Privacy for students is often a motivating factor in satisfactory study habits, and space is necessary for group activities and interaction. During the expanding stage, furniture and household items may need replacing, and thus many families find it necessary to have two incomes to maintain an acceptable standard of living.

Contracting families

As children leave home, the financial strain eases and the couple's needs are similar to those at the beginning-family stage. They may modify a house, or they may decide to move to another dwelling—a decision which will be influenced by their financial resources and their physical ability to maintain their current accommodation. Housing for older and aged people has been discussed in greater detail in Chapter 8.

Housing mix

A mixture of housing types in the same area can attract people at different stages of the life cycle and prevent any particular group from becoming predominant. Mixing or integration of different housing densities provides for a social mix of people and also places less strain on those resources and facilities that specifically cater for individuals at a certain lifespan stage. Young singles and young couples often remain living in the area in which they grew up because they can afford to buy or rent medium-density housing such as a unit. Similarly, older people who no longer want the maintenance associated with a detached house have the option of moving to smaller accommodation in the form of medium-density housing. Redevelopment or gentrification of older inner city areas may also bring younger generations into ageing suburbs and thus promote a more heterogeneous community.

Decisions

As resources are usually limited, each family will have to consider all options related to housing. The final choice will ultimately depend upon values, needs and the available economic resources. The major housing decisions that families may have to make are listed below:

- Whether to rent housing. Rental housing, although not requiring a large initial investment, may not provide security for the future. However, it may be appropriate at certain stages of the life cycle.
- Whether to build, buy or renovate housing.
- Is the price suitable? What is the price range that can be afforded?
- What type of dwelling in which to live? Will a particular kind of dwelling satisfy present and future needs? Is moving intended at a later stage?
- How much external and internal privacy is required? Is the location quiet, free from traffic, industrial noise and pollution?
- Does living space provide facilities for meal preparation, dining, sleeping, privacy, storage, recreation and individual and group activities? Is this important?
- Does the location offer the community facilities required, including transport, schools, health and medical services? Which facilities are most valued?
- Is the dwelling designed for convenience? How much time is the family willing to spend on maintaining housing?

- Are all the services required by the family connected to dwelling, e.g. sewerage, telephone, gas etc.?
- Is the building structurally sound? Does it need major repairs? Is the family willing to renovate a dwelling?

HOUSING FOR DISABLED PEOPLE

Disabled people have the same basic needs as other individuals, but often require certain facilities to satisfy specific needs arising from their handicap or disability. These facilities may include ramps instead of stairs, larger bathroom facilities and wider doorways that enable a wheelchair to be manoeuvred. Disabled or handicapped people with low incomes, or little economic flexibility, may not be able to afford to have their house modified, or to buy an existing home which is suitably equipped. Features in housing that are appropriate for the aged are often appropriate for disabled people. These features have been outlined in the previous chapter.

UNCOORDINATED HOUSING DEVELOPMENTS

Between 1961 and 1965 the New South Wales Housing Commission built a large-scale housing estate at Green Valley, a suburb about 40 kilometres south-west of Sydney and a few kilometres west of Liverpool. Between 1961 and 1965, the population grew from 1003 to 24 602 and although the estate satisfied a desperate need for low-cost housing, a lack of coordinated social planning produced many problems for residents. In other capital cities of Australia, similar housing estates were established with the same lack of planning for necessary community resources.

Over the last two decades state governments have become more mindful of developing areas for housing without consideration of the necessary community facilities. If the urban sprawl of the major capital cities is allowed to continue without check, areas can be populated without thought to the support networks required by individuals and families. Medium-density housing has been seen as one way in which the urban sprawl can be checked and ensure that existing community facilities are utilised to a greater extent. However, housing on the fringe areas of metropolitan areas is usually still cheaper than the equivalent space in medium-density dwellings in established suburbs.

Between 1966 and 1969, Professor T. Brennan undertook a study of

Green Valley which was documented in a book called *New Community: Problems and Policies* (1973). Many of the results of this study are outlined below. While the area of Green Valley was developed three decades ago, a study of its development is useful when investigating all dimensions of housing. At the time Green Valley was established, there was little industrial development in the area and thus very few employment opportunities. As many of the families living in the area were eligible for public housing because of unemployment, the lack of job opportunities further compounded their problems. Many of the families living in the area at this time were single-parent families headed by females—who had even fewer opportunities than males to obtain full-time or part-time employment.

The problem of unemployment was further complicated by the lack of an efficient transport system in the area. Bus services to Liverpool and other areas were very limited, and were not coordinated with rail services from Liverpool. Many employees were forced to travel long distances to work, which increased costs and meant that parents were often away from home for over 12 hours a day. Such a situation does not provide conditions conducive to family and social interaction. Furthermore, employers tend to discriminate against job applicants who have to travel a long distance to the workplace. Lack of transport facilities also hinders interaction outside the housing development. For many families who move to new areas, away from kin and friends, social isolation can result: with a low income and thus little likelihood of owning a car, visits can be a problem.

Green Valley was planned to the extent that roads, sewerage, electricity and telephone services were available. Many community facilities were lacking, however, in the early days: there were few child-care centres, pre-schools or baby health centres (pre-schools were not established until 1970). The lack of such facilities furthered hindered parents in their quest to obtain employment as there was nowhere to leave children during working hours.

Medical and dental facilities were inadequate. As there were few shopping facilities, shopping usually had to be done in Liverpool—with inefficient transport systems, this could be an arduous chore particularly for women with young children. There were insufficient schools built to cope with a rapidly growing population and those that did exist became overcrowded. Social, recreational and service clubs (e.g. Apex and Rotary), which are present in most communities were lacking. Voluntary agencies, upon which low-income families rely heavily, were not established until the later years of development.

Social and family support systems are an integral part of any community as they help promote interaction. If individuals and families become isolated through a lack of private and public transport, inadequate recreational and community facilities, and the absence of kin and friends, social and psychological welfare can be detrimentally affected.

In the development of Green Valley, it would appear that the external physical environment had a greater effect on the wellbeing of the family than did the internal environment. In any program of decentralisation or community development, the planning of the total physical environment must be coordinated. Not only must an environment provide the necessary facilities, but it must also be aesthetically pleasing and stimulating.

PUBLIC HOUSING ACCOMMODATION

DEVELOPMENT OF PUBLIC HOUSING IN AUSTRALIA

During the first part of the nineteenth century, there was an acute shortage of building materials in Australia and thus a shortage of suitable family housing. During the gold rushes many 'jerry-built' houses were erected: they were lacking in sanitation, drainage, lighting and ventilation, and were later to form slum areas. It was not until 1906 that the New South Wales government specified sanitary, light and ventilation standards for housing, with minimum room sizes. While these new laws forced housing standards to rise, it was not a large improvement, as builders applied only the minimum standards in order to reduce costs. Only higher-income families could afford quality housing.

In 1912 the Housing Act was introduced to establish a Housing Board, which eventually built 315 houses, eight shops and a community hall. Throughout the 1930s depression the housing situation worsened. The government did build 56 flats during 1936 and 1937 to let to low-income families, but by the outbreak of the Second World War there was a desperate need for 120 000 houses—a need which still existed at the end of the war. In 1941 the New South Wales Housing Commission was established, but little work was undertaken until the end of the war.

The introduction of the Housing Assistance Act in 1981 provided for two programs: a home purchase assistance program and a rental housing assistance program to provide rental accommodation for those most in need. Other important features of this act included assistance to those most in need; special funds to be earmarked for pensioner and

Aboriginal housing, and flexibility to state housing authorities in how assistance was provided. In 1982, the Commonwealth government initiated a private rental assistance scheme in order to provide assistance for low-income earners who were renting accommodation in the private sector.

In 1973 the Australian government created the Department of Housing and Construction. The main objective of this department was to ensure individuals and families secured accommodation which was within their budget. Government policy aims to set housing standards and to control the home-building industry through an appropriate supply of land, finance, materials and labour. By integrating housing policy with government environmental objectives, land can be developed for housing and satisfactory living environments can be provided. Housing is provided for special groups, including migrants, Aborigines, the aged and repatriation beneficiaries. Decentralisation projects and the preservation of old housing areas in inner city locations are also concerns.

Objectives

The objectives of public housing are:

- To improve existing conditions by enforcing demolition and repair of substandard housing.
- To sell houses to eligible persons who are unable to buy them by other means and thus increase home ownership.
- To develop land for public housing accommodation.
- To provide good-quality housing, available at low rentals, for low-income families and pensioners.
- To support and encourage the private rental sector.
- To provide emergency housing.

In 1990 a new Commonwealth–State Housing Agreement (CSHA) covering all states and territories commenced. Part of this agreement includes a process to ensure that priorities for all groups such as youth, people with disabilities, Aborigines and the aged are met. CSHA provides funds for specific programs including rental assistance for pensioners and Aborigines, mortgage and rent relief, crisis accommodation and assistance for local government and community housing programs. Under the current agreement, eligibility for public housing will continue to be met by the states, with priority given to those most in need. Given the depressed state of the economy and cutbacks in government expenditure it is unlikely that expenditure on public housing will increase in the near future.

Access to public housing is no longer seen as housing for middle-income groups as it was following the Second World War. Unlike some other developed countries, in Australia, public housing is directed at those individuals and families with low incomes. Thus, public housing in Australia is seen as part of the welfare system, which can often carry negative images. Many social scientists have argued that more money should be and can be spent on housing through a redistribution of wealth, and thus provide acceptable accommodation for not only low-income earners but lower-income earners. This could be achieved to some extent through the abolition of taxation advantages that some property owners have, such as negative gearing.

Eligibility for public housing

Each state has a separate housing authority and eligibility for public housing varies accordingly. To become eligible for housing assistance, an applicant must be able to demonstrate financial incapacity to rent or buy private accommodation. A family or individual may be eligible in a variety of circumstances including:

- When present accommodation has been condemned as dangerous, unhealthy or overcrowded.
- When an aged couple is sharing accommodation with other people.
- When suitable housing is not available at a rental the family can afford.
- When there is extreme ill-health in the family.
- When a family or couple is forced to live apart because there is not enough money to pay for accommodation large enough to house all members.

Although many individuals and families may be eligible for public housing accommodation, long waiting-lists may prevent immediate housing. The increased demand for low-income housing has become difficult to satisfy as land and construction costs rise. Only a certain amount of money is allocated each year to maintain current accommodation and build new accommodation.

Public housing rentals in most states have been fixed at about 80 per cent of what private landlords would charge for similar accommodation, but assistance is such that families usually pay no more than 20 per cent of income on rent. As a result of social and economic factors, the demand for public housing in the 1980s has soared and this has meant substantial waiting lists. Single-parent families now form the majority of applicants for housing assistance.

Criticisms of public housing

Over the past few decades many criticisms have been levelled at public housing accommodation. Some of these are outlined below. It must be noted that in recent years many of these criticisms have been addressed at the design and placement of public housing.

- Often housing is functional but lacking in aesthetic appeal.
- Most of the units and houses look the same. This similarity is highlighted by their close proximity to each other. By utilising the same design for many dwellings, costs can be reduced.
- Public housing estates are too large. For such projects to be economically feasible, they have to be planned and built on a large scale.
- Historically, public housing has been built in areas where there are insufficient community facilities. The main reason for this is that land is cheaper in undeveloped and outer urban areas.
- People with similar problems are often clustered together, thus families do not have the opportunities to interact with a wide social mix of people.

Recent developments

Many new public housing developments are based on the townhouse concept. This type of dwelling is versatile as it provides accommodation for different family formations with private garden space as well as common garden space.

Home purchase assistance

- Subsidised loans are available to public housing tenants to purchase accommodation on the private market or to purchase their Department of Housing home. Loans are at a fixed interest rate, with a maximum loan rate and maximum property value applying. Other loans are available to assist moderate income earners who do not qualify as low-income earners but may not be able to obtain finance from lending institutions.
- The Mortgage Assistance Scheme is designed to provide short-term financial assistance to people who are facing serious financial difficulties in repaying their home mortgages as a result of an unexpected change in their circumstances.
- Pensioners and low-income earners may be entitled to assistance with bond money, first rent payment and moving expenses if forced to move due to exceptional circumstances.

- Each state has a home purchase advisory service which provides advice and information to the public on a wide range of home purchase matters, including sources of housing finance, government assistance schemes and the steps to take when buying or building a home.

Supported Accommodation Assistance—SAAP

SAAP was introduced in all states and territories in 1985 and brought together the former programs of the Women's Emergency Services Program, the Youth Services Scheme and the Homeless Persons' Assistance Program. SAAP which is funded jointly by the Commonwealth and State governments provides funds for a range of supported accommodation and related support services. Services include crisis accommodation and support services for homeless persons. Within this program, homeless youth have been identified as a priority target.

The Crisis Accommodation program (CAP) is totally Commonwealth-funded and the objectives of this program are to provide support services for people who are homeless and/or in crisis to help them move towards independent living. Under this program assistance is also given to women with or without children who are escaping from domestic violence.

To ensure that the social and psychological needs of all individuals and families are satisfied, our society has a responsibility to ensure that the physical environment is designed to promote satisfaction of these needs.

Review questions

1. Which resources are the main determinants of how well individuals and families can satisfy housing needs?
2. How do needs of families change?
3. How do values influence choice of housing location?
4. Describe the physical needs of families in relation to housing.
5. Outline the problems that may arise when the physical environment is inadequate.
6. Explain what is meant by overcrowding.
7. Describe the psychological needs of families in relation to housing.
8. Why do some families place a higher priority on certain housing needs?

9 Describe the social needs of individuals and families in relation to housing.
10 How is housing classified according to density?
11 What proportion of Australia's population lives in low-density housing?
12 Discuss how low-, medium- and high-density housing could be utilised at various stages of the life cycle.
13 Outline the advantages and disadvantages of medium-density housing.
14 Explain what is meant by a 'housing mix'.
15 With reference to housing, what disadvantages may Aborigines sustain?
16 It is often stated that owner–purchasers have an advantage over those who rent accommodation. Explain.
17 Outline the advantages of renting housing.
18 During a family's life cycle, certain housing decisions may be made. Outline these decisions.
19 Discuss how uncoordinated housing developments can affect the wellbeing of those who reside in them.
20 What are the objectives of public housing authorities?

Case study 9.1

A dual-income family

After three months of searching for a home they can afford, Colin and Louise have found nothing they like. All the homes in their price range are either too small, in great need of repair or maintenance, or in areas too far away from where they want to live. Louise is six months pregnant and feels a house and garden are necessary for a family with children. Colin is unsure about buying a house at this stage, as neither Louise nor himself particularly like gardening or spending a great deal of time on maintaining a house.

Louise has taken leave from her job but intends returning six months after the baby is born. When this happens, they will have even less time available to maintain and/or renovate a house.

They are currently living in a two-bedroom unit, on which they have a mortgage. They like the unit as it is relatively new, easy to care for, close to employment, and close to Colin's mother who will mind the baby when Louise returns to work.

QUESTIONS

1 Why does a conflict exist here?
2 What factors are influencing Louise's belief that a house and garden are necessary for children?
3 Do you believe a free-standing home to be essential for the socialisation of children? Give reasons for your answer.
4 What priorities do Colin and Louise have on any form of housing in which they decide to live?
5 What are the present housing needs of Colin and Louise? How will these needs change with the birth of the baby? When may these housing needs change again?
6 When Louise returns to work after the birth of her child, what physical aspects of housing may aid the smooth running of the household?
7 What housing alternatives do Colin and Louise have? Next to each alternative, list the values and goals that may be influencing each alternative decision.
8 Are there any other alternatives that Colin and Louise have not yet considered? Discuss.
9 What resources do Colin and Louise have to help them make this decision? Which resources are limited? Which resources may they not be aware of?
10 If Louise decided not to return to work, how might this affect their decision about the type of housing in which to live. Explain.

CASE STUDY 9.2

FAMILY ON THE MOVE

Phillip and Jean Martin have three children: Peter, aged 16, Christine, 14 and Debbie, 10. Phillip is employed as a fitter and machinist with a company that contracts labour to construction sites. This involves the family moving to each site where Phillip will be working—the time spent on each site may vary from a few months to a year. Usually the company provides temporary housing at a low rent, or it subsidises the cost of renting a house in a nearby town. Wages from this type of work are good, and Jean and Phillip have managed to save about $20 000 in the last eight years.

Jean is often very lonely, as Phillip's job requires that he work a great deal of overtime. She finds it difficult to make friends because she has to move so frequently, and as the children grow older they are becoming resentful as they have to change schools frequently and make new friends each time. Jean also feels that the lack of stable schooling for the children is detrimental to their educational achievement.

Phillip has offered to get a permanent job as a fitter and machinist in a town or city so the family can settle down and establish a home base. Jean, however, knows that Phillip would not really like this as he enjoys working on different sites. She has also considered the possibility of buying a house so that she and the children can live in one place while Phillip works elsewhere. This would enable the children to have a stable education, and allow Jean to make friends and perhaps return to work.

Jean and Phillip cannot decide between alternatives: they feel the family should stay together if possible, but that all individuals within the family must be considered.

QUESTIONS

1 For each family member, explain the needs that each may have.
2 Analyse the needs for each family member, given the stage in their life span, and discuss the extent to which these needs may be satisfied. To what extent will values determine this?
3 Who is making the decisions in this family? Explain.
4 What values are influencing the lifestyle of this family? Can you differentiate between individual and family values?
5 Does this family have clearly defined goals? Explain.
6 Why are Jean and Phillip having difficulty in choosing a course of action for this family?
7 What resources does this family have to help them choose a suitable course of action?
8 If Phillip and Jean decided to buy a home, what factors would they have to consider in their choice?
9 Communication is an important resource. To what extent is this resource being utilised in this family?
10 Explain why this is a management problem.

CASE STUDY 9.3

A FAMILY LIFE CYCLE

Joanne and Russell have been married for three years. They are currently renting half a house in a suburb about 30 minutes from the city by train. They have been informed by the real-estate agent that when their lease expires in three months, the house is to be put up for sale by the owner and they will have to move.

Joanne and Russell have been saving with a building society since they were married, with the goal of one day obtaining a home loan to purchase housing. As they now have to move, Joanne would prefer to use the money they have saved as a deposit to buy a home unit—provided they can obtain approval for a loan. Russell, however, does not want to move to a unit as he feels that it would be too small and there would not be sufficient outdoor space. Joanne believes that if they do not buy something they can afford now, they will have to wait a long time to be able to buy a house. Meanwhile, house and unit prices will rise, they will be paying more for rent, and the value of their savings will be eroded.

Russell has suggested that they move further out of the city to an area where they can afford to buy a small house. Joanne likes the area in which they are currently living, as it is close to family and friends and her place of employment. She would like to continue working in the city for a few more years, or at least until they make the decision of whether or not to have children. Russell does not really mind where he lives or works, provided he can get a job in a similar field to that in which he is working now.

QUESTIONS

1 Define the conflict in this situation.
2 How are Joanne's values influencing her wish to purchase a unit?
3 How are Russell's values influencing his desire not to buy a home unit?
4 Why do families make different choices as to the form of housing in which they live?
5 What are the alternative decisions that Joanne and Russell could make?
6 Outline the advantages of their present location.
7 If they were to buy a house in the outer suburbs, what would be the advantages and the disadvantages?

8 What would be the advantages and disadvantages of buying a unit?

9 What forms of housing could Joanne and Russell utilise through their life cycle? Explain how this would be dependent upon whether or not they choose to have children?

10 Which resources could Joanne and Russell use to solve this problem? Which resources may be limited?

SURVEY

HOUSING

This survey may be used as a guide for interviewing families living in a variety of housing situations. It may help to establish patterns in families' choices of dwelling as they move through different stages of the life cycle. Move importantly, it may establish if the current housing situation of a family satisfies their particular needs.

A Composition of household

1 Number of adults in the household ____________________

2 Number, sex and age of children

____

____

____

____

____

3 Any relatives (grandparents, etc.) living in the household

____

4 Total number of people in the household

____

B Dwelling type

(Tick the appropriate spaces)

1 a free-standing house ______ b unit or flat ______

c townhouse ______ d villa unit ______

e	part of house	_____	f	semi-detached house	_____
g	duplex	_____	h	retirement village	_____
j	high-rise	_____	j	Housing Commission	_____
k	terraced house	_____	l	caravan	_____
m	other	_____			

2 a Rented ____________________

b Owned/Paying mortgage ____________________

3 External material of building

a	brick	_____	b	timber	_____
c	fibro	_____	d	weatherboard	_____
e	cement-rendered	_____	f	stone	_____
g	aluminium	_____	g	combination	_____
i	other	_____			

C Physical environment

(Fill in or tick the appropriate spaces)

1 a kitchen ____________________

b bathroom (no.) ____________________

c separate toilet ____________________

d combined bathroom/toilet ____________________

e lounge-room ____________________

f dining-room ____________________

g combined lounge and dining-room ____________________

h family room ____________________

i laundry ____________________

j number of bedrooms ____________________

k garage ____________________

l carport ____________________

m workshed ____________________

n sewing-room or study ____________________

o other rooms ____________________

TOTAL ____________________

2 **a** Children's outside play area (if applicable)

____

b Outside living areas

____

c Views from house

____

D Community facilities

(Fill in the spaces applicable to each family)

a Distance from shopping centre

____

b Distance from child-care centre

____

c Distance from pre-school

____

d Distance from primary school

____

e Distance from secondary school

____

f Distance from wife's employment

____

g Distance from husband's employment

____

h Availability of public transport

____

i Availability of private transport (e.g. car)

____

j Distance from recreational, sporting, leisure interests, etc.

____

____

____

____

k Distance from family doctor

____

l Distance from family dentist

____

m Distance from public library

____

E Social network

1 Distance from children's grandparents

a Paternal ______________________________

b Maternal ______________________________

2 Distance from close relatives

____

3 Distance from friends

____

4 Amount of social contact with family (kin network)

____

5 Amount of social contact with friends

____

6 Amount of social contact with neighbours

____

F Previous accommodation

1 What types of dwelling have you lived in since you were married?

____

____

____

____

2 a Where did you live prior to this location?

____

b Why did you move?

____

G Present accommodation

1 **a** What were your main reasons for choosing this particular accommodation?

____

____

____

b Are you satisfied with this accommodation?

Yes or No ______________________________

Reasons

____

____

____

2 **a** *Given more money*, in what location would you choose to live?

____

b Why would you choose this location?

____

____

____

c Which type of dwelling would you choose (e.g. townhouse, terrace, unit, etc.)?

____

3 What factors do you think a family must consider when it moves from one housing situation to another?

____

____

____

____

INFORMATION AND CONCLUSIONS

1 **a** Is the total number of rooms (excluding garage or carport) adequate for this family size?

____

b Is there a separate bedroom for each child?

____

2 Is there sufficient space for the privacy and activities of each individual member?

____

3 Is there space for family activities and interaction?

____

4 Does the outdoor living area satisfy the needs of the family?

____

5 a Which community facilities are important to this family?

____

b Are these facilities located within reasonable distance of the family home?

____

____

6 a With whom does the family interact most—kin, friends or neighbours?

____

b Is this group located nearby?

____

7 Has this family changed housing situations as needs and resources have altered?

____

8 Upon which aspects of housing does the family place highest priority (e.g. space, internal arrangement, community facilities etc.)?

____

____

____

10

Families, communities and support networks

What are communities?

The term *community* is often used to refer to many different social groups and types of social organisation—the Australian community, Aboriginal community, overseas community, local community, urban community, rural community, business community, prison community, medical community, educational community, legal community, ethnic community, school community, gay community, neighbourhood community etc. Just as it is difficult to define the term 'family', it is equally difficult to define the term 'community'. Among social scientists there have been many attempts to define the abstract term of 'community' and the debate over a definition continues. There is argument as to what exactly is meant by the term 'community', yet like the term 'family' it is used frequently and widely.

One of the problems encountered with defining 'community' is the confusion between what a community is in reality, and what it should be, or what people would like it to be. Communities are often discussed in terms of ideal types rather than real types. Again, this has similarities with defining the family—there sometimes exists a confusion between what people perceive or believe families should be, and what is actually the case.

Many people hold a belief that in times gone by communities were characterised by a small population sharing a sense of belonging, solidarity and common norms, working for the common good, assisting each other in daily activities and looking out for each other. Similar things could be said about ideal family types. It is unlikely that either ideal families or ideal communities were as common in the past as is sometimes believed. However, families and communities are often idealised and are seen by some people as something better or more desirable than what we have now.

The mass media, particularly television, have had a strong influence in the promotion of idealised families and communities. Indeed the basis of some of the most popular long-running television series have been contented and happy families, who have encountered and solved their problems living within a fairly self-contained and mostly harmonious community.

Definitions of community

Definitions of community usually stress such things as networks of social relationships, locality, common ties such as residence or occupation, territory, interrelationships, sense of belonging, common norms and social interaction. While there may exist variations in definitions of community all have one thing in common—people.

Community may be perceived or defined in the following ways:

1 The population which resides in a particular area. (Used in this way it refers to geographical or physical location, e.g. the Australian community.)
2 As social groups which have a special sense of shared identity and social relationships. (These groups have particular kinds of relationships irrespective of location, e.g. ethnic communities.)
3 A social system, which exists in a particular location. Communities are ongoing systems of interaction within a locality, and which have some degree of permanence. (That is, a social system in a particular location in which there are emotional and personal relationships among members, e.g. the familiar and local area in which individuals and families live and interact.)
4 As an ideology, they are an expression of what should be, rather than what it is—this is sometimes referred to as 'the good life'.[1]

1 R. A. Wild, *Australian Community Studies and Beyond*, George Allen & Unwin, Sydney, 1981, p. 14, and M. Waters & R. Crook, *Sociology One* (2nd edn), Longman Cheshire, Melbourne, 1990, p. 379.

Location

The main problem with the first definition is that it only refers to geographic location or territory, it does not take into account social relationships and interaction. This definition does not define true social communities.

Social interaction

The second definition of community takes into account social interaction but not location or geographic area, e.g. ethnic community, Aboriginal community, medical community etc. While individuals and families may consider themselves as belonging to these wider communities they do not usually share a common geographic location; therefore the group of people cannot really be regarded as a true social community. An example of this situation would be a large ethnic community, where community refers to all people of a particular ethnic background who reside in Australia, e.g. the Italian community. Sometimes particular ethnic communities can be classified as true social communities. This happens when a certain location is populated primarily by people of a particular ethnic origin, e.g. Greeks, Italians, Lebanese, Vietnamese etc. However, even in communities where the binding tie is social interaction and not location, support systems and networks may exist which are beneficial for individuals and families who consider themselves part of that community. For example, Aborigines who are scattered all over Australia have access to support systems established for the Aboriginal community. As well, they have access to social interaction with other members of that community. For this reason, perhaps there is a need to place more emphasis on the social relationships that exist among people rather than with the spatial organisation of people.

Location and social interaction

The third definition of community is more acceptable to sociologists as it takes into account both social interaction and location. This definition is probably the one that individuals feel most comfortable with when they talk about the community or locality in which they live. Most people have feelings of belonging or attachment to a particular geographical area; like home, the area feels familiar and comfortable. The local community may not be a homogeneous group; that is, not all the population may share the same values and beliefs.

Elements of consensus, cooperation, competition and conflict will always exist in communities and the norms, values and beliefs of the larger society will be reflected in the local community. These elements of consensus, cooperation, competition and conflict can often readily be seen in reports and stories in local community newspapers.

IDEAL COMMUNITIES

Perhaps one of the reasons that many people yearn for idealised communities is because they believe the community in which they live does not enhance their wellbeing, or provide for the development of positive social relationships and social interaction. Or it may simply be that people perceive ideal communities as offering something more than what they currently have. The concepts of city and community are frequently proposed as alternative forms of social organisation. The city is seen as cold and impersonal, while the community is seen as warm and personal, that is as 'the good life'.[2]

Dr M. Scott Peck wrote about communities in his book *The Different Drum*. The following quote is from this book and shows that while people may reside in the same location they do not necessarily form relationships with each other, nor interact with each other.

> I personally know of this isolation and fragmentation. From the age of five until I left home at twenty-three I lived with my parents in an apartment building in New York City. There were two apartments to a floor, separated by a small foyer and elevator. As there were eleven storeys above the first, this building was the compact home for twenty-two families. I knew the last name of the family across the foyer. I never knew the first names of the children. I stepped foot in their apartment once in those seventeen years. I knew the last names of two other families in the building; I could not even address the remaining eighteen. I did address most of the elevatormen and doormen by their first names; I never knew any of their last names.[3]

To many readers it may seem improbable that people could live so closely with each other for a long period of time yet virtually have no interaction with each other. However, for many people, contact with neighbours is limited and may consist only of a friendly greeting and a short chat. For other people neighbours can become good friends and act as a support system for each other. Social relationships may develop

2 Waters & Crook, *Sociology One*, p. 226.
3 M. Scott Peck, *The Different Drum*, Rider & Co., London, 1987, p. 27.

among neighbours when people are home for longer periods during the day and have the opportunity and time for socialising. This is more likely to happen when children are very young and mothers may not be participating in the paid workforce. Neighbourhood relationships may also develop as people retire and have more time to spend outside.

Local communities

When we talk about our local community, we often think of the immediate area in which we spend a large proportion of our time, in social activities, in leisure and recreation, in shopping, and in going to school, that is, in day-to-day activities. At the same time, many people frequently move out of their local community in order to go to work, or to visit relatives and see friends. Also, many of the daily activities we are involved in are controlled by social institutions and systems which are physically outside our local community, for example the mass media. Social relationships in a community do not exist alone, they are subject to outside forces and interdependent relationships exist with other social institutions and subsystems of society.

Community boundaries

A major problem is deciding on the geographical boundaries of a community. This decision may not be difficult when studying a country town, but it may be difficult to identify community boundaries when studying a large metropolitan area. In a metropolitan area distinct communities may be identified if there are obvious geographical boundaries such as waterways and parklands which separate one community from another. However, this is not always the case and sometimes amidst the urban sprawl of a city it is impossible to work out where one community ends and another begins. Also, perceptions among individuals regarding the boundaries of their communities will also vary. This may be determined by where they live and by the formal systems and informal support networks which they utilise in their daily activities.

Changes affecting communities

Local communities do not exist in isolation—they will be affected by economic, political, legal and social changes, as are individuals and families. For example, legal changes at a state or federal level may override local government regulations. This has happened in metropolitan areas where state governments have introduced legislation which effectively prevents local councils from zoning land for low-density housing. Thus local councils have little option than to allow medium-density housing in areas once zoned for single dwellings only. Economic changes can mean that state and federal government subsidies to local governments are significantly reduced and this can affect the quality and quantity of supports that are provided in local communities.

Interaction among communities

While the communities listed in the first paragraph of this chapter may not be considered true social communities by some social scientists, it is important to note that these communities provide supports, both formal and informal, to their members. The school community while providing academic programs will also provide other programs which assist in satisfying needs of members and thus contribute to wellbeing. Welfare programs and extra-curricular activities provided within the school and the wider educational community can assist in the physical, social and emotional development of community members. In so doing, there is often interaction with other specific communities or the wider community. For example, work experience for students relies on systems established within the school but it also requires interaction with other communities, particularly the business community. Ethnic communities provide support for their members through the provision of social clubs, food outlets, celebrations of cultural events. Individuals and families who do not belong to these ethnic communities often enjoy the facilities and activities provided by them.

Stratification of communities

Communities are also stratified, that is, individuals and families are arranged in a hierarchy. Those at the top of the hierarchy have access to more of the social and economic resources available in society and those at the bottom of the hierarchy have access to less of these resources. Thus, within most communities there is an unequal distribution of resources. For this reason it is likely that those who have access to more of these socially valued resources are likely to interact with other individuals and families who have similar amounts and types of resources. Also, within the geographic area of the community, individuals with similar amounts and types of resources are likely to live together, or in similar types of residential areas.

Needs for support

Individuals and families rely on each other, their local community and the society in which they live, to satisfy needs and wants in order to secure the wellbeing of members. It is impossible for individuals and families to provide all basic needs, and for families to undertake their functions, without interaction with and dependence upon other subsystems of society. For example, the majority of families can provide housing for their members through participation in employment. However, some people may not have access to paid employment and may not be in a position to purchase or rent housing in the private sector.

Other families may be able to satisfy most needs but if they experience a crisis such as family breakdown, they may need to use other supports to assist them through the crisis. In the case of family breakdown these supports may include counselling and/or access to public housing. Many single-parent families, particularly those headed by a female, need to rely on the support system of social security for income support following marital breakdown. However, within a few years of marital breakdown occurring, many of these single female parents are contributing to the economy through paid employment in the workforce.

The subsystems of society include the economy, education, law, polity and the family; these subsystems interact with each other and are dependent upon each other. Individuals and families participate in the economy in order to obtain income upon which to live; at the same time the economy would not exist unless there were workers to produce the goods and services and consumers to consume the goods and services generated by the economy.

While political and legal systems may determine the laws and regulations by which we live, these laws and regulations are devised by individuals and groups from the society in which we live. Laws and regulations are determined in response to the needs and wishes of individuals and families who make up the society. Laws and regulations usually reflect the norms and values of society and they are required to maintain a stable and cohesive society. Within a community, local government regulations may be an important support system. Most of the regulations are enacted for the common good and to maintain harmony within the community.

Within society, support systems exist for individuals and families in both the private and public sector. Within each subsystem of society, supports also exist to assist individuals and families who may have specific needs for support. These specific needs may be lifelong, as in the case of disabled people, or they may only be required at a certain point in their life. Support systems may be provided by government agencies—federal, state and local, or by non-government and voluntary agencies. Many of these non-government and voluntary agencies receive government assistance and subsidies to provide community programs and activities which provide support to individuals and families on both a continuing and emergency basis.

Support systems and networks

Families have responsibilities to satisfy basic needs of members to ensure the overall development of members and to enhance wellbeing. Families undertake a wide and diverse range of functions, including physical, economic, social, emotional, educational and psychological. These functions involve families in caring for, socialising and educating dependent children. Many families are also involved in caring for elderly family members who may or may not live with them. To undertake the myriad of tasks that are associated with performing these functions, families rely on both informal support networks and formal support systems. Informal support networks may be referred to as social support systems, the family unit itself being a support system. Formal support systems refer to those systems which exist outside the family group, upon which most individuals and families are very dependent. Indeed the majority of families could not satisfy needs and wants and promote the wellbeing of family members without utilising or interacting with other support systems and networks. These external or formal support systems include education, employment opportunities, access to housing, leisure and recreational facilities, transport and other amenities.

Levels of support

Informal support

Families are social groups: members interact with each other and have certain obligations and rights in relation to each other. When discussing family functions, roles and support networks, families need to be seen in the broadest sense—as *sets of relationships* rather than as structures.

Family members rely on each other for support and at the same time provide support not only for immediate family members but also for family members who live in other households. Reciprocal relationships exist: family members *receive* support and assistance, and also *provide* support and assistance to other family members who may or may not reside in the same household.

The social support provided by families to members living in a household extends to relatives living in other households, as well as to neighbours and friends. Support, again, is often reciprocal: friends, relatives and neighbours rely on each other through social relationships, providing assistance that often cannot be provided by formal support systems. This informal support can take many forms and may include such activities as grandparents babysitting grandchildren; adult children undertaking household and maintenance tasks for elderly parents; taking elderly parents shopping or to appointments; lending money to children; being available; and such favours as waiting in the home of kin for service people to come and repair household equipment etc.

Neighbourhood supports

Informal social supports also exist in neighbourhoods, and these are enjoyed by individuals and families. These informal social supports may include social functions, chatting with a neighbour, neighbourhood children playing together, collecting the mail and minding a pet while a family is on holidays, doing the shopping or hanging out the washing for an elderly neighbour etc. Sometimes informal support systems and networks can become semi-formalised; Neighbourhood Watch and Safety House Schemes are examples of where this has happened.

Formal support

Many factors affect the capacity of families to support members. These factors are *social*, *demographic* and *economic*.

In brief, *social factors* relate to changing social values, norms and ways of living; *demographic factors* relate to population trends and where and how people live; *economic factors* relate to economic conditions and the economic resources available to individuals and families. These factors are complex and interrelated and are influenced not only by those events and conditions in Australia but also by events which happen worldwide. For example, economic recessions in other countries can affect economic conditions in Australia and contribute to increased interest rates, higher inflation, higher unemployment levels and a lower standard of living. Similarly, social changes, particularly over the past two decades, have contributed to a variety of family formations and to changes in roles of family members.

All families have needs for formal support, but depending upon personal and family resources, some families may have a greater need than other families for more formal support services. Some families may have needs for formal support of child-care services when children are young, whereas other families may have access to informal social support networks of relatives and friends to provide child care for young children. In large families where there is a wide age range of children, social supports may be utilised within the family unit by having older children assist with the care of younger children.

Families have different needs for formal support. Some families may be dependent on formal economic support systems of social security income assistance in the form of Family Allowance or Family Allowance Supplement. This type of support would assist in providing basic needs of food, shelter and clothing. Other families may receive income through participation in the formal system of the paid workforce. Some individuals and families may wish to participate in the paid workforce but are not provided with the opportunity. Families rely on a variety of resources provided through both formal and informal support systems to allow them to function adequately and to provide for the needs and wellbeing of all members.

Not all families will utilise all the resources provided by all formal support systems. Some individuals and families will have a greater need for particular support systems at a specific time in their lifespan or life cycle. For example:

- families with young children may have a need for formal child care or pre-school experiences;
- families with primary school children may have a need for schools and sporting and recreational facilities;
- older people may have a need for services specifically directed at maintaining health and mobility;
- single parents may need access to economic support systems, advisory services and single-parent support groups;
- young people may need access to employment agencies and recreational facilities;
- middle-aged people may need access to recreational facilities and retraining facilities;
- older people may need access to public transport systems and community centres.

Access to many of the resources which families rely upon are determined to some extent by Commonwealth, state and local government policies which provide for a range of government and community programs and services.

Social policies

The policies which are formulated by governments in relation to social security, taxation, education, employment, health, housing and community services are formulated to take account of the differing needs of individuals and families. These policies influence the nature and level of formal support resources available to families.

The types of resources which are available to families have changed considerably over the last few decades and are affected by prevailing social attitudes and economic conditions. For example the expansion of child-care services has been a response to the increased number of mothers, both married and unmarried, remaining in and re-entering the workforce; this increase has been a result of social, economic, political and legal changes. Similarly, governments have responded to the increase in the number of single-parent families which has occurred over the last two decades. This response has been in the form of income security, subsidies for formal child care and re-training schemes to encourage single parents to re-enter the workforce.

With Australia's ageing population, social policy is currently focusing on the provision of formal and informal support systems for the aged. To encourage aged people to remain in independent living for as long as possible, formal support systems have been established to meet this goal. Thus, the formal support system of Home and Community Care has been expanded rather than the formal support system of aged people's housing. Responses to high youth unemployment levels have been in the form of expanded educational programs and income support through Job Search Allowance and the Young Homeless Allowance.

Government concern for family support

The 1992 *Survey of Families in Australia* examined the characteristics of families and the nature of family support. It was undertaken by the Australian Bureau of Statistics and randomly surveyed 21 300 private households and special non-private dwellings. Government and non-government organisations with an interest in this survey were specifically interested in examining the capacity that individuals have to support one another, and how such support can be supplemented or assisted by government, community and employers. This survey used a transaction approach, that is it looked at people over a period of time to investigate interdependence among people.[4]

Interdependence of formal support systems and informal networks

While the number of formal social support services for families have grown, there has also been an increased emphasis on equipping families with the *coping skills* (resources) to assist their own members. Thus, while formal support services are available to assist and supplement family roles, individuals and families are encouraged to use these services to ensure crisis situations are avoided. This is reflected in the policy of maintaining aged people living independently in the community. This policy assumes there are family members or neighbours to provide the necessary support. Informal social support networks in the form of families provide much of the care required for frail aged people.

Formal support systems are at risk during economic recessions. Funding cutbacks often occur and this can mean services are reduced and less people have access to them. When this happens there is a greater reliance on informal social networks. However, not all individuals and families have access to these networks.

While individuals and families may rely on formal support services, at the same time they may be providing informal social support to aged relatives, neighbours, and through participation in environmental groups, childrens' sporting groups, Neighbourhood Watch, playgroups etc. A single parent may be dependent upon social security for income support but may contribute to the maintenance of other informal support systems in the community, for example assisting with reading programs at the local primary school. Similarly, an aged relative may need to use a community resource of home help to assist with cleaning and household maintenance, but may provide social support within their family by reading to young children, and thus developing communication skills, imparting history and providing affection. This interdependent support can benefit all—individuals and families rely on the resources provided by other people but also act as support systems. This two-way process contributes to the wellbeing of all involved in these complex interactions.

Support systems and social networks provide resources for

4 Australian Bureau of Statistics, *Families in Australia: A Guide to Content and Procedures*, Canberra, 1993, p. 1

individuals and families. These systems may be informal and exist within and among families, relatives and friends. They may be formal and established by all levels of government, or they may be provided by non-government or voluntary organisations. Individuals and families will have different needs for support during their lifespan or life cycle, and these needs may be satisfied through a variety of support systems.

Community wellbeing

Access to support systems is important for all individuals and families as the resources provided assist families in satisfying needs. This contributes to the wellbeing of individuals and families. Community wellbeing is dependent upon the wellbeing of people living within the community. When there is a lack of formal and informal support systems and networks, wellbeing of individuals and families is threatened. In Chapter 9 there is an example of how community wellbeing can be affected by lack of formal and social supports. You will need to refer to the section on unplanned housing developments for more detail, as it illustrates the effects of lack of both informal and formal support systems on the wellbeing of individuals and families.

Individuals and families who have the social and economic resources to satisfy needs and wants are more likely to participate and be active in the community, and thus make a positive contribution. Individuals and families who do not have the resources to satisfy immediate needs are unlikely to be able to participate effectively in the local community and make a positive contribution to the welfare of others.

Accessing support systems

Over the last decade considerable efforts have been made to make information concerning social security and other support systems readily available through a variety of outlets that people may visit, including public libraries, schools, rest centres, community centres, shopping malls, medical centres and the CES.

The information is presented in a more user-friendly manner than in the past, making it easier to read and understand. Single leaflets in a variety of languages are available for each pension or benefit which is paid through the Department of Social Security. Similar leaflets are also available for other support systems which are available for individuals and families. Medical personnel, health workers and social workers also disseminate this information when they believe an individual may be eligible for a particular form of assistance. However, despite the wide availability of information regarding social support systems, not all individuals are aware they may be eligible for assistance.

Part of the educational process is teaching children and youth a variety of information skills. In the first instance these information skills are used to access information which is relevant to their formal education. There is a need to extend the use of these information skills to all aspects of their life.

In Chapter 4, the development of competence has been discussed in detail. Children need to develop the knowledge, skills and abilities which will provide them with the competence to earn a living, take care of themselves, form relationships and to participate effectively in society. Competence also refers to the ability to interact effectively with the environment, to adapt to the environment, to solve problems and reach goals. To access all available resources throughout their lifespan, individuals need the skills and competencies to do so. Perhaps there is also a need to educate people that there is nothing wrong in seeking and accepting assistance when it is required. Some families try to satisfy needs without seeking assistance to which they are entitled.

TYPES OF SUPPORT

Outlined below are the types of informal and formal supports that are available to individuals and families. These supports may not be available in all communities, yet at the same time there may be other support systems which are available in a community but which are not included here. As many of these supports have been discussed throughout this book, it will be necessary to refer to specific chapters for more detail. The supports identified here are provided by the public and private sector, by various levels of government—federal, state and local—as well as by individuals, families, community groups and organisations, and by private enterprise.

EMPLOYMENT SUPPORTS

Employment supports can refer to supports which assist people to maintain employment, or it can refer to supports which may be available to obtain employment. Child-care services and cleaning services provide supports for working families. These are formal supports, but the same services, particularly child care, may be undertaken in an informal manner by other family members and friends.

Major formal or non-family sources of employment support which may assist in obtaining employment include the Commonwealth Employment Service (CES), private employment agencies, employ–

Figure 10.1 The Commonwealth Employment Service (CES) provides support for unemployed people. (Photo: D. Lowe)

ment advertisements, education and re-training schemes. Income support which relates to unemployment includes Job Search Allowance, Newstart Allowance, Young Homeless Allowance and the unemployment benefit. The JET scheme administered by the Department of Social Security is a voluntary scheme to assist sole-parent pensioners to get into the workforce. Assistance is provided with education and training programs, job seeking and child care. Retraining schemes for unemployed workers are provided by government organisations, TAFE colleges, voluntary agencies and community groups. Volunteer centres in each state help find voluntary work for people. This often provides job skills, as well as making people feel useful through contributing to the community.

Family members may provide help to individuals to look for work or to get a job, position or apprenticeship. Family members may also offer assistance and advice on preparing resumés and applications and presenting for an interview. In many families where one adult partner works part-time or not at all, he or she often provides the support required for the other partner to work full-time.

Often it is the wife who provides the physical and emotional support for a husband to pursue a career. Parents in a family often provide informal support for teenagers who have part-time jobs, merely by supplying the transport to and from the workplace. (For further details of available employment supports refer to Chapters 4, 5 and 7.)

INCOME AND FINANCIAL SUPPORTS

Income supports can refer to income received as wages or salary, or income received from receipt of a social security pension or benefit.

Social security benefits which provide income support include age pension, invalid pension, widow's pension, sole parent's pension, sickness benefit, special benefit, unemployment benefit. Other allowances which contribute to income support include family allowance, family allowance supplement, rehabilitation allowance, carer's pension, job search allowance, young homeless allowance, rehabilitation allowance and mobility allowance.

Pensioners and recipients of benefits may be entitled to some fringe benefits. These fringe benefits may include a reduction in gas and electricity expenses, rebates on council and water rates, reduction in telephone rental, a range of free pharmaceuticals and reduced fares for Commonwealth government railway services. Fringe benefits provide income support by reducing outgoing costs for individuals and families dependent upon social security for income support.

Other financial support is provided through a variety of resources. Most states have credit telephone lines which provide financial counselling and the Salvation Army provides a financial counselling service. The Department of Social Security has a Financial Information Service (FIS) which provides information to people who have been retrenched or made redundant or who are planning for their retirement. Officers of FIS can also help with information on social security matters, taxation and investments.

Individuals and families often provide informal income support for each other. Money may be lent or given to family members to help out during periods of financial strain or stress. Indirect income support can also take the form of food and accommodation given to adult children living in the family household. This may also occur for family members who return home for short periods of time, as may sometimes happen with single parents and their children.

Education supports

Formal education supports take the form of pre-schools, kindergarten, primary and secondary schools, colleges and universities, and distance education. These facilities may be government supported or they may be private organisations. The amount of economic resources required to attend private educational institutions is greater than that required to attend government educational institutions.

For families who have difficulty in meeting costs of education, allowances are available for families who meet assets and means tests. Financial assistance is available through the Student Assistance Scheme, Austudy, Abstudy, Isolated Children Scheme, scholarships and postgraduate awards. Adult education courses are available to assist

Figure 10.2 Community resources are often accessed for leisure activities, such as this primary school playground on a weekend. (Photo: D. Lowe)

people to learn new workforce skills and/or enhance literacy and numeracy skills. Through the Department of Immigration courses are available for adult immigrants to acquire language skills and courses are provided for job seeking, vocational skills and study skills. Similar courses are run through Outreach, administered by TAFE. Outreach addresses the special needs of women, migrants, Aborigines, the unemployed and isolated people.

The Department of Employment, Education and Training (DEET) offers a specialised library for occupational, educational and training information. State government departments which are responsible for employment, training and further education provide vocational counselling services for young people and adults, and assistance in developing job seeking and application skills.

There are many informal education supports. Families play an important role in the education of their members, being actually involved in the educational process and supporting the role of the educational institutions which members may attend. Families, particularly adults, provide emotional support and encouragement of children attending school and tertiary institutions. Families usually provide the fees, materials and equipment required for education, supporting young as well as adult children during the years of formal education. Many of the activities in which children are involved in the community also assist in the educational process. These activities may have a social or sporting focus but they form part of educational experiences. Such activities can include individual and team sports, children's clubs, Cubs and Brownies, Guides and Scouts, Venturers,

Young Achievers and other youth groups.

Australia, like other developed nations, now sees education as something which continues throughout an individual's lifetime, rather than as something which occupies only the early stages of the lifespan. For this reason, the amount and variety of educational facilities have expanded over the past decade. Individuals may spend a large proportion of their early life in education and while they may eventually move into the workforce in a full-time capacity, it is very likely that they will move in and out of formal education as the need arises. This will be necessary in order to learn new skills required to participate in a rapidly changing workforce. This continuing education may take the form of both short-term and long-term courses.

Housing supports

In the previous chapter housing supports have been discussed in detail, so it will be necessary to refer to Chapter 10 for more information. When individuals and families have the resources to provide for their own housing, many of the other needs of individuals are also met. When housing is adequate and satisfactory, the wellbeing of individuals and families is enhanced; when housing is not adequate, needs may not be met and this may contribute to the illbeing of individuals and families.

The primary formal support required for housing is the income or assets required to purchase, pay off, or rent housing. However, there are many other resources which assist in this process. In the private economic sector assistance is provided in the purchase of housing through banks, building societies, credit unions, insurance companies and other financial institutions, real estate agents and through legal and conveyancing firms. The cost of these services varies.

Other formal support services include home purchase advisory services, government-sponsored home loans for low-income earners, mortgage assistance schemes, rental assistance and tenants organisations. Government and non-government organisations provide housing for low-income earners, crisis housing, refuges, Aboriginal housing, housing for people with disabilities, pensioner housing and retirement villages, hostel and nursing home accommodation. Many housing assistance schemes also provide related services—these are also outlined in this section.

Families often provide informal support to other family members who may be establishing their own housing. This can take the form of monetary support or it may be through the provision of household equipment and help with repairs and maintenance. Housing support is often provided to adult children and aged relatives who are living in the family household. Self-contained accommodation may be made available in a family home to provide housing for a young couple or for an elderly relative.

Transport supports

Transport supports are provided by the public and private sector. Many individuals and families outlay significant economic resources for the purchase and maintenance of private cars. The economic resources needed to purchase and maintain a car may be beyond the reach of some families and this can limit the flexibility of families, particularly when public transport facilities are limited. While the primary use of a car may be for transport to and from place of employment, private cars are used for many other activities. These activities may include the transport of children to and from school or child care, for shopping, for payment of accounts, for banking, for appointments, for children's activities, and for other activities such as social outings and holidays. Older children may have access to a family car to use to travel to and from part-time employment, as well as for personal social activities.

Public transport networks are provided for communities; however, some communities have more services than others, and some have better coordinated services than others. Also, the services available on the weekend may not be sufficient to provide for the needs of those living within a particular community. For a parent with young children, negotiating public transport can be a very difficult and daunting task. The difficulties of public transport for parents with young children can make a social outing stressful rather than pleasurable.

Many recipients of social security benefits are entitled to public transport concessions on bus, rail and ferry services. Many private bus and coach companies provide concessions to social security card holders. Holders of pensioner concession cards are entitled to free driver's licences and motor vehicle registration fees, and a concession on the Third Party Insurance levy.

These benefits may extend to disabled people, including those who have impaired vision. Some airlines offer a discount to blind people and the sighted person who accompanies the passenger. For a very nominal fee people with functional disabilities are entitled to use community transport. This is usually provided through local councils under the Home and Community Care Program. The Department of Transport administers the Taxi Transport Subsidy Scheme for people with severe

Figure 10.3 Public transport systems are necessary for many people to participate in society. (Photos: D. Lowe)

and permanent disabilities. This scheme allows people with such disabilities to travel in taxis at concessional rates. For disabled drivers, car spaces close to entrances are provided in shopping complexes, in car parking areas and near other community facilities such as public libraries.

HEALTH SUPPORTS

Access to health and medical supports is through the private and public sector. Many people choose to invest in private health insurance. The benefits available from private health insurance are dependent upon the amount of insurance paid. All taxpayers contribute to Medicare which provides access to health services for all people. However, people who are only covered by the support system of Medicare may not have access to the same services as those who have private health insurance.

Many communities have a community health centre which provides a wide range of advice, support and health care to all age groups. Community health centres focus on geriatric assessment, aids for the disabled, Aboriginal health, drug and alcohol counselling, ethnic health, sexual assault services, domestic violence, women's health, family planning, parenting, mental health, rehabilitation, child health and immunisation, and domiciliary and community nursing services. These centres also provide referral to appropriate health services, doctors and counselling. Baby health and early childhood health centres are important facilities provided by community centres. Community centres also provide classes in preparation for parenthood. In each state, the Family Planning Association provides clinical and educational services in the areas or reproductive and sexual health.

Pensioners who have a concession card will be entitled to a range of pharmaceuticals at reduced cost, free dental treatment at some public hospitals, and may be eligible to receive free hearing assessment and rehabilitation, including the provision of hearing aids. Also, pensioners may be entitled to assistance with the purchase of eye glasses. For people with disabilities, Telecom will supply additional equipment free of charge to allow easier use of the telephone at home. Most states provide services for isolated residents who need financial help to travel a long

Figure 10.4 Hospitals and medical centres are a primary health support in a community.

distance to get specialist medical treatment.

Individuals and families provide informal health supports to individuals. These supports relate to physical and emotional health. Parents provide informal health support to children through the treatment of minor injuries and ailments. Parents take the initiative to utilise formal health services when they think it is necessary, and educate children regarding personal health care. This type of care often extends to elderly relatives, particularly frail aged people.

Within local communities there are often health support and self-help groups. These may include branches of the Alzheimer's Association, Arthritis Foundation, Asthma Support Group, Coeliac Society, Compassionate Friends (for bereaved parents), Cystic Fibrosis Foundation, Epilepsy Association etc.

PERSONAL CARE AND HOME HELP SUPPORTS

These supports are closely related to health supports, as they enhance the physical and emotional health of the recipients. Formal supports in this area are provided through the Home and Community Care program, which is a joint Commonwealth/State government program. This program aims to assist people who need basic support services to continue to live in their own homes in the community. The program provides a range of services including home help, for example house cleaning and lawn mowing, personal care, such as bathing and dressing, respite care, home nursing, food services such as Meals-on-Wheels, home maintenance and modifications, community transport, dementia support, carer support, podiatry and occupational therapy. Community Aged Care Packages (CACPs) operates in a similar way to Home and Community Care. CACPs are targetted to older people who have complex care needs: care is provided to frail aged people who live in their own homes.

Many of the supports outlined above are also provided through informal networks of family, friends and neighbours. An individual who is caring for a person who is in need of constant care and attention may be entitled to a carer's pension and formal support to carry out duties of care. As Australia's population ages, these informal support systems will become even more important.

LEGAL SUPPORTS

Obviously the most important formal legal supports that are provided in a community are the laws and regulations that protect individuals and families. While solicitors and barristers provide legal advice and act

Figure 10.5 Courthouses represent the legal protection provided to individuals and families. (Photo: D. Lowe)

for an individual or group in a legal proceeding, the costs of such often prohibit people from using their services.

There are other legal services available which are free of charge and can provide information on courses of action to pursue. The Chamber Magistrate at the local courthouse can provide assistance and give referrals if necessary. Community Justice Centres provide a free mediation service for people in disputes—the most common disputes include neighbours and family members. The Family Court of Australia has a free professional and confidential counselling service available for personal and family problems arising from separation and divorce. Free legal advice is available in most areas of law from a Legal Aid Office. However, legal representation is subject to a means test and merits test. Law societies in each state may also offer legal advice and referral to other services by telephone. Anti-discrimination and Equal Employment Opportunity departments in each state and territory provide support for individuals and families who have sustained discrimination.

Local government differs from the Commonwealth and state government in that it can only establish regulations, not laws. These regulations primarily concern development within the boundaries of the local community. These regulations relate primarily to zoning of land and construction of buildings.

Child-care supports

Formal child-care supports have increased dramatically over the last decade. There has been an increase in the number of child-care centres, before- and after-school care facilities and holiday care facilities. Family day care is also a formal child-care support which is administered by local councils. Despite the increase in formal child-care facilities, informal child care is still the most utilised form. (Formal and informal child-care supports have been discussed in more detail in Chapters 4 and 6.)

Emergency help supports

Many individuals and families have access to someone, whether a friend or relative, who can help them in an emergency or in times of crisis. However, for some individuals and families this is not the case. Also, the assistance that can be provided through informal networks may not be sufficient. Emergency assistance may be required as a result of domestic violence, assault, drug use, family breakdown or other personal circumstances.

Many organisations exist in local communities which offer practical help and assistance during a crisis or emergency. These voluntary or non-government organisations include the Anglican Home Mission Society—Care Force, City Missions, Salvation Army, The Smith Family, St Vincent de Paul Society, Red Cross Society etc. The organisations listed here are perhaps the more well-known but there are many other less well-known organisations that assist people in the same way. While these organisations may provide assistance in an emergency they also provide ongoing welfare services for individuals and families. Government organisations which provide emergency and crisis assistance include Family Crisis Centre administered through the Department of Social Security, Alcohol and Drug Counselling and Rehabilitation, Life Line, Youthline, Kidsline etc.

Disabled supports

Many of the supports provided for disabled people are through informal social networks of family and friends. However, there are many community groups that directly provide support services for disabled people. As many of these groups are self-help groups they also provide indirect support. Resources include craft and activity centres, employment centres, multi-purpose centres, disabled aids and equipment, disabled driver training, centres for visually impaired people, independent living centres, learning difficulties support groups, therapy centres, Handicapped Children's Centres, Down Syndrome Association, Autistic Association, Multiple Sclerosis Society etc.

RECREATION, LEISURE AND SOCIAL SUPPORTS

There is a wide range of support available for leisure and recreational pursuits. These supports may be formal and be provided by both government and private sectors. In many areas throughout Australia, neighbourhood centres have been established to assist in developing support networks among residents and combat isolation often experienced by individuals and families. Many of these centres are located near public housing developments and offer a wide range of activities including arts and crafts, sport, bingo and video nights, coffee

Figure 10.6 Public and private leisure facilities are available for individuals and families in our society. (Photos: D. Lowe)

mornings and lunches, ante-natal classes, food preparation classes, budget management classes, health and fitness classes etc.

Semi-formal supports often exist in the community, where facilities are provided by local councils, but the activity is coordinated by interested people. In the case of children's activities parents may be involved in the overall organisation and administration of the activity. Many recreational and leisure pursuits occur through informal networks, that is activities organised by individuals and families. However, in their leisure and recreational activities many families use facilities that have been established by governments and local communities, e.g. parks and picnic areas.

There are many private leisure and recreational facilities that are available in the community for use by individuals and families. Movie theatres, entertainment centres and fast-food outlets are examples of some facilities used by the majority of individuals and families. Often these facilities are found together in large shopping complexes and malls, which are also often considered leisure centres.

Some entertainment organisations, including football and racing, give concessions to holders of social security concession cards. For older people, senior citizens' clubs are important supports for social interaction, leisure and entertainment. While these centres may be classified as formal support systems, they provide the opportunity for informal interaction.

The following organisations, facilities or activities which cater for a wide range of interests, ages and abilities may be available in local communities. While each group or club may have a specific focus, they also provide opportunities for social interaction. It is this social interaction which can ease isolation and loneliness for many people. Often, from these clubs and groups, informal social networks are developed. Sporting clubs have been included below and while not all individual sports have been listed it has been estimated that over a third of Australia's population belongs to or is associated with a sporting group, club or association.

- Arts and crafts groups
- Gardening, flora and fauna groups
- Car clubs
- Historical societies
- Environmental groups
- Astronomical societies
- Museum clubs
- Collectors' clubs
- Dance schools and groups
- Photography, camera and film clubs
- Chess clubs
- Board game clubs
- Television and radio clubs
- Philatelic Societies
- Bridge clubs
- Music bands and orchestras

- Drama and theatrical groups
- Friendship centres
- Social clubs
- Toastmasters' clubs
- Business and Professional Womens' clubs
- Quota clubs
- Parks
- Scout and Guide halls
- Camps and conference centres
- Sporting clubs
- Orienteering clubs
- Fishing clubs
- Physical culture classes
- Marching and baton twirling clubs
- Shooting clubs
- Rowing clubs
- Learn-to-swim classes
- Libraries
- Sole parents' groups
- Playgroups
- Churches and related social groups.
- Writers' groups
- Musical and choral societies
- Service clubs
- Apex, Rotary and Lions clubs
- Lioness clubs
- Youth clubs and groups
- VIEW clubs
- Community centres and halls
- Sporting fields
- Athletics clubs
- YMCA facilities
- Bushwalking and caving clubs
- Dog training clubs
- Keep fit classes
- Lifesaving and rescue clubs
- Martial arts clubs
- Model aircraft clubs
- Tai Chi clubs
- Running and jogging clubs
- Swimming pools
- Women's centres
- Step-parents' groups
- St John Ambulance

Listed below are other organisations and groups which may exist in a local community. These groups also provide for the welfare and wellbeing of individuals and families.

- Alcoholics Anonymous
- Overeaters Anonymous
- Weightwatchers
- Crossroads Association (self-help support organisation)
- Gamblers Anonymous
- Narcotics Anonymous
- Stroke Recovery Association
- Amputee Association.
- Solo Parents of Australia
- Family Life Movement of Australia
- Parents without Partners
- Grief Support Group
- Marriage Guidance Council
- Association of Relatives and Friends of the Mentally Ill
- Resident and Ratepayers Association
- Pensioners' Association
- Prisoners' Aid Association
- Civil Rehabilitation Committee (assist wives and families of prisoners)
- Ombudsman's office

- Precinct groups
- Progress Association
- Small Business Advisory Centre

Local Government Supports

Checking the local government guide in the telephone directory can provide an indication of the variety and extent of resources provided by local councils. While the resources provided by local councils will be similar, variations will occur depending on the composition of the population, location and the economic resources of the local council.

For example, older areas may have established parks and recreational areas and there may not be a need to spend a large proportion of the budget on construction of new roads, but instead on the maintenance of existing roads. Councils in this situation may be able to direct more funds to other services such as child care or community centres. Newer communities may have to allocate a greater proportion of economic resources to establishing roads and other services and they may not be able to allocate as much money to other community resources. Newer communities may have a younger population and may need to direct a greater proportion of income to services for children and youth. Older, more established areas may have a greater need for services which meet the needs of an ageing population.

Sometimes local councils survey residents to determine changing needs. This provides the opportunity for particular groups of people to have input into local council decisions. A local council may wish to determine if the recreational and social needs of aged people or youth are being met or could be better met. This is referred to as *needs*

Figure 10.7 Libraries provide services and facilities for individuals of all ages. (Photo: D. Lowe)

assessment. While public meetings may provide the opportunity for some residents to express their views, a wider range of views may be obtained through a survey of a sample of the population together with invitations to interest groups to present submissions. Residents of a community also have opportunities to express opinions and concerns to their elected local councillor.

Local councils have responsibilities for property services which includes roads, curbs, guttering, garbage collection etc., and human services which include libraries, community centres, recreational centres etc. Responsibilities may include:

- early childhood centres including immunisation
- kindergartens
- community and information centres
- parks and ovals
- hire of function centres
- activity centres for disabled people
- netball fields
- beach information
- garbage collection
- emergency and rescue services
- tree preservation
- complaints concerning noise littering and footway parking
- zoning of land for residential, commercial, industrial and recreational use
- children's services
- child-care centres
- public libraries
- senior citizens' centres
- womens' rest centres
- community halls
- recreation centres
- swimming pools
- tennis courts
- golf links
- animal impounding and registration
- bushfire control
- meals-on-wheels
- regulation of the types and sizes of buildings that are constructed

Contact your local council for an outline of its major responsibilities as well as a directory of community resources available in your area. Through payment of rates, residents actually provide for the resources that are established and administered by local councils. While local councils may receive other forms of income such as government grants, council rates are the primary form of income for most local councils.

Community-based services

In recognition of the importance of the local community in the lives of individuals and families, family support programs are usually community-based. Most studies have shown that when individuals and families look for help beyond informal family and social networks, they prefer to use formal support services if they are located within the local community. People perceive community services as more accessible, flexible and sensitive to local circumstances. Also, services which are community-based may be more familiar with the social, cultural and ethnic composition of the community.[5] Support services have become multidimensional in order to focus on looking after whole families. For example, the JET program for single parents not only provides for retraining; it also provides the child-care facilities to allow the parent to attend an educational institution.

The availability of social support is an important variable affecting individual and family wellbeing and stress. Not all individuals and families have access to social networks of family and friends to help them satisfy needs. Also, the type of support that is sometimes required cannot always be provided through social networks. The majority of individuals and families rely on both formal support systems and social networks to satisfy needs and enhance wellbeing.

Longitudinal studies in other countries have shown that when support programs of early intervention are provided to disadvantaged children in the first six years of life, there is a greater likelihood that these children will grow up to complete secondary and post-secondary education and to be employed. These programs offer early childhood experiences which their families, due to a lack of social and economic resources, are unable to provide. Individuals who have been exposed to such programs are more likely to be socially competent members of society—that is, they are able to participate effectively in and contribute to the society and community into which they were born. While these support programs may be expensive to initiate and operate, the long-term benefits suggest they are cost-effective for both the individual and the community.

Support services are resources—some individuals and families may use more, some may use less. The use of particular resources by an individual or family at one point in time may reduce future reliance on support services. To cater for the diverse needs of individuals and families, variety and flexibility is required in the types of services available through formal support systems.

5 I. Wolcott, *Family Support Services*, Australian Institute of Family Studies, Melbourne, 1989, p. 12.

REVIEW QUESTIONS

1 Outline some of the difficulties encountered in establishing a definition of community. Consider the community in which you live. Can you determine the boundaries of your community?
2 What are the two major elements of a community?
3 Why is location alone not a sufficient basis for a true community?
4 Do you think it is desirable to interact with your neighbours? Justify your answer.
5 If your state government decided to close down your local hospital, what may be the implications for the local community?
6 With reference to stratification within your community, identify particular areas.
7 What personal needs for support do you have? How may these differ from your friends? How does your community meet these needs?
8 Distinguish between (a) support systems and social networks (b) formal support systems and informal support systems.
9 To which informal support networks do you and your family have access? Draw a network map, showing all the relationships among the people that form part of the network.
10 How may a neighbourhood provide informal supports? Why may some neighbourhoods have more informal supports or networks than other neighbourhoods?
11 What factors influence the amounts and types of formal support systems that will be utilised by individuals and families?
12 Within the framework of the lifespan of an individual, list the formal support systems that may be used at each stage. (Stages may include infancy, early childhood, play age, school age, adolescence, young adult, adulthood, mature age.)
13 Within the framework of the family life cycle, list the formal supports that may be used at each stage. (Stages may include beginning, expanding and contracting, but you may also need to identify substages.)
14 Discuss the relationship between community wellbeing and individual and family wellbeing.
15 Describe the procedures you could follow to access formal support systems if you were eighteen years of age, unemployed and homeless. What formal support systems may be available in this circumstance?
16 Describe the procedures you could follow if you were a single parent with two young children, unemployed with nowhere to live. What formal supports may be available in these circumstances?

17 Why may the resource of private transport provide more flexibility than the resource of public transport?

18 Contact your local community centre to find out what services they offer and the information they can provide about formal support services.

19 Explain how both formal support services and informal social networks may be used together in the care of a frail aged person.

20 What resources are provided in your community for recreation and leisure? Distinguish between those provided by the public sector and those provided by the private sector.

11

FAMILIES AND CHANGE

While the social institution of the family has experienced many changes this century, it cannot be assumed that the family is breaking down, nor can it be assumed that the family was a stable and static unit in the pre-industrial era. When studying changes in family life it is necessary to analyse whether family life in the past was as ideal as is sometimes believed—i.e. have the changes been as dramatic as they appear, or is it that more publicity is now given to the family and the changes occurring within it? For example, it has been suggested that the incidence of mental illness, suicide, neurosis, wife-beating and child abuse is higher now than it has ever been, and that this is due to the inadequacy of families in meeting individual needs, as well as the increased stresses of living in an increasingly complex society.

The late 1960s and the 1970s was a period of significant change in most developed countries. It was a period marked by:

- the rise of women's liberation;
- higher education retention rates;
- availability of reliable contraception;

- legalised termination of pregnancy;
- an increase in both divorce and living-together relationships;
- declining birthrates;
- delayed marriage;
- increased workforce participation of married women;
- greater tolerance of homosexuality;
- an increase in the number of people choosing to remain single.

Earlier chapters have discussed changes in family structure and composition, family functions and tasks, and the allocation of roles within families. The purpose of this chapter is to present a summary of the changes which have occurred within the family during this century, and particularly during the past few decades.

FAMILIES TODAY

FAMILY SIZE

The most dramatic decline in family size occurred during the second half of the nineteenth century: the family of five and more children had virtually disappeared by the beginning of this century. Currently, most families choose to have only two children, although there is an increasing tendency to have only one child or to remain childless. Recent research shows that most young women expect to have children, although they expect to have only two children. The increased number of single-parent families means that many children will live in households in which there is only one adult member present.

The natural increase in population has fallen steadily since 1971 and much of the slow population growth which has occurred over the past two decades is due to immigration rather than to an excess of births over deaths. During the early 1990s there was a slight natural population increase resulting from more births and fewer deaths in the period.

EX-NUPTIAL BIRTHS

Until 1950, ex-nuptial births remained stable at about 5 per cent of all births, decreasing during the Depression and war years. Since the Second World War there has been a steady increase in ex-nuptial births (See Table 11.1) due in part to changed social attitudes and increased social services. In 1991, 23 per cent of all births were ex-nuptial. Also, over the past few decades there has been an increase in the age of

Table 11.1 Ex-nuptial births as a percentage of total live births in Australia, 1901–91

Year	Percentage	Year	Percentage
1901	5.99	1979	11.00
1921	4.75	1980	12.40
1941	3.84	1981	13.20
1961	5.11	1983	14.70
1965	6.97	1986	16.90
1971	9.27	1989	20.30
1975	10.71	1991	23.00

Source: Australian Bureau of Statistics data

mothers at first ex-nuptial birth. Some of this increase may be due to older women who make a conscious decision to have a child and raise it alone. With the increase in ex-nuptial births there has also been a decrease in the number of children born within the first eight months of marriage. Pre-marital pregnancy is no longer a strong reason for marriage.

Family size and composition

The traditional or ideal extended family pattern was not a common feature of Australian society last century. Many Australian families during the nineteenth century lived an isolated existence, having little contact with kin and neighbours, and this tendency towards isolationism continues today. The traditional family pattern of two adults and two children still remains popular, although other family formations have become significant, including single-parent families and blended families. Many children will experience more than one type of family structure—they may be born into a two-parent family, move to a one-parent family situation and then back to a blended family situation.

Most research suggests that while most people live in a two-generation family formation, they do interact regularly with other family members, particularly grandparents. For many families an extended family situation exists in that people maintain relationships with relatives who live outside the immediate household. These relationships provide a social support network for individuals and families.

Marriage patterns

For most of this century, and particularly since the Second World War, Australians married at progressively younger ages. Since 1977 this trend has reversed and age at first marriage is now higher for both men and women. In keeping with this trend, Australians are now older when they have their first child. Also, there is a trend to delay having children until the second five years of marriage. This contrasts with the situation following the Second World War when couples were likely to have their first child within the first two years of marriage.

While the majority of individuals still choose to marry, a significant number choose to live alone or to live in de facto relationships. Following divorce, many individuals choose to remarry although more men than women make this choice. This indicates that men may favour marriage more than women.

Divorce patterns

Following the Family Law Act of 1975–76 the divorce rate rose sharply in the late 1970s and early 1980s. However, while the divorce rate is now higher than before 1975 it appears to have stabilised. Approximately 35–38 per cent of marriages will dissolve through divorce. It cannot be concluded that marital disharmony has increased, as prior to the Family Law Act divorces were difficult and expensive to obtain—many couples may have separated but not divorced, or remained living together as they could not afford a divorce. It cannot be concluded that family life was more harmonious at the beginning of the century merely because there were fewer divorces.

It has been suggested that with increased life expectancy, it may be unrealistic to expect partners to remain in the same marriage for a long period of time. It may become common in the future for people to have a series of marriages or relationships throughout life.

Women

Perhaps one of the most significant changes during the second half of this century has been the increased workforce participation of married women. More than 60 per cent of married women are in the workforce in a full-time, part-time or casual capacity. The reasons for this increased workforce participation include changing social attitudes, economic conditions, employment opportunities, increased educational qualifications, greater availability of child-care facilities etc. This trend is likely to continue as females are born into and socialised into a society which regards workforce participation of mothers as the norm rather than the exception.

Despite the increased participation of women in the paid workforce, there has not been a corresponding increase in male participation in household work. Recent studies indicate that many women undertake two roles—at home and at work—and that women undertake the greater proportion of unpaid household work, regardless of whether they work outside the home.

YOUTH

The economic situation and competition for jobs has meant that education retention rates have risen significantly. Youth are staying at school for longer and are more likely to pursue some form of post-secondary education in order to gain skills and increase educational qualifications. With limited employment prospects, youth unemployment levels are also high, although unemployment levels are higher for those without educational qualifications. This situation has increased the financial dependency of youth upon families, a situation which can contribute to stress and conflict within families. It has also been a contributing factor to delayed marriage.

THE AGED

Australia's population is ageing, as a result of increased life expectancy and a decreased proportion of young people in Australia. Increased life expectancy and the trend to earlier retirement as a result of the economic recession means that many men and women can expect to live for many decades following children leaving home, and retirement from the workforce. The higher proportion of older and aged people who are not in the workforce has increased the demand for appropriate support systems and community resources. As Australia approaches the next century there is increasing concern about the care of the aged. With the trend away from institutional care to home-based care, many individuals and families will have to face the challenges and problems of caring for the frail aged.

IMMIGRATION

The contribution that immigration has played in the growth of Australia's population is very significant. Nearly one-quarter of

Australia's population were born overseas and since the Second World War, approximately 30 per cent of natural increase in population has been due to children born of migrant parents. The emphasis that migrants place upon family reunions, that is, relatives migrating to Australia to join families already settled here, and the tendency to live in the same neighbourhood as relatives, indicates the importance placed upon family and kin.

Changes in functions and tasks of families

The popular belief that the family is becoming obsolete is based on the idea that the pre-industrial, pre-technological family was a self-contained unit performing all the functions necessary for its own survival. It is highly unlikely, however, that this was in fact ever the case. With industrialisation, there have been some changes in the functions of families, but these functions have not been eroded to the extent that the family is no longer serving a useful role in our society.

Physical functions

As in the past, families still have the primary responsibility to provide its members with adequate food, clothing and shelter. Health care has been largely taken over by more expert organisations and agencies. Families no longer have to rely on charity for help, as they did last century, if they are unable to provide basic requirements for members. Social service benefits are now available for families who lack the necessary economic resources to provide for basic needs. However, voluntary agencies play a major role in financial, and particularly, non-financial supports for individuals and families in need.

Economic functions

It is doubtful that pre-industrial families produced all the goods necessary for their survival. It may have been necessary to trade and sell goods that were produced by family members, in order to obtain other needed goods and items—it is unlikely that families were ever completely self-sufficient. Nevertheless, the family's role as a producer has been eroded to a large extent with the advent of industrialisation: the family now consumes rather than produces goods.

With the growth of the consumer society this century, and the increasing array of available products and services to choose from, a family's task of allocating economic resources is more difficult and complex than it was 100 years ago. This places great strains on low-income families who are living in a consumer-based society but do not have the resources to participate as fully as they would like. It is for this reason that, in many families, both partners work to increase income.

Educational and social functions

The role of families as educators have been taken over by other efficient and specialised institutions, but the family still retains the major role in the reproduction and socialisation of children. Compulsory school attendance, and a longer absence of children from the home during the day, have not eroded the family's influence in the socialisation process, although children and adolescents are subject to more socialising influences outside the family than they were in the pre-industrial era.

The rapid pace of social change has made it increasingly difficult for parents to guide adolescents into adulthood, but although there is now a generation gap that did not exist prior to industrialisation, adolescents still perceive the family as being a major influence in their life. Adolescents may go through a period where they reject family values, but in adulthood they generally adopt values that are similar to those of their parents.

Families still allocate roles and related tasks among their members, although roles may be less differentiated on the basis of sex than they were 50 years ago. The function of families in protecting members from violence seems to have disappeared prior to industrialisation. Society does not allow the family to physically settle its internal and external disputes.

Emotional and psychological functions

With the increased awareness of the need of children for love and affection, families today undertake this function in a more enlightened manner than they did prior to industrialisation. Most parents are aware of the need to encourage the development of each child as an individual. Society views the connection between emotional nurturing and satisfactory individual development as being very important. Indeed, emotional child abuse is often seen as being more serious than physical child abuse as the effects of the former may be more long-lasting.

Cultural functions

Through families, children internalise from birth the customs, traditions and beliefs peculiar to the culture into which they were born. As children interact with others outside their immediate family they also become familiar with different customs and values. In Australia, a country with a variety of ethnic and cultural groups, children are likely to be exposed to and become familiar with more than one culture.

Moral, spiritual and religious functions

The majority of families teach children the attitudes, values and standards of behaviour considered appropriate in our society. The extent of religious instruction given will, of course, vary with each individual family. Whether families performed this function prior to industrialisation is doubtful—at that time the main responsibility in this area lay with the church.[1]

Adaptive functions

This is perhaps one of the most important functions performed by families today. Rapid social changes associated with industrialisation and the development of technology require families that are highly adaptive to the demands of other institutions within society. Families act as agents of change—socialising and preparing members for a constantly changing society, and for the changing demands within families.

Factors affecting families

The factors outlined below have been discussed in greater detail in other chapters. While attempts have been made to isolate these factors, all changes which affect families are complex and interrelated.

Political and legal changes

The introduction of anti-discrimination laws and the implementation of equal pay legislation has influenced the increased workforce

1 H. Mol, 'Family and religion', in J. Krupinski & A. Stoller (eds), *The Family in Australia*, Sydney, 1974, p. 108.

participation of married women, which in turn has had a significant impact on the structure and functioning of families. 'No fault' divorce implemented through the Family Law Act of 1975–76 has provided men and women with alternatives to unsatisfactory marriages.

The development of social welfare throughout this century and the expansion of services since the Second World War has meant that families in need are no longer dependent on charity alone for support. Further, social welfare provides an option for people living in intolerable situations, such as domestic violence. There is a greater range of support services and community resources available for individuals and families with varying needs. These services and resources are provided by government and non-government organisations. An important development has been the expansion of formal child-care services which enable parents in many families to work outside the home.

Technology

The availability of reliable methods of contraception for both unmarried and married people has meant that women, particularly, have more control over their lives. This has enabled them to pursue other things in life apart from wifehood and motherhood. Technology has also provided families with more labour-saving devices, more consumer goods, faster transport, complex communication systems and convenience foods. It has also changed the nature of work outside the family unit and provided individuals with more leisure time. However, for married women who are in the workforce, leisure time is often utilised in undertaking household tasks and maintaining the technology of the home.

While technology has had many positive consequences, it has also had negative consequences. It has removed many of the unskilled jobs available for young people and increased the number of jobs which require low levels of skills and repetitive work, many of which are performed by women. Technological advances have meant that many workers have become redundant. In an economic recession, the chances of obtaining another job are severely reduced, even if retraining is undertaken. For older workers, it may mean permanent unemployment and forced early retirement. With this comes a reduction in living standards.

Mass media and advertising

The development of the mass media has provided many opportunities for advertising goods and services, and thus creating in families a sense of need. For many families, these perceived needs, and a socially acceptable standard of living, can only be satisfied with two incomes. In recent years however, for many families, two incomes have been necessary in order to provide basic needs. Whereas the family remains the primary influence in socialisation, the media plays a significant role in socialisation of children and adolescents from a very young age. Television serves as a transmitter of fads and fashion, as well as providing models of behaviour, both desirable and undesirable. In recent years there has been much concern expressed about the amount of violence shown on television and the negative effects that this may have on both children and adults.

Social attitudes

Since the 1970s, individuals have placed greater emphasis on personal autonomy and independence. These value and attitude changes have contributed to the increase in age at marriage and the delay in childbearing, and an increased number of people who choose to live alone. Social attitudes have changed and many practices that were once subject to social disapproval are now tolerated and even encouraged. These include divorce, ex-nuptial children, de facto relationships, single-parent families, childlessness, homosexuality, workforce participation of mothers etc.

Economic factors

The 1970s witnessed the beginning of an economic recession and a sharp rise in unemployment and 1980s opened with the highest levels of unemployment since the Depression of the 1930s. While unemployment rates continued to decline for the remainder of the decade, following the high rates of 1983, in the early 1990s unemployment rates had exceeded the levels of 1983. The high inflation rates of the 1980s and consequent increases in interest rates has meant that the goal of owning a home has become more difficult to achieve than it was in the 1950s and 1960s. In relation to real earnings, housing prices have risen markedly. In the early 1990s the economic future for many individuals and families was bleak: youth are wondering if they will ever secure employment and older employees who have been retrenched have to accept the possibility that they will never be employed again.

Throughout this century until the mid-1980s, the real value of wages rose. However, over the past decade real earnings have declined and there has been a growth in casual and part-time work, particularly among young people and women. The decline in the real value of wages, combined with lack of wage increases, has contributed to a higher incidence of poverty for women and children. The economic constraints of the 1980s and 1990s have placed pressures on family formation, as individuals often delay marriage and childbearing during difficult economic times.

Religious influences

Australian society still seems to expect some moral guidance from religious institutions—a large number of children are sent to Sunday School even though their parents may not attend church. There appears to have been some resurgence in church attendance over the past decade, perhaps as a consequence of people looking for something else during a period of time characterised by uncertainty. There has been a growth of religious groups outside the mainstream churches. Perhaps these groups offer individuals and families more than the more well known or traditional churches have been able to do so. However, in the 1986 Census, 25 per cent of the population were recorded as having no religious affiliation.

Since the introduction of civil celebrants in the early 1970s a significant number of couples choose to marry outside the church, that is, in a civil ceremony. Prior to the Second World War, civil marriages remained fairly constant at about 10 per cent of all marriages. In 1983, the proportion of all marriages celebrated by a civil celebrant had risen to nearly 40 per cent. By the early 1990s this figure had been exceeded. Despite the increasing popularity of civil celebrants it appears unlikely that they will replace the church in their role of performing marriage and name-giving ceremonies.

Religion may have exerted some influence on family stability prior to industrialisation, but it is doubtful whether this influence has been as great as economic, legal and social factors in preventing family dissolution.

Summary of changes

- Marriage is occurring at a later age.
- More couples are opting for de facto relationships rather than marriage.
- Values of independence and personal autonomy are more apparent.
- Decline in family size since the mid-nineteenth century.
- Couples are having children later in marriage.
- Increase in the number of ex-nuptial births.
- Wider availability of abortion during past two decades.

- More couples are choosing not to have children.
- Increase in the divorce rate.
- Greater proportion of single-parent families.
- Greater number of blended families.
- Children are likely to experience more than one type of family formation.
- Youth are dependent upon families for a longer period of time.
- Men are more likely than women to remarry.
- Higher levels of education are attained for both men and women.
- Dramatic increase in workforce participation of married women.
- Expansion of formal child-care facilities.
- Significant increase in life expectancy for men and women.
- Expansion of social welfare services this century.
- Movement toward greater equality of men and women.
- Technology has provided a wider range of goods and services from which to choose.
- Family members have more freedom, independence and leisure time.
- Over the past decade there has been a decrease in the value of real wages.
- Unemployment levels have risen.
- Widening of the gap between rich and poor.
- Most individuals and families have experienced either directly and/ or indirectly the effects of the economic recession.

It is fairly evident that although the family has experienced many changes during this century, it does not appear to be diminishing in importance within our society. It is virtually impossible to predict future changes that may affect the family as a social institution, as it is not really possible to predict future political, economic, legal, technological and social developments which may contribute to such changes.

Bibliography

Books

Alford, K., *Production or Reproduction: An Economic History of Women in Australia 1788–1850*, Oxford University Press, Melbourne, 1984.

Amato, P., *Children in Australian Families: The Growth of Competence*, Australian Institute of Family Studies, Prentice-Hall, Sydney, 1987.

Anderson, C.H., *Toward a New Sociology*,The Dorsey Press, Illinois, 1974.

Anderson, C.H., *The Political Economy of Social Class*, Prentice-Hall, New Jersey, 1974.

Anderson, M. (ed.), *Sociology of the Family*, Penguin, Melbourne, 1971.

Aspin, L.J., *The Family: An Australian Focus* (2nd edn), Longman Cheshire, Melbourne, 1987.

Baldock, C.V. & Cass B., *Women, Social Welfare and the State in Australia*, Allen & Unwin, Sydney, 1983.

Baldwin, D., *All About Children: An Introduction to Child Development*, Oxford University Press, London, 1983.

Batten, R., Weeks, W. & Wilson, J. (eds), *Issues Facing Australian Families*, Longman Cheshire, Melbourne, 1991.

Berger, P.L., *Invitation to Sociology: A Humanist Perspective*, Penguin, London, 1963.

Bostok, E.A., *Talking About Women*, Wayland Publishers, London, 1973.

Bottomley, G. & de Lepervanche (eds), *Ethnicity, Class and Gender in Australia*, Allen & Unwin, Sydney, 1984.

Brennan, T., *New Community: Problems and Policies*, Angus & Robertson, Sydney, 1973.

Brewer, G.F., *On the Bread Line: Oral Records of Poverty*, (For the Brotherhood of St. Laurence), Hyland House, Melbourne, 1980.

Burns, A. & Goodnow, J., *Children and Families in Australia* (2nd edn), George Allen & Unwin, Sydney, 1979.

Burns, A., Bottomley, G. & Jools, P. (eds), *The Family in the Modern World*, George Allen & Unwin, Sydney, 1983.

Callan, V.J. & Noller, P., *Marriage and the Family*, Methuen Australia, Sydney, 1987.

Carmichael, G.A., *With This Ring: First Marriage Patterns: Trends and Prospects in Australia*, Australian Family Formation Project Monograph No. 11, Department of Demography, Australian National University/Australian Institute of Family Studies, Canberra, 1988.

Castle, R., Lewis, D. & Mangan, J. (eds), *Work, Leisure and Technology*, Longman Cheshire, Melbourne, 1986.

Choo, C., *Aboriginal Child Poverty*, Brotherhood of St. Laurence, Melbourne, 1990.

Connell, W.F. et al., *12 to 20: Studies of City Youth*, Hicks, Smith & Sons, Sydney, 1975.

Connerton, P. (ed.), *Critical Sociology*, Penguin, Harmondsworth, UK, 1976.

Cooper, D., *The Death of the Family*, Penguin, London, 1971.

Coulson, M.A. & Riddell, C., *Approaching Sociology*, Routledge & Kegan Paul, London, 1980.

Curthoys, A., Eade, S. & Spearitt, P. (eds), *Women at Work*, Australian Society for the Study of Labour History, Canberra, 1975.

Dickey, B., *No Charity There: A Short History of Social Welfare in Australia*, Allen & Unwin, Sydney, 1987.

Dobriner, W.M., *Social Structures and Systems: A Sociological Overview*, Goodyear, California, 1969.

Dunlop, R. & Burns, A., *Don't Feel the World is Caving In: Adolescents in Divorcing Families*, Australian Institute of Family Studies, Monograph No. 6, Melbourne, 1988.

Dwyer, P., *Public and Private Lives: A Sociology of Australia*, Longman Cheshire, Melbourne, 1989.

Edgar, D., *Introduction to Australian Society*, Prentice-Hall, Sydney, 1980.

Edgar, D., Keane, D. & McDonald, P. (eds), *Child Poverty*, Australian Institute of Family Studies, Allen & Unwin, 1989.

Encel, S. & Berry, M., (eds), *Selected Readings in Australian Society: An Anthology*, Longman Cheshire, Melbourne, 1987.

Encel, S., Mackenzie, N. & Tebbutt, M., *Women and Society: An Australian Study*, Cheshire, Melbourne, 1974.

English, B.A. & King, R.J., *Families in Australia*, Family Research Unit, University of New South Wales, Sydney, 1983.

English, B.A., King, R.J. & Smith, S.S., *Families in Australia: A Profile*, Family Research Unit, University of New South Wales, Sydney, 1978.

Erikson, E., *Childhood and Society* (2nd edn), W.W. Norton, New York, 1963.

Fallding, H., *Marriage and the Family in Australia*, Angus & Robertson, Sydney, 1957.

Ford, B., *The Elderly Australian*, Penguin, Melbourne, 1979.

Galvin, M. & West, P., *A Changing Australia: Themes and Case Studies*, Harcourt Brace Jovanovich, Sydney, 1988.

Game, A. & Pringle, R., *Gender at Work*, Allen & Unwin, Sydney, 1983.

Giddens, A., *Sociology: A Brief but Critical Introduction* (2nd edn), Macmillan, London, 1986.

Goffman, E., *The Presentation of Self in Everyday Life*, Pelican, London, 1959.

Goode, W.J., *World Revolutions in Family Patterns*, Glencoe Free Press, New York, 1963.

Goode, W.J., *The Family*, Prentice-Hall, New Jersey, 1964.

Goodnow, J. & Pateman, C. (eds), *Women, Social Science and Public Policy*, George Allen & Unwin, Sydney, 1985.

Graycar A. & Jamrozik, A., *How Australians Live: Social Policy in Theory and Practice*, Macmillan, Melbourne, 1989.

Hamnett, S. & Bunker, R. (eds), *Urban Australia: Planning Issues and Policies*, Nelson Wadsworth, Melbourne, 1987.

Hancock, K. (ed.), *Australian Society*, Cambridge University Press, Melbourne, 1989.

Harper, J. & Richards, L., *Mothers and Working Mothers*, Penguin, Melbourne, 1979.

Harris C.C., *The Family and Industrial Society*, George Allen & Unwin, London, 1983.

Hollingworth, P., *The Poor:Victims of Affluence*, Pitman, Melbourne, 1975.

Hollingworth, P., *Australians in Poverty*, Thomas Nelson, Melbourne, 1985.

Hoult, T.F., *Dictionary of Modern Sociology*, Littlefield, Adams & Co., New Jersey, 1969.

Hurlock, E.B., *Child Growth and Development*, McGraw-Hill, New York, 1949.

Jennett C. & Stewart, R.G. (ed.), *Three Worlds of Ineqality: Race, Class and Gender*, Department of Political Science, Faculty of Arts, Australian National University, Macmillan, Melbourne, 1987.

Jupe, J. et al., *Child Development and the Family*, Macmillan Education Limited, London, 1985.

Kondos, A., *One Among Many: Living in Urban Australia*, Cheshire, Melbourne, 1971.

Krupinski, J. & Stoller, A. (eds), *The Family in Australia: Social Demographic and Psychological Aspects*, Pergamon Press, Sydney, 1974.

McDonald, P.F., *Marriage in Australia: Age at First Marriage and Proportions Marrying, 1860–1970*, Australian Family Project, Australian National University, Monograph No.2, Canberra, 1974.

Maas, F. & Hartley, R., *On The Outside: The Needs of Unsupported*, Homelesss Youth, Australian Institute of Family Studies, Policy Background Paper No, 7, Melbourne, 1988.

Maher, C. & Burke, T., *Informed Decision Making*, Longman Cheshire, 1991.

Marchant, H. & Wearing, B. (ed.), *Gender Reclaimed: Women in Social Work*, Hale & Iremonger Pty Ltd, Sydney, 1988.

Mercer, J., (ed.), *The Other Half: Women in Australian Society*, Penguin, Victoria, 1975.

Myrdal, A. & Klein, V., *Women's Two Roles: At Home and Work*, Routledge & Kegan Paul, London, 1956.

Ochiltree, G., *Children in Australian Families*, Longman Cheshire, Melbourne, 1990.
O'Donnell, C. & Craney, J. (ed.), *Family Violence in Australia*, Longman Cheshire, Melbourne, 1982.
Park, R., *Poor Man's Orange*, Penguin, Ringwood, 1949.
Probert, B., *Working Life*, McPhee Gribble, Penguin, Australia, 1990.
Reiter, R.A. (ed.), *Toward an Anthropology of Women*, Monthly Review Press, New York, 1975.
Richards, L., *Having Families*, Penguin, Ringwood, 1978.
Richards, L., *Nobody's Home: Dreams and Realities in a New Suburb*, Oxford University Press, Melbourne, 1990.
Ronalds, C., *Anti-Discrimination Legislation in Australia: A Guide*, Butterworths, Sydney, 1979.
Rowland, D.T., *Ageing in Australia*, Longman Cheshire, Melbourne, 1991.
Ryan, E. & Conlan, A., *The Gentle Invaders*, Thomas Nelson, Sydney, 1975.
Sargent, M., *Sociology for Australians* (2nd edn), Longman Cheshire, Melbourne, 1987.
Scott Peck, M., *The Different Drum*, Rider, London, 1987.
Simms, M. (ed.), *Australian Women and the Political System*, Longman Cheshire, Melbourne, 1984.
Stephenson, R., *Women in Australian Society*, Heinemann Educational, Melbourne, 1970.
Summers, A., *Damned Whores and God's Police*, Penguin, Sydney, 1977.
Thiering, B., *Created Second*, Family Life Movement of Australia, Sydney, 1973.
Vamplew, W., *Australians: Historical Statistics*, Fairfax, Syme & Weldon Associates, Sydney, 1987.
Waters, M. & Crook, R., *Sociology One* (2nd edn), Longman Cheshire, Melbourne, 1990.
Western, J.S., *Social Inequality in Australian Society*, Macmillan, Melbourne, 1983.
Wild, R.A. (ed.), *Australian Community Studies and Beyond*, George Allen & Unwin, Sydney, 1981.
Winch, R.F., *The Modern Family*, Holt, Rinehart & Winston, New York, 1963.
Windschuttle, K., *Unemployment: A Social and Political Analysis of the Economic Crisis in Australia*, Penguin, Ringwood, 1979.
Young, M. & Willmott, P., *The Symmetrical Family*, Penguin, London, 1973.

Journals, Papers and Articles

Australian Institute of Family Studies, *Family Matters*, no. 20, 1988; no. 21, 1988; no. 22, 1988; no. 23, 1989; no. 24, 1989; no. 25, 1989; no. 26, 1990; no. 27, 1990; no. 28, 1991; no. 29, 1991; no. 30, 1991; no. 31, 1992; no. 32, 1992; no. 33, 1992; no. 34, 1993.
Australian Journal of Sex, Marriage & Family, vol. 9, no. 2, May 1988.
Australian Journal of Social Issues, vol. 11, no. 2, 1976; vol. 24, no. 3, 1989; vol. 25, no. 1, 1990; vol. 25, no. 2, 1990.
Brewer, G., *The Impact of Work on Family Functioning: A Review of the Literature*, Occasional paper no. 3, Institute of Family Studies, Melbourne, 1983.

Brock, J. ven den, 'Accommodating the aged in the latter part of the 20th century: An architect's viewpoint', *Australian Journal of Social Issues*, vol. 24, no. 14, November 1979, pp. 274–84.

REPORTS AND RESEARCH PAPERS

AUSTRALIAN BUREAU OF STATISTICS

Australia in Profile: A Summary of Major Findings, Canberra, 1988.
Australia's Children 1989: A Statistical Profile, Canberra, 1989.
Australian Demographic Statistics, Canberra, 1989.
Australian Families and Households, Census of Population and Housing, 1986, Canberra, 1989.
Births Australia, 1991, Canberra, 1992.
Deaths Australia, 1991, Canberra, 1992.
Demography, New South Wales 1991, Canberra, 1992.
Divorces Australia, 1991, Canberra, 1992.
Education and Training in Australia, 1992.
Estimated Resident Population by Country of Birth, Age and Sex Australia, Canberra, 1992.
Family Formation and Dissolution, 1982, (R.J. Cameron, Australian Statistician), Australian Government Publishing Service, Canberra, 1985.
Families in Australia: A Guide to Content and Procedures, March 1992—May 1992, Canberra, 1993.
Families in Australia: Selected Findings, Canberra, 1993.
General Social Survey, Australian Families, Canberra, May, 1975.
Household Expenditure Survey, Australia: Summary of Results, 1988–89, Canberra, 1990.
Income Distribution Survey, 1986, Canberra, 1988.
Labour Statistics Australia 1988, Canberra, 1990.
Labour Force Status and Other Characteristics of Families Australia, Canberra, 1989.
Marriages Australia, 1991, Canberra, 1991.
Overseas Born Australians 1988: A Statistical Profile, Canberra, 1988.
Social Indicators No. 2, Australian Government Publishing Service, Canberra, 1978.
Social Indicators No. 4, Australian Government Publishing Service, Canberra, 1984.
Social Indicators No. 5, Australian Government Publishing Service, Canberra, 1992.
Women and Work, Canberra, 1992.
Women in Australia, Canberra, 1993.
Year Book Australia, No. 69, (R.J. Cameron, Australian Statistician), Australian Government Publishing Service, Canberra, 1985.
Year Book Australia, No. 71, (Ian Castles, Australian Statistician), Canberra, 1988.
Year Book Australia, No. 72, (Ian Castles, Australian Statistician), Canberra, 1989.
Year Book Australia, No. 73, (Ian Castles, Australian Statistician), Canberra, 1990.

Year Book Australia, No. 74, (Ian Castles, Australian Statistician), Canberra, 1991.

Year Book Australia, No. 75, (Ian Castles, Australian Statistician), Canberra, 1992.

Year Book New South Wales, No. 71, (John Wilson, Deputy Commonwealth Statistician), Sydney, 1988.

OTHER

Australian Council of Social Service (ACOSS), *Poverty: The Acoss Evidence*, Sydney, 1976.

Australian Ethnic Affairs Council, *Australia as a Multicultural Society*, Australian Government Publishing Service, Canberra, 1985.

Australian Institute of Family Studies, *Family Wellbeing: Proceedings of a Workshop*, Melbourne, 1987.

Bittman, M., *Juggling Time: How Australian Families Use Time*, Prepared for the Office of the Status of Women, Department of the Prime Minister and Cabinet, 1991.

Department of Immigration and Ethnic Affairs, *Australia's Population Trends and Prospects, 1985*, Australian Government Publishing Service, Canberra, 1986.

Family Research Unit, University of New South Wales, *Australian Family Research Bulletins*, no. 1, 1973; no. 2, 1975; no. 3, 1976; no. 4, 1978, Sydney.

Foreman, L., *Children of Families*, Australian Government Social Welfare Commission, Sydney, 1975.

Henderson, R.F., Professor (Chairman), *Poverty in Australia: First Main Report of the Commission of Inquiry into Poverty*, Australian Government Publishing Service, Canberra, 1975.

Hoekstra, M.H., *The Aged and Housing in Perspective*, Ian Buchan Fell Research Project on Housing, Faculty of Architecture, University of Sydney, 1976.

King, R., *The Dimensions of Housing Need in Australia*, Ian Buchan Fell Research Project on Housing, Faculty of Architecture, University of Sydney, 1973.

King, R., (ed.), *Children in High Rise Flats*, Research Project on Housing, Faculty of Architecture, University of Sydney, 1974.

Reed, J. & Oakes, K., *Women in Australian Society: 1901–1945*, Australian Government Publishing Service, Canberra, 1977.

Report to the Minister for Social Security, *Families and Social Services in Australia*, vols 1 and 2, Australian Government Publishing Service, Canberra, 1978.

Ruzcka, L.T., *Reflections on Zero Growth of the Australian Population*, Research Report of the National Population Inquiry, No.7, Australian Government Publishing Service, Canberra, 1974.

Women's Bureau, Department of Employment and Youth Affairs, *Facts on Women at Work in Australia, 1979*, Australian Government Publishing Service, Canberra, 1980.

INDEX